OPERATION
SHIELD

ALSO BY JOEL SHEPHERD

Cassandra Kresnov novels

Crossover
Breakaway
Killswitch
23 Years on Fire

A Trial of Blood and Steel novels

Sasha
Petrodor
Tracato
Haven

OPERATION SHIELD

A CASSANDRA KRESNOV NOVEL

JOEL SHEPHERD

an imprint of Prometheus Books
Amherst, NY

Published 2014 by Pyr®, an imprint of Prometheus Books

Cover illustration © Stephan Martiniere
Cover design by Jacqueline Nasso Cooke

Inquiries should be addressed to
Pyr
59 John Glenn Drive
Amherst, New York 14228
VOICE: 716–691–0133
FAX: 716–691–0137
WWW.PYRSF.COM

18 17 16 15 14   5 4 3 2 1

Library of Congress Cataloging-in-Publication Data

Shepherd, Joel, 1974-
    Operation shield : a Cassandra Kresnov novel / Joel Shepherd.
        pages cm.
    ISBN 978-1-61614-895-9 (pbk.)
    ISBN 978-1-61614-896-6 (ebook)
    1. Life on other planets—Fiction. 2. Androids—Fiction. I. Title.

PR9619.4.S54O64 2014
823'.92—dc23

                                                                      2013040041

Printed in the United States of America

CHAPTER ONE

Vanessa saw stars, then bright colours, felt hands under her arms, dragging her. Cold, and sweat, and a struggle for breath, voices yelling and nearby gunfire. Her boots were skidding, dragged along the floor. Then a massive shock, and the whole station seemed to lurch. Reverberations on tacnet—she still had tacnet, it didn't need her conscious to run. Someone forced a mask over her face, tightened the strap, then a flood of cool oxygen.

Into an airlock then, emergency overrides holding both doors open, armoured bodies rushing them through. Then a cramped space, shielded lights, she felt herself picked up and dumped into an acceleration sling, straps pulled tight about her on automatic as other bodies found their slings, someone's tac-sergeant yelling to move move move!

Thrust hit them harder than seemed reasonable, slamming the slings down and out, absorbing the G that built and built, her vision darkening . . . and then stopped, and she was floating the other way, then rebounding as the sling's auto-tension sorted itself out. More voices, questions, someone wanting the ship feed but receiving a negative. Marines didn't get ship feed, they buckled up and just presumed they were never more than a second from being plastered into some bulkhead by sudden manoeuvers. Marines who got ship feed sometimes got cocky and thought they could see a clear window in which to unbuckle, only to discover that a three-meter drop at ten Gs was the equivalent of falling off a thirty-meter building at one G—and they broke just as many bones.

"Ricey?" She could hear someone asking. Rhian, she thought. "Ricey, you okay?"

"Her vitals are stable," came Cai's voice.

"I'm okay," she murmured. She couldn't recall what had happened. One minute they'd been evacuating Antibe Station bridge with assistance from *Mekong*'s marines, and the next everything had gone wrong.

"Fast approach!" the sergeant was shouting again. "Two minutes! Could manoeuver any time!"

If some fool on station was dumb enough to fire on them. Who would be dumb enough, with *Mekong* parked barely three clicks off their stern? But someone on station *had* fired on them. Were they suicidal or what?

There was no manoeuvering, just a two-minute wait, then a more sensible deceleration. A crash of grapples, then secondary arms, as *Mekong* grabbed the limpet in a tight embrace. More movement, and she was unstrapped, then hauled floating to the disembark. Vanessa protested she was okay but was ignored. Disembark whined open, air equalising with a painful inner ear pop, and then they were floating up the passage that separated *Mekong*'s habitation cylinder from its engines.

Into the central spine, and Vanessa shrugged away her assistance; she really was feeling a little better, her vision clearer, no longer so dizzy. Rhian—because it *was* Rhian, she could only now see—made her grip more gentle but did not remove the hand.

Central spine was rotating, and now they took a service elevator to the outer rim, and gravity kicked in.

"We fire on station?" one of the marines was asking.

"Fucking felt like it," said another.

"Any idea why they shot at us?" asked one more.

"Guess they don't like us," said Ari, typically deadpan.

"Fucking dumbass Torahns. They'll be lucky Captain doesn't blow them away."

Vanessa wanted the bridge, but Rhian dragged her to medical instead, down narrow, dog-legged corridors past *Mekong* marines and crew, then into a narrow side corridor to a medical room, where she was loaded into a chair while a med came and peered in her eyes and asked questions.

"Dunno," Vanessa answered. "Maybe they gassed the corridor when we got out."

They'd been cooped up in Antibe Station's bridge for about fifty hours. Antibe Station had stopped trying to cut their way in when *Mekong* had arrived, but they hadn't been very friendly either. *Mekong* hadn't asked for their safe release; *Mekong* had demanded, and Antibe Station had said yes, pleased enough just to be rid of them but also left with no choice when a Federation carrier parked nearby leveled full firepower at them.

The med looked questioningly at Rhian, who shook her head. No gas. The med attached various sensors and hooked them up to various things that beeped, while Vanessa took deep breaths and tried to stop her heart from racing. That was an unpleasant sensation. The only time she'd experienced something similar was in her previous life, as an office worker straight out of uni. She'd been to the doctor, who told her it was likely a panic attack . . . ridiculous, because she didn't *get* panic attacks. The doctor had smiled and said that's what they all said.

She didn't think this was a panic attack, though. All that had stopped once she'd joined the CSA, many years ago. She might have had panic attacks as an office worker, but in the CSA, despite all the hard work, stress, and danger, nothing close—most nights she'd slept like a log.

A marine stuck his head in the door and informed all present that their berthing assignment had been issued.

"Wow," said Ari. "I've never had a berthing assignment before. Is it fun?"

"It's overrated," said Rhian. "You go check it out."

"You go," Ari told Cai.

"Berthing assignments don't excite me," said Cai, leaning on the straps of the med-room take-hold.

"I'm under orders to escort *someone* to see the berthing assignment," the marine said impatiently.

"I'll go," said Vanessa hopefully.

"You stay," said the medico firmly.

"I'll stow it," Rhian muttered, heading for the door and the marine's escort. She was the logical choice as the most experienced spacer present. Vanessa had the feeling the nostalgia of space travel had long since worn off for her. Rhian had family back on Callay and would rather be back there than anywhere.

A few minutes later, Captain Reichardt himself ducked his lanky frame under the low doorway to medical. He wore a spacer's jumpsuit and a leather jacket with patches denoting his ship, and Third Fleet, of which *Mekong* was part. Anyone not familiar with Fleet might not immediately recognise him as a Captain; spacers were a sparse and practical lot, hats and ostentatious insignia could catch on things, or become a variable-G hazard. But everyone who served on *Mekong* sure as hell knew.

"What happened?" he asked her, a mild Texan drawl.

"Attack of the vapours," said Vanessa. "Delicate constitution."

He nearly smiled. "My toughest marine sergeant says you CSA SWATs are the only grunts she knows crazier than Fleet Marines. I was shocked, 'cause I didn't think her capable of compliments."

Vanessa shrugged. "Had some help." With a glance at Cai.

Reichardt followed her gaze. "Good to meet you in person," he said to Cai, extending a hand.

Cai leaned and took it. "Likewise."

They'd met in cyberspace, though. Cai's friends had destroyed a League warship that had been trying to nuke Droze at the time. Cai's friends had then jumped, though no one thought they'd gone far. Everyone was now pretending Reichardt had done it, though *Mekong* had been somewhat out of position for that to be true. Likely someone would discover the truth of it eventually, but for now, better for *Mekong* to take the fall than have everyone know the truth.

"Excuse my bluntness," said Reichardt, "but what are you?"

"A GI," said Cai.

"I'm the Captain of a Federation Fleet carrier," said Reichardt. "I'm currently at the center of the biggest blow-up in Federation-League relations since the war. Billions of lives hang on what we do here. Excuse me if I require more information."

Cai seemed to think about it for a moment. "I'm a GI made by the Talee. Don't ask for a designation, Talee don't use them, and any number I gave you would be meaningless."

"Why did they make you?"

"A number of reasons, most of which I'm not at liberty to discuss with you. But mostly, for recon."

Reichardt frowned. "To spy on humanity?"

Cai shrugged. "You call it spy. I call it recon. Talee won't interact with humans directly, as you've noticed. But this puts them at the disadvantage caused by a lack of information. I'm an answer to that, among other things."

"What other things?"

"Like I said, can't discuss it."

"Great," said Reichardt. "Just great. Your buddies just blew a League warship to bits over Droze, but you're not allowed to talk about it. You tell them that they can't both violently intrude into human affairs, and then maintain a safe distance, both at the same time."

"I have," said Cai, with a very faint smile. "Many times."

"And what do they say?"

"Can't talk about it."

"Why not?" asked Ari, from somewhere behind Vanessa's head. "Why the secrecy? Talee are more advanced than humanity, that's pretty obvious. What's to fear from interacting?"

"Many things," said Cai. "Again, I can't discuss it. But understand that they don't do this from some unthought impulse, something reactionary and unreasoning. They reason very well, I think. And they have reached a series of well-thought conclusions, conclusions that encompass my purpose here. But I can't discuss those conclusions. There is too much at stake to risk the gain of some false impression. False impressions between species of differing psychological makeup could be very dangerous."

"So you're like a translator," said Reichardt, leaning one hand against the doorframe. Spacers rarely stood unsecured. "Someone who can understand both psychologies. A go between."

Cai thought about it for a moment. Then nodded. "Perhaps."

"But your brain is structurally human?"

"I'm a GI. GIs can be modified."

"To see things both ways," Ari finished, nodding in wide-eyed comprehension. Cai said nothing.

"So let me tell you how things stand," said Reichardt. "Right now we're tucked in close to station, so Pantala's anti-ship missiles can't frag us. They've got some super hightech stuff down there, at these ranges if we break away from station, the only way we'll survive is if we jump clear. So for now, the station is our shield.

"The reason we can't jump away is because of our mutual friend Commander Kresnov, currently occupying Chancelry Corporation HQ down on Droze. We're her firesupport—without us threatening her enemies from orbit, she's dead. We're clear so far?"

"I was here from the beginning," Cai said calmly. "I know all this."

"Between species of differing psychological makeup," Reichardt said with an edge of sarcasm, "misunderstandings can be dangerous. Are we understanding each other?"

"Perfectly."

"Good. As things stand, both I and Commander Kresnov have committed a technical act of war against the League. And Commander Rice here too. Pantala space and New Torahn space in general is still technically League territory, and we've violated it. League warships will be arriving here as soon as word gets back to them, and likewise Federation warships shall be arriving on the back of the message I sent. We can only hope that they don't come in shooting, or it'll look like the Battle of Sirus Junction all over again.

"My excuse, and Commander Kresnov's, is what she uncovered in Chancelry HQ on Droze. Something that not even you're aware of, I don't think. But I can assure you it's big, and definitely within the Federation's security interests. I've no guarantee the Grand Council will see things that way, but I can hope, otherwise its all of our necks on the block.

"So, my question to you is this. What are your friends going to be doing, during the time between when all these ships start arriving, and now?"

"Watching," said Cai.

"Do you need to talk to them?" Reichardt pressed. "Because if you do, I can coordinate those communications. On the other hand, if you're thinking about using those fancy network capabilities I'm told you have to gain covert access of my ship's coms to talk to the Talee in private, I promise I'll blow you out an airlock. This is my ship, and you ask permission first. Are we clear?"

"Very clear," Cai affirmed. "I don't need to talk to them. They are aware."

Reichardt frowned. "Of what, exactly?"

"Of many things."

Reichardt scratched his head. "This is going to be like having a fucking leprechaun aboard, isn't it? Talking in fucking riddles."

"I could wear a little green hat if you like?" Cai offered.

"What's a leprechaun?" Vanessa wondered.

"Strange little people whose purpose in life is to piss off starship Captains."

"But that's me," said Vanessa.

"Tell me about it," said Reichardt. "What's wrong with her, Doc?"

"Couldn't say," said the medico, watching various screens. "Give me a few hours."

"You've got ten minutes," Vanessa said drily.

"Watch her," said the Captain, pointing a warning finger at Vanessa, backing out the door. "She's my unlucky charm."

"Hey!" Vanessa retorted. "You're still alive, why so negative?" *Mekong's* Captain was gentleman enough to give her a dry smile as he left.

Naturally the emergency alarm sounded the first time Sandy let Kiril come with her to see the weapons bay.

"Kiet, what's going on?" she asked as tacnet emergency lit all channels. Something in the parameters she'd laid out had been breached. About the bay, captured weapons systems were firing up, engines whining, running lights flashing. Much of this they were planning to run automated if they had to; they didn't have the manpower otherwise.

There was no reply from Kiet. Sandy led Kiril to the center of the bay's wide ferrocrete floor, the safest place when automated systems were activating, and ran a full tacnet scan. It showed central Droze, the corporate zones, five primary districts arrayed around a central, neutral hub. About that hub, Droze city sprawled away into the night, but that was not a main concern. She was in occupied Chancelry Zone, and the four other corporate zones were all unfriendly. In the past, before the united Torahn government had been formed, they'd shot at each other. Now they prepared to do so again.

Immediately she saw it highlighted—something had crashed in Central Zone. But the weather was bad, and the only view was a com tower camera on maximum magnification, which showed only the remains of a rotor nacelle amidst residential rooftops and a few trees. And now came a mass of new highlights, activity around the encircling corporate zones, tanks and AMAPS moving, spikes in registered com traffic, weapons bay doors sliding open. She snapped quickly into the secure matrix, where Kiet and a few of his network specialists had been probing corporate nets on systems Sandy and Cai from orbit had helped design . . . and ran straight into a blank wall. She was locked out of her own system? What the hell?

"Kiet!" she snapped. "Either respond or I'll presume you incapacitated and have you removed from command!"

Tacnet declared that Kiet was in D-2, eighth floor. So was Rishi. Sandy began breaking into defensive barriers, unlocking complex systems she knew far better than Kiet did, and certainly better than Rishi . . .

"Sandy, what's going on?" Kiril asked. He wore his favourite 3D glasses, linked to slate and booster they gave him a good overlaid display of his surroundings—not as fast as uplinks, nor as detailed, but pretty cool for a six-year-old. Across the bay an AMLORA was firing up properly, a howl of engines, a giant six-legged bug now straightening, then walking with huge, thumping steps toward the main elevator. "Sandy, look, the AMLORA's moving!"

On the Armoured Mobile LOng RAnge system's back was a huge launcher and enough missiles to level city blocks. The legs would let it operate in places wheels couldn't go—not fast, but better for concealment and camouflage. Here in Chancelry they'd captured six. The other corporations between them had about fifty. If it came to an artillery contest, most of Chancelry's rounds would not survive the opposing missile defences, and would then be destroyed by counter battery fire, along with most of the Chancelry complex.

Sandy smashed a couple of final defensive barriers, hard enough to give tacnet a wobble . . . visual portions crashed, then rebooted from 3D static, confused and struggling.

"*Sandy!*" Kiet shouted at her. "*Leave it alone, I have it under control!*"

"Are you deploying?" She could see it now, portions of tacnet the barriers had hidden. GIs, Kiet's troops, moving fast toward the crash site. And sideways, toward the Dhamsel Corporation border.

The secure network had once gained some connectivity with surrounding corporate systems, not a big presence, mostly through the overarching intranet that linked the neutral spaces between corporate entities. Now it was all shut down, the surrounding corporations must have physically cut the intranet, and with it, nearly a week's work.

"Rishi, talk to me," Sandy demanded, holding Kiril close to her side as vehicles crashed and hummed into life around her. "Rishi, if you've entrusted a major operation to Kiet then you're about to get into trouble, he's not up to it."

"*Sandy, we got a response from some Heldig GIs,*" came Rishi's voice, terse, preoccupied. "*They wanted out, they attempted escape, but someone just shot them down, we don't know who.*"

If she weren't sliding into combat mode, Sandy might have sworn. They weren't supposed to make a move without her, she'd thought they were agreed on that. But with this rabble of recently freed GIs, it wasn't always clear who was in charge. Logic said her, as the highest designation and unchallenged, most experienced and lethal combatant. But Kiet hadn't agreed with her methodology on freeing the other corporations' GIs, and on his side were the majority. Rishi's GIs, the former Chancelry experimentals, were split between the high designations, who wanted to help but had no sense of how, and the lower designations, whom no one trusted.

"That's wonderful," she said. "Would you like my help, or do you want to wait until everyone starts dying?"

"*You're not the only one with combat command experience,*" Kiet retorted.

"In case you've forgotten," she said, "I'm the only one who Captain Reichardt will listen to. And without the threat of an orbital strike, and mutually assured destruction, we'd have all been dead a week ago."

"*We are not going to allow some Feddie squish to veto our freedom!*" Kiet snapped. "*Now leave us alone, we're busy!*"

The link disconnected—a block, because tacnet never truly disconnected. He'd fucking blocked her.

"Kiril, let's go," she said, and grabbed the boy up.

"But I wanna stay!"

"Tough."

She took off running, rifle in one hand so it didn't bounce, Kiril in the other. The latter burden made her somewhat slower than she'd have liked, but as the ferrocrete stretched toward the underground tunnel, she adjusted her steps to short leaps, skipping out to five normal steps, then eight, then ten at a time. It made her fast, but she had to watch Kiril's head on the ceiling, and keep the trajectory low so he wouldn't bounce painfully with each impact.

The huge steel elevator doors were already opening on her uplink signal, and she got inside and signalled the lift up. It went, slowly, as Sandy scanned tacnet for the nearest unoccupied armour suit.

"That was fun," Kiril announced of his ride, rubbing a bruised backside. "Where are we going?"

"To synthetic assembly," said Sandy, checking her rifle and wishing she were already armoured . . . but walking around in armour for a week wasn't practical, any armour needed downtime maintenance, they had it on a roster system that left most of them unarmoured much of the time.

"Where?"

"The GI factory," Sandy explained, slotting the grenade mag, chambering a round.

"Why are we going there?"

"Because if someone drops artillery on us, that will be the safest place."

"But it's not deeper underground than the other basements," Kiril said doubtfully. "I looked at it on my glasses, and I think the other basements are safer."

Six years old or not, there was no coddling Kiril about nasty possibilities. Which was something of a relief, because she wasn't good at it anyway and had no idea how to take care of children beyond what she'd seen third-hand from others.

"I don't think they'll want to damage the GI factory if they can avoid it," she said. "The people who ran Chancelry are hiding over with the other corporations, and they want their headquarters back. The GI factory is one of the most valuable bits."

"Wow, did you know there are big power cables running down the wall here?" He was pointing at things only he could see with his glasses.

On tacnet, Sandy could see the other corporations firing up to full mobilisation. Exactly how tacnet knew, given their limited resources here, she wasn't sure. Had Kiet deployed new intel assets?

"Why won't Kiet listen to you?" The elevator was nearly at the top now, above the ferrocrete ceiling that would perhaps stop a couple of armour-piercing AMLORA rounds, but no more than that.

"Kiet thinks all the other corporations' GIs should be freed right now," said Sandy. "I was trying to be patient."

"You mean he was being *im*patient," said Kiril with wise emphasis. "Danya tells me all the time, me and Svetlana, don't be impatient. He says we can get hurt if we're impatient. Is Kiet going to get hurt?"

"Worse," Sandy said grimly. "Everyone else will."

"Sandy, when are we going to rescue Danya and Svetlana?" Looking up at her with those big, serious eyes.

Sandy looked at him for a moment. There was probably some kind of adult-to-child moment to be had here, that she'd know how to do if she'd had some practise. But with her head full of tacnet and combat reflex, it wasn't her thing.

"I don't think they need rescuing, Kiril. They're in Rimtown and they've lived in Rimtown all their lives, like you. I'm sure they're much safer there than here."

Probably shouldn't have said that either, but it was true.

"But I want them here!"

"I know." There was a dull, unpleasant feeling as she said it. Something twisting deep in her gut. "But the corporations have us surrounded and out-gunned, and I couldn't bring them here if I wanted to."

"We have flyers in the bay," Kiril retorted, pointing back that way. "We could fly to them."

"We'd be shot down." The elevator reached ground level, A-5 building of Chancelry HQ, wide aprons and heavy, triple-layer security doors leading to the outside. "Besides, we don't know where they are and if we tried to contact them, that contact could be traced and lead the corporations straight to them. Come on."

She bent for him, but he went on his own. "I don't need to be carried," he muttered, walking fast.

"Well, then you need to run," said Sandy. "Can you run?"

"I can get there on my own." Kiril walked across the apron to new secure doors that Sandy was already opening with a mental uplink. Within lay a long internal corridor. Out on the courtyard space between buildings, another AMLORA was positioning, missile launcher angling skyward.

Sandy kept up. "I promised Danya and Svetlana I'd look after you. You don't want me to break my promise to Danya, do you?"

Kiril said nothing for a moment. Then held out his arms. Sandy picked him up and resumed running, slower this time, as the low ceiling would not allow bounding. She opened doors in their path with uplinks, patched directly into the local network. Building 5-A became the much larger 7-A, which remained a mess after the uprising, externals shot to hell, all windows gone and much of the outer facing walls and offices. One part of the internal corridor sagged where the wall had caved, ceiling threatening to collapse, but once she squeezed through the gap the floor was relatively clear, shielded from external bombardment.

Rishi had led her Chancelry GIs in an uprising that had sheltered here and in a few other buildings, trying to gather enough firepower together to survive against what Chancelry unloaded on them, trying to recapture these buildings. Then Sandy's force had arrived, with Kiet and his older desert dwellers, come in from five years in the sands to right this one, horrid injustice. The Chancelry uprising would have been put down if they hadn't arrived when they had.

7-A adjoined to 2-A, a detour around ruined adjoining passages, through a cold and dusty night and air that smelled of sulphur. It wasn't breathable to humans save with lung and bloodstream micros that filtered the toxins; even Sandy had had them added, being synthetic didn't make her immune to bad air. Then through more heavy, secure doors, into a waiting atrium that this time demanded realtime ID, then to the top of some stairs.

"Su and Alice will be down there," Sandy told Kiril. "They'll be monitoring all the GIs' systems. Do you think you can stay with them until the emergency passes?"

"Can I help them?" Kiril asked, brightening a bit. He loved technology. Down in the bowels of Chancelry's experimental synthetic-person assembly plant, there was plenty of that.

"Sure, but only if they ask you to, okay?"

Kiril nodded. "Sandy, is there going to be fighting?"

Developments on tacnet did not look promising. A lie might have been parental. "Probably," she said. "But I'll try to stop it from reaching here."

"Be careful," said Kiril as she left.

"I will," she assured him . . . and uplinked to Su and Alice to tell them Kiril was on his way down. They'd have no problem, they liked Kiril and could always use someone to carry small things or bring coffee.

She closed the entrance up behind him and ran, across courtyards, dodging debris no one had yet bothered to clean up, several burned-out vehicles, a destroyed AMAPS from before they'd gained control of Chancelry's defensive grid, a lot of broken glass. A link opened from orbital relay; that would be *Mekong.*

"Reichardt. Commander, what's going on?"

"A bunch of GIs launched an operation to free the neighbouring corporations' GIs without me," Sandy formulated silently, easier than speaking while she ran. *"I'm assuming they've isolated the killswitch lockdown, but I've no idea how long that'll last, a group of Heldig GIs tried to escape by flier but they were shot down in neutral territory, we've various units converging on that spot now."*

"Sounds like your revolution just met with a counter revolution. You have no control at all?"

Sandy skidded to slow down, then dodged through the main door atrium of building 9-R. Here the last few armour suits were racked against the wall, several being occupied even now by late-arriving GIs, additional ammo, and weapons too.

"I'll have control once it all starts to go wrong, Kiet's not much of a tactician. I did tell you we were at odds over tactics where the remaining corporate GIs were concerned."

She pulled off her jacket, emptied pockets, and slammed her back into the spread torso armour—this was only light stuff, League-issue urban armour, not the quality of her CSA gear. But in urban spaces with heavy firepower, a bit of extra protection, plus carrying capacity, never went astray.

"Commander," came Reichardt's reply, *"you should know that I cannot provide direct support to any operation that is not under the direct command of a Federal officer or agent."*

"Mate, just shoot when I say shoot, okay? This was a very broad interpretation of the Federal Interest from the very beginning, you know the stakes as well as I, don't go pulling all this semantical crap now."

"This reply is not adequate." Reichardt didn't seem very amused. She was asking him to commit to firing orbital warheads on her say-so that would kill tens of thousands of people here on Droze. He'd wear the responsibility without any of the control, and he hated it. But she didn't have a choice.

"This situation is not adequate." She sealed the armour up with a whine and click of interlocking joins and powering micro hydraulics. She left the helmet off for her preferred headset, additional sensors, and processing. *"But it's all I've got."*

She took off running.

The main entrance to Chancelry HQ was not defended by a wall of any kind, just a pedestrian space, a few gardens, then civvie roads, light rail, and shopping. Everyone in Chancelry worked for the corporation; inside the zone there were no outsiders to defend headquarters from. But they had parked a big fuck-off tank out front, so described because its multiple rapid-fire auto-cannon, street sweeper anti-personnel systems, and missile launchers gave nearby residents an unmistakable message.

She took off running up the main street. Up ahead, she didn't need tacnet to tell her the shooting had started. The night sky was lit up with rapid flashes and random tracer. Now an explosion, a lingering flash. Then another.

A new connection lit up her internal visual. CEO Patana, Dhamsel Corporation. *"Commander! You end this provocation at once!"*

With the intranet cut, she had no way of telling what was going on in the other HQs. The idea had been to create a new uprising, like they'd accidently caused with Rishi here in Chancelry, but with alternate routes created to ensure they could see what was happening. Now they were blind and had nothing like the force to attack the other corporations directly as they'd done initially here. Damn Kiet for moving too soon.

"The true provocation is the continued utilisation of any synthetic person in armed bondage," Sandy replied, bounding now at over 60 kph down the suburban road. Now eighty. Admitting she wasn't in control would be dangerous. *"Release them all now and this stops immediately."*

Tacnet showed Kiet's troops crossing the border into neutral land ahead, under heavy fire. Civilian areas, joint administered between the corporations, and they wouldn't risk excessive civvie casualties. But they could zero on the roads, avoiding buildings.

It didn't take her long to get close—she could see the deployment clearly, support lines with heavy weapons ahead, scattered across apartments and street corners, others deployed ahead, across neutral territory. In there, tacnet updated periodically, new hostiles where identified, fire positions, trajectories. It looked relatively restrained, too many civvies around for the heavy stuff. And here ahead there were more civvies, running in the streets, a few carrying kids and terrified. Fucking Kiet, she was going to wring his neck.

"Get indoors!" she yelled at them, pointing. "Stay indoors, armscomp will shoot at the roads, not the buildings!" A few complied, the others kept running. A support line GI on the corner saw her and connected on direct talk.

"Commander, we're holding the support line in case Dhamsel tries to cut off the retreat . . ."

Sandy leapt, ignoring that soldier, onto a neighbouring rooftop, then up to an apartment balcony—she didn't need some greenhorn explaining to her a fraction of what she already knew. She could see Dhamsel Zone from up here, then across the built-up neutral zone, the other corporate zones beyond. Dhamsel was the problem, they shared a long flank with Chancelry, now crawling with what tacnet identified as military vehicles.

Chatter indicated the advance party had reached the crash site, visuals showed a military flyer demolishing half a house amidst a sprawl of debris. Big apartment building nearby, civvies now running for cover, probably the reason the companies hadn't just blown the wreck. The flyer couldn't have held more than twelve people, Sandy thought Kiet might have lost more than that already. She uplinked to Reichardt again and got his Com officer instead.

"Get me Cai, please," she asked.

"*Cai,*" came the reply, remarkably fast considering relay distances.

"We have the corporates' killswitch channels locked down, but they'll be trying to unlock it."

"*I know, find me a point of access and I'll try and stop them.*"

Cai had been instrumental in making that happen over the last week. Sandy didn't even know exactly what his technology was, except that it was a vastly superior version of what she had, an ability to manipulate huge volumes of network data in very short time frames. Over the last week he'd helped them to infiltrate corporate networks via the intranet and to isolate corporate security channels and codes that they would use to trigger the killswitch—the ultimate failsafe against their own GIs. Access to Chancelry's own codes had helped them know what to look for, but of course the other corporations had known that and had changed to backups.

"Look," she said, having a reasonable view up here, and being somewhat confident opposing AMLORAs wouldn't take out this building with all the civvies around, "Kiet's trying to help the escapees, but if the corporations break your barriers and trigger the killswitch, every GI they have will be dead instantly."

"*You're sure they'll do it?*"

"Very. Rishi's uprising scared the crap out of them, they've had all their GIs in lockdown for a week."

"*Cassandra, the only reason we're able to maintain those blocks on the killswitch channels is because of the hardline infrastructure in Central Zone . . .*" There was a working pause, even Cai needed to stop talking when the info-overload hit him. "*With Kiet attacking Central Zone they now have an excuse . . .*"

"I know," said Sandy. "But a lot of that stuff is built into civvie infrastructure, they can blast some of it but not all of it." She called up her own schematics, searching for the intranet structures, the only infrastructure still connecting Chancelry networks to the other corporations. Nodes, junctions, and interfaces highlighted in Central Zone and Chancelry Zone.

How long until they figured it out? She did some fast calculation . . . assuming they'd tried to use the killswitch on those GIs who were escaping, and it hadn't worked . . . the blocks would show up in a few minutes of processing their systems. More minutes to hunt solutions, various departments consulting, arguing . . . how scared were they of their own GIs? Only the higher designations, not the regs, most of whom didn't even have killswitches. Which left her with. . . .

Missile fire, her eyes flicked to it, zigzagging madly across the dark sky. Then dove, and a bright flash, in a target zone far away from the current fighting. Another, then one more flash. Two intranet nodes disappeared from her schematic.

"Kiet!" she shouted. "They're taking out the intranet! We're out of time, get all your people out of wireless range!"

"*I can't do that, we have more GIs breaking into Central Zone from Dhamsel! You can't see them on tacnet because they're keeping silent, they don't want to draw fire!*" Gunfire in the background, heavy explosions—big weapons, she reckoned. Not attacking, just hemming them in. It matched with what she could see on the streets.

Another explosion took out one more intranet node. They had to buy more time.

Her subconscious saw the cannon fire coming her way before her conscious mind could process it, and she leaped for empty air on reflex as the balcony and chunks of the building wall disintegrated around her. Fell, hit a rooftop, and slid, then leaped for the road as concrete crashed behind her.

"Cai, get me a full intranet diagnostic," she called as she thudded to the road. "What are they going to hit next?"

She ran up the road as Cai processed—that had been tank fire, someone was evidently scanning the horizon and looking for anyone high up, possibly they'd figured it might be her. Not *that* worried about civvie casualties then.

"*Cassandra, right here*," said Cai, and several points formed on tacnet in Neutral Zone, forming a network. "*Their analysis will tell them if they take out these five points, intranet will collapse.*"

"Kiet, I need a team!" Sandy was already running, past several more GIs in heavy suits, missile launchers on their backs awaiting tacnet's next targeting assignment. "Infranet protection in Central Zone, if it goes down they'll reestablish killswitch channels and we'll lose all of them!"

No reply from Kiet, tacnet showed him engaged in heavy fighting, probably he couldn't fight and command like she could. Fuck him—she enabled her own command structure on tacnet, a little trick Kiet wouldn't know she had, overrode Kiet's protocols and established her own secure coms.

The security wall was breached, but she jumped an intact section, saw missiles streaking overhead to intercept flying targets farther up that might have been engaging Kiet's forces. GIs from the rear line were leaping the wall after her, pulling off Kiet's reserve line to do so.

"What if Dhamsel outflanks us?" one asked.

"You wanna save the other GIs or not?" Sandy snapped.

Here in Central Zone the roads were more built up, multi-level apartments and lower four-storeys. The roads were grid pattern, and Sandy paused at a building wall to peer around a tacnet-blind corner . . . and rolled back as heavy fire blew brickwork thirty meters back down the road. Tacnet tagged the shooter as some kind of armoured vehicle and tried to lock a missile onto it, but already it was moving and they had no visual fix, the anti-armour missiles on the heavy suits moved too fast to acquire mid-flight and would probably get jammed anyway.

"D-5, D-7, pincer left, blockers hold here, E-4 get ready to flank right." She ran fast left across the road, GIs with her, fire pursuing—Kiet's forces were too far into Central Zone to be of any help here, and these corporate units (Chancelry, she thought) were threatening to cut Kiet's retreat.

She jumped for rooftops, leaping across sloping tiles, springing long and low across intervening yards, then slamming down flat for cover as heavy fire intercepted from five hundred meters left. Tile fragments and chunks of roof went spinning, Sandy locked and returned fire, not a challenging shot even at half a K, but the target was armoured. The corporations had prepared well for this, her killing options were limited.

She kept moving, more GIs running with her, several in heavy suits loosing missiles at whatever tried to shoot at them, big explosions from that side and a notable reduction of incoming fire. But their move was noted now, and the response ahead would be concentrated.

Two buildings from the end of the block, a rooftop AMAPS opened up on them from a hundred meters with rotary machine guns . . . or tried to as Sandy shot it first, sliding on a rooftop, then dropping to a back yard as rapid-fire grenades came in from somewhere, big explosions sprayed fragments every-where as she ducked behind a wall. That brought all the other GIs down off the rooftops as well, one of them injured. More grenades came in, then rapid-fire mortar, Sandy already scrambling down a narrow lane between building and wall to the road, and the cross street beyond, but still no direct line of sight.

"E-4 flank right," she called to the units she'd sent over that way, "we'll try to pin these guys here!"

"*If we don't get cut to pieces first,*" someone muttered.

A huge airburst overhead, and the air was full of shrieking shrapnel, road-side trees above Sandy lost limbs and windows shattered. Sandy hurdled the side wall to the next property, not wanting to expose herself on the street with artillery coming in, and tried to duck up the narrow front garden of this apartment building. Immediately she was under fire from the crossroad ahead, one of the facing buildings, rounds shredding the wall between her and the road as she plastered herself against the next wall, gained a tacnet visual from someone behind her, and popped up to fire. She hit the window the rounds had come from, but the shooter was gone, displacing as well-trained soldiers learned to do against GIs—shoot once, move like hell, cover, and shoot again.

"Dammit, these guys are well trained," she announced. She couldn't stay under this arty, but moving across that road was going to cost her. "Someone get me a visual on that road." If she had a visual she could use missiles and dig the fuckers out.

Tacnet showed her someone smashing into a building, running down a corridor, and peering out a window . . . a brief glimpse of the road ahead, buildings on either side, vehicles down below, a few civvies and one big one . . . it flashed, something boomed nearby, and the feed went dead. Sandy locked a missile request into tacnet for that location, pointed her grenade launcher across the road, and fired. Raced and dove through the hole it made in the wall, smashed across a room, up a corridor, then kicked and punched a ragged hole in an adjoining wall—civvies were all in the basements, thank god.

BOOM! as her missile request hit the place opposite her new position where the tank had been, only she doubted it was still there. Grabbed a scanner off her belt, found a window and tossed it to the road—if she'd done it from her previous position it would have been seen and grenaded. This one bounced, little cameras recording all directions, tacnet recording positions dutifully, now fixing the tank, an AMAPS just across the street . . .

Already the missiles came in, blew the tank to hell and most of Sandy's apartment building with it. The next thing she knew, she was under rubble and would certainly be dead if she'd been a straight, and with several tonnes on her, her armour might break, but she wouldn't. She heaved it off her, smashed some uncooperative bits, and crawled out amidst the debris to the sound of massive fire coming up and down the road, her GIs now rounding that previously lethal corner and shredding anything that didn't run away.

Then pressed on, fast, knowing they were leaving a lot of enemies hiding in buildings to ambush them on the way back, but GIs survived in high-intensity battlespace by moving fast and not allowing the enemy to concentrate firepower. They'd nearly gotten stuck against that roadblock, and Sandy hated it. Direct thrusts into intensely hostile battlespace were not what GIs were made for, she had little firesupport here; the enemy had all the advantages of well-prepared terrain and tactics, and she'd already lost four of the roughly fifty GIs who were accompanying her now on this thrust into Central Zone against Kiet's previous orders, plus several more wounded who'd fallen back or were holding the lines of retreat open. The farther she pushed in, the more surrounded she'd become.

Advancing over rooftops was a pain, leaping and running from one to the next, under fire from surrounding buildings, some of which they could silence with return missile fire, but anti-missile systems were taking out more and more of those. Worse, they were under observation here, and enemy tacnet was dropping light arty and missiles on them that only fast evasive action could save them from. But they had to stay off the roads because one tank or AMAPS could turn those narrow canyons into deathtraps.

By now the surrounding circumstance was chaos; Cai and now Ari announcing in her ear that various corporate networks were showing signs of instability. Internal trouble they said, sign enough that there were GIs breaking loose in there, though exactly on what scale these particular revolutions were, there was no way to tell.

Ahead the first intranet nodes were only a few hundred meters away. Sandy put a grenade through a nearby apartment window, leapt for cover behind a rooftop eave, fire snapping past, then dropped to ground level as a missile blew a neighbouring rooftop to hell. Ran at ground level until space ran out, then sprang back up, bouncing off a high wall to make a new rooftop, other GIs bounding forward amidst sporadic incoming . . . a crash as AP grenades blew one of them flying into a wall, more indirect fire hurtling in as Sandy slid once more and fell to the ground, cover from more explosions.

Pressed against a wall as concussions blasted masonry around her, she discovered that she wasn't enjoying this at all. She couldn't do anything about all this incoming; they were exposed here, the enemy were using indirect fire, always the best policy against GIs, and no amount of synthetic physical toughness would save them from accurate high explosives. But if they didn't capture the intranet nodes and stop the corporations from reactivating the killswitch . . .

A burst of cannon fire ended a GI's run across the rooves ahead, and Sandy sprinted across a yard, over an adjoining wall, and found the fallen GI on a carport rooftop, arm and part of the chest gone, blood everywhere, dying amidst convulsions. It was Angela, nice girl, low 40s designation; a few days ago Sandy had chatted with her about music, clothes, and the strangeness of civvie fashions. She'd never see any of that now. Before she could think another thought, another huge airburst had her rolling for cover and blew another of her team off a rooftop onto the road.

"Cai!" she yelled. "I need to make contact with all the corporate GIs if you can swing it! I can't protect all these intranet nodes, just this one closest will be a struggle, I'm getting shot to hell out here and if we keep going we're all dead!"

Then she saw the AMLORAs rising. Not heading for her, she realised a second later, watching those trajectories unfold. Heading for . . . Chancelry HQ.

"Reichardt!" Crawling into a narrow space between buildings for better cover as more arty came in. "Kressler and Heldig just launched AMLORAs, target Heldig and fire now, one orbital round to my fire control."

A pause that felt like a lifetime. "*I see only three AMLORA rounds fired,*" came Reichardt's reply. "*You're asking me to kill thousands of people on that?*"

"One round to my fire control," Sandy repeated, leaping back up to rooftop level, where tacnet identified a target. "It will take four minutes to arrive, if AMLORA firing has ceased by then I'll detonate it short of the target." Landed and lay flat on the rooftop, scanning apartment windows nearly a kilometer away. A human face appeared, with laser ranger, a tacnet-filler. Sandy fired, a slight pause then the head blew off. She moved before they could counter-track her.

Detonations back at Chancelry HQ, but she had no time to observe what they hit. If Reichardt refused her, they were all screwed, the corporations were testing them, a failure to respond would encourage more of the same.

"One round to your fire control," said Reichardt. *"On its way, good luck."*

Sandy skidded over rooftops like a crazed pebble bouncing along the surface of choppy water. Hurdled an intervening street and paused at a good vantage over a minor industrial complex ahead. The infranet node was under that somewhere.

"Hello, all corporate CEOs," she announced on general frequency. "This is Kresnov. If you all look skyward, you'll find your defence screen radars showing you an incoming orbital round from where *Mekong* parked them in geostationary over your heads. That's what happens when you launch AMLORAs at Chancelry HQ. One of you is about to die, I haven't decided which yet. Keep firing AMLORAs and the rest will follow."

It would come in several thousand Ks too fast for anti-missile defences to stop. Not quite a nuclear-scale blast, but enough to make a permanent geological feature where a corporate HQ had once been.

GIs smashed into buildings for cover overlooking the industrial complex and used that to gain line of sight. Missiles took out a tank, several AMAPS, but their ammo was now getting short. Fast, close engagement silenced more targets, then GIs were blowing holes in factory walls and dashing inside, Sandy joining them.

A fast run through one warehouse complex, someone uncovered tunnels beneath buildings that hadn't shown up on the schematics. Sandy jumped down a ladder, into a dark space filled with pipes and cables, and followed several junction signs until she reached a wide open space with big fuel cell generators in industrial steel containers, a lot of power routings, and a bunch of ceiling wiring along the aircon that looked like it was probably coms.

"This is why they can't blast it from the air," she announced, transmitting visual feed from her headset. "It would take out power for half of Central Zone." Power in Droze was serious, with no native water and air that got lethal in poor weather; power could be life and death.

"If their security situation gets bad enough," said Rishi at her shoulder, "they might blast it anyway." Rishi wore a heavy suit, new shrapnel holes in the armour, the back-mounted launcher smoking from a recent shot. She'd no sooner spoken than two of the five remaining nodes disappeared. On a nearby rooftop, tacnet prioritised a visual feed showing two fireballs rising.

"Just because they're underground," came Poole's voice, *"doesn't mean they can't blow them by hand."*

Looking at this, she could make a few schematic guesses about the intranet nodes—they relayed the signal above ground via a mass of antenae scattered over these buildings. Above ground, that could be jammed, but jamming would sever corporate forces' own communications. Besides which, nodes like this ran networks underground, and you had to cut those lines of transmission as well as block the wireless frequencies if you wanted to jam the network, because the network would adjust information flows and leapfrog severed sections by alternate means. Thus Cai's instruction that these five primary nodes all had to go down simultaneously to block the signal. Three left.

And three minutes left on the orbital round. Sandy gave orders, deploying a defensive perimeter about the industrial complex. She was above ground between buildings when a call came in. It was Patana, CEO of Dhamsel Corporation.

"You're about to commit a warcrime by the Federation's own statutes," he told her.

"Don't care," said Sandy. "Let your GIs go, peacefully, and cease all offensive actions, or those incoming rounds will multiply."

"If your Captain agreed with that rationale he'd have fired more than one round already. Furthermore, not all of our GIs want to leave."

"Good," said Sandy, walking to a corner near the complex perimeter. "Then you won't mind dropping your internal emergency alerts and allowing full observation privileges to our Captain in orbit."

"Commander!" one of her soldiers cut in. *"I've got GIs, escapees!"*

Sandy looked, saw broken visuals, running men and women, a few armed, none armoured, some wounded. Looking desperate and bloodied, like they'd just run through heavy fire without the means to fight back.

". . . lots dead!" one of them was shouting, as Sandy's troops laid fire back up the road they'd come down. *"We heard about your uprising, we heard what they were doing . . . corporates locked us up, a few of us they just killed . . ."*

"*We had to get out!*" a girl shouted over the top of her friend, eyes wild. "*We had to get out, they were gonna kill us all, I heard them talking!*"

"*. . . we can level Chancelry HQ well before any orbital warhead gets here, and we will if you do not terminate that round immediately!*" Patana was yelling at her. "*You have twenty seconds to terminate or we open fire!*"

"Most of my people aren't even in Chancelry HQ," Sandy said coldly, crouched on the complex perimeter and watching escapee GIs rushing across the street ahead, pursued by tracer fire. "Better yet, you just selected yourself for targeting. Everyone in Dhamsel Zone now has two minutes to live, unless you comply."

"*Ten seconds!*" Patana shouted. Sandy didn't need audio analysers to hear the tremble in his voice. "*Kresnov!*"

"See you in hell, motherfucker."

"*Commander!*" Reichardt overrode her. "*You're not going to kill thousands of people just because you're pissed off . . .*" Sandy cut him off. She had fire control, it was out of Reichardt's hands now. If Patana fired, everyone back at Chancelry HQ was dead, Kiril included. If she backed down, same thing. Only this way, she'd take that asshole with them.

AMLORAs launched, lots of them. She could see them on tacnet, bright flares against a dark sky. But immediately, she didn't think they were heading for Chancelry.

"Incoming!" Sandy yelled, as a dozen other voices echoed it, and GIs took off running to get clear of the industrial complex. "They're going to blast it!"

Across from her was a market building with a truck drive-in at the rear. Sandy raced into it, down the slope, and tore through a roller door to basement parking.

"Cai, we're about to lose the intranet!" She slid behind several large vehicles, other GIs rushing in around her. "Do something fast!"

A series of huge thuds, and the ground rocked and shook. The concussion made her ears pop, shook light fittings from the ceiling.

"*Commander, I can't do anything,*" said Cai helplessly. "*I'm not a magician, the intranet is the only thing preventing the reestablishment of killswitch channels.*"

Save shooting her own AMLORAs at them. Which would most likely not do enough damage and would invite counterstrike that would surely level Chancelry HQ, and would not be responded to by Reichardt because she'd have shot first. Time moved at a crawl. She stared at the tacnet picture, stared at it so hard her brain nearly bled, like staring at a chessboard so hard you could force some new, miraculous move to appear from the harsh reality of squares and pieces. But no matter which new angle she considered it from, the reality was the same—checkmate.

"*Those AMLORAs were not fired at Chancelry HQ, Commander*," came a new voice. CEO Huang, Kressler Corporation. It was an integrated com, patched into multiple receivers, Reichardt included. "*The Federation is just over a minute away from a strike killing several thousand League citizens for no commensurate reason. When League Fleet arrives, this will be presented to them as an act of war.*"

"*No way, Commander!*" Kiet interjected. "*The minute you terminate that round, they'll use the killswitch!*"

"They'll use it anyway." Sandy got to her feet. Past the combat reflex, she could feel very little but dawning horror. GIs sheltering in the basement loading bay were also standing, staring at her. Hers was a command channel, not usually accessible to regular troops, but now it was open. She didn't remember changing those settings, but she must have.

Reichardt cut in. "*Commander, you are a Federation operative. You cannot single-handedly commit an act of war and expect to retain the Federation's support in whatever you choose to do next.*"

Think about the long game, he meant. Think about the larger things at stake. That was easy for someone sitting in orbit thousands of clicks away to say. Someone who did not have to look into the wide eyes of fellow synthetics who had only just managed to break free, hoping for freedom and a long life, now to realise they were all about to die.

Forty seconds. High above, the round was entering atmosphere. Tacnet showed the intranet gone, all remaining nodes removed. Corporate GIs had no autistic mode, no defence against the killswitch signals; even if they could turn their uplinks off, the codes would reactivate them, anywhere within range. Her own had been shut off, barriered behind so many layers that even Cai couldn't get in there without direct cable access and several hours with serious barrier breakers. But this was what it was built for. A big red button, labelled "press in case of revolution."

"Don't do it," she whispered. "Please."

"*We won't do anything,*" came the response. "*We haven't done anything. Terminate the round now, and we'll talk.*"

Lies. She ought to let the round land, for preemptive revenge. But whether it landed or not, they'd still use the killswitch. The only question was whether she'd betray the trust the Federation had placed in her by granting her a commission in the process.

"*Don't you do it, Commander!*" Kiet shouted. "*You can't back down now!*"

A girl walked to her, a GI, unarmed in a torn and bloody tracksuit. She looked scared. "Don't forget about us," she begged. She grasped Sandy's hands. "Don't let this happen to any more of us. Promise you won't."

Fifteen seconds.

"I promise," said Sandy. Escapees hugged each other. Her own troops looked at her disbelievingly, then back again, with mounting desperation. Surely they hadn't gone through all of that for nothing?

Ten seconds. Any closer and the round would do damage. Sandy triggered termination and saw the signal on firecontrol abruptly vanish. Time passed, a frozen stillness. Then a great, rolling boom, like some unworldly thunder. If she'd been outside, she would have seen a great light high above, a brief and secondary sun.

"*Very good,*" said Huang with satisfaction. "*Now we can complete our transaction.*"

Some GIs fell immediately. Others screamed and thrashed. The implants in their brainstems turned white-hot and exploded. Straight human brains had no nerve receptors, but in GIs it wasn't that simple. Sandy forced herself to watch, as others cried, or embraced the dying, or turned away to stare at the walls. This she was going to remember. This would not be for nothing.

CHAPTER TWO

Justice Rosa was a cyclist. Sandy hadn't thought the activity more than one of those odd, antiquated things that for some reason hadn't died yet, despite the many more hightech forms of transport available. But Justice needed to interview her for his book, and liked to cycle at least 250 kilometers a week, and so thought to combine the two. A lot of Tanushan roads had cycle-lanes, something she'd barely noticed before. They were just wide enough to ride two abreast, and since all traffic was automated, there was no danger from vehicles—just pedestrians, who Justice complained often thought the cycle-lanes belonged to them, despite being clearly marked otherwise.

Sandy hadn't expected how nice it was. Tanusha was both awesomely huge, busy, and hightech, but also pretty on the small, intimate scale. Walking let you appreciate a neighbourhood, but it was too slow to see any more than a tiny sliver of the megacity. Cars and maglevs were faster but reduced the city's details to an air-conditioned blur. Cycling held a middle speed, about 40 kph, air on the face and sun on the skin, everything to look at with no glass between you and it, much the same freedom she loved about surfing. And cycling you could observe how neighbourhoods changed, from the crowds and soaring towers of city hubs, to sudden bridges over Tanusha's many river tributaries, to green parks and patches of urban jungle. A game of cricket on a roadside field, the whack of bat on ball. Roadside buskers, music, and singing. The whine and hum of a big VIP cruiser coming to land at a riverside transition zone. Children laughing and shouting in a school playground.

"So where do GIs fit in with the nationalism debate?" Justice asked her, long brown legs pumping easily. Sandy could have managed a massively larger gear, of course, but she got a better exercise-heartrate kick from the smaller one. Much of a GI's musculature response was mechanical and wouldn't count as exercise in the short term, but if she pushed it long enough, constant use triggered nutrient flow, meaning blood, and a thumping heart to push it all around just like in regular humans.

"GIs are born with nationalism built in," said Sandy. "That's the joke of it; we're not allowed to choose."

"So when you were a soldier in the League, you loved the League unconditionally?"

"Yes."

"Is that all foundational tape teach, do you think?"

"No," said Sandy. "It's just like a child and her parents. The bond is instinctual; you can't second-guess it. Children love their parents because they have to, that's their environment, they're stuck with it. It's a part of them and determines their welfare, so they'd better love it, because its survival is their survival."

"Hmm," said Justice. They pedalled over a short bridge. Sandy recognised this stretch of Derry District, where a terrorist bomb had gone off a few months after her arrival in Tanusha. Nearly six years ago now. She and Vanessa had responded to that one, briefly, and had been relieved that no one had been killed. Cycling around the city, it struck her how much personal history she'd accumulated in this place. "Sociologists will tell you that minor nationalisms will spring up wherever a commonality of people share a unique bond that at the same time separates them from everyone else. Race, religion, etc."

"Gender," said Sandy.

"Gender nationalism," Justice mused, as they left the bridge, between tall apartment towers. "Interesting concept."

"Gender's the one that struck me the most, arriving in civvie life. I mean, race, religion, and all that are interesting, but it's all blending together, and both Federation and League have done a pretty good job at making a single, bigger nationalism, or set of nationalisms, for everyone to belong to. So you live in Tanusha, and you're Indian, or African, or whatever, but you're Callayan first, and Federation too . . ."

"No, most Tanushans are Tanushan first," Justice disagreed. "There's no snob like an urban snob."

"But gender's the thing that transcends everything else, the thing that no amount of modernisation can change. People cling to gender types the same way they yearn for sex, it's primal."

"Please don't tell me you're becoming a feminist," said Justice. "All that trivial, girly fluff Tanusha's feminists want to destroy is the stuff about femininity I like."

"No, I've grown to quite like the fluff too," Sandy admitted, smiling. "After a military upbringing, pointless decoration is lovely."

"Yes."

"Just not on me."

"Nobody's perfect," said Justice.

"And I'm alarmed at how many people define their gender identity by the fluff, without realising that it *is* fluff."

"Well, you'll get that in any prosperous, self-indulgent society," said Justice. "And it's by no means just a female problem."

"It wasn't a gender-specific observation." She remembered something that made her grin. "Rami Rahim had a piece about men messing with the penis genome in the gene-screen labs. Apparently despite all laws against it, penis size in the general population is increasing so fast that soon sex will be impossible. Women will need larger vaginas to accommodate, and he went on to describe a world where there were no people left, just giant walking genitals."

Well, it was funny when Rami did it. Comedic delivery wasn't her strong point.

"I think you're avoiding the question you know is coming by talking about sex." Sandy frowned at him. Justice's expression was impenetrable behind his cycling glasses and the rim of his helmet. "You do that when you're uncomfortable with a line of questioning."

"I wasn't aware this was a 'line of questioning,'" Sandy replied. "Unlike you, I cease hostilities with my dayjob; a conversation's just a conversation."

"This is my dayjob," said Justice. "Now that all these GIs are arriving in Tanusha, it's inevitable they'll all acquire some kind of synthetic nationalism. What form will it take?"

He was right; it wasn't a question she was particularly comfortable answering. "I guess that depends on how they're treated."

"What difference will that make?"

"People who are well treated are less likely to form a defensive group nationalism in response."

"I'm not sure that explains the Chinese community," said Justice. Traffic lights ahead, and they slowed, an intersection between apartments, a large shopping mall, and a university campus nestled in garden grounds. Students queuing at the lights to cross. "On most Federation worlds Chinese communities have stuck together irrespective of how well they've been treated—on most worlds very well."

"Not on worlds where they're the majority, which is plenty. They disperse like any dominant group."

"Yes, but we're talking about minorities." They stopped alongside waiting cars and students. A student peered at her curiously, as though recognising her. "GIs in Tanusha will always be a minority. And they'll always be very different from the surrounding population, which is arguably why Chinese minorities tend to cluster, as do plenty of other ethnic minorities."

"Excuse me," the student asked her. "Are you . . . ?"

"Get mistaken for her all the time," Sandy explained with a smile. The student clicked a photo on her portable, not believing her. The lights changed, and they cycled off. "Look, you can't generalise about GIs. We don't have an ethnicity. We speak English because that's the League's dominant tongue, lucky for us it's the Federation's too. But we understand nothing of the cultural origins, and none of it holds any significance for us. Ethnic and religious nationalisms are formed by shared history, but GIs are relatively new, we've very little of that either.

"Nearly all of my best friends are non-GIs. My only best friend who *is* a GI has probably gone even more that way than I have. She's married a non-GI, adopted kids, and is so fascinated by early childhood development that she's made it her other profession—a biological process that GIs are completely divorced from."

"Not completely," Justice disagreed. "It has some bearing on early GI neurological development too."

"And our early neurological development has turned out to be far more unpredictable than the League initially thought. We're a big, wide bunch of different personality types, and the longer we're allowed to evolve in peaceful, civilian environments, the more diverse we'll become. I'm asking everyone who they're voting for in the next election, those who have citizenship and can vote. So far it's a completely even split. The kind of nationalism you're talking about comes from a homogeneity that I just don't think GIs have. We don't cluster."

"But you're tracking their voting intentions."

"Sure."

"So obviously you're concerned about how this new synthetic community will turn out, surrounded by strange non-synthetic civilians who are often distrustful. And you're keeping other tabs too, no doubt."

She was helping people she trusted to run full-scale psychological analyses on them. But she wasn't about to share that now. "It's interesting," she said shortly. "We synthetics are all just as interested as you straights, trust me."

"There is one other factor that can lead to the creation of a group nationalism," Justice continued, as they pedalled into pleasant, leafy suburbia. "A powerful, charismatic leader."

"Then you're lucky they've only got me, aren't you?" Sandy said drily. "Dull, practical, loyal servant of the Federation that I am."

Justice smiled. "And there's one factor that makes some people wonder if GIs aren't especially vulnerable to a powerful, charismatic leader. You've got a caste system. It's your dirty little secret."

"Well, for one, your analogy stinks. Lower castes in old India didn't happily submit to rule by the upper castes, they all hated the upper castes, they only obeyed with a knife to their throat."

"Sure," said Justice. "What you have is worse. It's the caste system the Indian upper castes would have loved to have, where their power and privilege were actually founded in something real. Lower-caste Indians proved it was all bullshit the first chance they got. But your lower-caste GIs, they really can't outdo you in anything, can they? And a lot of them worship you. As might be natural, given that you're the one who saw the light and led them to this promised land."

"I'm not Moses," Sandy said testily. "And even if I were, you'd still have nothing to worry about, because leading the Israelites was like herding cats. And still is, if my Jewish Tanushan friends are any indication."

Justice smiled. "Agreed. But if you and your GIs are the Israelites, and the Federation is the Roman Empire, then one of us has cause for concern. Because the Israelites gave birth to something that turned Western civilisation on its head, and the Roman Empire inside out. And a lot of Romans, if they'd known it was coming, would have killed every last Jew long before the Nazis thought of it."

Danya sat on the stairs overlooking the dingy basement, as Anku scanned his booster on a cluttered table. Svetlana walked around the basement, peering at the junk piled onto shelves or tables. A lot of it was salvage, and some surely stolen. Anku was a collector of odds and ends, far enough away from their usual haunts in Rimtown that few there had any leverage on him. And he owed them a favour.

"This better be worth it," said Anku, reading data off a separate screen. He was hooked in, a cord to the back of his head, but not directly to the booster. Given where Danya got it from, that could be dangerous. "With the number of guys after you two, you must have done something serious."

"We didn't do anything," Svetlana retorted, handling some interesting-looking tools.

"Don't touch those," said Anku, barely looking at her. She made a face and put them back. "Rimtown Home Guard wants you, Whalen Home Guard have the word out; they're looking for you too. And who's that junk shop family over in Steel Town? Ting?"

"They say we stole from them," said Danya, chin on arms, arms over raised knees. "But we were helping someone."

"So you did steal from them."

"For a good cause."

"The best cause I know is me," said Anku. "Word is you stole the Ting's GI, joined the uprising."

"How can a couple of kids steal a GI?"

"That uprising killed a lot of people. Artillery came down all over Droze, now we've got drones and flyers all over, Home Guard shooting them, them shooting Home Guard . . ."

"Home Guard are stupid," said Svetlana, checking out several useful-looking lengths of cord. "What's the point of shooting at drones, the corporations just make more, and people get killed."

"If Home Guard don't shoot at corporate drones," Anku asked, "what's the point of Home Guard?"

"Good question," Svetlana replied.

"Boss everyone else around," said Danya. "Home Guard are about power here, fighting the corporations is just an excuse."

"Bingo," said Anku with a smile, still peering at his screens. "Well done, young sir, the prize is yours."

"What prize?"

Anku gestured to the room. "Pick something of absolutely no value. Anything at all." All who knew Anku knew he placed value on every piece of junk he collected. He sat back in his chair and rubbed both his chins. "Well, the defensive barriers on this are amazing. Military grade, probably AI constructed. Who did you say gave it to you again?"

"Friends," said Danya. "I have the passcodes."

Anku looked dubious. "Well, it better be a gift, because if you stole it from someone, those people will want it back. This is League military, probably spec ops. With this you could gain control of some serious systems."

It had been a gift to Svetlana from their GI friends. Just before the attack, one of them had realised the advance meant leaving Svetlana all alone. She'd given her a bag of some stuff, with the carelessness of a middle-designation GI who didn't know much about civilian society, and what was and wasn't considered suitable equipment for the possession of children.

"What kind of systems?"

"Anything with wireless access. Of course you need uplinks, internal or external . . . in your case external of course, since you're kids. You have an external unit?" Danya nodded. Anku looked a little jealous. "Well-equipped little buggers. Use that to acquire a wireless gateway, and this booster should break you in. Lots of uses for conniving little trolls up to no good."

"Valuable?"

Anku's face turned suddenly thoughtful. He tried to shrug offhandedly, fingers interlaced in his long, greasy ponytail. But Danya caught the glint of greed in his eyes, the suppressed eagerness. "Could be. You want me to look for some buyers?"

Danya kept his bored expression in place with far more convincing ease. "No. Not a good time for us to go around advertising ourselves. Someone would dob us in just for our stuff."

"People will do that anyway," said Anku. "If you did it through me, I'd make sure no one knew who the seller was."

Danya shook his head. Put a hand into his backpack and pulled out a heavy black pistol. Anku's eyes widened. Suitable equipment for children indeed. "We can defend what we've got. And I'd rather defend a useful tool than a shitload of cash we can't spend without showing our faces in public."

"I'd be careful who I showed that to," Anku warned him. Everyone knew the corporate bounty on guns and their owners. It was an easy way to make money, and for the corporations to keep their threat levels down beyond the walls. No one collected on Home Guard, because Home Guard killed informers. But a street kid with a gun was just a bounty awaiting collection.

"I am," said Danya. Something buzzed on his earbud. Frequency chatter, probably Home Guard. Svetlana pulled AR glasses and activated; they fed off the receiver in her backpack.

"Flasher drone," she said, observing what it showed her. "Home Guard are watching it."

"The feeder drone still there?" Danya asked. That was the high-altitude one, a feeder because it sent a constant feed back to the corporations. Who were putting so much countermeasures up lately, Home Guard had stopped bothering to shoot missiles at them. Missiles were expensive, and limited.

Svetlana nodded. "Yep. And another one up over West Side."

"Wow," said Anku, watching them. "You two did hit a treasure trove. Nice gear, kids."

"Friends," said Danya, putting the gun away. "Svet, we better go."

He felt nervous being in one place for too long. And more nervous being outside and moving. Anku had several ways out of his basement, then along some dark corridors, past some people sleeping in the central corridor, dirty limbs amongst tangled blankets—it was safest, protected from further artillery by layers of concrete. Power was out once more, which probably had something to do with all the shooting in the corporate zone. But now when he stopped at the rear exit to peer out the glass doors, the sky in that direction was silent once more. A few hours ago it had been like a Pantalan static storm but with streaking missiles and scattering tracer. Now nothing, save a few long-burning fires aglow against the night horizon.

"Parking," he said, leading them to the adjoining parking exit instead. Nervous habits, born of life on the streets of Droze. The parking exit led into a covered section protecting a few vehicles and an armed security guard with a mechanical cybernetic arm who stared at them. The kids pulled down hats and hoods against the cold and made for the road. They paused at the sidewalk. Once beyond the covered area, aerial surveillance would spot them. Them and thousands of others in this region of Droze; the streets were quiet but not *that* quiet. If the people Danya feared were looking for them really were, they'd have no way of sorting their heat signature from those other thousands. But children made a smaller signature, surely. And they'd know there were two of them.

He pulled out his own AR glasses. The booster Anku had been lovingly examining was hacked nicely into the Home Guard feed, which gave them visuals on the feeder drone. It was approaching a position where it could look down this street with no cover. Luckily the corporations had poor satellite surveillance, something about a hyperactive sun and poor planetary magnetics . . .

"Wait a moment," he said, waiting for the drone to pass.

"You don't really think the corporations are after us?" Svetlana wondered.

"They know who we are, Svet," said Danya. "CEO Patana himself threatened us when I was with Sandy before the attack, I saw it. Or he threatened Kiril. They think they can get to Sandy through us."

"I bet that was Sandy," said Svetlana, eyes alive, nodding toward the corporate zone. The fireworks, she meant. "I bet that was her blasting them all to bits!"

"She's not a superhero, Svet. GIs die just like anyone."

"She got Chancelry, didn't she?" Svetlana had been *so* impressed. Chancelry Corporation were the all-powerful overlords of Droze, Pantala, and all the immediate universe. Even the gang bosses and Home Guard commanders of Rimtown and the other, outer districts of Droze lived in terror of earning Chancelry's displeasure, for all Home Guard's tough talk of warfare. Now, their friend Sandy had torn through their heaviest outer defences and occupied Chancelry HQ. It was like Abraham's tales in his little Rimtown mosque of a man named David who had once killed a giant. Although Danya didn't think David had been a GI, and Sandy had been using better weapons than slingshots.

"She had a lot of help getting Chancelry. For all we know most of her GIs died taking Chancelry; we've no idea how many of them survived."

"I bet lots!" Svetlana said hotly. "They wouldn't have captured Chancelry if they'd lost too many! And I bet she rescued Kiril too!"

It was a total non-sequitur, but Kiril was the dominant recurring thought for both of them. And she had no proof of it either. Danya would have argued the point, but it was too hard. Svetlana wanted to believe. Being younger, she had that luxury. As the oldest, he never had. And now that logic forced him into possible conclusions he couldn't bear to face. Kiril was over there, in the direction of all that shooting an hour ago. Had been over there, out of sight and unreachable, for more than a week. He could have died in the initial attack on Chancelry and been dead over a week, there was no way to tell.

He and Svetlana had taken two days to reunite after the attack at one of their emergency rendezvous spots. Since then they'd been hiding from various drones, spies, and people out to get them. As scary as that was, Danya didn't find it nearly as scary as wondering what had happened to Kiril. It was a fear so great he was almost tempted to let the corporations grab them, so long as he could know Kiril's fate. But that was stupid—Kiril had been in Chancelry, and the other corporations now knew as little of what went on in Chancelry as he did.

As they waited, Svetlana pulled some flatbread from her pack, tore some, and offered half to him, eating hers. He ate. It was dry now, three days old, and Danya dreaded buying more for fear that shopkeepers might be alerted to them. Corporations did that sometimes, to get the people they wanted. They had cash, Svetlana had salvaged a pair of boots and a knife the GIs had also left, which Danya had since sold. Svetlana could always steal some more, but he hated it when she did that; she was so good at stealing that he wasn't sure she always saw the point of money. And they could get a lot more cash if they sold some of their newer acquisitions . . . but as he'd told Anku, where could he spend it? When the bounty on you got high, you trusted no one.

The drone was passing. "Svet," said Danya as she prepared to move from their wall. "I have an idea." Svetlana waited patiently. So trusting. Sometimes he wished she wasn't. She had more confidence in him most of the time than he did. "Do you remember Janu?"

"Of course. The Wilkie job." Wilkie were a rival family out in Al Khartoum. Danya and Svetlana had been offered good money to spy on one of their establishments from an opposing attic for a week. They'd taken it with trepidation, but far from getting screwed, or killed, they'd been paid well, and even thanked. "That was good money."

"Svet, if you're sure you heard micro drones the other night . . ."

"I did! I heard them buzzing, you were asleep so you didn't . . ."

"I know, I believe you." Svetlana was placated. "But if they're using micros, we're not going to be able to stay hidden very long. I mean, we don't even know whose micros they are, and I was thinking . . . if Home Guard and the Tings and whoever else knows the corporations are looking for us too, that only gives them more reason to find us, so they can get a big bounty."

Svetlana nodded impatiently. "So what about Janu?"

"I was thinking maybe he'd help us."

Svetlana blinked. "But he's a mobster. Danya, he has people killed, he could just hand us over to the corporations, or the Tings, and . . ."

"No." Danya shook his head firmly. "He's never taken corporate money, and he deals in all the stuff the corporations ban, so they'd rather him dead. Home Guard don't like him either because he shows them up on their turf. He's got a lot of people and technology, so if he helped us, we wouldn't have to worry about these fucking drones. And best of all, he's got contacts in the corporations with all his blackmarket stuff. I reckon if anyone could get in contact with Chancelry, find out if Kiril's okay, it would be him."

Svetlana's eyes widened at that. He knew he had her. "You think?"

"Maybe. This standoff with Chancelry could go on for weeks. Svet, I don't know if we can dodge these drones for weeks." And he didn't want to spend more weeks not knowing about Kiril. He didn't need to say it, she felt the same.

"But what can we give to Janu? All we've got is weapons, and he's got plenty already."

"I know." He stared past the wall at the cold, empty street and boarded shopfronts. "I'll think of something."

CHAPTER THREE

Sandy knelt in the shower stall and sobbed. It wasn't her accustomed reaction after a fight. But that fight had sucked. Her brain kept replaying that trapped, horrid sensation of the advance across Central Zone rooftops, unable to move fast on the streets thanks to defensive fire, cross-fired from all sides, and pinpointed by enemy arty. Tacnet was usually her friend, the puzzle that presented solutions. This time it had shown her nothing but a giant cage, slowly contracting on her.

The numerical certainty of losing friends with every few passing seconds as the rounds came in, and knowing there was nothing she could do to stop it save to keep advancing, condemning even more of her troops to die . . . she could see the blips on tacnet disappearing even now, accompanied by that rapid, pounding concussion. The memory brought on panic. She never panicked. Deep in combat reflex, the sensations of combat did not usually register on that emotional side of the brain in the same way they did with regular humans. But she was changing, older now. Her brain had new pathways, had exercised new emotional connections that hadn't been there a few years ago. And this felt just awful.

And she'd failed. Nearly all of the attempted escapees were dead, save for a few that Kiet's troops had moved away from the initial crash site in time to be clear of the killswitch frequencies. Possibly as many as several thousand GIs, spread across the four remaining mega corporations. Mostly not experimentals like in Chancelry, just combatants, of whom the corporations had become suddenly terrified, following events here. Of course she'd known she would fail; Kiet's plans were crazed wishful thinking based on idealistic rage. But his incompetence had forced her to try, and had put her into an unwinnable trap. Never again.

"Sandy?" The stall door opened, and there was Kiril, worried. "Sandy, are you crying?"

"Yeah." She raised her face to the hot water, so that there could be no telling between water and tears. "Yeah, kid, I'm crying."

Kiril came into the stall with her and hugged her. Sandy was baffled. It was a dumb thing to do; he was getting all wet. It was also awkward, because she-of-no-parenting-skills-whatever now had to worry about female adult nudity and young boys, which wasn't something she'd ever been concerned with before. What would Rhian say that could make sense of such behaviour?

She'd say that Kiril was actually the smarter, because getting wet and being nude were stupid and irrelevant, and Kiril ignored them both by trying to make her feel better. Because kids were like that; while adults tried to navigate between grown-up obstacles, kids ploughed straight through them with utter unconcern to go for what mattered to them. And she recalled Danya and Svetlana telling her what a sweet boy Kiril was, how he liked to hug and liked to make friends. Too sweet for a street kid, and Danya had worried about it, fearing he'd make friends of the wrong kind.

Sandy hugged him back. To her surprise, it did make her feel better. She held him for quite a long time. It made him very wet, which was completely selfish of her, but neither of them cared.

"Come on," she said, and kissed him roughly. "You need to get dry."

"Hey, Sandy," he said cheerfully. "I'm having a shower in my clothes!" Like it was the most amusing thing ever.

Sandy smiled. "Well, that's no good. Do you have some dry clothes?"

"Yeah, Ratnika helped me wash some earlier."

"Well, let's go and get them, and let's thank Ratnika."

"I already did, she's really nice."

It was well past midnight, and she left Kiril with Poole in medical, with instructions to let him fall asleep on a spare bed when he got too tired. Medical was a mess with injured GIs, tended to by other GIs like Poole with barely enough field medic skills to cope, and she had no business leaving a six-year-old boy in such an environment. But all three AMLORA rounds fired on Chancelry HQ had hit the 4-A building beside the main armoury, where small-arms reserves were stored, which were not the strategic weapons the companies were scared of, and led to speculation they'd been trying to stir a counter uprising amongst Chancelry's GI regs, and disabling local defences. Sandy was having all network traffic scoured for backdoors into local systems in case their local regs had been contacted, and all regs were under surreptitious watch. In the meantime, Kiril would never be more than a few meters away from her or Poole. Given what she was about to do, she knew that now, it had to be Poole.

GIs had gathered on the ground floor to 9-R. Sandy walked through the main hall, past stacked ammunition boxes, lounges, and meeting rooms now converted into infantry-ready rooms, where GIs congregated between armour rosters. The past few days it had been a social space, this conditioned air filled with the smell of mess hall food and the sound of rock music. Now it was silent, save a few dutifully holding to their maintenance tasks on armour or weapons.

The lobby was where they gathered, high glass walls and public sculpture, where Chancelry HQ presented its public face. A modernist human figure, towering up the sides of open-cut floors, balconies overlooking the space below. Sandy found something about its human distortions darkly ironic.

The gathering of GIs was maybe forty strong, all armed, a few armoured but mostly not. Tired, some showered, a few injured, they wore whatever odd combinations of civvie or military clothes they could scrounge. Kiet's desert dwellers had their military fatigues, League issue and now a little old, cast-offs from the war that they were. Rishi's Chancelry experimentals had only company fatigues, black and navy blue, with the civvie stuff they'd "borrowed." Some of the former had long hair, or braids, or other unorthodoxies. They were old by GI standards, some even older than her. League soldiers stationed on Pantala before the crash, they'd been abandoned by the retreating League with the rest of the population, their berths on escaping ships granted to Droze VIPs instead. Rather than participate in the civil war that followed, they'd withdrawn to the deserts, where they'd been surviving for the past five years.

The Chancelry experimentals on the other hand were all green and new, neat haircuts and wide eyes. In Sandy's old Dark Star unit the veterans had said such GIs were so new they squeaked. Chancelry had bred them to die, entire batches living and dying in experimental surgeries, barely knowing each other existed, their environments so tightly controlled they'd not even questioned the need to step outside. Until Sandy had arrived and exposed the truth to one of them: Rishi. Who had done the human thing and freaked out completely, and led an uprising that would have failed had not Sandy and Kiet led his desert dwellers on an explosive attack that had saved them in time, while also getting them trapped in this place, enemy corporate forces encircling all sides.

Kiet and several others were talking loudly while most listened. There were looks of disbelief and despair. Confusion as to how it had all gone so wrong. The civvie world thought GIs emotionless, but Sandy knew that could not be further from the truth. GIs could control emotion when necessary. But when it came out, it was more pure and less restrained than in straights. Most GIs Sandy knew would make terrible poker players.

Kiet saw her coming. Broad shouldered, he was Asian featured, squat and compact like a lot of male GIs. "You let them live!" he shouted at her furiously. "You traitor!"

The crowd parted as Sandy approached. She walked to him, vision already tracking well into multi-spectrum, muscles tensing in the onset of combat reflex. Kiet saw, eyes widening, and took a ready stance. Sandy reached for his throat, quite slowly and deliberately. Kiet swatted her grip away, giving Sandy contact, which quickly reversed into a series of technical hand, arm, and wrist grips, basic Wing Chun, and ending with Sandy pulling his guard aside for a direct face punch that she declined to take.

Kiet's eyes widened further—a 41 series, fairly advanced and with extensive experience of both life and combat, he wasn't accustomed to losing. Consciously of course he *knew* she was more advanced but had perhaps yet to understand what that really meant in practical terms. He tried again, another fast flurry, Sandy again refraining from a headshot, then another, then a fast reversal into a chest punch that she *did* take, which travelled ten centimeters and knocked him flying four meters backward.

Surrounding GIs caught him as he tried to regather his wits. Not having expected this. "What the hell does this prove?" he snarled at her.

"Not entirely there, are you?" said Sandy. Her calm was not that of disinterest, feigned or otherwise. It was deadly implacable. She advanced on him.

"So you can beat him in a fight," said Rishi from one side. "He's right to ask, what does it prove?"

"You assumed command over me," said Sandy. "Odd thing to do, for someone who's not as good a soldier."

Another flurry, this time Kiet brought a kick into play, but Sandy blocked with a raised leg, twisted an arm grip to cost him balance, reversed his counter to throw him completely off balance and into a humiliating arm lock. Kiet grimaced, forced down to one knee as Sandy applied simple pressure.

"This isn't that hard," she told him. "It's not that my hands move faster, they don't. It's that my brain processes everything you're doing with no blind spots at a much faster speed. You can't surprise me. By the time your brain has formulated a possible attack, I've already seen it coming."

She released him, and he backed off, flexing his arm and circling. Sandy followed.

"But today," she continued, "despite your disadvantages, you led good people into a fight against overwhelming odds. Once engaged, your focus of concentration became so small that I had to intervene to try and save the intranet, our last and only hope of saving those other GIs . . ."

"I had to act because you weren't going to!"

"I was waiting for an advantage." She lunged, Kiet defended, only to find it was a feint as she went low and swept his legs. He fell with a crash, rolling quickly up, but she was already there. "We managed to put in a block against their killswitch without them knowing. That took time. We might have had other covert successes, we were starting to penetrate their networks, we could have found others on the inside and set up something planned, like what happened here with Rishi, only more thought out . . ."

"We did that!" Kiet retorted. "We *made* contact. We started an uprising in several corporations, and it was working! It was then or never!"

"And you did all that without telling me?"

"Yes!" It should have hurt more than it did. She wasn't here to be loved by these people. It didn't even interest her. "We knew you'd never agree, and we saw our chance and went for it! You'd have waited until everyone was already dead!"

"And now they are dead," said Sandy with cool contempt. "Congratulations to all of you; with intellect and reasoning like that, the corporates are right, we deserve to get wiped out."

Deathly silence. All looked troubled. A few looked angry. Many were pale, upset. Some near tears.

"We fought for freedom!" said Kiet with emotion. "We fought the good fight!"

"No. You fought the bad fight. The good fight is where we get everyone out alive. That's not what happened. You didn't reason." She put a finger to her temple. "You felt." She thumped herself on the chest. "You thought with this. This isn't for thinking. This is." Back to her head. Silence in the room. All were staring.

"The thing with being a high-des GI is that you're not only smart, you feel," she said. "You feel with such intensity that sometimes it can be overwhelming. But feeling is not thinking. You can't substitute one for another. Just because it ought to be true, doesn't mean it is. Just because you feel it, doesn't mean it's there.

"Now I can understand how you'd all do something this stupid. But I want you to look around now, and not search for excuses, or point fingers of blame, but just consider what it's cost. I wanted what you wanted too. I wanted it so badly. But they're dead now."

A tear ran down her cheek. She hadn't thought she'd been speaking with that much intensity, but she must have been. Even past combat reflex, the emotion showed. She certainly was changing; a few years ago it couldn't have happened.

"Now figure out why it happened, and how you might be led better in the future. I'm not volunteering, my loyalties are Federation first, and God knows I'm not perfect, sure as hell the Federation isn't either. But I'm Federation first for a reason, and I think my way does the most good. If you don't buy that, fine. But I think you all just ran out of options."

"You're going to use this as an opportunity to blackmail everyone into joining your Federation cause?" Kiet asked incredulously.

Sandy gave him a look that could have melted lead. "You're lucky I let you live," she said icily. "You're lucky *they* let you live." With a glance around. "After what you just pulled, who would ever care again what you think?"

She strode out. GIs made way for her, with deference. A caste system, Justice had said that day cycling in Tanusha. Herself at the pinnacle, a caste of one.

CHAPTER FOUR

Vanessa was surprised they let her on the bridge during an action stations alarm, but there was an observer station behind the captain's chair, squeezed against the rear wall and bulky overheads, and she slid in and did the straps. It wasn't like the movies, no flashing lights and blaring alarms, just a short alert message that had sent everyone sprinting with high-speed deliberation. And alerts on uplinks, not the yellow of General Quarters, but a blood-red action stations, accompanied on her internal vision with an instruction to hit the bridge.

Reichardt said very little, just sat in the central Captain's chair and watched the steady flow of incoming information. With everyone strapped into stations along the narrow, bending length of the bridge, there was actually very little activity. People sat and watched their screens, plugged into all kinds of incoming data that was mostly passed from station to station in silence.

Vanessa's observer post had three screens with various overlapping data displays that she could manipulate but not input. One showed *Mekong*'s position, squeezed in behind Antibe Station in low Pantala orbit. Around it, trajectories of inbound Torahn vessels, mostly freighters, though suspiciously many and coordinated. The New Torahn united government had no navy as such, but it did possess a merchant fleet. Arming a merchant was a simple thing and was usually ineffective against genuine warships like *Mekong*. But *Mekong* was stuck sheltering behind Antibe Station, the only way it could maintain low orbital proximity around Pantala without Pantalan ground defences shooting it down. They were trapped down here, the only way they could protect the forces occupying Chancelry HQ. Reichardt hated it.

A second screen showed incoming. There was no telling yet what it was, trans-radiation showed a jump arrival, mid-system and closing fast, Pantala its obvious target. Current position and trajectory indicated it had come from League space. And it wasn't transmitting IDs. A combat jump, yet not the most hostile approach it could have made.

"Helm, thoughts?" Reichardt said after more tense seconds had passed.

"Sitting duck here," said Helm. Helm was always a starship's second-in-command. "But if we leave, Kresnov's dead."

"Worse, we'll concede authority," Com added. "We're staking our position, we can't concede we've done anything wrong."

"Does us no good if we're dead," Helm replied.

"We don't know it's hostile," said Reichardt. "League only know there's a Federation infiltration here, but they don't know its nature, and they don't want a new war any more than we do."

"And the locals normally won't welcome them any more than us," Arms added.

Listening to them, Vanessa wasn't certain any of them were arguing what they actually feared or believed. It sounded more as though each of them were taking a position for its own sake, making sure all the angles were covered. It impressed her.

"Helm," said Reichardt, "how long before elapse?" Elapse was the point at which their time ran out, before which they had to run or no amount of rapid acceleration could get them clear of the incoming kill zone.

"Seven minutes, nine seconds."

Reichardt studied those trajectories, nodding slowly. "Didn't come in that hot after all, did they? Gave us some time."

"Triple option scenario," said Helm. "Talk, run, or shoot."

"Last's out," said Reichardt. "It's talk or run, or both. Commander Rice, the Federation perspective, if you please."

"Commander Kresnov found evidence that the League is entering a period of intense sociological instability, technologically induced," said Vanessa, her mike carrying clear to everyone's ears. Also, she suspected, being recorded in the ship's log for later review by people who could probably have them all shot if it went wrong. Assuming they needed to. "This is evidence that a previous League scout tried to nuke Droze and kill a million people rather than let get out. If the League's about to fall apart, the Federation needs to know. I submit that protecting that data, and transmitting it to the Grand Council, is worth any sacrifice or risk at this point."

"Agreed," said Reichardt, fast enough to surprise her. Fleet Captains were usually cagey where their vessel's security was concerned. "But if the scout was going to nuke Droze, what will these guys be willing to do?"

"Taking out this station to get us would be a lot easier than nuking Droze," Helm added.

"Depends if these are regular League Fleet," said Vanessa. "Do League Fleet captains usually know what their scouts are up to? The scout captain made a decision based on information these captains may not be privy to."

"Usually they'd not be aware unless . . ."

"New entry, new entry!" Scan cut them off, the screen flashing once more as new points appeared on the system map. "Two four one degrees nadir by three two, AU point 86! Computer reads the size of that entry wave as three vessels, one of them a carrier."

"Getting serious now," said Helm in a low voice. "That stagger pattern looks like an entire combat squadron."

Now Vanessa's mouth was dry. Hell of a way to learn appreciation for the scale of decisions Fleet captains had to make. Those incoming ships could have fired already, scan wouldn't read it. With this much velocity, incoming fire would get here real soon and destroy anything vessel or station sized it hit. But staying here and talking to them would not elicit a response for several minutes more, it taking that long for the light wave to travel there and back. Already the light delay was showing them only what these ships *were* doing, several minutes ago. And they, of course, were only seeing where *Mekong* was, a similar time before.

"We're staying," said Reichardt. "Open a channel." Com did that. "League warships, this is Federation carrier *Mekong*. We are insystem on Federation business under Article 213 of the Federation charter. We are not hostile to League vessels, repeat, we are not hostile to League vessels. More Federation warships are inbound to this location, ETA imminent. Their intentions are not hostile, repeat, not hostile to League vessels. Awaiting your happy reply, *Mekong* ending."

"Nice," said Com. "Real nice."

"Famous last words," said Helm, to a snort of laughter. "Article 213 of the Federation charter? What's wrong with Article 98?"

"Invokes direct threats," Reichardt explained. "This is still technically League territory, they might take it wrong. The Commander knows Article 213, don't you Commander?"

"Not a fucking clue," said Vanessa. "Which means it's obscure, and they'll have to waste time searching for it, then figuring what it means."

"Creating indecision over implications," Helm completed.

"Real nice," Com repeated.

Several minutes later, League warships began cycling jump engines to shed velocity. But the real relief didn't start until they got an incoming transmission, thirty-three minutes later.

"Hello, Federation carrier Mekong, this is League carrier Defiance."

"Defiance," Helm muttered. "That's fucking Colou, wonderful."

"We are inbounds on League business in League territory, and you have committed an act of war by being here. Any hostile move on your part shall ensure your destruction. Defiance ending."

"She don't like you, Captain," said Arms.

"Howdy, Jess," said Reichardt. "Say now, that's not very friendly of you. You see, problem is, we're expecting a whole big bunch of Federation warships jumping in here any hour now, and if they all come in with your attitude, you, me, and most of this system are all going to be little smoking pieces. So my suggestion is this—why not leave the technicalities of whose fault this is to the lawyers, and not come in swinging your dick and ruining everybody's day?"

He disconnected and swivelled in his chair from amidst his encircling displays to give Vanessa a wry look. "Captain Jessica Colou, she's a mad old witch. We nearly killed each other a few times in the war."

"How nice," said Vanessa. She wondered if the diplomats in League and Federation had adequately taken into account that out here, the first line of diplomacy was heavily armed Fleet captains whom the distances of space had empowered to make their own decisions, and who continued to carry all the grudges from a thirty-year war that had killed many of their friends, and seen the captains in question trying to kill each other on numerous occasions. "She's unstable?"

"No, she's completely stable. But she's mean."

"Least she didn't shoot at us," Helm volunteered. "That's a change."

Svetlana waited in the vacant room several doors down from Janu's headquarters. That was a dull corner building, apartments atop a drive-in podium, various vehicles parked on the broken pavement. At regular intervals a new one would drive in, and men would open the garage doors, offering a glimpse of dark interiors and a lot of activity. When loaded, trucks would exit on the opposite side of the corner. Other trucks or pickups would drive out empty.

Janu worked in trade. Most of what he traded, the corporations didn't care about. And that stuff, Danya had once explained, worked as a cover for all the stuff they *did* care about, like weapons, pharma, biotech, and luxury stuff. Rumour was, a lot of his stuff was itself smuggled from corporation supplies, from people inside who were on the take. The corporations really didn't like that, because they hated having people in their own organisations who answered to the likes of Janu on the wrong side of the barriers.

There was nothing in the room save peeling walls and empty sockets where electricity had once been installed. Svetlana entertained herself by listening on her earbuds and watching the skies with AR glasses. That was cool—even staring at the ceiling and walls she could see passing drones, as though she were outside. Danya had gone in alone and told her he could be some time, assuming Janu wanted to talk to him. Stupid for both of them to go in; this way if something went wrong, only one of them was at risk. If it went right, he'd call her on the earbuds.

This was Aurangzeb, and it had taken much of the day to get here, hitching several rides, walking alleys and shadows the rest. It was a busy neighbourhood, dusty roads bustling, street stalls and flashing lights, food smell sizzling the air amidst the dust and diesel, and the acrid tang of recharge batteries. Peering back the wrong way down the street, Svetlana could see luozi being unloaded from the back of a pickup, legs tied, kicking as they were carried. A Muslim man in robes and skullcap accompanied the unloading, talking to the pickup driver—that was a butcher then, and the luozi would be killed halal. Somewhere near, the muezzin was calling the faithful to prayer.

Svetlana liked it here more than Rimtown, but street turf here was all taken and newcomers were unwelcome. The richer the pickings, the more organised their protection, and Danya insisted the better living wasn't worth getting killed for. But Svetlana still thought that one day, when Kiril was grown up, they might try it. Maybe take someone else's patch for a change, be the aggressor rather than the victim. Nice change that would be. Danya scowled at her whenever she'd suggested such a thing, but maybe he'd come round.

Damn, he'd been gone a long time.

Word on the street was that League and Federation ships were arriving in system. Their booster hack on Home Guard transmissions had let them listen to various guardies talking about how they'd fight League *or* Federation, make them wish they'd never come here. Laughable. Svetlana was ten, but she knew stupid when she heard it. Everyone here liked to talk—Home Guard, Companies, gang bosses. But in the end, if the other guy had a bigger gun, talk meant nothing. She'd seen big talkers get blown away like it was nothing, had known loudmouth street hustlers who Danya had said, he'd *said*, like he could see a vision or something, that guy won't last. Too much talking, he'll rub someone the wrong way and that'll be that. And sure enough, another month, another year, talk would reach them of the hustler in question, dead in some alley. No one asked questions, no one needed to.

Sometimes Svetlana wanted to talk with the loudest of them. If she had the biggest gun, she could.

She took the pistol from her backpack. Danya hadn't taken it, he'd said it wouldn't do him any good, he'd be surrounded by guys with guns who knew how to use them. Besides, the GI had given it to Svetlana, and the other stuff. The pistol was cold, black and heavy in her hands. Not very advanced as these things went, but simple powder cartridges were good for Droze, nothing jammed in the dust, and they didn't need to be recharged. She checked the magazine for the hundredth time, then smacked it back in firmly. And held it up, pointing at a wall, like she'd seen Sandy hold hers, briefly. Sandy hadn't liked handling guns around children. Sandy was from a place where children were always safe.

It didn't interest Svetlana very much. Safe was something far outside her experience. Guns had always been too dangerous before, in case someone dobbed them in. Now, there was no choice, and Svetlana kind of liked that. A line had been crossed by having this cold, heavy thing in her hands. Now, the fear was not entirely on her side of the divide. With this, she could share it around.

She peered out the window again. Between slats, she could see the usual men milling around the front of Janu's place, talking, leaning on crates, lighting a cigarette. No sign of Danya. He'd said he'd send her a signal on the earbuds if everything was okay. He hadn't. Well, she wouldn't panic. She didn't trust the earbuds as much as she trusted Danya anyway. Maybe Janu had jamming.

But she shouldn't stay here. If something had gone wrong, they'd know that where there was Danya, there would be Svetlana. A vacant room overlooking Janu's corner would be obvious once they thought about it. Lucky it wasn't the only one.

She slipped out the door, into a stripped-bare corridor, lightless save for the pale sun through the window behind. Moving silently, she heard footsteps coming up the stairwell. Several people, she thought, heart thumping as she moved quickly to another doorway—she'd scoped it before, another empty room, this one without a view. Through the door and leaving it open a slit, she crouched in darkness, peering through the gap. Back down the hallway, men appeared. Big coats, pistols, and a short shotgun. AR glasses, probably uplinks too.

They moved fast, indicating with professional intent, closing on the doorway Svetlana had just left. A fast kick, and they went through it fast. Svetlana left equally fast, before they could come out again and search surrounding rooms. She went quickly along the hall, around a corner, then down the next stairwell toward a rear exit. But there might be a guard on that exit now, better she took a side room and waited.

Her heart was thumping, but not from personal fear—she'd dodged tough guys before, she was good at dodging, and sneaking, and had the knack of knowing where to be when people weren't looking. Danya. If Danya was in trouble, she'd thought, men would come at her to that room . . . and here they were. Janu had Danya and had tried to get her too.

Panic threatened as she skipped down stairs in the dark, then up the next length of hall. But she would not panic. She was armed.

Chancelry synthetic assembly felt to Sandy like something between a temple and a morgue. A morgue because there were body parts everywhere and the sweet smell of mortality lingering in the air. And a temple, because here was creation, enabled by science, yet still inexplicable for all that.

A GI factory, she'd told Kiril. Narrow spaces between machines, vats, tubes pumping nutrients, endless rows of growth and assembly. You couldn't see most of the function, light interfered with it, and besides, transparent materials weren't efficient construction. Just displays, regulators, lines and figures representing temperatures, densities, unfolding phases in a multi-layered process. It made her feel melancholy to be here. To walk these aisles and observe the machinery. Mostly automated, horrendously expensive, casually sterile, not requiring spotless whites here, where internal processes were locked away from the surrounding world.

Regular humans grew. Nine months, that was all, and incredibly efficient. She'd seen the costings for this place, and they were eye-wateringly expensive. No real word on where all the synth-organic foundational material came from, but a few guesses. GIs couldn't exist without this. All this money, this technology, mechanisation. The product of organisation, of industry and political will. You didn't go to all this effort without wanting anything from it. Anything selfish. Anything designed to gain benefit, to make all this expense worthwhile, on some vaster, civilisation-spanning balance sheet.

Who would make a GI just for fun? Just for the pleasure of her company, to watch her grow up, learn to walk, look cute in a pretty dress, and gurgle her first words? She could feel muscles flexing as she walked, strain from the recent fight, a few light impact and shrapnel wounds that hadn't penetrated. All parts from these machines. All for some purpose. It hadn't bothered her before, the simple fact of being synthetic—it was like a straight human being female, or male, or something else specifically physical and unchangeable. It was what you were, and you were stuck with it, unknowing of any alternative. And besides, being a GI was fun, there was great ability, sensory perception, sensation. Who wouldn't want this? Who wouldn't want it . . . if only they could be free to use it as they chose?

What had Weller told her, explaining the Bhagavad Gita? "Just do your duty. Be what you are. It's not your fault you're a killer, you are how they made you. The fates understand. Yours is not karma to suffer, but karma to inflict on others."

So maybe that's what we are, Sandy wondered, slowly walking the aisles and running her eyes over displays. Karma in human form. The arrow of fate, shaped by others, aimed with trembling hands. It was an argument to embrace entirely her truest nature, abandon all trace of moral consideration, and kill anything in her way. And it scared her, because right now, it felt so damn attractive.

The aisles opened onto a space. Here was a holographic table, white light against the machines. By it sat a woman, black-haired, Caucasian, thin.

Perhaps middle-aged. In a grey jacket and pants, lots of pockets, where one might have expected a white lab coat. This place was an automated facility, not an experimental or sterile laboratory. Workers here operated machines. And some, like this one, monitored unfolding designs.

She rotated a holographic shape as Sandy approached, zooming in on a seriously 3D model that looked like some crazed plant's root system. Pathways highlighted, then others, calculations appearing, calibrations, balances, and feedback loads. Only when she zoomed out a little more was it apparent that the model was a part of a synthetic brain.

Sandy put her hands on the table and looked at the model. The woman kept working. Whether she noticed or not, she gave no sign.

"What designation?" Sandy asked.

"Forty-five. Middle gestation." Her finger pointed to the bulky contraption opposite. It was wrapped around entirely by tubes that fed from the walls and ceiling. Somewhere in there was a tank filled with fluid, thick with micros. Floating in that, a growing synthetic brain. A small object, to be the subject and product of such a large machine as this.

Middle gestation, she'd said. "How much longer?" Sandy asked.

"Another month. But we'll run out of gestation nanos before that. They die too fast for self-replication, and we're short on spares right now."

There were sixteen synthetic brains in various stages of gestation. Each would normally become a GI when the plant was in full operation. Now the plant had been taken over by GIs. Automated though it was, the various systems feeding into the plant took far more effort to keep working than Sandy had been prepared to spare. But in this as in many other things, she'd been outvoted. Shutting the plant down would be an act of synthetic abortion, and these GIs, having just gained control of their own reproduction for the first time in synthetic history, were very pro-life. So now they ran it. GIs making GIs. With absolutely no idea what they were doing, save what some of them with basic medical and technological training could figure out.

That was where Margaritte Karavitis came in. "Progress on normalisation?" Sandy asked expressionlessly.

Margaritte took a deep breath. "A little. But the fundamental structure is what it was designed to be—a 32-class deviation. This GI will have sensory processing imbalances leading to autistic tendencies. That can't be changed."

The other reason Sandy had been favouring abortion. "What'll happen if she lives beyond Chancelry's max lifespan?"

"I don't know," Margaritte admitted. "It's the unpredictable variation in the design that leads to valuable results."

"But it's not likely to be pretty."

"Not the GI, no. It wasn't designed to be."

Sandy stared at her, unblinking. Margaritte never looked her in the eyes. Never looked anyone in the eyes, lately. She kept working.

"Why didn't you escape?" Sandy asked. "You had plenty of time in the uprising. Everyone else got out."

"Fate," said the Chancelry employee. She refused to say her rank, and no trace of her identity could be found in Chancelry's systems. Network experts had looked everywhere, but likely it had been erased. And they didn't have enough access to other corporate networks to search them too. Now, with recent developments, they had no access at all. Some Chancelry employees had been executed. Margaritte stayed alive by working here, with expertise none of her artificial creations nor their new friends possessed. She'd made no attempt to escape, nor sabotage her work, nor display any extreme degree of fear at the fact that she was the captive of combat GIs bent on revenge who'd killed some of her colleagues. Sandy found her a puzzle.

"I hear you lost quite a few of your people just now."

"Not my people," said Sandy.

"No?"

Sandy felt no obligation to discuss it further. "I want those full reports on all the standard design deviations," she said.

"I'm quite busy here," Margaritte pointed out.

"You can find time."

"Not if you want these GIs in gestation to have less defective lives than they otherwise will."

Sandy didn't want these GIs born at all. That was Kiet's choice, and those of his friends and supporters, more numerous than hers. She wondered what point there was to Kiet's plans, birthing all these GIs, if he was just going to get them killed in harebrained attacks. A straight human might have ground her teeth in visible frustration. Sandy pursed her lips, thinking dark thoughts.

"A 43 series had seizures yesterday while listening to music," she said. "Can music trigger it?"

"Yes. Depending on the condition." Still checking through the holographic construct, slowly rotating. "European classical is worst for some reason. Something about the processing of high harmonics."

"Was it worth it?" Sandy asked. "Doing this to all these GIs? Implanting defective foundational structures on purpose?"

"That other GI, Kiet, was down here before making all kinds of threats," said Margaritte. "I don't know what it gains you, you either kill me or you don't."

"It was a serious question," said Sandy. "Was it worth it? Don't presume I don't understand your reasons. I understand them perfectly."

Margaritte paused, and looked at her. It was the secret a League scout had tried to nuke Droze to prevent getting out. That League uplink technology, derived from the synthetic neurobiology used to create GIs, was causing second- and third-level neurological associative disorder across vast swathes of the League population. It threatened civilisational collapse, which threatened in turn to take the Federation with it. And it scared the shit out of everyone who understood the implications.

There was a little fear in Margaritte's eyes. But only a little. "I did what I had to do," she said shortly. And returned to her work.

"So why stay here now? Why not run away when you had the chance?"

"It's called responsibility," said Margaritte. "Some of us accept it."

"The four-year max lifespan," said Sandy, pressing implacably. "Your idea?"

A faint snort. "I'm flattered you think me so important."

"I've no idea how important you are, you hide your identity. Interesting choice, for someone accepting responsibility."

"There's a vast difference between accepting responsibility and committing suicide."

"Not so vast," said Sandy. "I might let you live, but I have little enough say around here. The others only let you live so long as you're useful. You can't seriously expect mercy, given what you've done here. Yet you chose to stay."

"How can you decide whether or not to be merciful, if you don't know what I'm responsible for?"

Sandy considered that for a moment. "Clever enough strategy," she conceded. "Save that simply being involved in this makes you guilty at any level. How many GIs has this program created, then killed for your research?"

Margaritte shook her head. "It's not my research. That's not my department. I just build them." A slight sideways glance at Sandy. "I might have made you."

"You know Renaldo Takawashi?" Takawashi was lead researcher for League Recruitment, the monster government authority tasked with producing military-level GIs for the war. The head of Sandy's "project," such as it was.

"I might."

Sandy shook her head. "Trying to capture my interest won't help you. Your life's not in my hands. It's in theirs."

"And they want these GIs to miraculously come to life." Margaritte pointed to the gestation tanks. "It won't happen without me. My clock is ticking very slowly."

Sandy left the facility via the secure lobby, with a wave to the security camera, and Baku on its other end, up in the control room. Multiple secure doors cycled her through, though ID security systems had been disabled, not recognising anyone now in charge.

A call came in, blinking on internal visual. Vanessa. *"Hey. Any word on your regs?"*

"Psych eval didn't like what it was hearing," said Sandy. "They're confined to quarters."

"You locked them up?"

"No choice. They understand Chancelry did bad things, but they're conditioned for service. We're pretty sure the other corporations tried to hack our networks and make contact with them, create a counter uprising, but we can't find any more than traces, so we don't know what they did or said."

"So the regs swapped one restrictive overlord for another."

"I didn't say I liked it," Sandy snapped. "I didn't design the fucking things." Silence on the other end. The last doors cycled through. Sandy headed for the elevator. "I'm sorry. Tell me something else I can do and I'll do it."

"Try talking to them? There are variations of reg intelligence, pick a leader, elevate him or her, try to convince him."

"Might work if I had weeks, and spare personnel." The elevator closed on her, and rose. "The only person I'd trust to talk to regs and maybe make some progress is me, and I don't have time. What's up at your end?"

"Federation Fleet just arrived. Carrier Murray and seven others. Talking not shooting, there's a preliminary agreement to meet at Antibe Station. Some dissention from the League because we've got two carriers and they've only got one."

"You'd think that after we won the war, we shouldn't have to keep reminding them that they can't match us in a pissing contest." It felt odd to say it. During the war, she'd been on the other side.

"This is technically League space. Reichardt thinks the fact they only sent one carrier might suggest they have trouble elsewhere."

"That would fit. On the other hand, they've only got seven left, they can't be everywhere. Who's attending this meeting?"

"We're discussing that. New Torahn Assembly members are up here already. Murray's commanded by Wong, he outranks Reichardt, so he's leading for Federation, we understand there might be another Feddie bureaucrat on board too."

"Can't be anyone senior, their response time is too short to have come from Callay. I want you there."

"For what?"

"To represent these GIs."

"I'm flattered. But like you, I work for the Federation, I don't get to choose."

"Put the case. GIs are a fourth party here, they currently hold Chancelry HQ and League's most important secret data by force of military arms. And they'll be prepared to use that as leverage if necessary."

A short pause. Sandy was entirely sure she knew why. *"Can I say that this is them talking? Or you?"*

Entirely sure. "I work for the Federation, Vanessa. Like you said. They'd send their own representative up if they could, but there's no way to do it right now, unless the corporations grant overflight, and League probably won't allow it anyway, because they obviously want us trapped down here."

"Well, Sandy, if you're not commanding them, you'd better make it clear to our new arrivals who is. Because otherwise this delineation between you and them is going to get very blurry, and for your sake I'd hate to see that happen." Sandy accepted the warning silently. Federation had already been given cause to doubt her loyalty in this matter. *"Is it Kiet?"*

"He thinks so. Others have been given reason to doubt it lately."

"Well, get it sorted out, and I'll present it to them."

"Whoever it is still can't be there physically, and I'm not trusting an uplink. They'll still request you represent them, with my recommendation."

Another short pause. *"Not Rhian?"*

"Rhi will insist on you as well. We know who the talker is."

"Gee, thanks. Well, I'm not flying solo on this, you're going to have to get everyone to agree what your position is. Then I'll present it to the best of my ability, if they let me."

"Tell them if they don't let you, League data vital to Federation security might go missing."

Another, this time longer, pause. The slow-moving elevator finally stopped, opening onto the secure lobby where she'd dropped off Kiril at the beginning of the shooting. *"Is that you speaking or them?"* Vanessa repeated warningly.

"Is there some civilian freighter insystem?" Sandy asked, walking the cold lobby. "Headed for Federation space in the next few days?"

"Uh, sure. I think. What for?"

"Best you don't know." An emergency alert came through on tacnet. Internal alert, nothing strategic. "I gotta go, take care."

She switched to incoming traffic. Got a lot of garbled voices. Then something clear . . . *". . . bullet wound, lower face. Self-inflicted."*

"Who?"

"Kiet. Kiet shot himself. Taking him to medbay."

Sandy swore and took off running.

Medbay was crowded, GIs clustered in open space between beds, trying to see. Sandy wanted to get through but had no path without pushing. Then Poole was climbing on a bunk and shouting at them.

"He's okay! Now the lot of you fuck off, give us some space, you can't block the aisles and expect us to treat injured people!"

GIs backed off, pulled others back. Many saw her as they retreated and gave misgiving looks. A few looks were plain hostility. All were armed, a few in light armour, a lot of those older-looking, untidy haircuts, a few scars that even on GIs would never heal. Kiet's friends, the ones who had rushed down here.

Sandy held her ground as they filed past. None dared threaten her. It was the caste system again, the invisible shield. And dammit, she thought,

Justice's phrase was now permanently stuck in her head, a needle in her mind, jabbing her at unpleasant moments.

Sandy walked to the bed. Poole had stuffed a lot of bandages into Kiet's mouth to stop the bleeding. To her alarm, Kiril was here, handing Poole more bandages and tearaways from the neighbouring bench. He had them arranged in little piles, quite neatly. Surely she had to send him away . . . but then, he'd been helping Poole for over a week now, around cases more injured than this one. GI injuries were never quite as messy as straight humans', nor did they cause quite as much pain. Where else would she send him, with the regs locked up for fear of counter rebellion, and the HQ under further threat of attack?

Dahisu and Asma were also here, two of Kiet's best friends, and they weren't leaving for anything. Rishi too, de facto leader of the Chancelry GIs.

"Dahisu tackled him before he could shoot," Poole explained. "Gun went off, not a clean shot." Dahisu said nothing, eyes dark. "He lost a few teeth, tongue cut to hell. Piece out of jawbone, cheek. Maybe he'll talk again with surgery, but it'll take more than I've got."

Asma was staring at her furiously. Dahisu wasn't. He looked maybe Filipino, brown and Asian, longish hair completely non-regulation. Asma looked Sudanese, blacker than black. GIs and ethnicity. Sandy sometimes wondered why they weren't all made more racially generic, instead of these matching features and names. Socialisation perhaps, and empathy with regular humans.

Sandy searched for Kiet's signal on uplink. He was there, dormant. Sandy connected but got nothing. She pushed past Poole and stood over him. His eyes were closed, so she slapped his cheek. Eyes slitted open. She connected again.

Click. *"You idiot,"* she told him. *"Of all the dumb solutions, this is the dumbest."*

"You never tried it?" Slitted eyes fixed on her, as though he knew something. Had someone told him?

"Yes." She wouldn't lie. If truth mattered anytime, it mattered now.

"Then shut up."

"My reasons were better than yours."

"Like what?"

"I got tired of being the cause of one too many massacres."

"Good people?"

"*Bad people,*" she corrected. "*Federal Intelligence Agency, when it existed.*"

"*That's a worse cause than mine. I got a bunch of good people killed.*"

"*No,*" Sandy formulated. "*I was trying to stop killing. I had this dream I could have a peaceful life. I dreamt that my creators couldn't actually dictate my life, that I could be free to choose. But it turned out I couldn't, because being what I was made people hunt me, and kill my friends, and my dreams all evaporated into pain and loss as far as I could see.*

"*You never tried to stop being what you are. You like being what you are. You're quite happy to blast whatever gets in your way. And you were right, the reason I delayed so long in trying to save the other GIs was that I didn't see a way to do it yet. Maybe they all would have died anyway, my plan or yours. Killing yourself doesn't help anything, it just adds one more body to the pile.*"

"*It was my idea.*" Quietly. "*I was sure it would work. We're so strong, when we're angry. We took Chancelry HQ, I mean, it was amazing. So I arranged another uprising, we used our contacts there . . . and now they're all dead.*"

"*And now you're quitting.*" Sandy stared down at him, eyes hard. "*The GIs here are only a fraction of it. There's so many more, in the League. Increasingly many in the Federation. You've fallen at the first hurdle, but you've learned from it. The whole race is still yet to run.*"

"*And what can you do? What can you possibly do for us, leashed to your Federation?*"

"*Kiet, look at me.*" He looked, pain-filled eyes above a mouthful of bloody bandages. "*Leashes run both ways.*" Deliberate pause, staring at him. "*Just watch. You'll see, I promise.*"

"*Sure.*" Bleakly. "*I'm not going anywhere.*"

CHAPTER FIVE

Svetlana could tell it was one of Janu's trucks from the lights, glaring in the dark street. Still there was no power, no streetlights or glowing shopfronts, but that only made it easier to hide by the verge, against some stacked wheels out front of an auto repair shop. She had to be fast, the cold was closing in, and the wind whipping dust down the street—shopkeepers and others along this stretch of Aurangzeb were moving everything inside for the night, grinding down the shutters. Blue light danced and flashed in the sky to the east, the promise of a storm. Soon this street would be deserted. It was this truck or never.

No one saw the small shadow in the dark, flitting from the piled wheels as the truck passed. No one saw that shadow clinging to the rear fender as the truck bumped along the road, unilluminated save for the glaring front lights. It pulled up in front of Janu's yard, and the guards gave it the walk around, failing to see the shadow roll under the stationary truck, then grab axle and exhaust and let herself be dragged the short distance inside Janu's shop.

Internal lights then, run from a generator somewhere. Svetlana lay on her stomach beneath the front wheels and peered around. That front axle had nearly cost her fingers when the driver turned the wheel; she hadn't understood what the mechanism would do. It made her mad at herself, for not knowing—you had to know stuff, or the lack could hurt you.

It was a warehouse, unsurprisingly. Piles of crates and boxes, and cleared space for tables where men and a few women were preparing things. Loading and packing, often talking, music playing over speakers. The place smelt of exhaust, cigarettes, and various, probably illicit, things she couldn't identify.

The driver got down from his cabin, talked with someone, walked around to the rear of the truck. Svetlana looked around three-sixty, moving as little as possible. When she thought everyone was in the right positions, she moved, a fast dash for stacked boxes. The move brought no alarm, and she kept moving, fast and crouched down an aisle.

Here boxes were stacked on shelves. In gaps through a shelf, she saw movement, and paused as someone walked by on the other side. Pressed herself low, ready to roll under the nearest shelf if anyone appeared up the far end of the aisle. No one did. She thought of the gun but realised that holding it would be stupid—if she got into a firefight here she was dead, these guys all knew guns far better than she, besides which she needed two empty hands while sneaking.

The far wall was air-conditioning ducts, which were sometimes good for sneaking, but these had no way in, just bolted to the wall. She stayed low between ducts and shelves until she could see the work space where boxes were being unpacked. These looked like plastic containers of some sort. Shampoo bottles. Janu smuggled shampoo? It was rare enough. She and Danya had had fights over shampoo; she liked it and Danya said she didn't need it, so she'd stolen some and didn't tell him. Of course he'd found out, he always did. And no matter how angry he got he always forgave her.

She moved when it felt right, when the music was loud and a few packers were distracted with conversation, just floated in the shadow near the wall, headed for the next corridor. That revealed a stairwell inside a doorway, which she took, because obviously Janu would be on an upper floor, if only because it bought him extra seconds if anyone attacked.

The next corridor up was lit also. Svetlana walked quietly along a wall, pausing when she heard voices. They came from up ahead. Someone was standing in a side doorway, back to the hall, talking. Svetlana edged into a near doorway and waited. They were men, and their conversation was . . . nothing interesting. Names she didn't recognise. Gossip. So Janu hadn't let Danya go, was holding him in here somewhere against his will, and his men thought it so unimportant they were talking about something else entirely.

Anger was good. Anger helped her forget how scared she was. But fear was all relative anyhow. In Svetlana's life, fear of doing something dangerous for food only lasted until the pain in your stomach was so great you were more scared of that than you were of the dangerous thing. After a while, learning to overcome that fear became preemptive—you didn't wait until you got hungry to do the dangerous thing for food, you did it *before* you got hungry, because you knew if you didn't, you'd just end up where you were before. After a while, it became habit, and you got used to doing dangerous things because you had to, because there were no good options, only bad and worse.

Svetlana was so much more scared of losing Danya than she was of being hungry, she couldn't have put it into words. Danya always knew the bad options from the worse ones. Sometimes he could even find a good one. There were only two things in Svetlana's life she loved more than herself, and both were brothers. And this brother in particular kept her alive.

Janu was talking in the next room. Danya sat and stared out the window. Janu's office was makeshift; the room had probably once been a standard office for some logistics company long gone with the crash. Now it was converted into Janu's head office: a big desk, some shelves, a few pictures. A man with a gun sat in a nearby chair, watching him.

They'd have gone after Svetlana, Danya knew. He thought desperately of something he could do, anything, to get her a warning. The gun in the man's hand looked big and cold. Currently it rested in his lap, but if he tried anything stupid, that would change. Svetlana was smart—about short-term things, probably smarter than he was. She could see and solve the immediate problem immediately. Planning for things beyond tomorrow, she struggled with. She'd see Janu's men coming, Danya was sure of it. They'd not catch her too. Please God.

Janu reentered the room with a final dismissal of whoever he was talking to. He strolled, this man in a suit, neck undone. An unremarkable-looking man, dark-skinned, middle-aged, with serious, bug eyes. He pulled a thin, custom cigarette and lit it.

"Don't be scared, boy. Companies won't hurt you."

Danya said nothing. Hurt, won't hurt, it was all tactics at this level. Like in any game, tactics changed as opportunities presented themselves.

Janu offered him a cigarette. Danya ignored it. "You should try one. I smoked my first when I was younger than you. Gave me a taste for the finer things." Danya thought it smelled like someone had caught a rodent and set fire to it.

Janu pulled up a chair and sat, with an offhanded gesture. "It's nothing personal, boy. Just business. You're right, I don't normally do business with the corporations. But this here, this is a whole new game. You're hot material. I don't hold onto material this hot, not for anything. You'll burn me. So I do a deal. It's someone else's problem."

"You know why the corporations want me?"

Janu blew smoke. "Leverage over Kresnov. She's alive you know. In case you were wondering. Her last attack on the other corporations failed though. For some reason, someone thought the best leverage against her was you. What can you tell me about that?"

"We're her friends. She doesn't like people who hurt her friends. She's pretty much the most dangerous GI ever made. What does that tell you? About this being safe, what you're doing?"

A flicker in Janu's eyes. A consideration. Respect, perhaps. "Fair enough, boy. Fair enough. But Kresnov's stuck in Chancelry HQ, and she can't teleport through walls. And I'm not going to hurt you. I'm just doing a deal."

"Handing me over to people who will kill me if they have to, to stop Kresnov."

Janu held his hands wide. "Hey. I'm sorry. If I cross the corporations on something this big, I'll have ten artillery rounds through my roof any time soon. You think I'm going to suicide for you? Doesn't work that way, boy. You made a mistake coming here. You want to find your brother, that makes you wooly-headed, yes?"

Damn, it did, Danya thought through gritted teeth. Stupid stupid. He'd wanted that so badly, he'd convinced himself that these other things were true, that it turned out were not. Getting played by other people was one thing. Playing yourself was the worst, the most dangerous. He almost never did it . . . save where Kiril and Svetlana were concerned. His judgement wasn't sound then. But usually he knew that, and compensated, like a drunk compensating for listing balance.

"You didn't need to tell the corporations I was here at all," he bit out.

"My call," said Janu. "Too late now, they're coming. Maybe Home Guard will make a problem though." He tapped the cigarette. Burning rodent-smelling ash fell into the tray. "There's a good chance you'll live through this, if you're smart. So I'll tell you something for free. You know what I did, before I became a businessman? Before the crash?"

Danya said nothing.

"I was an economist. That means I was an expert, in economic transactions, the fluctuations of prices and goods in an open market. An academic, if you will, I taught at Paulson University on Wade, then I came out here to teach on the frontier. I was idealistic, you see. The frontier was the new direction of humanity. It was where all the new economic theories could be tested. And of course, I arrived here just in time for one of the biggest economic calamities of modern human history.

"What I do here, none of it's personal. And if you care too much, and let that get in the way of your judgement, you're finished. This here is just another form of economic distribution. The crash was just a transition, you understand that? And in truth, I think I'm better at this form of economics than the other one. This one is more pure. Fewer rules."

"You had a wife," Danya said, remembering.

Janu nodded, distantly. "Until the crash, I had a wife. And a kid. She'd have been nearly your age. Nothing's fair, boy. Remember that. The game makes its decisions for us."

Until someone like Sandy comes along, Danya thought, and single-handedly upsets the biggest game in town. He decided he didn't believe it. People could make their own game. If they had enough leverage. But few people did.

Somewhere out beyond the doors, something went pop! Then pop!pop!pop! Janu and the armed man looked at each other, an instant of wide-eyed alarm. Shouts and yells then from outside. The popping got louder, graduating to full-fledged bangs that rattled anything loose. Janu rushed behind his desk for a drawer, and the armed man stood, covering the door. Something smacked a wall.

The door opened, and something sailed through it. The armed man fired, splintering the door. Danya dove at the man's back, knocking him sprawling. The grenade went off, an impossibly loud noise with flashing light and smoke, and Danya struggled to clear his head and vision to climb on top of the sprawled man before he could bring his gun to bear.

But the man recovered faster, and threw him off. BangBang! And the man fell as he'd been trying to get up, just went, like a puppet with its strings cut. And here through the smoke walked a small figure with AR glasses and a backpack, a pistol in both hands held like the ungainly steel contraption that it was. And firing, firing repeatedly, eyes wide and staring. Janu went down, with whatever he'd been trying to get from his desk.

Oh my God, Svetlana, what have you done? Second thought, we have to get out of here right now.

"Svet, let's go!" He grabbed the fallen man's pistol, tried to ignore the widening pool of blood on the floor, and went for the door.

"No, Danya, not that way! This way!" Svetlana was going for the windows.

Danya opened the door anyway and saw the room beyond. Two more bodies, one struggling to crawl, on hands and knees, hacking up blood. Screams of pain from somewhere farther beyond. For a moment, he stood frozen in horror. Svetlana?

"Danya! Come on!" She yanked the window, and when it wouldn't budge, fired at it. The gun clicked empty. She swore, reaching quickly to her pocket for a new mag. Her hands barely even shook. Reloaded, she fired two shots, careless of whoever might be living on the other side of the road, then reversed the pistol and hit the shattered glass with the butt. It collapsed, and she scampered through, onto the verandah rooftop outside.

Danya followed, with a look at Janu slumped against the wall behind his desk, a stupidly awkward pose, head lolling, eyes blank. Nothing's fair, huh?

Out onto the verandah rooftop, now there were shouts rising from the road below. Svetlana was running ahead, looking for a way down . . . no, she'd spotted a way down, a truck parked ahead, she could jump onto its roof and . . .

Danya saw running lights of something flying, low and fast above nearby rooftops. An eruption of flares and a fast-banking manouver told it was under fire. Counter-fire from somewhere else and a huge explosion on the ground a block away.

"Svet, move, move!"

She leaped, nimble-footed onto the top of the truck, then onto the cabin, and Danya followed as a corporate flyer roared overhead, lights blazing in a hurricane of downdraft. Another followed it, and as Danya followed his sister onto the cabin, then with a thump down to the road, crazy heavy gunfire tore Janu's corner of the road to bits and kicked up a huge cloud of dust. Not aiming at them, Danya realised—aiming at anyone on the road who might be shooting skyward.

Svetlana was already running down the road, keeping to one side, weaving amid parked vehicles, streetside stalls, and whatever else had not yet been rolled away, seeking cover. Danya ran hard and caught up, surely if the flyer wanted them dead they'd be dead, at this range they didn't miss much, and these two were *low*, so much lower than they usually dared to fly.

Svetlana reached an alley and ducked up it. It was narrow, blocked in parts by pipes, half-crumbling walls, and junk. Another alley, and then a ground-level window to a basement. Svetlana fell and rolled inside. A light thud as her feet hit the ground inside.

"It's okay!" she called up. Danya followed, a tighter squeeze. Inside was a horrid old washroom, sink and toilet long unused but smelling rank all the same. Svetlana led them to a corridor then paused, gun held in both hands, looking anxiously back at Danya. "What do you think? They won't put people on the ground around here?"

Corporations usually avoided it, not wanting prolonged shootouts at point-blank range. Even with corporate superiority, they lost people doing that, or got them wounded, then they needed to be rescued, and then the rescuers got wounded . . . a big mess. Often they'd do it with GIs, who were far better at close quarters and were more expendable, but lately the corporations had stopped trusting their own GIs. Small wonder.

"I don't think they'll risk it without GIs," Danya concluded. "But they might. Svet, are you okay?"

He checked her up and down, looking for holes. He'd heard that people in shoot-outs could get hit and not realise it; he'd even seen it once, a gangster who'd run into Treska's joint after some random shots and looked fine until one of the patrons had pointed out he was bleeding. Then a collapse, and two minutes later he was dead.

"I'm okay," she said. "I don't think any of them really got a shot off." That guy with Janu certainly had; Danya recalled seeing bullets blow holes in the door. Must have missed her by centimeters, probably hadn't bargained on her being so small.

"Svet . . ." he just stared at her. And had absolutely no fucking idea what to say. What did you say when you just saw your ten-year-old sister blow a bunch of people away?

Telepathic as they were, she knew his thoughts exactly. "It wasn't hard," she insisted. "They weren't ready. There were just some of them in the room between me and Janu's room, and I listened long enough to make sure you were in there. Then I just walked in, and they were all just standing there, it was easy."

Easy. She was blinking at him with that utterly calm demeanor that he knew was at last half a fake, a put-on for his benefit; she did that when she was trying to prove something. But now the calm was wearing off, and her hands were starting to shake. The shakes were spreading, slowly, within which the calm stare remained desperately fixed and level. Like a wall of sand, slowly collapsing from the steady vibration.

He hugged her, frantically hard. She returned it.

"Danya, the AR glasses showed me the corporate flyers were coming. They were going to take you. I'm not going to let them take you. I don't care what, I won't let them."

Now she could barely stand, the shakes were so bad. If not for Danya's grip, she would have fallen. "I'll take care of it, Svet," he insisted. "That was my mistake going to Janu. It wasn't your fault, it was mine. I'll make it better, I promise."

Exactly how he'd do that, he had no idea.

CHAPTER SIX

Lt Nadaja was yelling at her troops when Vanessa arrived, armour chafing in places where the formfit straps wouldn't adjust well enough to her small frame. Lines of *Mekong* marines, crowding the branching approach corridors, grasping secure straps in the dull red light of standby emergency. Vanessa shouldered past, a crush of armoured elbows and secured weapons now shoving a hole as someone came through the other way—here in the side alcove several medics waited, fast-response equipment ready in case of wounded. *Mekong* crashed and thumped as the final grapples attached the main passage.

"Sandy, have any idea what that shuttle was?" Reichardt asked when she reached him.

"No," said Vanessa, taking a retractable handhold and fervently hoping it wouldn't be needed. "It definitely left from Dhamsel's pad, Sandy's not happy about it." Wasn't happy about much at the moment. Vanessa worried about her. "It dock yet?"

"Ten minutes ago, combat approach. Damn good pilot too."

"Hey," interrupted a corporal, pushing in to confront Vanessa. Faceplate shoved up, tough guy, shrapnel scar through one cheek. "You comin' out to play, civvie? You know your patterns?"

Vanessa gave him a distasteful look. "Seems like the corporations want their player in the game," she answered Reichardt, ignoring the corporal.

"Hey," said the corporal, "you go out there on that dock, in this formation, you answer to me. I don't care what you were in civvie street, you're with the marines now."

"Fuck off rookie," said Vanessa. The corporal's eyes flashed. He nearly smiled, and left. "So we at war again or what?"

"Not yet," said Reichardt, laconic as ever. Vanessa had seen him under fire, so dead calm he almost looked bored. "Forgive the greens; they bark at strangers."

"They're not my usual standard," said Vanessa, loudly enough for those around her to hear. "I suppose I'll have to make do."

Marines wouldn't like that, they rated themselves far above any non-military agency. Usually they'd be right. To emphasise her point, Rhian emerged at her side, similarly armoured and armed.

"You good 39?" asked Rhian.

"Armour's a tight fit. Apparently there's no small marines."

"If we come under fire you could just make like a turtle, pull your head in."

Vanessa smiled. Rhian's jokes were improving with age also.

"39?" asked Reichardt.

"Her GI designation," Rhian explained. "She got one in Tanusha. Combat GI, 39 series, that's my designation. Outdrew it from a standing start, ten meters face to face."

Now even the surrounding marines were staring.

"S'all progress, baby," said Vanessa, checking her weapon for the eleventh time. She popped some gum, offered more to those around her.

Dismount came hard, troopers hitting the dock with weapons out and seals tight, just in case *Mekong* had to break dock fast and blow it all to vacuum. Reichardt followed, Vanessa and Rhian in tight formation, other marines fanning out to secure the back corridors. All shutters were down along this stretch, Antibe Station had been impressive once, the export hub for some of League's biggest weapons industries during the war. Now four-fifths of it was cold and unoccupied, and this one remaining business zone had seen better days.

Dockside was big, ten meters high and forty wide, and not much cover save for the big support gantries on the spaceward side. Ahead they could see three berths up the station curve, and no visible people. Reichardt walked with his marines, in full armour like the rest, face invisible behind the armoured visor. They held a line down the dock, local tacnet informing them that others were advancing on the right flank, behind the vacant frontages, clearing corridors.

"*Local net's completely down*," Lt Nadaja informed them. No surprise, considering what Cai did to them a few weeks ago, Vanessa thought.

"*Watch your transmission spacing*," said one of the sergeants. "*If they jam us we might have to fry something.*" Because a marine unit operating on hostile territory ran tacnet off their own wireless. Jamming tacnet was nearly as hostile an act as shooting . . . or marines chose to take it that way.

Four berths down they secured berth 11 and waited for *Murray*'s shuttle to come in. That took some fancy flying, to move a shuttle in a one-G barrel roll with the rotating outer rim, and not lose a wing on gantry supports designed to hold monster tonnage freighters and warships. The shuttle unloaded Captain Wong and his contingent of twelve marines, and they continued up the dock. No way were both carriers going to dock in this environment; *Murray* stood off at five clicks, ready to manoeuver or shoot if trouble started.

Then they saw them. An opposing wall of League marines across the dock, similarly armed and armoured, slowing, emerging below the angle of the high overhead. It wasn't a combat deployment, there wasn't much cover to begin with, but it looked impressive, at least a hundred armoured soldiers in a row. Vanessa's mouth felt dry to look at them, her heart now thumping.

"*Steady*," said Nadaja, a low voice as they walked.

"*Welcoming ceremony*," someone else observed.

"*Wedding reception*," said another.

"*Turkey shoot.*"

"*Stow it*," said Nadaja.

Vanessa wondered what the League marines were saying. How many of them had been in the shooting war, now seven years ended but many of its participants on both sides still active. Sandy always said the war had never truly ended, the fundamental disagreements that had driven it still bubbling away.

"*Okay, hold it here*," said Reichardt when they were close enough. "*Nadaja, Rice, Chu, with me.*" Wong gave similar orders to his small contingent, and the two captains, plus six personal guard in loose protective formation, continued toward the wall of League troopers.

Audio clicked on Vanessa's vision, and she accessed. "*Keep your eyes peeled*," said Nadaja tersely. Rhian was receiving this too, tacnet confirmed it. "*Two shots end the League's immediate problem.*"

A thousand questions and possibilities flashed through Vanessa's head. She knew Nadaja hadn't been pleased with Reichardt's decision to come out here, almost to the point of shouting at him. That was serious, as those two were close. Nadaja thought League might suffer the consequences of killing two Feddie captains here? Damn unlikely, that would start a war . . . but marine commanders weren't employed to consider wider politics, just to deal with what landed in their lap.

Not impossible though. Sandy said League was in serious sociological trouble, possibly on the road to disintegration. Which would make war inevitable anyway, of one sort or other. If League got desperate enough to try and manage their own troubles without Federation interference . . . or if they figured the consequences of two dead captains was less than the Federation finding out what Sandy had found on Droze . . .

In that case, they'd all be dead. Possibly the League captain too. Maybe she'd figure that out, if she knew what was going on.

A League trooper with Lt stencils on shoulder armour walked forward to meet the captains ten strides out and popped his faceplate. "Captain Calou is waiting," he said, pointing to the inner wall. "Conference room."

Reichardt shook his head. "Right here." He pointed to the deck. "Get us a table and some chairs."

The League Lieutenant looked at them, then beyond to the Federation marines. Then back, to his own side. "I'm not sure that's wise," he said drily.

"An opinion," Wong remarked. "How much do those go for these days?"

The Lieutenant scowled. "Captain Calou is waiting for you inside."

"Yeah, well, we're not on great terms with the locals," Reichardt explained. "They just recently regained command and control, which controls things like environmentals, access, which in a small room can be a problem. It's the dock or nothing."

The Lieutenant closed his faceplate, walked a few strides off. They waited. Faceplate down, targeting visuals active, tacnet showed Vanessa a mass of red threats and targets. If anything happened here, they'd all be cut to pieces, even Rhian. She kept special watch for sudden movements, raised weapons. Nadaja was clearly worried about a rogue, either League intelligence plant or a disgruntled regular with a score to settle. Tacnet could identify some such movements before she could, but she didn't trust it.

The Lieutenant came back, faceplate up. "She's coming."

A few minutes later, a black-clad woman appeared from the corridor beside an insurance frontage. She wore no armour, not even an emergency breather, just a captain's leather jacket and rough pants. Dark features, perhaps North African, black hair pinned back tightly. She walked to the two Federation captains, the only person on the dock unarmoured, looking faintly smug. To her side, Vanessa could feel Nadaja bristling, to see her captain shown up like this. First strike for psychological warfare.

"Captains," she said. Behind her, several of her armoured marines were carrying chairs. "Shall we sit?"

Chairs were placed. "Let's mingle," Wong suggested, pointing to the waiting troops.

"I don't think so," Calou said coolly.

"Three people from our side. Three people from your side. Put them together in the middle for a chat. Relieves some tension, no one loses advantage."

Calou thought about it for a moment. Then shook her head. "I don't think so."

Wong shrugged and sat. Reichardt unhooked his helmet completely. Vanessa sensed Nadaja even more unhappy than before. Wong removed his helmet also.

"Wait just a moment," said Calou. "Someone will join us."

"Representative Protocol says captains only," reminded Reichardt.

"Or captain equivalents, nominated by other captains. I so nominate."

Who the hell, Vanessa wondered? *"Someone who just came up on that shuttle, I bet,"* Rhian volunteered, unheard by the captains.

"Great," Vanessa formulated. *"So the corporations have a representative."*

Another soldier laid down sound suppression, little omni-speakers on slim retractable stands, they made a circle about the chairs. Activated, they hummed and buzzed, then all sound from outside the circle faded to dull mumbles, like hearing underwater.

"Visual analysis gives a seventy-nine percent probability that one of your personal guard is a GI," Calou said to Reichardt. "And a forty-six percent chance of the other one too." Vanessa smiled. Reichardt said nothing. "Curious reversal, given the reasons for the war."

"Not so curious," said Reichardt. "Yours all ran away to fight for us."

Calou's eyes flashed. "Not all."

A man walked from the doorway Calou had come from, also unarmoured. A GI, clearly, from the muscular intensity of his stride. African. Familiar.

"Rhian," Vanessa said in a low voice, using real vocals for fear that formulation would not capture the right tone. "No trouble, huh? Leave him for Sandy."

"Yeah," said Rhian. And nothing more. Vanessa didn't like that, but there was nothing else to do.

Mustafa Ramoja took a seat at Captain Calou's side. He and the captain exchanged the kind of look that suggested they were engaged in uplink communication. Both pairs of eyes went to Vanessa.

"Hello, Commander Rice," said Ramoja, in that deep, intelligent voice of his. "Good to see you well."

Vanessa activated externals. "Sandy says hi." Ramoja's deadpan never changed. *Sandy says you're dead*, that really meant. He knew.

"And Rhian Chu, I'm sure," he continued, looking at Rhian. Rhian said nothing. The rifle in her hands only needed to move slightly, a flex of the index finger, and problem solved. At the cost of everyone and everything else.

"Don't push your luck," Vanessa advised him.

"The League has two pressing questions," Calou began. In this environment, of course, what the League wanted, and what Calou wanted, were synonymous. "One, why did you fire on this station?"

"They fired at us during personnel retrieval," said Reichardt. "We told them what would happen if they did, they didn't listen."

"I'm informed several station personnel were killed, and one whole station section is now inoperable until repairs."

"That will happen when you attack a warship's boarding crew," said Reichardt.

"Second thing," said Calou. "What happened to *Corona*?"

"I killed it," said Reichardt.

Silence but for buzzing omni-speakers.

"There were a hundred and twelve souls aboard *Corona*," Calou said softly. "Why did you take them?"

"Their captain was trying to nuke Droze," said Reichardt. "There are more than a million souls on Droze. Y'see that second number? That's bigger than the first number." He tapped his head knowingly. "Smart folks we Feddie Fleet captains."

Calou glanced at Ramoja, then a pause. Certainly an uplink discussion. Perhaps Calou wasn't yet convinced what *Corona* had been trying to do. *Corona* had been a ghostie, a recon vessel, answerable to League Intelligence. Folks like Ramoja. Calou was not.

"We've acquired telemetry that suggests *Mekong* could not have made that intercept," said Ramoja. "Pantala says they couldn't hit it from the ground."

"Your telemetry's wrong," Reichardt said calmly.

Ramoja gazed at him for a long moment. The deadpan stare reminded Vanessa of Sandy. There was a depth there. A calm. It was in the psychology of all high-des GIs. None of this wash of impulsive thoughts and reactions that regular humans struggled, and occasionally succeeded, to control. "How did you gain control of this station?"

Reichardt smiled and said nothing.

Ramoja knew . . . something. Vanessa was certain. Exactly what he knew was unclear. But probably League Intel knew a lot more about the Talee than Federation Intel.

"League will demand immediate withdrawal," he said. "Your intervention here has violated the Five Junctions Treaty on numerous levels. Technically it is an act of war."

"Which League can't afford to reciprocate," said Reichardt.

Wong held up a hand, demanding attention. All looked. "Diplomatic though my esteemed colleague is, on official Federation diplomacy, my seniority is established." Reichardt nodded. "Federation regrets this matter. Federation will remind League at this point that this mission was only pursued in conjunction with League Internal Security Organisation, of whom Mr Ramoja here was most recently Callay's senior-most operative."

Calou shifted uneasily. "League is aware. League and ISO have settled their differences. We are united in our demand that the articles of Treaty must be followed, and Federation must withdraw."

"However we arrived at this point," Wong continued, with the air of the trained diplomat that he was, "Federation cannot ignore facts come to light on Droze. Facts regarding League's internal stability."

"An internal matter," said Ramoja firmly. "Not the Federation's business."

"With respect, Mr Ramoja, the scale of these discoveries make it the business of every member of the human species."

"This will not be discussed here," Ramoja insisted.

"Then somewhere," Wong replied. "Federation withdrawal from New Torahn territories is incumbent upon the formal establishment of higher-level negotiations. Failure to comply with this condition will see the Federation presence in New Torah become permanent, I am quite confident my council will back me on that."

Silent consultation between Ramoja and Calou.

"I assure you that Federation involvement in this matter is inevitable at this point, internal or not," Wong insisted. "All that remains to be seen is how deeply involved Federation becomes. Cooperation would significantly lessen the degree."

One did not need to be a diplomat to recognise the threat. Either League lets us get involved, or we'll get involved anyway. With or without your permission.

"We are not that weak yet, Captain Wong," Calou said grimly. "Understand that League will take any violation of sovereignty as an act of war."

"We are not talking about violations of sovereignty, only negotiations."

"Brought about by duress from *this* violation of sovereignty, and the threats of more to come."

"Which we hope to avoid by talking. And Captain Calou, Mr Ramoja, Federation is concerned that your reluctance to even enter negotiations may indicate that the League's internal problems may be even more severe than previously thought. Which may alarm members of the Grand Council into even more stern action than may currently be the case."

Oh, clever, thought Vanessa. The more you refuse to talk, the more alarmed we get, thereby making the thing you fear most, more likely.

"Captain Wong," said Ramoja carefully. "Let me be quite clear about this. Do not be fooled into thinking that the League is so outmatched by the Federation's firepower that you can push us into anything. If our internal matters were as severe as you suggest, we might just decide to go down swinging."

Just as clever, if far more diabolical. It was the suicide ploy—we're not scared of dying, push too hard and we'll take you down with us.

"Which only underlines how correct Federation is to be concerned," Wong concluded. "Please. Federation self-interest drives all external policy, as you know. League stability and survival is in this instance also Federation self-interest. I offer you negotiations as a means of keeping Federation involvement in League affairs to a minimum."

Further, silent deliberation between Calou and Ramoja. Clearly League had been keeping this quiet for so long that agreeing to talk to the Federation about it, and thus acknowledge the problem existed, was a huge step.

Admitting it did more than damage League security; it undermined the entire League philosophy, the raison d'être of League existence—that progress was all good, all the time.

"We must consult with higher government," said Ramoja finally.

"As shall we," said Wong. "When they arrive."

"How many more are arriving?"

"The barest minimum," Wong placated. "Merely those who can make the preliminary arrangements we make here more permanent. If ship numbers bother you, one Federation vessel may depart for each new arrival."

"We shall consult," Ramoja repeated.

It was a finality. Nothing more to discuss until we've consulted on this much.

Wong nodded, looking satisfied. Primarily he'd hoped to force League to talk about their little techno-social problem, structured talks involving the Federation so the Grand Council would be directly involved. That much now seemed possible.

"Now," said Ramoja. "The corporations."

"Can negotiate for themselves, surely?" Wong suggested.

"They have agreed for now to delegate that function to us," said Ramoja, with careful deliberation.

It was Wong and Reichardt's turn to glance at each other. Whether words passed between them on private link, Vanessa couldn't tell.

"So a League recon vessel attempts to nuke Droze," said Reichardt. "Droze attempts to shoot it down, fails, is saved by me. Now Droze turns around, presumably with the backing of the full New Torahn government, and throws in their lot with the people who just tried to kill all of them."

Ramoja waited patiently. With no intention of answering what had not been clearly phrased as a question. And probably not if the phrasing changed, either.

"I take it," Wong tried with greater diplomatic subtlety, "that this means League is declaring New Torahn sovereignty to be void?"

"We have always declared it void," said Calou. "The Torahn systems have always been, and remain, League space."

"Only now you're choosing to enforce it," Reichardt completed.

There wasn't a lot the Torahns could do about it. League had let them go because they were expensive and superfluous. Now they had something League needed, and however reduced the League's Fleet capabilities, they were still infinitely more than New Torah's little group of lightly armed freighters and planetary defences could handle. New Torahn sovereignty had been useful when League had discovered its catastrophic new problem, providing a safe place to conduct experiments on advanced origin biotech far away from the prying eyes of ethics monitors and journalists. New Torah had accepted, no doubt desperate for cash and eager for leverage over their old masters. But now the secret was out, and forced to choose between a new Federation overlord or the old League one, they'd gone with what was familiar. No matter that *Corona* had tried to nuke them.

Suddenly Vanessa was very suspicious. *Corona* answered to ISO, as did Ramoja. *Corona* had acted without full knowledge of the situation and would have killed Ramoja too, had it succeeded. So the corporations trusted that Ramoja had nothing to do with it. Now they struck a deal with him to get the ISO onside? No more nukes? You don't need to kill us, we can keep a secret? But what use would that secret keeping be, unless the Federation agreed to it too?

"Now," said Ramoja. "About the Federation's very illegal occupation of Chancelry corporation on Droze."

"Not the Federation's occupation," Wong corrected. "I understand it's more of a civil conflict, almost all of the occupiers are either former League GIs or Chancelry domestic GIs."

"Yes," said Calou, "but the *almost* in this regard is quite significant. Kresnov is yours, and she leads them."

"She didn't lead their last action, I promise you," said Reichardt.

"How can you promise me?"

"It was reckless, poorly planned, and ultimately unsuccessful. Kresnov is rarely any of those, and never all three." Reichardt leaned forward a little. "The real answer is that League's own GIs don't like you." He jerked a thumb back at Rhian. "What's happening in Chancelry is a rebellion. Kresnov's role in it was largely accidental."

Calou snorted. "Yes, she seems to get accidentally involved in a lot, doesn't she?"

"I believe," said Reichardt, turning in his chair, "that Commander Rice can speak for Kresnov?" Wong looked displeased. Clearly Reichardt hadn't cleared this with him first.

"In a limited capacity," she said, externals activated. It gave a fair approximation of her voice, if slightly metallic. "The GIs occupying Chancelry tell me to tell you that they've had meetings on it and have voted. There's hundreds of them, though they won't of course reveal their precise numbers, given their current strategic situation. They began with a number of demands, but now they've whittled them all down to one single demand. This demand has been transmitted to departing system freighters and will be spread independently around League and Federation systems regardless of what we do here."

Everyone was looking at her now, even Wong. He in particular looked most unhappy with this talk of departing freighters and spreading.

"What demand, Commander?" asked Calou.

"Universal emancipation. For all GIs, everywhere. That it become policy, agreed to by all sides through negotiation. Otherwise, they won't agree to anything."

"Emancipation!" Wong was furious. He had her in Reichardt's quarters on *Mekong*, no time for her to change from armour, the narrow space barely big enough for the three of them. "This is Kresnov's idea, isn't it?"

"I think at this point the distinction is meaningless." Vanessa's helmet was under her arm, her back to the door. Reichardt poured her a drink, non-alcoholic.

"Upon this negotiation," Wong thundered, finger jabbing back toward the dock, "hang the lives of billions. We are this close to getting a deal on inclusive negotiations on the gravest internal threat space-faring civilisation has yet faced, and you throw emancipation into the works! Without consulting me first!"

"You were consulted," said Vanessa, sipping Reichardt's drink. Ice tea. "I was going to speak for the GIs in Chancelry. You never enquired what I'd say, what *they'd* say. What did you think they'd say?"

"It's out now anyway," said Reichardt. "League and Federation public will hear the demand."

"Like they've heard it a thousand times before from various activist groups," Wong retorted, "all ignored because they know League will never allow it. Hell, League never did allow it, it nearly upset all the Five Junction Treaty talks. We got the Nova Esperenza agreements on limits to GI production, and that was that . . ."

"All of which they subsequently ignored," Vanessa said sourly.

"Exactly! GIs have always been the League's battlefield trump card, the creation of GIs was the reason for the entire war . . ."

"No, synthetic life sciences were the reason for the war," Vanessa corrected. "Of which GIs are but one particularly useful application. They wanted to get one up on the Federation in a synthetic bioscience arms race."

"And the fact that GIs are so central to League ideology," Wong continued, most unaccustomed to being interrupted, "only illustrates what an absolutely farcical illusion it is to believe that League will ever allow full emancipation to its synthetic citizens!"

"Least of all now that the main search for a cure to their new crisis is to use GIs as guinea pigs," said Reichardt.

"Yeah," Vanessa muttered. "Least of all."

"So what's she thinking?" Reichardt sat on his bunk, back to the narrow corner. "Kresnov's not stupid. And we're not stupid either, so you drop this shit about how that might not be her idea."

Vanessa said nothing. She wasn't the only one who knew her friend.

"It's not her *official* idea," Wong said darkly. Brooding. "She'll let her new friends make that claim themselves while maintaining her neutrality. But she's smarter than all of them, she's the real puppetmaster, and now with divided allegiances."

"No," said Vanessa very firmly. "Absolutely not. She's shed blood for the Federation, she's lost friends for it, she believes in it. She just disagrees with your course of action."

"If the League's internal problems are as bad as the data she found suggests," Wong retorted, "all human civilisation could be facing existential threat. FTL starships are weapons of mass annihilation in the wrong hands; if the League suffers an outbreak of borderline psychotic nationalism and sectarianism of the kind that we know only too well human beings are capable of, half the species could wind up dead."

"More than half," Reichardt murmured. "I ran the scenarios at Academy. Wouldn't be much left at all."

"Now, I'm sorry for Kresnov's GIs," Wong continued, "I truly am. But down there in Chancelry are a few hundred. There's nearly a hundred more in the Federation, perhaps a hundred thousand in the League."

"More," said Vanessa. Sandy had been quite sure.

"And I'm negotiating for the survival of the human race." Wong's expression said that he didn't think any more needed to be said. And he was right, it didn't. "So I think, that at some point, we all need to choose what's most important. You included, Commander."

CHAPTER SEVEN

Usually when Sandy walked in on Kiril in the medbay, she'd find him sitting on a spare bunk talking with one or another GI, or playing with his beloved AR glasses. But this time, he sat slumped, looking tired and uncomfortable. That wasn't like him.

"Kiril?" Sandy sat quickly on the bed alongside him. "Kiril, are you feeling okay?"

"My head hurts."

"Where does it hurt?"

Kiril pointed to his forehead. "And I keep seeing lights."

"Lights?"

"Yeah. It's like, when I close my eyes, I see green, and blue, and red. And they all move around."

Sandy uplinked fast. *"Poole, get here now."*

"What's up?"

"I think Kiril's uplinks are propagating." No reply from Poole. "Kiril, can you open your eyes for me?" He did that. "Now here, follow my fingertip with your eyes, can you do that?"

He nodded and did so. Poole appeared around a corner, walking fast.

"His pupils are dilated," Sandy told him, as Poole took over the examination. "Response time's a little slow, what do you think?"

"Well," said Poole after a moment, "I can't tell from here, I don't have the equipment. There's only one place that does."

Margaritte Karavitis stared at the scan display with goggles on, reaching now to toggle and shift her 3D view. Kiril lay as still as he could beneath the scan. He'd wanted his own goggles on, but Margaritte had said that would mess with the scan. He was a no-trouble kid on a lot of things, but he really didn't like not being able to see cool stuff that other people were looking at. Sandy thought he'd get on well with Ari.

"It shouldn't do that," said Poole. Poole had his own feed and didn't need goggles. "He's only had them two weeks, even given for the differences in kids . . ."

"They propagate faster in kids," said Karavitis.

"What do?" Sandy asked suspiciously.

"Uplinks. Any uplinks. No matter you try to slow them down, a child's brain is more malleable, late-generation uplink tech will integrate faster into a younger neurological structure because it gets more feedback."

Sandy glanced at Poole. "Seems logical," said Poole. Who would know such things, when the knowing was illegal in both League and Federation? Who experimented on children? Simulations were advanced, but even the most advanced simulations available still could not replicate with reliable accuracy the finer details of human brain function. And experimentation on subhuman-level sentient species were incredibly difficult these days, given ethical under-standing of just how semantical "human-level sentience" actually was.

"Why'd they do it to him?" Sandy asked.

"No idea," said Karavitis, studying her display. "I'm a synthetic neurolo-gist, not an integrationist. This is organic."

"I'm not asking for a scientific explanation," Sandy said coldly. "There are reasons organisations do things. They have objectives in mind. Unless you've been living in this basement the past five years straight like a hermit, you'll have some guesses."

"Pretty damn close," said Karavitis. She highlighted a spot on her display. "You see this? This is making a baseload pathway between the . . . well, if you're not a neuroscientist you won't know the words—between this bit here, and here. A child's brain will see that and respond twice as fast as an adult's, maybe faster."

"So why do it?" Sandy fought the urge to point a gun at Karavitis's head. Doing this to children was an extreme moral stretch even for Droze's corporations. But Karavitis wasn't directly responsible, and besides, they needed her. And it had never been Sandy's style to make threats she couldn't follow through. "We didn't find any other kids they'd done it to, despite them having abducted plenty."

"Kiril," said Karavitis, "I'm going to stimulate a small portion of your uplinks. Can you tell me if you hear or see anything different?"

Now Sandy really was about to point a gun at Karavitis's head. She looked at Poole. Poole shook his head faintly. "It's normal," he said. "It's how you tell what stage the propagation is at."

Sandy couldn't know, her uplinks came built in.

"Will it hurt?" Kiril wondered.

"Nothing in your brain hurts, Kiril," said Karavitis. "The brain has no nerve endings, so it feels no pain."

"So why does my head hurt?"

"That's an involuntary secondary reaction, like all headaches."

"That's bullshit, that's what that is," said Kiril, with the air of a boy pronouncing something he'd heard his elder siblings say. Poole grinned. Sandy would have, but she found nothing in the situation amusing.

Karavitis did something. "Kiril, what do you feel?"

"Everything sounds funny," said Kiril. "It sounds like the whole room just got bigger."

Karavitis glanced at Sandy. "That portion of the brain is audio, plus it cross-integrates some spatial functions. His baseload is already about one-thirty percent of what a child's would normally be; his brain's adapting."

"Make it stop," Sandy demanded. It wasn't safe at this age. Children's brains needed balance; you made one part hyperactive, and it changed all the other parts, just like making one leg longer would change the walking gait and throw everything else out of whack.

"I'm not sure that I can," said Karavitis. Gnawing a lip, black bushy curls falling in her face. Hair that looked like it hadn't been brushed in months. "The patterns are different, I don't recognise them."

"Recognise them from what?" Sandy asked dangerously. "Not from adult patterns, children's patterns won't look like adult patterns. From *other* children's patterns?"

"I told you," said the other woman patiently, "organic biology isn't my field. But the synthetic stuff they've put in his head is, mostly I only see it in GIs, where the entire neural structure is calibrated from day one to account for multiple augmentations. My understanding of what happens when you put it in any organic's head is sketchy, let alone a kid's head, but I can guess what it's doing by looking at its growth. And this thing isn't doing anything normal."

She highlighted the display. Several sections illuminated, a 3D-map of Kiril's brain. "Normally these points propagate much more slowly, plus they'll do what we call a phased stagger, where one point of neural outreach will advance and pass on its knowledge to the rest of the nano-formations, which will process and integrate accordingly. But this is all simultaneous."

"You're saying it's growing too fast to be safe?" asked Poole, now with a frown of concern.

"It's not a matter of safe," said Karavitis. "It just shouldn't be able to do what it's doing. Without progressive mapping the nano-formations don't know where to grow. They can't grow, they've got no instructions. But these grow anyway, without the processing interval."

"Like they already know where they're going," Sandy murmured, gazing at the display. "Fucking Talee research base." Poole looked at her. Karavitis remained studiously noncommittal. "All the neural synth tech the League got from this place were derivations, the basic technology with adjustments to human type. There had to be more pure strands of Talee tech they never used." Suddenly she was frightened. "You can't get this shit out of him?"

Karavitis shook her head. "Even if I had the expertise, which I don't. Someone who did would tell you no, it's too integrated. You'd take big chunks of brain with it."

"Then I want to know exactly what it is."

"Those files they erased," Poole reminded her. "They'll have copies, but we're not exactly in a position of leverage . . ."

"We've got an expert in orbit," said Sandy. "Let's use him."

The mall had been nice once, some old-timers said. In the crash, Home Guard had used it for staging and supplies, and the corporations had hit it, leaving half of it a collapsed ruin. Danya and Svetlana sat in what had once been a kitchen of some mallside restaurant, huddled in long sleeves and hats against the cold. Svetlana had her AR glasses on, looking for drones. Somewhere farther down the mall, stray dogs barked.

Danya examined the booster unit. His own glasses gave him a graphical display of receptive targets and sources he could potentially lock into besides the Home Guard feeds. Quietly monitoring local and supposedly "secure" networks, they could move around like this for quite some time and have real eyes and ears. Would have been damn useful the past five years. But it made them a target too, and they couldn't live like ghosts forever.

"Danya, what did Mama do before she came to Pantala?" Svetlana asked suddenly.

Danya thought about it for a moment. It took a mental adjustment. That was another world, the world with Mama. "She worked in insurance," he said, remembering.

"What's insurance?"

"Insurance is where you pay a company some money each year, and if something bad happens to you, they pay you even more money back. So you're covered, in case something bad happens."

"Who'd pay a company money?" Svetlana asked incredulously. "What if the company was the one that made something bad happen to you?"

"Companies elsewhere aren't like they are on Droze. You can trust them."

"And what good's money if something bad happens to you anyway?" Svetlana adjusted her glasses settings. "Why not pay money to make sure something bad *doesn't* happen?"

"I guess even offworld sometimes they can't stop bad things happening," Danya reasoned.

Silence for a moment. Down the mall, dogs were still barking. Sometimes the strays found scraps, left by other street kids or wanderers. The mall was a common place to look for a sleeping spot. You wouldn't do it more than one night at a time, because it could be dangerous sometimes, thieves or worse targeting the helpless to steal their stuff. But tonight, Danya feared thieves less than he had, and preferred some place farther away from regular folk.

"Why did Mama come to Pantala if she worked in insurance?" Svetlana asked then.

"Pantala was rich," said Danya. "She thought she could make more money." She had been making money too. Danya remembered a big apartment. He'd been younger then, maybe Kiril's age. Before Kiril, then. Svetlana just a baby, he remembered her as a baby, a little thing all squished up in her bedclothes. Remembered being shown her, straight from the tank, all pink and wailing.

Confident Mama. Single woman, big apartment, new city. Bit of a wasteland, but you could build anything if you had enough money, he remembered her saying so. They'd all called Droze the sandbox, even before the crash. But the companies kept the money pouring in from big military contracts, and no one thought about it. Until the war stopped, and the money with it.

Confident Mama. Three kids, no father, just a donor bank and gene labs. They were all three of them pretty well set, gene wise, Mama had wanted for them all the best in life. He remembered her saying so, tears on her face as she held him in the crowds of the transit camp with the cops yelling and the sirens and roadblocks blaring and flashing, and everyone pushing and screaming for a seat on some departing transport. She'd only wanted the best, please forgive her.

But they hadn't gotten a transport. There'd followed a smaller apartment, then troubles, then a lack of food. Kiril, in the tank even as the trouble started, but Mama hadn't terminated, no, she didn't believe in that kind of thing. A new baby, Danya remembered holding him in the water queues, remembered Mama getting milk from company officials, company people were all about town back then, still trying to help, you could ask them for stuff and not get shot. Thank you, she'd said, as Danya had held the baby, and Svetlana had cried and clutched her teddy.

Then the queues had been less orderly, lots of people yelling, and Mama didn't like the kids in line anymore, even though it had helped to get them more stuff. Then locked doors and crouched with other neighbourhood parents and kids as the riots ran up and down the streets outside, and then the shooting started . . . and then it was concrete and basements, watching the walls shake and dust rain down as explosions crashed and boomed above. Running from one place to another, terrified of shooting but desperate for water and food. Bodies in the street, things burning. Lots of shooting.

One day Mama had gone out and not come back. Danya remembered crying and being terrified, but also being so preoccupied taking care of Svetlana and Kiril that he hadn't had time to cry and be terrified for very long at all. He'd put it off, crying for Mama, and by the time he remembered again, it was too late, and he'd almost forgotten her face.

"I think she was right," Svetlana decided. Danya looked at her in surprise. "I'd like to have money."

Ah. Of course she did. "I think you're quite a lot like Mama, Svetochka," said Danya. Svetlana looked pleased at that. Danya put an arm around her. Svetlana would never blame Mama for dumping them in this mess. Kiril neither. They were too young to know anything else and could not recall that there was an alternative. Mama was a mythical figure, of distant memory to Svetlana, and of only tales for Kiril. And their older brother had no business tarnishing that figure with doubts and crude, blunt observations born of a lifetime staying alive on the streets of Droze, like what kind of fool moved to a government-run munitions town in the last throes of an ending war and brought three kids into a world that, suddenly without all its money, and her money, she had no chance of supporting . . .

It was the scariest truth that he knew. Adults were stupid too, and there was nothing to look forward to in growing up, except that you might be a bit stronger and wiser, and people wouldn't treat you quite so much like shit all the time. Or if they did, you could do more about it.

Truth was he didn't much like it when Svetlana asked questions about Mama. He always tried to tell her the truth, but with Mama, he couldn't. And he didn't like to think about it, because unlike Svetlana and Kiril, he was old enough to remember things that they'd happily forgotten or never really known.

Outside the kitchen, on the floor where the restaurant had been, a dog started barking. Danya got up and looked. Sure enough, it was barking at them; it could smell them. Most of the mutts weren't dangerous, just suspicious and territorial. A few he'd even been friendly with, the ones that licked and wagged their tails. Not so much different from street kids, they just got by how they could.

"He'll go away in a minute," said Danya. He looked around for something he could throw . . . but that could be awkward, he didn't want to make any more noise.

"He'll give us away," Svetlana warned.

"I'll chase him."

"Don't," said Svetlana. "There's a pack out there, packs are dangerous."

"I don't think it's a pack, it's just some mutts in the same place . . ." He finally noticed what Svetlana was doing. The pistol came with a silencer, and she was screwing it quickly into place. "Svet, what the hell . . ."

Svetlana rolled quickly to the edge of the bench, got up, and sighted the pistol on the benchtop. Danya could have stopped her, but he wasn't about to wrestle a loaded gun off his sister over a dog. Besides, he couldn't quite believe she'd do it.

The gun thumped, just a small thud of compressed air. The dog stopped barking. It looked puzzled, wobbled slightly, then sat down, panting heavily. With a jet of arterial blood shooting out of it at least a meter, like water from a punctured pressure pipe. Both kids stared in horrified fascination. Or Danya did. Svetlana calmly unscrewed the silencer, all business.

Still panting, the dog lay down, with a glassy, slightly desperate look. Not knowing what was wrong with it, but wanting it to stop. The jet of blood reduced to a trickle, and the dog lay still.

Danya crouched back down and stared at his sister. Silencer back in a pocket, she had the safety back on the pistol like Sandy had shown her.

"What?" she said stubbornly. "That dog was going to get us killed."

"It wasn't; it was just barking."

"And attracting attention! There's people looking to kill us!"

"Dogs bark all the time, you think the people after us have sensors looking for barking dogs? They'd get a thousand readings all over Droze."

"We can't take risks anymore, Danya," Svetlana retorted, jaw set stubbornly. "I'm not getting killed over some stupid dog."

"So that's going to be how you solve every problem from now on, huh?" This new turn scared Danya in ways he couldn't put words to. Svetlana could be ruthless. "Selfish" was a hard word to use about someone you loved more than your own life . . . but there it was. Only her definition of selfish included her brothers and anyone else who happened to be important to her. Most of her life, it'd just been them three. Lately, it had come to include Sandy. Who Danya was starting to think had been a very bad influence in this one respect. "Someone annoys you, shoot him?"

"If that someone's trying to get us killed, yes!" Svetlana settled back against the counter, knees drawn up, arms about her legs.

"Svet, any number of people might nearly get us killed. It's not always on purpose, sometimes things are just dangerous! You can't just shoot everyone who worries you!"

"They were going to take you away!" There was panic in her tone, the calm cracked. "They were going to take you like they took Kiril, and I was going to be left all alone!"

"Svet, this isn't about that." He held her arm firmly, knowing that he lied—it *was* about that, of course it was. How could it not be? "That wasn't a bad thing that you did." Dead eyes staring at the ceiling. Screams and blood. He'd had nightmares of seeing her or Kiril like that. He'd wanted them free of all of that kind of thing. But now they were in it neck deep, and there was no getting out, and Janu's people were after them with revenge on their mind, and there was just no getting out of this that he could see, nothing that would stop the two of them ending up the same way . . .

"But if this is how you start dealing with everything," he continued, forcing himself, "well . . . people shoot back, Svet. And they've got much bigger guns than that one, and there's more of them, and . . ."

Something hit the counter with a thud, then a bang! and acrid smoke everywhere. Stunned from the noise he tried to scramble for his own bag and gun, then realised that Svetlana's was in her pocket, and she was pulling it out. He grabbed her, holding her arm, and something heavy came over the counter and fell on them, gloved hands pulling him off with effortless power.

He was being dragged then, something pressed over his mouth regardless how he struggled, but he didn't pass out like he assumed; they weren't trying to smother him. A mask to keep gas from his lungs. He heard voices instead, muffled from inside helmets.

"*Rear's clear.*"

"*Two bags, some field kit. Two pistols.*"

"*We got them,*" said the man holding him. "*Objective secured, returning to rendezvous.*"

"*This is Ramoja,*" came the reply on an audible speaker. "*Good job.*"

CHAPTER EIGHT

Sandy moved quickly in the lower hallway of 9-R building, fine-tuning systems on her armour, quickly selecting weapons and ammo, an extra harness for grenade rounds, more lateral rotation through the torso; mobility was going to be important here. On local tacnet she had Droze primary spaceport, out beyond the northern periphery, visible defensive grids downlinked to her from *Mekong*.

"*If this was my sitrep, Sandy, I couldn't confirm what they're up to,*" Vanessa warned her.

"They grabbed the kids," said Sandy, running through armour systems on linkup. A right arm flex, and the armour flexed in response, harnessed to a wall of the hallway with a couple of underarm straps. "There's nothing else it could be, you don't drop a combat shuttle from orbit onto Droze outskirts with a sudden tacnet linkup with corporation defences for any other reason."

"*That you can think of,*" Vanessa cautioned.

"*That I can think of*'s been all I've had for the last twenty-two years, Vanessa." Amp down feedback, lateral flex up two, rebalance the power ratio to the shoulder mount, recalibrate, pump up the feedback once more . . . "Corporation defences were set to shoot down League orbital descents just an hour ago, now they're locked down, they've done their deal and now they both want me out of the picture. Grabbing the kids is the best way to do it."

Poole came stomping down the hall in heavy gear, loaded with extras and not yet calibrated. Rishi followed, unarmoured. Dahisu, Kiet's best friend, likewise.

"They're at the spaceport," said Rishi, frowning. She leaned against a wall, arms folded. "You going to attack it?"

"No, I'm going to go and ask nicely if they'll let me have my kids back." Poole handed her some loaded webbing. "You don't have to come. Someone should look after Kiril."

"Kiril wants his brother and sister back," said Poole, starting his own calibrations, unshouldering a massive rifle. "I think in poker it's called 'all or nothing.'"

"This isn't your fight."

"You think I don't like Kiril? I spend nearly as much time with him as you do."

Sandy stared at him for a moment. It was unexpected of Poole . . . and yet, somehow not. He was laconic, withdrawn. Some might say moody, for a GI. And also unorthodox and prone to confound. For him to forge a friendship with a six-year-old was surprising. Yet Poole often did things with the air of one raising a calculated middle finger to others' expectations.

"I don't get it," Dahisu said flatly. "You claim to be our leader, to lead all us GIs to something better. Now you're going to go and get killed for a couple of kids. I get tired of asking whose side you're on."

"So stop," said Sandy.

"Dahisu's right," said Rishi, still frowning. Her head still bore the scar where a bullet had nearly taken it off, when she'd attacked Sandy and her friends in service of Chancelry. Hers had been the biggest and most rapid turnaround in loyalties and worldview. "It doesn't make sense. How can you lead us if your loyalties are divided like this?"

"And your inability to understand makes me wonder if you're worth leading," said Sandy. She was processing on too many levels to get into the full emotive discussion now, gear calibrations, tacnet scan, comlink to *Mekong*, recalculating possible options now that it seemed they were two and not one. Rishi didn't get it, fine. She hadn't expected Rishi would.

"Help me to understand," said Rishi. "You helped me to understand before. I know I'm not like the rest of you, I'm young. But I know I can understand more, if you show me."

"Rishi," said Sandy, removing clothes down to her undershirt for a better armour fit. "I really don't have time."

"You do," said Rishi. "A League Fleet marine squad won't use corporate shuttles to get back to orbit, corporation vehicles all have embedded control systems and League don't trust them that much. The corporates would like those kids too, leverage over you and League. They'll have to refuel their own ship, take them another four hours at least."

Rishi was four years old, a 45 series. One iteration of synthetic neural tech below Sandy, though, making mere numbers misleading. Definitely far smarter at this age than Sandy had been, faster maturation with a lower plateau, like all GIs below her designation. Or all that she knew of.

Sandy slipped into the armoured upper half from below, thrust her arms in with the reflex ease that she tied shoelaces. "I like these kids, Rishi. I can't explain it, but I like them a lot."

Rishi's frown grew deeper. "Like motherhood?"

"I don't know."

"GIs don't get that," said Dahisu. "It's not written anywhere."

"Tell it to my friend Rhian on *Mekong*. She's a 39 series and she's the mother of three adopted."

"Liking kids and having maternal impulses aren't the same thing," said Dahisu skeptically. "Maybe you're trying too hard."

"To be human?" Sandy said drily, testing the arm and shoulder resistance and liking it. "Maybe you could try some self-respect."

"To be a straight," Dahisu retorted. "To be just like them."

Sandy might have shaken her head in disbelief, if she could be bothered. "There is no *them*. Nor *us*. That's what you're not getting."

Only she'd called them "my people" back on Callay, arguing with Director Ibrahim. And she'd felt that too, emotionally. Was this the curse of being high-designation, to be continually confronted with contrary impulses? Or was it rather the blessing, to ensure that no moral imperative was followed over a cliff?

"So all this mass production, experimentation, and murder was just a figment of our imagination then?" Dahisu snorted. You had to be fairly high-des, and fairly old, to do sarcasm like that.

"No," said Sandy. "The persecution isn't your imagination. But your conception of the persecutors is. Everyone not a GI is not the enemy. If they are, we're finished, you may as well shoot yourself now."

Dahisu glowered at that reference to his friend Kiet. "And you think you can make them like us by forming attachments with their kids?"

Sandy gave him her first dangerously contemptuous look. It had some effect. "This is like arguing with someone with the emotional range of a flea. I can't make them like us by doing anything, but my life experience tells me that many of them *already* like us or like some of us at least. But they probably won't like you, not because you're synthetic, but because you're showing every sign of being an asshole. I don't like assholes either. Give me an everyday straight or an asshole GI, I'll take the straight every day."

"Now after not letting me lead you in preference to a guy who turned out to be strategically incompetent, you're now complaining that I won't lead you because I have higher priorities. You're damn right I do. You want my help? Be worthy of it. Right now I couldn't tell why you're *worth* leading."

"We're your kind," Dahisu said darkly.

"That's not enough. Of all the standards to judge people by, that's about the worst."

"So why did you come to Pantala at all?" Rishi asked in simple curiosity.

For a brief moment, Sandy had no reply. Damn, she thought. Wasn't that a question. "I don't know," she muttered. "Maybe I came to save myself."

A few minutes later, Dahisu and Rishi were replaced by other, silent observers, Captain Wong was even less impressed.

"*As theatre commander of Federation operations in New Torah, I order you to desist from this venture.*"

"Fleet captaincy gives you theatre command of military operations in wartime," said Sandy. She was fully in armour now and taking her time with remaining preparations. There was, as Rishi had suggested, no mad rush. "We're not at war, and in peacetime the FSA is not within the Federation FBO."

"*Wartime or matters of wartime potential, Commander . . .*"

"Everything has wartime potential. You're late; I'm commander on the ground; I've never entertained the strategic judgement of orbital armchairs and I won't start now."

"*Commander, you are proposing an assault upon League assets located on a nominally League world over their alleged but unproven abduction of nominally League citizens! You might be able to squirm your way out of current League accusations of acts of war against them, but if you go ahead with this assault you will in fact have violated all the articles of treaty that keep League and Federation at peace!*"

"Federation citizens, Captain. Under asylum rules, status pending, Section 48 of the immigration act." She'd double-checked repeatedly, figuring how she might play it.

Short silence from the other end. "*Minors can't claim asylum.*"

"They can be granted pending status by ranking Federation officials. I'm certain I qualify."

"*You're not going to violate the treaty over two pending asylum claims who are not yet technically Federation citizens.*"

"For someone with no command authority over my decisions you seem very certain of what I will and won't do."

"When this is over, if you survive, I'll have you up on charges with process to criminal conviction."

"Good luck with that," said Sandy. "They're not taking these kids. They'll have a *spare*, two kids, so if I do anything at all that displeases them for years to come, they'll kill one without blinking and still have leverage. I'll be neutralised as a Federation asset, in which case I might as well die here anyway. Add to which their little brother has something in his head even Cai doesn't recognise, except to say it's certainly pure Talee, and if you want *his* cooperation in the next few years you're going to need his brother and sister back safe.

"Add to which, these cunts just abducted a couple of kids with lethal intent for nothing more than leverage. I'm going to kill them. If you don't mind."

She disconnected. Only now did she realise she was shaking. The armour picked up the motion and accentuated, rattling ceramic joints with a sound like hailstones. It scared her to be so scared. She'd rarely been this scared before. But she'd come to Pantala to try to unravel something important, something that had been eating away at her very soul, but that cause was all in bloody tatters and disappointment. Yet somehow, she'd found three kids who'd triggered something inside herself she'd been clueless had even existed. Lose something, find something else. And now the something else was going to be taken away as well.

Poole stepped in front of her, armoured and ready. He'd been playing these other roles lately, musician, medic, child minder, it was almost surprising to see him like this—a combat GI, his truest self, square jawed and armed to the teeth.

"Only a fucking idiot would try this," he said. "But of all the fucking idiots I know, you're my favourite."

"Thanks," said Sandy.

He searched her face. "You tell me it'll work, I'll believe you."

"That would make you the fucking idiot," said Sandy.

"I've played the part before," he admitted.

"Poole, stay here. This is my instinct. Me in a fight, I can vouch for, I can usually figure things through."

"You have a special affinity with violence," Poole nodded.

"You in a fight, or anyone else in a fight . . . I can't vouch for you. Not in this fight, this will be crazy."

"Read my psych report? I'm good at crazy."

Sandy smiled and put a hand on his shoulder. "I'm tired of losing friends, Poole." Her voice nearly cracked.

"Not many things that get me out of bed," said Poole. "Combat GI never really agreed with me, never saw the point. Got labelled a psych case real early, rather play my piano, play cards . . . you know I tried gardening once?" Sandy managed a smile, eyebrow raised. "Hydrohelios, nice flowers. Hydrohelios will get me out of bed. Mozart. A friend who understands why I'm me."

"Buddy, I've no fucking idea why you're you," Sandy laughed. "But I like you, so I don't care."

"And kids," Poole concluded. "Kids will get me out of bed. Pretty sure I don't want any, not like you and crazy Rhian. But if I don't help you get Kiril's brother and sister back . . ." he exhaled and made a vague, uncomprehending gesture. "Then what's the point? Of me being here at all? Combat GI, all dressed up and no one to blow away? Don't think I'd want to go home."

Want kids? Her? She nearly protested the thought. But Poole had said it now and . . . the fear got even worse. She didn't know what was happening to her.

"Cai? You reading me?" She sat in the pilot's seat of the combat flyer, a tight fit in full armour, linked into the expanding local tacnet. Poole sat in the seat before her, similarly belting in.

"*Hi, Cassandra.*" It was Cai, up on *Mekong.*

"What have you got for me?"

"*Like you suspected, they made a tactical level link from Fleet systems to Droze corporate nets when they went in, to neutralise the ground defences with redundancy backup.*"

Sandy nodded, running activation sequences in the cockpit, the engines beginning their low howl. "Via the uplink I've got feed to Antibe Station then down again, that gives me some windows into corporate tacnet . . . I've been working on it, I think I can buy time past their ground defences, get to the spaceport in one piece."

"You think?" Poole asked from the front.

"I think you can do better than that," said Cai. *"I've acquired access to a few of your network constructs, I hope you don't mind. But I think your interlink systems are about as close to Talee tech as I've seen. Let's see if you can handle this."*

Sandy waited. Nothing. *Handle what exactly?* she was about to ask but stopped herself. Whatever other technologies the Talee had, the one that had caused human and Talee kind to intersect was biosynthetic, and in particular neurosynthetic, which related to uplink tech for communications between natural and synthetic neurology and the wider communication nets. From what she'd learned from Vanessa and Ari, what Cai had done on Antibe Station hadn't been a matter of just beating opposing systems into submission with superior technology, he'd unleashed a separate communications construct into the station's systems and diverted information flows from the one onto the other, making them see, hear, and eventually think whatever he wanted.

So naturally anything he did here would involve . . . she rescanned the networks. And found, in the great walled divide that separated Chancelry occupied construct from the other corporations, a faint anomaly in an access portal that hadn't been there before, the kind of thing that probably only she or someone with similar capabilities, able to process massive data volumes simultaneously, would notice.

A simple touch let her in. And within . . .

"I'm not prepared to comprehensively infiltrate a League command system for fear of committing an act of war," said Cai. *"But I think it will adequately serve your needs."*

Explosions rattled the ferrocrete walls of Danya's cell. He stared upward in disbelief as the pale fluorescents flickered, then rattled again. Then a nearer, heavier boom! and bits fell from the ceiling. And BOOM! directly above, much louder than the rest and everything shook, and for a moment the lights went out completely.

And returned, dull red and ugly, hiding what little detail this storage locker had to show. Danya realised he was crouching, heart hammering, but there was nothing to hide under, the spaceport walls were heavily reinforced, built well before the crash but fearing Federation attack in the war, a League facility it had been then, the departure point for enormous quantities of military hardware.

Boom-thud-thud, the explosions continued. BOOM, the bigger one again, it sounded like an AMLORA, impressive, but it wouldn't damage these bunkers much. Who would be firing AMLORAs at the League-occupied spaceport? The corporations? Upset that League Fleet had dropped in on their turf? But they must have agreed to it in the first place, he knew they had defences against aircraft or spacecraft, for League to come down without getting shot at the corporations must have agreed to it—and besides, everyone was talking about how the corporations had caved and snuggled up to the hated League as soon as the Federation arrived.

Svetlana would say it was Sandy come to rescue them, but that was stupid. Sandy wouldn't commit all those resources just for him and Svetlana. Sandy was a soldier, an important one, and important soldiers didn't waste effort saving a pair of nothing kids. He'd told her that before they'd been separated, but Svetlana refused to listen, said Sandy would come for them, he'd see. He wanted to be with her, wanted to smash through these walls with his bare hands, she needed his guidance or she'd do something stupid trying to help with a rescue that wasn't. Yelling out to Sandy, who wasn't really there. Oh, God, she was going to get herself killed.

"Hey!" he yelled at the steel door. "Hey, out there, I want my sister! Get me to my sister, we'll be easier for you to guard if we're both together!" Now that you're under attack. Surely they'd figure that logic? Because the attack sounded pretty bad.

Boom boom, more AMLORAs, this time landing farther away. But the other explosions had stopped. Danya pressed his ear to the cold door, hoping the vibrations of further fighting would travel through the metal. Sure enough, he could hear thuds and feel impacts on his cheek.

And a heavy clank as the door opened, and he retreated as a League marine came in, armoured with weapon slung like she'd just thrown it over her shoulder in haste. He was grabbed without a word and pulled in a crouch running down the hall—his hands were bound in tight plastic cuffs, and every time he pulled against them they tightened painfully. The power here was emergency red as well . . .

"Get to supply junction!" the woman pulling him shouted at another marine who appeared in the far doorway. "Supply junction move!"

Into the next corridor, and there were several more marines running to intercept. "How'd they get in?" one asked.

"What's it fucking matter?" the woman snapped. "Get it deployed and shut it down. There's just a couple of them!"

"Tacnet's all screwy, coms are down . . ." Danya was thrown against a wall as they covered at a corridor junction. "I can't reach Beta and Delta, it's like there's interference . . ."

"Audio!" said the woman. "Radio backup, we can hear them at least." As someone fiddled to reset their coms. "This whole complex is reinforced, they can't blast through walls like the usual GI trick; they gotta come at us head-on, we can blast them with straight firepower."

Danya gathered himself against the wall, gasping breaths, wondering if he should make a dash for it . . . stupid, he concluded, there was no cover, and marines in armour were even faster and stronger than marines without armour.

Sounds came from one of the marine's helmets . . . audio, Danya realised, as they switched from tacnet to regular coms. Thumps and explosions, other marines yelling. Someone was in a firefight.

"Baker!" the woman shouted. Danya noted the chevrons on her armour—three, that made her a sergeant. "Baker, it's Leung! Sitrep!"

And a reply, amidst a lot more thumping and a lot of yelling, then some screaming.

"Baker!" Static. "Baker!"

"Oh, man," muttered one of the others. "GIs, it's fucking GIs." Because when your buddies were all shooting one moment, then all dead the next, it was the only answer, and all soldiers knew it.

"It's not just GIs," said Danya, sensing his chance. "It's Kresnov. Let me and my sister go or you're all dead."

It got him grabbed by an arm and dragged painfully through the next doorway. "This is Leung, pack and trap the junctions! She can't go through these walls, block her in, grenades and explosives, use indirect fire and blast round the corners, if you're waiting for line of sight you're already dead!"

It couldn't be Sandy, Danya managed to think past the agony of a wrenched shoulder as he was dumped this time at the edge of a minor hangar bay, small maintenance vehicles awaiting some larger aircraft to service in the adjoining main hangar. He could use the fear of Sandy against these soldiers, but he didn't believe it. It didn't make any sense, it went against every lesson, every life experience he'd ever learned. No way was it her, unless he and Svetlana had somehow become important in some way he didn't understand?

Marines covered the space, firing positions crouched behind the vehicles, behind a big maintenance loader, Leung herself crouched at Danya's side, tight to the wall. On her audio Danya could hear other marines talking, shouting, and crackles and pops that might be shooting. BOOM! went the AMLORAs overhead. Why were they doing that, when they couldn't hit anything? Distraction? Making noise to draw attention from the assault down here?

They wouldn't bring him and Svetlana together, he realised, brain churning in frantic overdrive. That would give whoever was attacking a single target—easier to defend maybe, but that wouldn't bother GIs. Better to spread them out, make it complicated . . . the attackers wouldn't know exactly where he and Svetlana were . . . only, dammit! He was being stupid, making the mistake of thinking he and Svetlana were the targets! Of course they weren't, why would a couple of street kids be . . .

"Let me and my sister go," he tried again. "It's your only chance."

Because if anyone could be persuaded, it was now, before the real state of affairs became apparent, and just how worthless they both really were. Leung's faceplate turned on him abruptly and she levelled a weapon at his head.

"Kresnov!" she shouted. "Kresnov, this is an all frequency output. I know you can hear me! Stop now or I kill the boy! You hear me? Stop now or the boy's dead!"

Over her audio, the shouts and yells continued.

"She can't hear you," Danya snarled. "She's not stupid. She's got everything turned off so you can't threaten her. You can kill me, but if you think she's angry now, wait until she finds me dead. She'll kill you slowly."

Svetlana had told him how she'd threatened that to Treska, who'd once been their landlord. But with Svetlana watching had made it fast instead. Leung certainly thought it was Kresnov. Was she fooling herself, or . . . ?

"Just pumped a fucking shitload of explosive down the B Central access!" someone was shouting on Leung's audio. *"Nothing can survive that!"*

And more adrenaline overload cursing and hooting in the background. *"Fucking got her, man!"*

Then yells, swearing, and panicked gasps of soldiers hitting the deck—not the same group, but someone else under sudden attack, and Leung yelling, demanding to know who this was because with tacnet down she didn't know who was talking when or where . . .

"*You didn't get her, you fucking fools!*" someone else was shouting. "*You blocked her and she went around you, now move before you're outflanked!*"

Leung looked back at Danya, weapon trembling. At least, Danya thought as he looked up the dark barrel, if they killed him first, it left Svetlana as the final bargaining chip. And if it was Sandy, as they seemed to think it was, they wouldn't dare kill Svetlana because then Sandy would have nothing to restrain her at all. And that could get seriously nasty. If it was her. If it was.

"Klimentou!" There was real fear in Leung's voice now, the pistol shaking. No, her whole arm was shaking. Danya had always been scared of the powerful people with the big guns. Seeing one of *them* so frightened her armour was audibly rattling was a revelation. "Klimentou! Oh, dear god."

Another unit, Danya guessed. Wiped out in seconds. Danya was grabbed once more and dragged not toward the open hangar but back the way they'd come, into the narrower hallway, others of Leung's soldiers moving ahead to clear the way . . . and disappeared in a flash of smoke and fire.

And shrapnel, Danya heard it ripping around him, then shooting and armour tearing as he fell, blinded, something wooshing past, huge impacts and simultaneous shooting, bodies falling, a faceplate caved in, another with an arm snapped the wrong way, another slammed back-first against a wall as a rifle was slammed into the neck ring and heavy rounds unloaded. Slid to the ground, blood spurting.

Another armoured figure crouching beside him, but not to threaten nor to check or comfort, as he stared up through the smoke and stench of explosive and scorched metal . . . one arm dangling, armour torn in places, reloading rapidly with just the one functioning hand.

"Danya, help, can you get some grenades?" Sandy's voice. He couldn't register what that meant.

"My hands . . ." She moved fast, he felt a pressure on the cuffs as he struggled up, then a snap and they were gone.

"Grenades," she repeated. "Don't bother with magazines, just grenades, follow me but don't move fast, I'm going to try and link with Poole and Svetlana."

And she was gone, possibly limping but gone so fast all the things he had to ask her were gone as well, where was Svetlana, who was Poole, what the hell was going on . . . but she needed grenades and the next thing he was scrambling for them, on the bodies of marines alive and breathing and talking just moments before, now . . . barely even human. A head was missing. Leung's body, kicked into a wall with such force the chest was all caved and the arm nearly severed, like she'd been hit by a train.

He found grenades, he didn't know how, and ran back into the minor hangar, only now there was another marine on the floor, caught in the open and plugged precisely between the eyes with a single shot. She hadn't needed more rifle ammo, no shit.

She wanted him to follow her? He stared about the ferrocrete walls, at dull red shapes that might have been clear as day to a GI's eyes but were only shadows and threat to his. Stuffing grenades into a webbing belt, five, and now a sixth and a seventh, and shouldn't he have a gun? Against Fleet marines, with Sandy swatting them like flies? What was the point?

He tried to think like a GI, of how she'd see the situation—flexible and unfolding. Yes she'd want him moving, closer to her and less vulnerable than if he stayed where he was, but obviously nothing was safe yet because otherwise she wouldn't still be moving. GIs were all about moving, all the time, when the fighting was on.

But ahead was the main hangar, big flyers and some aeroplanes down the ramp and sheltered from the bombardment above. Where the League assault shuttle the marines had come in was, he had no idea. But it was a big, wide space to cross on his own, just one accurate rifle that saw him coming would drop him, so he stayed where he was, crouched against the far wall by the vehicles.

Until he saw movement across the hangar. A man in armour, rifle raised, sweeping the hangar back and forth. And with him . . . even at this range, he recognised Svetlana. She was standing somewhat exposed, the man with him was obviously another GI, perhaps this Poole Sandy had mentioned, and if Poole was covering the hangar, no one hidden anywhere around it would live long enough to get a shot off.

He ran, and Svetlana saw him coming. Under the wheels of aeroplanes, Poole warning her to stay where she was, so it wasn't entirely safe, but she was jumping up and down with excitement and crying to see him safe. They embraced so hard they nearly fell and held each other so tight, her crying and him gasping not only for air but for the hope of returning sanity.

"Danya, this is Poole," said Svetlana against his shoulder. "He's Sandy's friend and he says Kiril is safe! Kiril's back in Chancelry HQ and he's safe!" And then Danya was in tears too.

Sandy was back, coming through a side door. Her left arm limp but the hand still worked, holding her rifle as the right arm hauled something else across the floor, something human sized and unmoving. A person, Danya saw. A man, full armour, leaving a smear of blood on the floor behind.

"Where's his friends?" Poole asked, voice cold.

"Pick your religion," said Sandy. Her helmet was off, wires and connections severed, the left side of her face a mess, multiple cuts and more blood than skin. It matted her hair and dripped. Danya's joy and tears died to look at her. She'd been shot up. She never got shot up . . . or he couldn't imagine she did. She slammed the man she was dragging up against a wall, and he struggled to sit, still conscious, still breathing.

"I want a witness," said Sandy. Danya didn't think she meant him and Svetlana.

"Sure," said Poole.

"Commander Mustafa Ramoja," said Sandy coldly. "I can't charge you with treason; you were never ours. But you pretended to be. Then you betrayed us all, and a bunch of my friends died. But that's not why you're dead. You're dead because you played this game, with me, and crossed me. You crossed the FSA. You crossed Director Ibrahim. You crossed Callay. You crossed the Federation. In this game, with these stakes, you don't do that and live."

"I know," said the man, looking up at her from his wall. Quietly. Sadly. "I'd do the same. And Cassandra, please know that . . ."

Sandy shot him, repeatedly, point blank, heavy caliber. Danya grabbed Svetlana and turned her away.

"No," said Sandy, trembling. "You don't get to kill my friends, abduct my kids, and have a sympathetic final word. Fuck you. Fuck you all."

She threw the pistol at the body and started walking back. And fell to one knee halfway there. Svetlana tore herself away and ran to her. Danya followed. Sandy embraced them both, sobbing, and they clung together, armoured synthetic and human child, an embrace of blood and hot metal and tears.

CHAPTER NINE

Return to Callay took three weeks, a succession of jumps through various systems, a few inhabited but most not, and one a blob of dark matter Fed Fleet Intel was pretty sure only they knew about and League did not. The freighter was Fleet registered, employed on this occasion primarily as a messenger, the simple movement of information back and forth across such distances was a task worth employing entire ships for.

Normally Sandy would have found three weeks of nothing a drag, but not this time. Danya, Svetlana, and Kiril found the ship incredible, especially the weightless core, where they'd go for at least an hour every day to float around and play various games they'd devised . . . and what a joy to see them playing. Or more correctly, Kiril would play, and Svetlana would play with him, while Danya supervised, all the while glancing around at various ship systems, or reading off some latest technical manual or a history of Callay or something for adults on the Federal Security Agency, since Sandy worked for them and Danya figured he needed to become an expert overnight.

And Sandy would go up with them, her arm bound in a tight cast and sling, side and leg tightly bandaged, and strange not to have any hair to float around in zero-G, it had all been shaved to accommodate the nano-environment bandage against the left side of her head and face. She'd been real close to losing an ear, which might not have transplanted and healed back very well, so she was glad. The doc said a few of the scars would be permanent, though very light, from up in the hairline to down the jaw. A small price to pay, by any measure. She had worse, elsewhere about her person.

Better yet, everyone got the chance to get to know one another. Sandy had never had the chance to learn all of the kids' stories, nor they hers, so they spent long hours around various games, lessons, or just looking at the observation screens, talking about things. And Sandy learned that as fun as they were, Danya could be too stubborn, and Svetlana could whine a lot, and Kiril could go off in his own little dreamworld and not listen to anything he was told, at which his siblings would roll their eyes . . . and it didn't matter. She'd known flawed adults too. And was one herself, for sure.

They got to know Vanessa, Rhian, Ari, and Poole as well. That pleased Sandy a lot, because as she told them, these were the people in Tanusha, aside from herself, that they could trust implicitly and who would always help them if they were in trouble. Vanessa struck up a particular rapport with Svetlana and told her stories about growing up in Tanusha, and parties, and getting in trouble, and boys, that had Svetlana in giggling hysterics. Rhian of course got on wonderfully with Kiril, having that way with younger children, and played games with him for hours. And Ari graciously took time away from various tech review manuals and construct design to talk with Danya about the way things worked in Tanusha from Ari's uniquely cynical perspective . . . and actually seemed to enjoy it.

"Kid's got potential," he admitted to Sandy one ship "evening" over a meal. "He's got a particularly brutal understanding of human relations. I like it."

"Yeah," Sandy said quietly. "He's learned that."

Poole remained Poole, engaging sometimes, other times withdrawing to listen to music, or to play virtual piano, or whatever else held Poole's attention for extended periods. But he seemed to like having the kids around and sometimes hung out with them as though just to hear them talk. Because kids didn't talk like adults talked, Sandy guessed, and Poole seemed to enjoy their non sequiturs and surprising conclusions. It gave Sandy ideas about what might be done to get Poole to engage more.

Arrival was at Hanuman Station, one of Callay's five stations, recently completed for Fleet Ops in high geostationary. FSA and Fleet Intel were waiting, debrief was an immediate requirement, and Sandy didn't resent it too much, so long as they cleared up any concerns about the asylum paperwork for the kids, to say nothing of guardianship. But the Intels waved it away, no problem, all fixed as they'd been informed in advance. Sandy didn't quite believe it but was happy the first debrief was a group one, Danya, Svetlana, Kiril, and her all together in a well-appointed lounge, real fruit juice for the kids, orders taken for dinner in a few hours (they'd been synched with Tanushan time the past two weeks to save the kids time lag), and an explanation for everyone of what debriefing was, and how long it would take, and were there any questions?

The kids were all adamant that Sandy should be at their own debriefing, at which the Intels just nodded, and said that Sandy was their legal guardian now, which meant that no one on Callay was actually *allowed* to interview them without Sandy present.

"No one?" Danya asked suspiciously.

"No one at all," the Intel lady named Togana confirmed with a smile. "Not us, not the police, not even your school teachers. A child's guardian must be present if the child is formally interviewed. That's the law."

"What can they do?" Svetlana asked, wide-eyed. "Can they get beaten?"

Togana blinked.

"Svet, the law doesn't beat people," said Sandy. "People can get arrested, then there's an investigation, and if they've done something bad they'll be either fined money, or put in prison. No beating."

Svetlana looked mistrustful. In her experience, bad people were only put off with the threat of a good beating, or worse.

The kids' briefing was after dinner and quite long at nearly two hours. Kiril got bored and did some drawing while Danya and Svetlana talked, but they seemed to enjoy it somewhat, telling all their tales of Droze and the things they'd done. The Intels just recorded, asking questions, keeping the stories flowing. They only wanted information, partly for what it could tell them of Droze and Pantala, and partly so they'd know just what kind of kids the infamous Commander Kresnov was bringing down to the surface. And Svetlana talked more than Danya, as Danya looked wary of talking too much, lest some revelations make someone here think badly of them. Perhaps he didn't quite believe they'd just let him and his siblings move in so easily. It had to be an enormous reality shock for him most of all; Svetlana and Kiril just accepted it as younger kids would, but Danya had that wary look of someone who thought he might be dreaming and kept expecting to wake up. Or was perhaps waiting, from hard experience, for that awful moment when the dream inevitably became a nightmare.

After the debrief it was late, and Sandy saw them all to bed. The Intels had a good room for all four of them together, with a reassurance that Sandy would be in later and would be just down the corridor talking with the Intels.

"The psychologist will be mandatory," Agent Gupta informed her as they sat in the same room the kids had been interviewed in. Sandy nodded, sipping a big mug of coffee. Good coffee, hard to get on spaceships and impossible on Droze. Small pleasures. The taste made her realise how much she'd missed her home. "I don't wish to be impolite about them; they seem like great kids, amazingly resilient. But they're also pretty messed up. You know that, right?"

"I know," Sandy agreed. "But I know what it's like to be messed up like that. And I think I can help."

"So why do it?" Gupta pressed. "Adoption is your right, like any Federation citizen. But three at once is a big task for someone who's never been a parent before."

Sandy shrugged. "Fell in love," she said. She wasn't going to explain it any more than that, because she didn't think there was any more to it. Except for all that deep, psycho-analytical crap that she sure as hell wasn't going to get into here. Leave that for some other asshole to make her life difficult with. "Different kind of love, but that's about it. Couldn't part with them, sure as hell wasn't going to stay on Droze, so they had to come here. And it's not such a big task with three. These three have been looking after each other in conditions that would have driven lots of adults to suicide. It would be the height of arrogance for me to think I can show them how to survive in the world."

"Then what do you see as your role, being their guardian?"

"To introduce them to civilisation and civilised attitudes. To show them how to make civilisation work for them. And to teach them how to be happy. God knows they deserve it."

There were the usual questions about Droze, about events, about strategic choices she'd made. But like with the kids, no real analysis, just an initial retelling of events in moderate detail. This would be analysed by all the relevant agencies (meaning just about everyone with a high enough clearance; she thought with a grimace at how many people that entailed), and once analysed, the follow-up questions would start. Those were the ones that worried her. This was just procedure.

It was two in the morning, Tanusha time, when she returned to her room. The kids were all up and waiting for her, looking worried. Even Kiril, struggling to stay awake.

"Is it okay?" Danya asked, sitting on his bed still in his clothes. Sandy was suspicious he might even have a bag packed, hidden under the bed. Like he might have to make a break for it any moment. His eyes showed that much.

"Danya," she said, and sat beside him. "It was just a long interview, it's just procedure. I'm important here, and these people won't mess with me. That means they won't mess with you either. Okay?"

Danya nodded, looking relieved but still not entirely convinced. Sandy kissed him on the forehead.

"Now," she said, "I'm tired, and I'm going to sleep. Our shuttle's tomorrow, 15:00 . . . quick, what's 15:00, Svetlana?"

"Three o'clock!" said Svetlana. She was sitting with Kiril, who was falling asleep against her shoulder, awkwardly.

Sandy smiled. "Poor Kiril, did your dumb brother and sister keep you awake worrying for no reason?"

"Yes!" said Svetlana, glaring at Danya. "I told him he shouldn't worry, I told him you were important here."

It wasn't the only reason the system would work for them. But Sandy didn't know how to explain to them that some parts of this system were actually pretty good and would have treated them well regardless of how much of a bigshot their new guardian was. It was too much of a leap to get them to understand that some systems didn't just brutalise the weak for the benefit of the strong. And again, maybe such skepticism would have its advantages too, in the long run.

Danya said nothing and got back into bed. Sandy wished she could tell him to just let go, for a little while at least. But truthfully, given what she was, and what her lifestyle would inevitably expose them to, she didn't know if she dared.

Vanessa, Ari, Rhian, and Poole all went down in the morning. All offered to stay, but Sandy firmly told them no. Rhian had a family to return to, Vanessa a husband, Ari his unendingly crazy life, and Poole . . . well, she didn't want Poole feeling he had to hang around with her out of some sense of obligation. Though she was damn well going to make another push to get him working full time somewhere, CSA probably. As soon as she was down.

For the kids there were medical checks, injections, micros and nanos, scans to make sure they wouldn't infect the Callayan population with some terrible offworld disease. Danya didn't like the shots either, so Sandy got the medicos to give him lots of reading material and took him through it step by step, vouching for each thing in turn.

"But you're synthetic," he told her. "How can you vouch for biological treatments?"

"'Cause I'm old and I'm smart and I've read a lot," said Sandy. "And if you don't take them, they won't let you go down."

More debrief questions for her, apparently someone downworld had responded with immediate follow-ups. This time the kids worried less and allowed someone from Fleet to take them down to loading, where massive inbuilt mechanisms loaded and unloaded huge cargo palates from newly docked warships. When she rejoined them, even Danya seemed impressed.

Then at 15:00, they went up to the zero-G hub where the scheduled shuttle was waiting. After three weeks in transit the kids were quite proficient weightless, and settled themselves in up at the front of the shuttle, while the usual Fleet personnel, including senior officers, strapped in elsewhere. Then a several-hour wait as the shuttle's deceleration brought it down from geostationary, and a particularly noisy and alarming reentry.

"I wasn't scared!" Kiril insisted, all wide-eyed and gorgeous, strapped into his big chair at Sandy's side. "Sandy, were you scared? Because I wasn't!"

"Sandy doesn't get scared, Kiri," called Svetlana from across the aisle at her window seat. Then stared out the window as the heat shields retracted, and the view showed ground and clouds.

Callay was green. Svetlana talked about it all the way down. Her world had been yellow and brown and mostly dead. This world was alive. At lower altitude, the setting sun glowed yellow and pink against the towering clouds. The shuttle bumped and jolted through the turbulence as the kids all stared out their windows and made exclamations to be flying between giant pink towers of cloud. Sandy smiled all the way down.

Sandy had half expected more procedures and delays at the Balaji Spaceport, but there were none—Hanuman Station had been the gateway, and they were clear from that departure. There was even a flyer waiting, an FSA courtesy, and Sandy took the kids across a rooftop pad in the last light of day, breathing in air that smelt like rain and flowers, and listening to chirping and shrilling insects, flitting batwings, and somewhere, a croaking amphibian. She carried Kiril, who was very sleepy but determined to stay awake, as Danya and Svetlana held onto their little bags containing all their worldly possessions.

"The air smells funny," said Danya.

"That's because it's alive," said Sandy. She put Kiril in the flyer's rear seat and showed Svetlana how to strap him in, then herself.

"Are there trees everywhere in Tanusha too?" Svetlana asked as Sandy ran the activation sequence from the pilot's seat, Danya at her side. She left the door open a bit longer, enjoying that smell too much.

"Everywhere," Sandy agreed. "But lots of people too, not like this. This spaceport is out in the wilds because it has to be a long way away from people, with all these military shuttles landing. Tanusha's got lots of trees, but . . . well, you'll see."

"Are we very far away?" Danya asked.

"A few hundred kilometers. Not far. Maybe forty minutes flying."

They flew for a while, not saying very much. Sandy supposed it was very strange, to actually be here, on another world, in the kind of flyer that had always meant trouble, viewed from below on Droze. Little of the wilderness below was visible in the dark, unless one had vision like Sandy's. A small cluster of lights here and there, a little town. A car moving on a rare outback road.

And then ahead there came an enormous glow that lit the horizon from side to far side. Closer, and the glow resolved into many colours and blinking lights. Thousands of lights. Then millions of lights. Then billions.

"Kiri!" Svetlana shook her brother's shoulder; he'd fallen asleep to the vibration of thrumming engines. "Kiri, look! It's Tanusha, Kiri!"

Approaching the outer perimeter, the air traffic became intense. Sandy flew mostly above it, as navcomp assigned her a lane, but not too far above. Svetlana and Kiril made awestruck sounds, staring down at huge towers surrounded by clusters of smaller but still huge towers, centering on gracefully tangling ribbons of light ground traffic in endless gleaming streams. And more towers, and more towers, in endless repeating but unpredictable patterns. Air traffic passing in trails, ahead and behind, predictable lines, following highways in the sky. Layers upon layers of it, dividing up the sky like a giant layered cake.

Sandy glanced at Danya as she flew one-handed. He stared in utter amazement, head turning this way and that, not saying a thing. All the cabin lights were off, yet still his face was lit with the glow from the ground. It shone through the cabin like white fire, turning everything silver and pale.

"Danya," she asked him, and he looked her way. "What do you think?"

For a brief moment, through the usual shield of wary concern, she glimpsed something else. Excitement. It was not the dominant emotion, not by a long shot. But it was there, real as the city that sprawled around them. Sandy thought it a good start.

"Amazing," he breathed, and went back to staring around him. "Amazing."

"I told you it was big," she said to them all cheerfully. "But you have to really see it, don't you?"

Kiril wanted to know how all the cruisers didn't bang into each other, so she explained the traffic control to them, and how she was steering along a centrally mandated skylane, a higher-altitude one for flyers. Svetlana wanted to know what all the towers were, and if they were going to live in a tower like one of these. Sandy laughed and said towers weren't that great because you couldn't have a garden. In Tanusha, short houses cost more than high apartments much of the time.

And then they were descending, to Svetlana's displeasure and despite her request to fly around for a while longer. Sandy told her she'd have lots more chance to go flying, but for now everyone was tired, not just Kiril, and it was time to go home.

The flyer landed at Canas District's third secure transition zone, actually a spot beside sports fields outside the Canas security wall. A groundcar was waiting, and they all piled into the third transport vehicle of the day (actually the fourth, Sandy reminded them after Svetlana said it, because the station was technically moving in orbit, and thus also transportation) and rolled the short distance to Canas security gate number three.

Automatic units scanned the vehicle inside and out, laser projectors peering through all windows, then the gate opened and they rolled inside. Up narrow winding streets, wheels bouncing on cobbles (why was it so rough? Danya asked) between decorative stone walls, across a little bridge with wrought iron light fittings, past the neighbourhood eatery packed with high-security residents seated along the streamside eating some very good Spanish food, then left around a bend and under some lovely tall trees. Then left again into a little driveway, the carport opening on automatic, sharply downslope, and into a very familiar parking space.

They got out, and Sandy couldn't quite believe she was home, it felt so surreal. Almost as surreal as the company she'd brought back with her. Through the little jungle of garden, up steps to the rear door, automatic locks came open, and a full system scan on uplinks gave her a return feed from the house, months of reports, all pouring in—most of them empty and unoccupied save for a few GI visitors come to check on the place. Almost as though the house had been lonely and was welcoming her back.

Months. Good lord, what months.

Before them the living space, polished floorboards and a high ceiling, a wall of windows opening onto the jungle/garden, open kitchen on the left, stairs climbing past it up to the second floor, all very mellow and light and spacious as suited her taste.

"This is your home?" Svetlana gasped, staring around in unrestrained excitement.

"No," said Sandy. "This is *our* home."

They couldn't believe it. Just couldn't. It wasn't the biggest house by any means, though quite nice by middle class Tanushan standards. But Sandy had seen where the kids had come from, and to them, this was a castle in the clouds. And everywhere else they'd been since leaving Pantala had been cramped and simple—the ship quarters, then the station quarters for a night. They'd never really seen how middle-class Tanushans lived, to say nothing of important residents of Canas high-security district. Sandy thought she'd take them to see one of Anita and Pushpa's genuine mansions one day.

Living rooms all downstairs, the bedrooms were all upstairs and unoccupied save her own, since Vanessa and Rhian, who'd once shared the place with her, had acquired separate lives and moved out.

Svetlana wanted her own room—demanded it, in fact—and ran excitedly around it and jumped on the bed when she got it: Vanessa's old room with the windows opening onto the big trees outside, where her pet bunbun had gone climbing each night. But Kiril wanted to be with Danya, so they got Rhian's old room across the hall, with the windows looking the other way toward the perimeter and the big flowering bushy tree that separated this house from the neighbours that way.

Then there were showers, and toilet stops, and pajamas the Intels had given them . . . and Sandy taking Danya aside to show him the house security systems, all of which were directly uplinked in her head, as were the broader systems of the entire district surrounding. That, to help him sleep. Some kids needed a glass of warm milk; Danya, a security briefing.

Then bed. Which lasted until Sandy sensed movement in the hall (she had hall sensors on directly, so she'd know) and got up to stick her head in Svetlana's room and found the bed empty. Smiling, she looked in the other room to find all three children wrapped together in the one big bed. Svetlana probably hadn't slept alone in her life. Sandy was half tempted to drag a mattress in there and join them, but this was their new normalcy now, and they needed it established as quickly as possible. Starting now, this was their home. Whether the kids would find that Tanushan normalcy actually agreed with them, or they with it, only time would tell.

She was awoken by running footsteps on the hallway floorboards. Children's voices, excited. Thumping down the stairs. She smiled. She hadn't expected they'd be up before her, though Rhian had warned her.

She got up, carefully, and checked all her bandages. Three weeks of healing, and it would be a few more before she'd get them off. The arm was partially functional now but still needed rest, healing itself at high speed as GIs with merely structural damage tended to do. She showered in the ensuite, dressed awkwardly, and checked herself in the mirror. Something of a mess, she looked. The hair now had three weeks of fuzzy growth, giving her an allover blonde buzz cut. Vanessa had said she still looked great, save for the bandage across the left side of her head. That short hair suited her, as it often did women with wider features.

Sandy had always liked it short, partly from habit, partly from agreeing that it suited her . . . but hair this short made her look like android model B from central casting. Longer hair could be mussed, lending that too-perfect face some unpredictability. Could be worn to one side, distracting attention from the effortless symmetricality of that central line. Some days Sandy was just happy to be going through life with the blessings of good looks, however she'd arrived at them. But other days, the big blue eyes gazed back at her with accusation.

Svetlana burst into the room. "Sandy, Sandy, there's a robot at the door!"

Sandy blinked at her. "There is?" She checked her uplinks. "Oh, yeah, it's just a delivery bot. The house knows when people are home and what's in the fridge and cupboards, and we don't have anything. So it ordered some groceries for breakfast."

"What should we do with the robot?" Svetlana asked, all breathless and earnest.

"Just take the bag and it'll go back to its vehicle," said Sandy. And she thought of Danya, downstairs facing an inoffensively humanoid delivery bot, his only experience of humanoid bots being things that carried rotary cannon and were programmed to kill. "It's not the slightest bit dangerous, please don't let Danya trash it."

"He's not going to trash it!" said Svetlana, scampering out of the room. "He just didn't know what to do with it, it looks kinda creepy!" And thundered back down the stairs.

Sandy looked back to the mirror . . . and found her previous train of thought all in tatters. For a brief moment, it offended her. Then she smiled. Good. Stupid, morbid train of thought anyway. Rhian had warned her of this too—they'll take over your life, your brain, your thoughts, everything, she'd said. And probably, Sandy thought as she went down the stairs after Svetlana, not before time either.

Everyone helped with breakfast. Sandy didn't even need to ask, nor Danya to direct, it just happened: Svetlana and Kiril setting the table, and Danya helping Sandy to see how the stove and frying pan worked, and then to cook, since she only had one hand. Bacon and eggs, they'd liked that when Gunter had made it for them in his apartment in Droze. Now they wolfed it down, with the appetites of kids who never knew when their next meal was coming. Sandy foresaw a problem, eating habits leading to massively increased calories, with massively decreased exercise. These kids were going to take up sports, or she'd have three little balloons in the house before long. Still, nice problem to have, she reflected as they ate, and Svetlana kept talking about the robot and teasing Danya for being scared of it, at which he laughed and tried to pinch her ear to make her shut up.

Danya laughing was the best thing Sandy had seen in weeks.

Then they all helped her clean up. Rhian would be jealous.

"Okay!" she announced, as they sat to drink a final cup—tea for her and Danya, juice for Svetlana and Kiril. "Today, we have some things to do. First, we're all going to take Kiril to FSA Headquarters, so we can check out his uplinks." It was the first thing she'd arranged, as soon as the freighter had entered transmission range of Callay on the way in. "And while we're there, you can see where I work.

"Next thing, we're going to do some shopping. Because you guys have basically no clothes at all, and I've got hardly any . . . well, anything, in this house, like we're going to need." And while she was at Headquarters, it occurred to her with halfway seriousness, she might ask for a raise as well.

"And then," she said brightly, "we'll have the rest of the day off, because I've been told quite pointedly by my various bosses that I'm not expected at work today" (they'd been even more direct than that) "so I figured I might show you some things in Tanusha. Where would you like to go?"

A clamour of questions and suggestions followed, entirely from Svetlana and Kiril. Danya was happy to go wherever they wanted to go, though he listened with great interest to Sandy's descriptions of the various places they might visit. While they talked, two waiting message lights illuminated her uplink vision, nothing urgent, just "call me when you've time."

Schedule decided, Svetlana and Kiril rushed upstairs to get ready. Danya remained at the table, cup in hand, gazing thoughtfully out the windows at the lush tangle of plants outside. Sandy sat beside him.

"I know you think I worry too much," he said, surprising her. But not really surprising her, because only a fool would think of Danya as an imperceptive child. "And, I mean, I can see how easy it would be, to just, you know. Relax. I mean, it's nice here."

Sandy nodded. "It is nice."

"And . . . I don't know." He sipped the remnants of his tea. "Maybe one day. But I just don't think like that, you know? You've seen where I'm from, you've seen . . ."

"Danya." She put her good hand on his arm. "You want the truth? I don't want you to change at all. Or if you change, I want you to decide for yourself how to do it. And I think you already know what maybe Svetlana and Kiril haven't worked out yet, that however nice this place is, it's not entirely safe either. Because I'm important, and I have lots of enemies, and a lot of the stuff that took me all the way to Droze? All that stuff started here. And it's still here, and it's found me many times before, and probably will again."

Danya nodded. Not looking at all surprised. "It's dangerous here?"

Lying was the standard thing to say to children when they asked things like that. "Yes," said Sandy. "Everyone's surprised I've become a guardian to children." She didn't say "adopted." It wasn't quite that, legally, though close. "I never thought I'd have children in my life before I met you guys. And the main reason why was because it's so dangerous. And look at me. You've seen what I am." She gestured with her damaged arm. "It's not pretty, and it's not safe. I'm the last person with any business taking care of kids."

Danya smiled. A very grown-up smile, slightly sad, and ironic. "You're perfect," he said. "For us."

Sandy knew exactly what he meant. And smiled back. "Look," she said. "I don't know what we are yet. All four of us together. I'd like to say 'family,' but 'family' is very contrived, isn't it? You guys are certainly family, but I'm not your flesh and blood, I'm not *anyone's* flesh and blood . . ."

"Semantics," said Danya.

Sandy blinked. She hadn't suspected he'd know that word, nor use it so well. "Maybe. But the point is that none of us are used to this. I'm not. You're not." Her smile grew broader. "None of us really knows what the hell we're doing. So here's what I think. We're a . . ."

". . . team," Danya echoed with her, at almost the same moment. "We've always been a team, me, Svet, and Kiril. That's what I'd always tell them, what Svet always needs to hear when she's off in Svetlana land, chasing Svetlana rainbows. It's all of us together. The way I see it, the team just grew by one more, that's all."

Sandy sighed and squeezed his arm. Stupid to think that Danya would need to have any of this explained to him.

"That's how I explain it to Svet and Kiril, anyhow," Danya finished.

"Okay, good," said Sandy, getting his very full attention. "But any team, whether it's military or sports or whatever, has different people doing different roles. In military teams, the two who make everything work are officers and non-coms, meaning sergeants. Officers have to look at the big picture, watch the broader environment, make sure nothing surprises the team. And the sergeant's like an officer, he's in charge, but he pays attention not just to the big picture, but also to the small picture—where everyone's standing, what they're doing, how they're feeling. He really runs the team, because it's his job to translate what the officer says into real actions on the ground, you get that?"

"You think you can be the officer, and me the sergeant?"

Sandy nodded. "That way, we both kinda know what we're doing. But here's the thing. Good sergeants don't just blindly do whatever dumb thing their officers tell them. Good sergeants think for themselves. And I gotta tell you, Danya, the main reason I'm happy to have you three in my life where I'd be reluctant with any other kids, is because you three can think for yourselves."

"And you don't have to worry about ruining our lives, because our lives were already fucked up," Danya quipped. Good lords, it was almost a joke. The truth, but spoken with humour, dry but real.

"That too," said Sandy. "In this culture, Danya, we think of kids as innocents. I couldn't inflict my life on anyone innocent. But you guys . . ."

"Trust me," said Danya, with a light in his eyes. "This is a big improvement."

Sandy grinned. "I'm so glad you think so. But keep your eyes open, because it'd be a damn shame to make it all the way through Droze, only to get knocked off in Tanusha."

It would be a horrid warning to give to most children. But Danya laughed and looked entirely more happy with things. Like suddenly he was on familiar ground.

After he'd gone upstairs to check on his siblings, Sandy checked her message lights. One was Vanessa.

"*Everything okay?*" Vanessa asked, with every expectation that it was.

"Just fine," said Sandy. "They're happy, Danya just made a joke, we're going to have a good day."

"*Wonderful,*" Vanessa said happily. "*Today I'm having a lot of sex. That's on top of a lot of sex yesterday evening as well.*"

"Currently between bouts?" Sandy asked.

"*Ice-cream sundae refreshment break.*"

"Want me to come and towel you off?"

"*Ooh. Now you're making me really horny.*"

The other light was Rhian's, with just the same question. Sandy told her about breakfast. "*That's not fair,*" Rhian laughed. "*I had to train my latest two from bodily functions on upward. Yours come combat drilled and field tested.*"

The doorbell rang. Sandy excused herself from Rhian's call and went to the door. It was Kushbu Iyengar, civil rights lawyer extraordinaire and friend of hers for the past five years.

"Cassandra!" A slim, grey and mild-mannered Tamil, he would have merely kissed her cheek, but the delight on his face deserved a hug, so she gave him one, one armed. "So glad you're back. Not that I ever doubted it." She released him. "Nor had the foggiest where you were, of course."

"I'm glad to hear it," she said. "Lovely to see you again."

"Oh, look, a little bird told me you had some additions to your household, and I knew I really shouldn't be bothering you on your first morning back, but I was just in the neighbourhood from visiting one of the Justices on other business, and I have some news I thought you'd find fascinating."

He indicated a folder he was holding, expectantly. "More arrivals?" Sandy asked.

"Yes!" said Kushbu, looking quite pleased. "There were another seven GIs arriving while you were gone, including three non-combat designations!" He beamed. Non-combats were relatively rare. He, Sandy, and others had worked often the past five years to lodge their asylum applications, Kushbu and his legal pro-bonos navigating that process while Sandy covered the security side, which was always the biggest hurdle to defecting League GIs wanting asylum. "Two of them have just fascinating stories, would you like to see?"

Sandy sighed, leaning on the doorframe, not moving aside. Kushbu looked puzzled. "Do you mind if I don't?" she said.

Kushbu blinked. "Of course, if you're too busy . . . oh, look, how silly of me, I really should have called first before surprising you like this, but I . . ."

"No no no," said Sandy sadly. "It was lovely of you to come. But I think it's time the Callayan asylum seekers began to manage without me."

Another blink. "But you'll want to sit in on the asylum applications, surely?"

"Kushbu, the system has become very accustomed to League GIs arriving here and claiming residency. There's quite a lot of opposition to those claims simply because of my involvement. Maybe it's time to see how things work without me."

"Cassandra, I assure you, your expertise on the security side of things and your personal familiarity with the confusion faced by our asylum seekers are invaluable!"

"But there are so many here now," said Sandy. "And a lot of them are quite capable of taking my place. I think it's time they did so. I think I've been too soft on them, and too willing to just let them ride on my coattails."

Kushbu looked taken aback. It hurt to see it. But she'd hurt a lot lately and was used to it. "Well, of course, Cassandra, if that's how you truly feel."

"It is. I'll talk to you again soon, and thank you for coming by. But I have other priorities now."

She gave him a farewell kiss on the cheek and left the gentle lawyer staring dumbfounded at the closed door.

FSA had acquired quite a team of experts. They clustered about Kiril now in the medical ward, a big, shiny room with wide windows and a large view over green gardens and Federal compound buildings. Kiril sat in a comfortable chair within the scanning paddles, an uplink receptive headset on. The head doctor, whom Sandy understood was an outside expert, chair of a prestigious institute, and quite famous in the field, asked Kiril cheerful questions and introduced him to various stimuli—listening to recorded sounds at various decibel levels and ranges, watching holographic images, tracking moving targets, then touching alternately some ice and a cup just hot from the microwave. They even gave him some chocolate to eat, then a biscuit, then some cheese, just to watch the different brain activity from each.

Other doctors compared it to the uploaded activity model Cai had given Sandy to take back to Tanusha. It was far beyond Sandy's expertise—there were few who knew better than her what to do with uplinks once established, but the process of getting them established was a field that ten years of solid tape teach and a genius-level IQ still was no guarantee of mastering. It pleased her, though, to have so many bright folks gathered around Kiril. Danya and Svetlana watched, with no complaint from the doctors, some of whom even explained as best they could what the various displays and technologies they were operating did. Danya looked cautious as always, but no longer paranoid. Just quiet and watchful.

"This one," said CSA Intel Director Naidu, after a warm embrace with Sandy and some minutes watching proceedings from behind the glass of an adjoining office. Nodding at Danya. "This boy's impressive. Thirteen, you say?"

Sandy nodded. "And nine months."

"So calm. Objectively, would you rate his intelligence?"

Objectively? Sandy smiled. "I'm not sure I can do objectively with these three."

"I've adjusted assessments for bias before," Naidu deadpanned. "It's not unknown."

"He's extremely clever. Top fifth percentile, my objective guess. I'd think each of them only had a fifty percent chance of surviving what they survived, that makes the odds of all three surviving one in eight. It's all due to him, Svetlana says so too."

"But he's paid a price for his wisdom."

Sandy looked at him sideways. "Compiling for the psych report?"

"We all have them, Cassandra," said Naidu, thumbs hooked into his belt beneath a considerable, authoritative belly. "Me, you, Director Ibrahim, all our close family and relevant friends."

"I'm not complaining," Sandy said mildly. "I'd be pleased to see this under your authority."

Naidu shrugged. "You're a Callayan citizen; that makes it primarily a CSA responsibility." In the ongoing struggle over the CSA, FSA overlap, where the former handled Callayan issues, and the latter Federal ones. Based in the same city, sharing many of the same personnel, including Sandy, the problem wasn't going away any time soon.

"Danya has stress issues," said Sandy. She didn't like *informing* on him like this, but it had to be done, someone would compile the psych report, and best they heard it direct from her to someone solid like Naidu. "And trust issues, as you'd imagine. He's not dysfunctional though, none of them are. In fact, given his environment until now, I'd say Danya is ultra-functional and completely adapted. The question is how well he re-adapts."

Naidu nodded soberly, uncommenting.

"Very clever," she continued, "very observant, very cautious. A real problem solver. Mostly non-aggressive, he'll do anything to protect Svet and Kiri, but he's an avoider. He keeps out of the way, tries to be polite, keeps a tight rein on his temper."

"Has he killed, do you know?"

"No," said Sandy, quite certain. "He might lie if he had, but Svetlana's very bad at lying, and she insists not. Danya might be able to keep a secret from Kiril, but I doubt he could from Svetlana."

Naidu pursed his lips. "I have to ask. It becomes a primary focal point with children."

"I know." She took a deep breath. "Almost completely selfless where Svet and Kiri are concerned. I don't know if his brain even truly understands the concept of 'I.' It's all 'we.'"

Naidu looked at her. She must have choked up a little as she said it. And Naidu repressed a faint, private smile beneath his greying moustache.

"And the girl," he said. "Lovely little thing, isn't she? But you'll need to feed her, she's so skinny."

"The way she eats she should have doubled in size by now. It's a metabolism thing from their upbringing, they've all got it." Svetlana was sitting alongside a doctor, peering at his screen as the doctor explained things. Far more trusting than Danya. "Svetlana has a very well-developed sense of 'I,'" Sandy said with irony. "Danya thinks in terms of 'we,' but Svetlana thinks 'I' plus everyone else . . . foremost of whom are her brothers, of course. Which makes her attachment possessive, I think. 'We' is not possessive; it's collective. Svetlana is possessive of her brothers, which makes her a lot more aggressive in her attachments.

"She's as clever as Danya, but she's never had that responsibility, never been the eldest. Maybe Danya looked out for her too well . . . I mean, she's incredibly self-sufficient by the usual standards of ten-year-olds, but she's adjusted to stress and deprivation by *wanting* things. And maybe she's compensated for Danya's caution by just going and getting things when he'd rather hang back."

"Selfish?" Naidu suggested.

"Intensely self-interested," Sandy corrected. Recalling what Naidu said about adjusting for bias and seeing his noncommittal expression. "An alternative survival response. And far more emotionally engaged."

"And thus capacity for negative emotion as well as positive," said Naidu.

"Hey," Sandy said coolly. "Me too."

"You control it well."

"So does she. She's still alive."

"Thanks to her brother," Naidu added. Sandy gave him a hard look. "Now this one, I hear, has taken life."

"Very recently. Danya was being held by a crime boss. The corporations were coming to take him. Good chance if she had not acted, Danya would be dead. Or in corporate custody, which might be worse."

"How many?"

"She says three. Danya thinks perhaps as many as five."

Naidu looked at her for a long, solemn moment. "How?"

"Handgun. Point blank. Walked through several rooms shooting until she reached Danya." She did not mention the flashbangs. A ten-year-old who remained clear-headed enough to use flashbangs to prepare a room before entering with lethal force scared even her.

Naidu took a deep breath. And murmured something Sandy couldn't hear. "In a ten-year-old, this is . . ."

"Determined," Sandy said firmly.

"*Developed*," Naidu replied carefully. "Alarmingly developed. Most ten-year-olds cannot muster the resolve . . ."

"Most ten-year-olds haven't grown up starving, seeing other ten-year-olds getting raped and murdered." She might have said it too loudly. Naidu's lingering look suggested as much. "She did what she had to do. She did it out of love."

"And in doing so demonstrated a capacity to conceptualise other human beings as deserving of death, and acting upon that conceptualisation. The literature says that if the child is placed into that situation through a social construct, like a child soldier, say, that's one thing. The catalytic influence was external, and the child can regain a normal growth path from that point on, if removed from the external influence and treated correctly. But for a child to reach these conclusions and act on them all on her own, at such a young age, is an indication of potential psychopathy."

"She's a good kid," Sandy said quietly.

"Has she shown remorse?"

"Why the fuck should she . . ." Sandy began, and caught herself. Another deep breath. "The pain is there. She'll never regret the action, but the pain of having to do it is there. I know what that's like. I can help her."

"Good," said Naidu, nodding as he gazed out the window. "Good. And the little one?"

"I can't even attempt an objective opinion with Kiril," Sandy said firmly. "He's gorgeous. He's kind, generous, brave, funny, and clever. Danya says he's the smartest of the three, and he's probably right. And I'm worried sick about those fucking things Chancelry put in his head."

Naidu nodded. And gave her a sideways look and a smile. "Very good," he said with a final, lighter note. And made to leave. "We'll talk longer once you're actually working again, I'm sure. Lovely to see you well."

"Hang on," Sandy said, with growing suspicion. Naidu stopped at the door. "You're not doing a damn psych report on the kids. You're doing it on me."

Naidu gave her a patronising look. "Cassandra, as interested as we are in your lovely kids, you are the Commander of FSA special combat operations, and you hold a continuing operational rank in CSA SWAT. These children now become a potential operational liability for you, one that League commanders recognised on Pantala and attempted to exploit. We are now going to have to protect these children, for the simple fact that they are our enemies' best chance of getting at you."

"And you want to know if such threats make me completely fucking unstable or what," Sandy added sarcastically.

"Well . . ." Naidu nodded at her immobile arm and the bandage on her head. "Apparently not unstable, since your rescue was successful. But very angry."

"Sure." With a glare.

"Let's just say from our interview I can conclude that there are safer places to be than between you and these children. But I only needed to look at you to know that."

They were all surprised to see her so beaten up. She'd seen them looking at her injuries in astonishment. Wondering if she'd screwed up. "There was no other way to do it," she said. "Heavy walls, narrow bottlenecks, they were pouring explosive into every opening; I had to take chances and expose myself. I just absorbed some near misses and kept on coming. Otherwise I'd never have broken through."

"Motherhood becomes you," said Naidu, smiling. "And have no fear, you'll have access to my final reports like everyone else with clearance, and you're free to challenge whatever you want."

He left. Motherhood? Sandy turned to look back through the office glass. Surely motherhood meant more than the willingness to soak up high explosive?

CHAPTER TEN

"**S**he's cut off all contact with the asylum process?" Ibrahim couldn't quite believe it. She'd been so passionate about it before leaving for Pantala. It had driven her to Pantala, no question. Had driven her to do questionable things, in the fear that the New Torah government were doing things to GIs that would have irreversible consequences for the entire species . . . if artificial humanity could be called a species.

"It appears so," said Naidu. Naidu technically did not work for him anymore, but on this matter he knew Cassandra best, and Federal and Callayan Security Agencies were close enough that they shared personnel and expertise on a needs basis. "She's still receiving reports, but I understand she's given no feedback, and she hasn't attended their meetings nor had contact with any of their personnel. Several of them are quite upset, they feel she's abandoned them."

Ibrahim looked at Vanessa. Vanessa wasn't happy to be here and showed it in her usual way, sitting on the desk in her old SWAT jacket, with complete disregard for protocol. "They broke her heart," Vanessa said tiredly. "The GIs on Pantala. Leave the girl alone, as if she hasn't gone through enough."

Ibrahim walked to the wall opposite her and leaned there, directly in her vision. Unable to avoid him, Vanessa rolled her eyes. "It was that fight, that last big one," she said. "I mean, she's been in bad fights before, she's lost individual friends before . . . in that one she lost about a thousand. They weren't friends, but . . . you know."

"The mass application of the killswitch." Even Ibrahim still could not quite believe the corporations had done that. If for no other reason than it had cost them a lot of money. But few things frightened the users and makers of combat GIs like the prospect of a mass uprising.

"She'll deny it, of course," said Vanessa. "But she really did have these big dreams of leading some rebellion. Not at the expense of her loyalty to the Federation, never that, but she thought somehow she could do one while serving the other, fold an uprising into the Federation cause."

"And she nearly did," said Naidu, sitting rumpled and grey-streaked in one of the FSA Director's office chairs.

Vanessa nodded. "And then it all blew up in her face. All her rebels were too eager and idealistic, and they just didn't want to listen to her when she told them to be cautious; they're GIs, I'd imagine it's easy to feel invincible when you're a GI, if you're not as smart as Sandy. You get a whole bunch of them together, overthrow New Torah Chancelry . . . they must have felt they could take on the universe."

"They're rebels," Naidu rumbled, old and wise. "They were rebelling. It's a state of mind, and Sandy was telling them to submit to a new ruler called the Federation. Like telling a life-term prisoner who's just escaped and is just enjoying his first pleasures of freedom that he now has to return to a different cell."

"And they wouldn't listen to her, so she just left them there," Vanessa finished. "Holding a bunch of cards, thanks to her, and with no real choice how to play them. But she didn't hang around to see them through, she just got her kids back and came home."

"To what effect?" Ibrahim pressed. Cassandra was important. The lynchpin in so many ways, she'd proven it time and time again. The isolated variable that could swing any number of ways. As FSA Director, Ibrahim knew that she was both an asset to be treasured and utilised, and a potential threat to be feared and guarded against. Either way, he needed to know. And her best friend was of course not happy about playing the informant . . . but most likely Sandy knew and would forgive her, it was all a part of the job.

"Everyone wants to fit in," Vanessa sighed and hung her head. Kicked absently at the green frond of a potplant by the desk. "Even Sandy. She knows she's not like other GIs, but still she feels responsible for them . . . or she did. Responsible for the things they do, responsible for the things that are done to them, she couldn't let them suffer like she suffered. I'm sure she didn't expect them all to embrace her and call her sister for her efforts, but somewhere deep down, maybe subconsciously, perhaps she did."

She looked up, brushed curls from her eyes. "And then they rejected her advice and rejected *her*, really. And Sandy's pretty tough emotionally, but she's not that tough. I don't think anyone is. And that's what she's protecting herself from now, by cutting herself off from them."

Ibrahim nodded. "And the children? How do they fit into this?"

Naidu cleared his throat. "Well, I certainly don't wish to suggest that her affections for them aren't substantial. But it is clearly a reaction of sorts. A shield, to hide behind and save herself from other pains. Cassandra's emotions are as real as anyone's, but we've never seen this before from her, nor from any other GI . . . except for lovely Rhian, of course. But Rhian was different, because Rhian had always had affection for children, and because Rhian developed her own motherhood attachments in her own good time. Cassandra's have arisen from a specific circumstance, and we'll just have to wait and see how it goes from here."

Ibrahim looked at Vanessa. Vanessa shook her head firmly. "Rhian's affection for children is itself a result of combat trauma. Remember Sandy's story of Rhian's experience in combat, the little girl who died in her arms as a result of a firefight Rhian had been in?" Naidu nodded with a conceding gesture. "Rhian was a far less developed individual then, had shown precious little interest in children or other civilian things, was just another simple-minded 39-series soldier until that happened. And if I had kids, I'd trust them with Rhian anytime, anywhere, more than nearly anyone. Where the emotion comes from doesn't matter, what matters is what it is, and Rhian's love of children is as real as it comes.

"And Sandy . . ." she shook her head, a little exasperated at having to explain this stuff in the Director's office of the Federation's most powerful security agency, ". . . Sandy has a lot of love, and being what she is, she hasn't had the same opportunities as most to express it. And I say this as one of those few people privileged to have been the recipient of some of it."

With a defiant gaze at Ibrahim. Don't forget that I love her, that gaze said. You can call me in here and order me to inform on her mental state, but there are limits to how you can order me where she's concerned. Ibrahim nodded, accepting that, and uncommenting. And wanting more.

"I just thank god for these kids," said Vanessa. "Sure, it's a rebound emotion to some extent . . . but Sandy would be nuts about them under any other circumstances too, and I say that as the person who probably knows her best. I mean, they're innocent and sweet and naive, and yet as old as the hills and deeply messed up by all the shit that's happened to them . . . they're practically smaller versions of her, when she first came here. They're *substitutes*, if you want the psych terminology, for what she wanted to feel for the other GIs. She tried to love them that much, and couldn't, so she gave that love to three more deserving. And," she added, with a warning stare at Naidu, "I think you underestimate the power of that love at your peril."

Ari passed through multiple levels of security and had the unnerving sensation of his uplinks going completely dead. Still active, but this place was completely shielded, like the Intelligence Committee rooms in the Grand Council. He surrendered his weapon, then a final door opened with a clack of heavy locks.

Within was a nice apartment, wide windows showing a seventieth-storey view across mid-eastern Tanusha. On the market it would have cost a fortune, but this one was CSA-owned, as was the upper half of this tower, certain security types having learned long ago not to centralise all their resources in the one headquarters campus. It was a studio apartment, though a huge one. Their secured guest sat in the sunken lounge reading holographic book displays, a tall, recently empty glass on the coffee table. At the kitchen bench watching over him was Amirah, very slender for a GI, eating a salad with a glass of rosé and reading a hand display.

"Hi, Ami," said Ari, and gave the girl a hug. She smiled at him, still eating, and offered him some salad. Ari put a fork in it.

"Bacon and . . . bits of toast?"

"They're called crudités," Amirah said flatly. "Eat it."

"It's delicious," their guest volunteered from the lounge. "She's an amazing cook."

Ari hadn't really thought bacon and bread would go in a salad, but he put the fork in his mouth and . . . he raised eyebrows at Ami. "Wow. That's really good!"

"It's called Roquefort Salad, it's French. Goes well with a rosé. Would you like some?"

"Can't, on duty."

"Me too," said Amirah with a superior smile, and sipped. GIs and their alcohol immunity. Amirah was a 45 series, two years defected from the League. Seven years old, she didn't truly remember who'd made her, high-designation GI memory being quite fuzzy until three or four. But she knew she'd been on a ship somewhere, only it had been boarded by civilian authorities who had taken the GIs into new custody. There she'd had news channels to watch and books to read, and within eighteen months knew that she wanted to follow other GIs to the Federation—meaning Callay, the only Federation world so far where GIs were allowed to live openly as new citizens. Some kind souls had smuggled her out to let her do that, and she'd worked her way through the Callayan asylum process.

Two months ago, the CSA had accepted her as an agent-in-training on the understanding that she'd probably end up as FSA as soon as she graduated, but Feds didn't recruit anyone who hadn't been at a lower level first, and had no training facilities for greenhorns. As a 45 series she was immediately over-qualified for paramilitary spec ops despite her lack of combat experience, but both Sandy and Vanessa thought she was too clever simply for shooting things and thought it wise to start socialising their new combat GIs by training in broader Intel roles. In which capacity, Amirah was doing an accelerated internal sociology course and enjoying it. And landing soft duty like this, keeping watch on other new GIs the authorities were less sure about, while reading her study books.

"What's the book?" Ari asked. "Psychology again?"

"Collected essays of George Orwell," said Amirah. "He's amazing, nearly six hundred years old and he's describing things I saw yesterday on the news."

"Yes, that's Sandy's contribution to the reading list. Ami, we might talk about some stuff that you're not security cleared to hear, so I'm sorry, I'm going to have to ask you to . . ."

"That's okay," said Amirah, collecting her salad bowl and wine glass in one hand, the half-empty rosé bottle and reader in the other. "Just don't let him devastate your brain with his logical conundrums." She left with a smile, and the secure door clacked and clanged shut behind her.

"Very clever girl," said their guest from his lounge chair, still reading from his display. "Suspiciously clever, for a seven-year-old 45 series. Enough to make one wonder if she's actually what she says she is."

"If you believe that GI designations are the final say in synthetic intellectual destiny, sure." Ari strolled over.

Their guest's name was Ragi. He was also a GI, though oddly, he claimed not to know his designation. In fact, he claimed to know hardly anything of his origins before arriving on Callay. He'd simply walked off a freighter at Nehru Station three months ago, while Sandy, Ari, and everyone were at

Pantala and told the authorities he was a League GI and wanted to claim Federation asylum. But asylum from what precisely, he couldn't say.

Ari took a seat on the sofa opposite. Ragi was of African appearance but of average size and build, most unlike the combat GIs, who looked and moved like ancient Greek statues come to life. He was almost slender, with a smooth, round face, faintly androgynous. He spoke like a man educated at the finest institutions and played chess like an AI. No expert who'd yet interviewed him had been willing to guess a possible IQ level, save to say that Ragi was by far the most intelligent GI they'd ever seen. That included Cassandra Kresnov and the recently late Mustafa Ramoja. They kept him here without uplinks because one look at a scan of Ragi's uplink hardware suggested that allowing him access to the network in any form could be quite dangerous. No one had yet seen anything like it, not the nature of the technology, nor the sheer density of synapse integration or bio-circuitry. As he'd recently seen some quite remarkable network capabilities utilised by a GI of entirely unfamiliar design and capability, those in charge of Ragi's fate now had an idea that Ari might be able to make progress with him.

"I'm Ariel Ruben," said Ari. "I work for the CSA."

"I know," said Ragi, turning off his displays. "They told me you were coming. They're very nice to me, save that they won't open the door to let me out."

"In our position," said Ari, "do you think it would be smart to let you out?"

Ragi smiled. "That's the sort of question a man asks who's been told his interview subject is extremely intelligent. The idea is to try and use my intelligence against me, by asking me to apply it in seeing things from your point of view, and indulges in a kind of intellectual flattery by supposing that I'm the sort of man who can see all sides. What if I'm not?" His delivery was mild, and completely calm, yet Ari sensed nothing of hostility or menace. And this GI, unlike most of those he'd known, was no more physical threat to him than the average civilian on the street. "I mean, who can truly claim objectivity in anything?"

Ari shrugged. "That's the sort of answer an extremely intelligent man would give who got his jollies messing up otherwise simple questions and throwing them back in the face of the person who asked them. Sometimes a question's just a question. You complained the door wasn't open, and I asked you if you thought it would be smart of us to open it for you. Do you think so?"

"I don't know," said Ragi. He seemed quite honest. "I suppose I don't know you well enough to answer. Or come to that, I don't know myself well enough to answer."

Ari sighed. "So it's going to be like that, then?"

Ragi made a face. "As though you'd expected anything else." He crossed his legs, hands folded, and made a pleasant expression. "So. I can't remember where I'm from, I have no active recollection of how I got here either, which might tell you that my type of synthetic human is somewhat susceptible to mental manipulation. Probably I'm not very old. And I know quite a lot of things, though I'm not sure how. I'm both a font of information and a black hole of ignorance, and I'm afraid all the other investigators and experts who've come to see me have left unenlightened as to my origins, and thus my prospects of ever making it out of this room. What would you like to talk to me about?"

"Politics," said Ari.

Ragi raised his eyebrows. "Really?"

"Or religion. Have you a preference?"

"Religious? I don't imagine so."

"You mean you've never thought about it?"

"If I have I can't recall."

Ari grimaced and scratched his nose. "You might be the stupidest smart man I've ever met."

Ragi frowned just a little. "Well, this *is* a different interviewing approach," he observed. "First politics, now religion and insults."

"Well, you know, when people talk politics and religion, insults soon follow. Do you support the League?"

"In what sense?"

"In the sense that they built you. In some GIs it inspires loyalty."

"While many others come here, I understand."

"Do you? Understand?"

Another slight frown from Ragi. "Why GIs come to the Federation?"

Ari shrugged. "Anything."

Ragi no longer looked so serene. "In the League they feel they are not free. GIs are designated roles in life. Here, they can choose . . . although it seems that here they often end up working in military or paramilitary roles also."

"Sure, but here they can quit if they want. I know one who works as a florist. You ever wanted to quit anything, Ragi?"

"I have no memory of it."

"You want to quit this room though. Why?"

"I think it would be nice to be free."

"Why? What would you do with freedom?"

A deeper frown. "I'm not sure. But I think I'd like to find out for myself."

"What good would that do? For a man who makes clever observations but draws no conclusions? Who sees everything but understands nothing?"

"How do you know how much or little I understand?" Ragi retorted.

"Which is better, League or Federation?" Ari asked, rapid fire.

"It depends . . ."

"Beep, wrong answer. That's the beginning of a very clever answer without a conclusion. Are you capable of conclusions, Ragi, or just clever answers?"

"It's a very technical question that you ask, there's nothing insightful in overlooking those technicalities just so that you can rush to an emotionally satisfying answer."

"The thing with emotionally satisfying answers is that they indicate the existence of emotion," said Ari. "In your case, I wonder. And it's really the simplest thing in the world to answer: which is better, Federation or League? Because that's what all the reasoning is for Ragi, so that you can draw conclusions. A mind that reasons but does not conclude is like a car that drives but never reaches its destination, a complete waste of time and space."

Ragi's frown was now intense. Then eased, as he thought of something. "You're trying to upset me. You think it can indicate some aspect of my psychology that has thus far escaped you."

"But here's the thing," said Ari, "I don't think I can upset you. I think upset is a state of emotional conclusion you're not capable of reaching. Like you're not capable of concluding if you like the League or Federation better."

"And so every response I give you will suit your prejudged conclusion. If I avoid getting upset, I'm an emotionless robot, and if I become upset, I'm simply trying to prove to you that I can."

"No, I've already told you, I don't think you can, full stop. If you did get upset, I wouldn't believe it."

Ragi raised his hands in exasperation. "Then why bother? Why are you here, Ariel Ruben? To judge me? To tell me if my life is worth living? Because I'd truly like to know, do you think I *like* being here, not knowing what I am or what I'm doing here?" There was definitely a quaver in his voice now, and anger in his eyes. "Why not try something useful, like helping to find some answers to these riddles, instead of attacking me as though they were all somehow my fault?"

"*That's enough,*" said Piyul's voice in his ear. "*That's a good reading right there.*"

"Good, great," said Ari. Ragi blinked, wondering who he was talking to. Ari smiled at him. "Look, I'm sorry about that—you were right, I was trying to upset you, I had a bet with my buddy Piyul I couldn't do it in less than five minutes, he said I could, he thinks I'm the most annoying person alive."

The poor synthetic looked completely baffled, with nothing to say.

Ari got up. "We're going to go and analyse that, and if it gets us the answers I think it might, we might be able to finalise what you are for the reports. And once we can do that, we should be able to get you out of here. Sound good?"

"*In English, if you please,*" said Director Chandrasekar on the vid screen. His hair was still perfect, Ari saw—no increased hours of pressure would come between the new CSA Director and his hair products.

"Okay," said Ari, "this is Piyul. Piyul helped to work up the latest GI-specific psych software, he used the other interviews on Ragi to get a baseline of mannerisms, responses, and stress readings. But he had to know where the stress and conflict lines kicked in, and on what issues and to what intensity . . ."

"*Wait a moment,*" said Chandrasekar on the screen. "*I'm not such a fan of psych profiles that I'd trust them to define anyone completely, especially of as low a base as you've established on this guy.*"

"Director," said Piyul, "it's different on GIs." Piyul was short and squat, a power lifter in his spare time, and much better with software and heavy weights than people. He had this odd habit of not meeting people's eyes when he talked, as though in a state of perpetual distraction. "Especially young GIs. They've much less psychological complexity, all the triggers and layers we use for the psych mapping construct become much more accurate."

"*Sure,*" said Chandrasekar, in a way that made Ari suspicious that he didn't already know that. He *should* know it. "*What did you find?*"

"Well, we're pretty sure his knowledge base is mostly tape," said Ari. Piyul preferred it when other people did most of the talking, even if it meant he lost some of the credit. "The patterns and repetitions when he's talking about things he knows are too similar each time. So if it's tape rather than experience, he's very young. So young that if he was created using the usual techniques, he couldn't possibly be this smart. Sandy at this age wouldn't have been much of a conversationalist, she wouldn't have even been in active service; her gestation was long, about five years."

"There was another GI who reached mental maturity very early with lots of tape teach," said the Director.

"Sure, there was Jane," said Ari. "But she was a combat GI, and she didn't have these network uplinks. Plus she had almost zero emotional range; there's a chance she evolved it later, but she was a modification, an overwrite, of a standard human psych template, with all the unneedful bits suppressed. Ragi still has all that, so he's much more a standard template than Jane, less modified, meaning he still thinks and feels much more like the rest of us.

"Plus he's just scary smart. He's not real experienced or mature yet, so I can still boss him around in a conversation on ground he's less familiar with. But intellectual range with GIs usually evolves as they grow older, and he's already very advanced. If he's any of the types of GI we're familiar with, it shouldn't be possible."

"And he's not a fighter," Piyul added, to Ari's surprise. He must be very interested in this one if he was volunteering conversation. "Lots of GI brainpower just goes into making them fast and dangerous, some huge percentage of Sandy Kresnov's brain is devoted to making her better at killing people. Ragi doesn't have that, being a non-combat. I'm betting it frees up a lot of his brain space for other things."

"So what do you think he is?" asked the Director.

"Something completely new," said Ari.

"Talee?"

Ari took a deep breath. The CSA Director had obviously heard *something* about recent events in New Torah. But at Ari's pay grade, he wasn't allowed to guess at what. "Sir, with respect, I can't talk about that. I'm not sure if I'm allowed to even confirm or deny a possibility."

Chandrasekar made a face. *"This is what happens when I lend you to the Feds.*

I suppose I'm going to get a call from Ibrahim any moment saying Ragi's now their problem?"

"I couldn't say," said Ari. "But it's not impossible."

He wondered how much Chandrasekar knew. Probably little, the Talee were the highest of high-priority secrets. He still couldn't quite believe that alien contact on the level it had happened had fallen to *him* . . . even if the alien in question hadn't truly been an alien, just a friend and creation of theirs. But Talee themselves were no secret. Talee had been known to various portions of humanity for a long time now, and everyone had sources and opinions on the subject. Especially men like Chandrasekar, who worked in intelligence-enabled security for a living.

"Very well," said the Director. *"I'll file the report with Ibrahim myself, save you the trouble. And I shouldn't have to remind you, if this security level is about to jump up to Talee and Talee-related matters . . ."*

"Won't say a thing," said Ari. Chandrasekar nodded grimly and disconnected.

"Save you the trouble?" Piyul asked. "You're still reporting to Ibrahim?"

"No," Ari lied. "Chandi just gives me shit about it, everyone always said I was Ibrahim's boy."

"Are you?"

"He doesn't sign my credit."

Piyul exhaled and looked back at the monitors to Ragi's apartment. Ragi was sitting on the sofa, reading books. A monitor showed the title, something huge by some twenty-third-century literary legend, two thousand pages long.

"Talee," Piyul murmured. "Wow." Ari said nothing. "Though you know, I still think all neuro-synth technology came from Talee, I don't see how the League made that breakthrough on their own. You know anything about that?"

"I know nothing," said Ari, getting up to leave. "I'm the stupidest smart man alive."

CHAPTER ELEVEN

"Cai," said Director Ibrahim.

All were gathered in the most secure room the FSA building contained. The numbers were rather small—besides Sandy it was FSA Director Ibrahim, FSA Operations Director Hando, Fleet Rear Admiral Hoi, and Fleet Intel Commander Lupicic. Even Chandrasekar's clearance wasn't high enough for this—he wasn't a Fed, and Talee were Fed business. Thus the presence of Fleet, who liked to behave like they knew more about the Talee than anyone, and probably did. Normally Sandy's clearance would not be high enough either, were she not the source of the intel in question. Not even Grand Chancellor Li could enter this briefing, if he'd known to try. He'd be briefed in turn, but later, once the security professionals had considered it and figured out what to tell him.

Sandy was more nervous about leaving the kids alone at home. Security was no issue; Canas District was so tight even the casual breaking of wind would register on someone's display somewhere. But they hadn't been alone since they'd left Pantala. Those three being alone had typically meant working and struggling and worrying, trying to make enough loose change to buy food and stay alive without treading on the toes of some heavy who might kill them like swatting flies. Now they'd have nothing to do. Play some games, read some books, watch some movies. Seriously? She knew Danya had woken hard last night, three times, gasping for air and braced for some emergency. And Svetlana, barely waking, had pulled him back down and held him like a giant teddy bear. Mental note, she thought, buy Svetlana a real teddy bear. Maybe she'd like her own bed better with something to hold.

How did you tell kids from that background to just switch off from every-thing they'd ever known? She opened an uplink now, a high visual of the living room, where she could see Kiril and Svetlana indeed playing a game, something holographic. For a moment she couldn't see Danya, but a new camera angle revealed him in the kitchen. Doing something. Cooking? It looked like he was reading from a recipe book. Had they ordered more food?

She hadn't known Danya could properly cook beyond bacon and eggs. What was he cooking?

Fleet Admiral Hoi asked her a question. About the most important development in Federation security since the end of the war with the League. And she'd much rather have watched Danya in the kitchen.

"No, sir," she answered Admiral Hoi. "No idea where Cai is. He expressed a desire to make his own rendezvous with a Talee vessel. Last I heard, Captain Reichardt was going to let him have a limpet, then arrange to 'look the other way' while the pickup was made."

"And how were the Talee going to communicate this pickup?"

"Again, sir, no idea. I'd advise awaiting the return of either Captains Reichardt or Wong. Being knowledgeable Fleet men, they could give you far better answers than I."

"And no one thought to detain this . . . Cai?" asked Lupicic. He was tall and bald, with a face naturally given to skepticism. "Ask him further questions?"

"No," said Sandy. "It might have come up, but everyone present, including myself, was of the opinion it was a bad idea."

Lupicic folded his hands on the tabletop. "Enlighten me, please."

"Cai is the first open contact made with an acknowledged representative of the Talee or any other intelligent alien species. That I'm aware of anyway, Commander Lupicic, you may of course know otherwise."

Lupicic smiled thinly.

"The last thing we're going to do," Sandy continued, "to said representative of a species far more advanced than our own, is piss him off. To use plain language. Cai was exceptionally helpful to us, and to the Federation's interests, on several occasions. To the point of actively intervening on two occasions in military conflict to ensure the Federation's success. That strikes me as a wonderful strategic success, a stunning success in fact, and possibly a vital one, in the struggles that lie ahead with the League, if the League's problems are as bad as they seem. We decided to pay Cai every courtesy, and to communicate our courtesies and heartfelt gratitude to his Talee friends when he reunited with them. A copy of which courtesies I included in my report, and you've all no doubt read."

"I concur with this decision," said Fleet Admiral Hoi, with what might have been a disagreeable glance at his Fleet compatriot. "Talee contact to positive ends is a staggering development—actual military *assistance* is beyond belief. My only complaint is that you did not put on a banquet in Cai's honour."

"We thought that sucking up should not be the Federation's style," Sandy said drily.

"If only that were true," said Hoi. He was a tough little nugget of a man, broad and grey with a toothy smile. Without the uniform, he'd have looked like farmer or the guy who came around to fix the electrics. He'd risen all the way through Fleet ranks from ensign to become commander of everything. Sandy didn't know him very well, but what little she'd seen, she respected.

"Plus the distinct possibility," Sandy added, "that if we'd decided to detain Cai, Cai might have decided otherwise. And we couldn't have done anything about it."

Grim assessment around the table.

"Commander," said Ibrahim. "Can you assess the evidence that Cai was acting a lone hand toward your situation? Or was he representing the thought-out policy of his superiors?"

Just like Ibrahim, he asked the central question every time.

"Logically any actor in Cai's position has a degree of operational autonomy," she said. "Like Fleet Captains, information takes so long to move in space, decisions cannot always be consultative, decision makers must be empowered to decide, with some degree of finality. Sir, there's no conclusive evidence either way, as you've read in my report, and Cai was deliberately vague on the question, as you might expect of a competent operative determined not to reveal too much about the Talee. But in my opinion, Cai did have general support, what you might call conceptual support. I find it inconceivable that an individual of Cai's capabilities would be allowed to make contact with us, against all established precedent, in that situation, and command the actions that he took . . . I mean, the destruction of a League ghost recon vessel and the effective network takeover of Pantala's primary space station."

Amazed silence. They'd read the report, but it still read like fiction.

"Talee have been so cautious," she continued. "This was an extraordinary break from that caution. I can't conceive that they would allow such a break to occur by carelessness. I think Cai was where he was meant to be. Now, whether all Talee are happy with the results, that's another matter.

Little enough a lowly soldier like myself is qualified to know about the Talee's internal organisation."

With a faintly hopeful look around the table. Hoi might have smiled a little. If they knew, or anyone knew, they weren't going to tell her.

"So if he was in your opinion just where he was supposed to be," Ibrahim continued, "why did the Talee want him there?"

"There's only one conceivable reason why a people so determined to avoid human contact in the past suddenly change their position," said Sandy. "Fear. Or whatever the Talee emotional or intellectual equivalent. Whatever's going on in League space, centered upon events on Pantala, the Talee don't like it. Now, whether that's out of concern for themselves or out of concern for us, I'm in no position to say. Perhaps both. Perhaps our fates and theirs are connected. Perhaps Talee have had something in their past that makes them particularly concerned about what they see happening now amongst humans. I don't know."

"Pantala was a Talee outpost, two thousand years ago," said Ibrahim.

"Yes," said Sandy. "Then mysteriously abandoned. And I'm betting, perceptive grunt that I am, that this is a pattern of settlement and abandonment Federation and League spacefarers have encountered before, out at the fringes of our existing territory, all highly classified from the rest of us. It suggests some kind of disaster. That would make a species concerned."

"It would, wouldn't it?" said Hoi. And no more, as Lupicic gave him an unimpressed sideways glance.

"Do you think Cai will be back?" Hando asked her. "Talee seem to have the ability to avoid our sensors when they choose, probably they can insert their own synthetic human copies into our populations as well, should they want."

"Oh, I'm betting they've been doing that for decades," Sandy said dismissively. "Probably there's a bunch of them walking around in Tanusha right now."

"Wonderful," said the FSA's Ops Director. "Now we have to figure how to tell Director Chandrasekar without violating the Feds-only rule."

"Agent Ari Ruben," Ibrahim began, in that slightly cautious way a man might bring up a contentious topic, "has some interesting ideas about a new GI arrival in Tanusha. A man by the name of Ragi, non-combat designation, massively intelligent, with augmented uplink capability so advanced to look at we're not yet willing to let him within contact range of a network. Given the capabilities Cai demonstrated, it seemed a wise precaution."

"Wait," said Hoi, hearing this for the first time. "He's Talee?"

"We don't know," said Ibrahim. "No recollection of his history, he just turned up on Nehru Station three months ago and requested asylum."

Everyone turned to look at Sandy.

"Apparently we've done the basic scans on him," she said. "He gave consent, but the new protection laws won't let us do anything more invasive without an external independent monitor . . . which of course we can't do because he's too secret."

"Wait," said Hando. "Apparently? You're not involved in this personally?"

"I'm attempting to rationalise my workload," Sandy explained flatly. "We've got a lot of GI experts here now; I don't need to personally supervise everything." No comment from Hando. Nor anyone else. "I don't think he's Talee; from what I can see he's crazy advanced, almost certainly one of the alternative neural growth methods—most GIs are number one, me and a few others like Ramoja and Jane are number two . . . *were* number two . . ." pause for a breath. "And Ragi looks like something else again. I've technical terms that won't mean anything to you; let's call him number three.

"Now if he's Talee, he's not nearly as advanced as Cai, because Cai's a combat GI, and he's got crazy network capabilities *plus* serious combat capabilities my synthetic colleague Rhian Chu estimates are not quite to my ability, but to combine both skillsets in the same brain at that level indicates that the Talee can do far more than the level represented by Ragi. Plus, Cai was a covert operator; if they're using other similar covert operators, that's some serious technology and knowledge, letting them roam around in our midst is a huge risk, so logically they'll be able to defend themselves, like Cai. So Ragi being non-combat, and Talee, doesn't make any sense, nor does the way he turned up here, delivered straight into our hands."

"So if he's not Talee, what?" asked Hoi. Sandy thought the Fleet Commander seemed a little agitated on this question. Was he expecting something from the Talee? Worried about something? Or just concerned that someone not-Fleet might have access to this much information on them?

"Presumably someone who wanted us to have him," suggested Ibrahim.

Sandy nodded. "So who is there in all human space, not Talee, who can make GIs to number three specifications?" She looked around the table. Probably they knew but weren't going to say it first. "Well, as I figure it, there's Renaldo Takawashi, and . . . well, Renaldo Takawashi."

Ibrahim frowned in that curious, intent way he did when he was right there with her on some very important point. "But what you discovered on Pantala suggests that Takawashi, and in fact no human anywhere, originated synthetic neural design. It's a Talee technology, as are all the different origin methods you're describing."

Sandy smiled. "Exactly. The League never invented neural synthology like they claimed, and Takawashi's a big, self-aggrandising, fucking liar. Like I always said." Tried to pass himself off as her Daddy. She hadn't fallen for it then and now had proof she was right. "So where did he get it from? There's only one place anywhere that was working on alternative GI development methods, and that was Pantala. Unless the Talee gave him the tech directly, and somehow I don't think they like him that much."

"And the first thing he does with this technological breakthrough," Lupicic said skeptically, "is give it to us?"

Sandy shrugged. "League doesn't control Takawashi any longer; we don't even know where he is. Speculation is he's accumulated that much wealth that he's operating like a shadow department within the League government, pulling everyone's strings within the only field he cares about, which is synthetic development, obviously."

"Doesn't explain why he'd just give us Ragi," said Lupicic, shaking his head. "I don't buy it. He's a loose cannon, sure, but a traitor? Because that's how League would view it."

"I saw a movie once," said Sandy. "Pretty old film, can't remember the title. But a senior soldier fighting for one side realises his side has created a doomsday weapon, and he has no choice but to defect and give this doomsday weapon to the other side to continue the balance of power and prevent mutual armageddon."

She looked about at them. Waiting to see which one of them got it first. Admiral Hoi looked quite unsettled. Points to Fleet for always being the first to understand what armageddon meant.

"You think Ragi that much of a threat?" Ibrahim asked, deadly intent.

"I don't know," she said. "Probably not, if he's not actually Talee he won't be as capable as Cai. But you've seen the reports. Can you imagine Cai loose in this city? Taking control away from us in city-scale networks, like taking toys from a baby? You guys were all scared of me when I arrived, but I'm nothing compared to that. I can do physical damage, sure. But the network encompasses everything. It's our civilisation's technological life support, and we're all wired to it. Everything is. If a single entity ever got that much control over it, well, you can see why Ragi might not *need* to be a combat model."

Returning home in her cruiser, she called back Justice Rosa.

"*Cassandra!*" he said, sounding genuinely pleased to hear from her. She quite liked Justice but was not yet prepared to judge whether that pleasure was mostly for her sake or mostly for the sake of the book he was writing and would no doubt gain great wealth and fame from. "*Glad to see you're back safely.*"

"Glad to be back safely, Justice."

"*And I hear your little gang of friends has grown by three?*"

"You hear correctly." Far too correctly, she thought sourly. Though it was too much to hope that news might have been silenced. Family details of high-security individuals like herself were repressed, so she wouldn't have to answer crap from any tabloids about it—and any tabloids who tried would likely end up in prison. But she'd have to answer *something*, sometime, she supposed.

"*A very remarkable development. I understand you'll be a little busy in the near term, but can we meet a bit later?*"

The previous routine. Sandy wasn't sure if she was looking forward to it or dreading it. Probably both. "Sure. How about give me a week, then try me again."

"*Of course. Schools?*"

"Being organised."

"*The psychology bureaucracy giving you their usual bullshit?*"

"Very much so," Sandy sighed.

"*Ages. Can I just know their ages?*"

Sandy had to smile. Justice liked to hold himself above the Tanushan tea house chatterati but now trafficked in personal gossip like any other. No doubt he could impress others with his level of access to her life. Still, better him than some others, and drip feeding the beast was probably smarter than starving it. "Two boys, six and thirteen, and a girl, ten. All wonderful."

"*Siblings?*"

"Yes. Orphans."

"*From Droze, wow. Well, best of luck to you, Sandy, it's a very noble thing you're doing.*"

"You know, it's really not." Justice had adopted a League orphan himself, she recalled. Having been a war correspondent there and seen the horrors.

"*I know what you mean. Oh, one more thing. Emancipation. Your idea?*" Oh, yeah, sure, Justice. Just slip it in there, I'll never notice.

"An independent development."

"*I do understand it's causing quite a stir in the human rights circles. Since it came from a rebellion on Droze, I put two and two together.*"

"You know if you do that long enough," said Sandy, "you can arrive at quite a large number that bears no relation to anything real."

"*The rebellion was League GIs left behind when the League pulled out five years ago?*"

"Yes."

"*And you happening to be there at the time is pure coincidence?*"

"Something like that."

"*What's happening to the rebels? We hear it's a standoff, so they haven't been wiped out yet . . . they captured the headquarters of Chancelry Corporation? This is New Torah Chancelry, right, the bit that remained behind, not main League Chancelry?*"

"Right again."

"*And they weren't wiped out, and now Federation is in there negotiating. Must be very important for the Federation to be there already. Unless there's more to the story than just some uprising of synthetic people, because as much as we all value synthetic rights, that does seem a thin reason for the Federation to be intervening in what is still technically League space, yes?*"

"Interesting," said Sandy.

"*Well, if you feel the need to get anything off your chest prior to a week's time, call me.*"

"I'll certainly do that."

"*Oh, and Sandy. I think I've settled on the title for the book.*"

"Yes?"

With the faintest trace of anxiety. *Heavily Armed Nympho* had been Vanessa's suggestion. "What, you don't think that would sell?" she'd replied to Sandy's disapproval, all innocence.

The Best Artificial Tits in Town had been Ari's effort. "I liked Vanessa's better," she'd told him drily.

And her various grunt squadmates had voted for *Blonde Ambition*. Had made a fake paperback cover of it, propped it up in the briefing room with all of them assembled, title over a photo of her arriving at some CSA formal function, a black-tie dinner, of all things. And poor, dumb GI Sandy, with little knowledge of how to exit a car in a fancy dinner dress, had managed to give the photographer a great look at thighs and underwear, now splashed across the book cover for all to see. "Fuck off, the lot of you," she'd told them with a smile, as the briefing room had fallen about laughing.

"*Twenty-Three Years on Fire*," said Justice. "*As we discussed before.*"

"Oh, okay." They *had* discussed it before. It was a touch more dramatic than she'd have liked, but what kind of idiot invited a self-promoter like Justice Rosa to write a book about her and was then surprised by a dramatic title?

"*Kind of catchy, isn't it? Good luck with the Tanushan education department, dealing with them can be worse than the CSA.*"

Disconnected. Sandy sighed, cruising along her skylane, a gentle bank between towers, and mulling things over. The thing with being home, as much as she loved it, was that everything got so complicated again so quickly.

She put in a call. Most people couldn't get through on this connection, but she would, once Ibrahim saw who was calling.

"*Hello, Cassandra*," said the FSA Director.

"I hate to be all big brother on my biographer," she said, "but he was just asking me questions, and he's a very smart guy. He doesn't know anything he shouldn't, but if anyone was going to solve this one soon, it might be him."

"*Hmm.*"

"The whole line of questioning was designed to show how much he knew, and he's got all his reasoning in very straight lines, no curves at all. I thought you should know."

"*You've a recording?*"

"Of course."

"*Well, I recall that he's an author, not a day-by-day reporter. Books don't come out often, so perhaps we can buy some time with a briefing.*"

"He does the other kind too. Might work though, he does enjoy an exclusive briefing."

"*Don't they all.*"

"He's got a book title too." All her employers were nervous about the book and had requested to be kept in the loop. "*Twenty-Three Years on Fire.*"

A pause. "*You know,*" said the Director, "*I think that's quite good.*" Which surprised her, because Ibrahim was hardly the type to go for commercial and catchy. "*What do you think?*"

"So long as I'm not in flames on the cover, or naked, I'll live with it."

"*Or naked and in flames. One can hope. Thank you, Cassandra.*" He disconnected.

She had to fight the impulse for gratitude. "Journalists," Ibrahim had once told her. "At your feet or at your throat. Never trust them."

Danya had baked a cake. Sandy was astonished. It was banana cake and smelled wonderful—half-eaten, the kids had already polished theirs off for lunch, with some baguette sandwiches Danya had also directed them in making.

"Where did you learn to bake a banana cake?" Sandy asked him, cutting her own slice and tasting. It was delicious.

"I don't know," Danya said with a shrug, sitting alongside Kiril on the sofa to help him read something. "I have this memory of baking things with Mama. I can't remember any recipes, I just always had this idea that I'd like to bake something again sometime. If I ever . . . well, you know."

He looked almost embarrassed. Not at baking, rather at admitting that he'd ever once dared to dream of a comfortable life. Maybe baking for him was like some kind of exercise, designed to convince his brain that he was actually here and things were better.

Sandy grinned, feeling happier than happy, and eating. "Danya, this is wonderful."

"I can follow a recipe, it's not hard." And he still remembered something of previous civilisation, before everything collapsed. It was what separated him from his siblings more than anything else. He knew what it was like to lose something and never to trust in solidity again.

"Oh, I know what would go perfectly with this," said Sandy around a mouthful. "The guy down at the restaurant makes his own ginger beer, you'll love it."

"We can have beer?" asked Danya.

"No, it's got no alcohol, it's fine for kids."

"Well, Kiril's reading," said Danya with irony. Kiril had barely looked up since she'd come in, eyes locked on the page, tongue in one corner of his mouth. Such concentration. "He's doing amazingly well." And Danya liked to supervise when that happened; Kiril's education had been a mission for him the past few years. Once, they'd hoped it might get them out of poverty, if Kiril could get a good job.

"That's okay, I'll take Svetlana. Svet!"

They walked together to the store. The kids had already been out walking around the neighbourhood together; Sandy said it was okay so long as they didn't leave the Canas walls. The automated security systems all knew them on sight and would track them and make sure they were safe.

"It's so pretty!" said Svetlana as they walked up the footpath of rough old stone, past stone walls, climbing vines, and thick overhanging greenery. "Why did they build it like this? I mean, everything else is so modern, but this looks old."

"It's what the architects call 'historical memory.' This is what lots of old stuff looks like on Earth. They thought the colonies shouldn't forget what old Earth looked like, where we all came from. So you have neighbourhoods that look like this, old Europe, old India, old China. This one's Spanish."

"What's Spanish?"

"Spain, it's a country in old Europe. You know flamenco music?" Svetlana shook her head. "Oh, I have to take you to see some. It's wonderful."

They crossed the little road bridge over one of Tanusha's minor streams. On the far side was the eatery they'd passed before in the car, people sitting outside having a late lunch by the water. Someone Sandy knew from the neighbourhood said hi, and Sandy was pleased enough to stop and talk—it was a high court judge, in Canas due to his proximity to sensitive information. She'd lunched with him and his wife before and enjoyed it. Svetlana wandered inside the eatery, intrigued by the old stone walls and delicious smells.

Two minutes later, a scream and some yelling. Sandy rushed the door as glass broke and found Svetlana beside an overturned table, one beer mug already hurled and another on its way, a table knife in the other hand. A man in a suit, security, was ducking the glass and coming at her.

Sandy caught his arm, pivoted him into a wall, and pinned him there by the throat. "I wouldn't," she warned, with a look back at his comrade, who was frozen in a shock of recognition. Local security, clearly. The comrade ducked again as Svetlana threw the second mug at him anyway, then rushed him with the knife.

"Hey!" Sandy abandoned the first man to whip Svetlana quickly off her feet, still one-handed, and nimbly removed the knife.

"No!" Svetlana was yelling. "Let's kill him, let's rip his fucking head off!" And other, most un-little-girl-like things.

"Svet, shush," said Sandy, carrying her effortlessly away with a rapid stride, back across the bridge. With everyone staring and in commotion behind. That didn't bother her for herself, she'd given up caring a fig for her reputation long ago . . . but Svetlana's reputation was something else. Then, as soon as they were around a corner, she put her down against a wall and crouched before her. "What happened?"

"They didn't recognise me!" Furious and tear streaked, breath coming in gasps. "Him and his fucking *friend*, they asked me to stand still for an ID scan, and I don't want to stand still for any fucking ID scan, and they said I had to or I'd be in trouble! I didn't do anything wrong and they were saying I was in trouble just for walking into the restaurant! And I . . . I called him some names, and he called me something back, and I got angry!"

"Svet, Svet . . . it's okay, it's okay. Don't be upset, you didn't do anything wrong."

"But they did!" Furiously. Such anger in those pretty young eyes. "Let's get them, you can get them, right?" Expectantly. Because that's what protectors did. Sandy just looked at her sadly. "Okay, so maybe we can't kill them . . . can we get them fired or something? Sandy, I don't want them here, I don't want to live here with them still here . . . !" as the panic threatened again, and tears.

"Oh, hush, hush." Sandy hugged her. She was so skinny, so slight, her body heaving. "Svet, it's my fault, I shouldn't have let you go in there alone, I didn't think security would be there. But they sometimes are, and it's their prerogative to check whomever they like, even kids. It's no big deal, Svet, they just do a vid feedback to HQ and run recognition software, takes ten seconds . . ."

"Why do they have to do that? Don't they know I'm with you?"

"I'll talk with them. I'll talk with them very hard, so they'll know you guys on sight and won't do all the procedure. I'll tell them you don't like it. But they were just doing their jobs, Svet, you have to stop being scared of people who are just doing their jobs, they weren't trying to hurt you at all. If anything they were trying to protect you."

"I don't want them to protect me! I've got you and Danya to protect me!"

Sandy sighed and held the shaking girl. She'd known this wouldn't be easy. Now she learned how and why.

Vanessa and Phillippe postponed a dinner engagement to help out. Sandy thanked them profusely—Danya and Kiril had been okay alone that morning and would probably be okay again, but it wasn't fair on them, and on Kiril especially. They knew and liked Vanessa, and it was about time they met Phillippe, who was lots of fun with kids and not so secretly itching to have some of his own. Plus he'd brought his violin, needing to practise at least five hours a day, so Danya and Kiril would get to see some truly amazing musicianship.

Meanwhile, Sandy and Svetlana were having a night out. First they took Sandy's cruiser and got some takeout, which was a long-established tradition in Tanusha, and some of the takeout places (or flyout places, they were often called) were top quality. They ate while flying circles about Tanusha, which traffic central frowned at and wouldn't allow more than one circuit, but most people circumvented with all kinds of trivial landings and takeoffs at places they'd no interest in visiting. Sandy having the security clearance she did, central didn't even query her route.

So they sat, and ate, and watched the sunset, and the never-endingly amazing view of one of humanity's biggest cities, as sunlight faded and the city lights came on, and Svetlana got that awestruck look in her eyes once more that she'd had on that first night's arrival. Even Sandy still got that look when she was not too preoccupied to notice.

Then they went to Safdajung District and landed amidst the flashing lights of a shopping district's major sale, and sent the cruiser on wheels to find itself a park in some underground lot. Svetlana's eyes goggled at the streetscape, kaleidoscopic displays and colours everywhere, thousands of people, streetside entertainers, daring outfits. But it was not the shopping nor the nightlife that Sandy had brought her to see . . . or not *this* nightlife, anyhow. The kind accessible to the mainstream crowds.

Down some smaller side streets, bustling with restaurants and entertainment parlours, a few very unsuitable for kids, but nothing could possibly shock a girl from the mean streets of Droze. Then some nondescript stairs beside a tavern entrance and down the most boring stairway yet seen, through the outer door, then a knock on the inner door, for those not thoroughly put off by the bland whitewash . . . and answered by a seven-foot-tall Asian man dressed like a woman. With what looked like a giant pineapple on his head.

"Cassandra, darling!" he shouted, and stooped to kiss her on each cheek with enormous ruby lips. "*Wonderful* to see you, and it looks like you've been in the wars again."

"You know me, Nánguā," she said.

"And oh, my goodness, who is this?" Stooping further to admire Svetlana. "Isn't she adorable? One of yours?" Looking at Sandy as though she must have done something naughty to acquire her.

"If only I could get them that way."

"Oh, I think this breeding thing is catching, even you synthetics will be doing it next." Sandy thought of the GIs operating the underground factory in Chancelry HQ on Droze and thought he wasn't far wrong. And to Svetlana, "Adorable child, my name is Nánguā, but if your Chinese is as bad as most of Tanusha's, you can call me Pumpkin. And what's your name?"

"Svetlana." Sandy didn't think it was so much shyness as astonishment. Svetlana had seen many things on Droze, but nothing like Pumpkin.

"What a lovely name! Now child, do you have anything to wear? You see, I don't know if Cassandra's actually told you what this is about, but this party's kind of about . . . well, *wearing* things. What do you like to wear?"

Beyond Pumpkin was a party worthy of a seven-foot-tall transvestite in a ball gown with a pineapple on his head ("If his name's Pumpkin," Svetlana asked her an hour later, "why is he wearing a pineapple?"). It was co-run by Togo, of course, one of Sandy's friends via Ari, whom she didn't get to see nearly often enough and was now delighted to have an excuse. Togo was one of Tanusha's cooler underground fashion designers, not those awful main-streamers with their displays of mass-market grotesquery; that was "beef steak fashion," clothing for cattle, disdained by those present.

These parties were fashion as fun, with little fitting rooms behind curtains rigged against the walls where local designers would run the latest hot fabric tech to knock up outfits in just a few minutes with the help of holodesigns and VR space, showing off their latest thought bubbles and outdoing each other for new ideas on a moment's inspiration, like musicians riffing competing solos in some downtown club. A person shouldn't walk into such a party if they weren't prepared to get changed numerous times . . . and there was of course also lively music, excellent if spontaneous catering, and lots of dancing and socialising.

It wasn't conceived with children in mind, of course, but it was hardly risqué nor swirling with illegality, and Sandy had just had a hunch about the kind of thing Svetlana might like to see. Might need to see. Nice people. Fun people. Crazy and wild and utterly unpredictable people of all shapes, colours, sizes, and preferences . . . and all completely harmless, creative, and non-threatening. This was not an image of human interactions that Svetlana had ever conceived of. Adults made her wary, and outside of her own little circle, people only interacted with other people for profit or power, in her mind at least.

But it was hard to sit on a bar ledge, with a glass of bubbly apple juice in one hand, amidst crowds of crazy-dressed, dancing, laughing people, and explain to an exotic black girl with hair like some fantastical spider and wearing ten-inch heels, exactly what her favourite colours and fabrics were, and still think of human interaction as something frightening and dangerous. The noise and crowds might have bothered Danya, but Sandy didn't think Svetlana would mind, and sure enough, soon she was ducking behind cur-tains and emerging in a pretty floral dress, then a girly "pop idol" skirt, then some tight and sparkly pants, and suggesting various hats and shoes from her new crowd of adult friends. Because Svetlana, when she was confident, could command a crowd like an empress. She'd seen genuinely scary things, and little things like public attention didn't bother her, so long as she had the power, or at least the upper hand.

"Well, *she's* a little princess," said Togo, sharing a more alcoholic beverage with Sandy by the bar. He wore a lavender, sparkly shirt, exposing strong black arms, and had a few more piercings than Sandy recalled. No one was bothering Sandy with the dress-up routine, seeing her arm and other injuries, but every now and then a new hat was placed on her head, with some new decoration, at an appropriately jaunty angle. The current one was a beret. Sandy saw it in the bar mirror and thought . . . maybe. When her hair was longer.

"She is a little princess," Sandy agreed.

"So now do you finally come to see the affinity between girls and dressing up?"

Sandy laughed. "I see almost as many boys here as girls."

"Yes, but when we were her age," pointing to Svetlana, "we were doing our dress-ups privately, in our mothers' wardrobes."

"Surely not," Sandy teased.

"No, it's true," Togo insisted. "And even more shy when the boy is heterosexual."

"You know, I hear heterosexual glamour boys are the new queers."

"Oh, shucks," said Togo. "Flatterer."

Over in Svetlana's corner, the curtain came back dramatically, revealing the slender model stepping out in short top and suspenders, with a . . . bowler hat?

"Hmm," said Sandy. Svetlana jumped around to the music, to applause and exclamation.

"I don't know if she's quite got the presentation down," Togo suggested.

"Not her fault, no one ever taught her how to dance."

"Sandy!" Svetlana yelled across the noise. "What do you think?"

"Suspenders great!" Sandy replied, thumb up. "Not sure about the hat though!"

"Nor if she's quite got the idea of ladylike volumes of conversation," Togo added, very amused.

"Oh, I hope she never gets that," said Sandy. "I hate it, all these demure girls who stare at the ground when they walk by. I want to tell them they'll walk into something." As Svetlana set about exchanging hats and taking new suggestions.

Togo laughed. "With you as a role model, I don't think you have to worry she'll grow up shy."

Sandy smiled. "Maybe." But then, she had advantages the kids didn't. Suddenly it worried her. Was she setting a bad example? Would they try to be like her? In one vital respect, they weren't, and never could be.

"Droze," said Togo, more somberly. "Good lords, that poor child. Is it really that awful?"

"Really," said Sandy. "She's lucky to be alive, they all are."

"And let me guess, the Tanushan psychology mafia are going to give you all kinds of grief before they let your little darlings into schools with other Tanushan children."

Sandy nodded, remembering Justice Rosa warning her of much the same. "She got into a fight today. With Canas security. No one did anything wrong, she just panicked and lashed out. She gets scared so easily."

"So you brought her here, to show her a place with lots of people and no fear." Togo smiled. "What a perfect idea."

"They're going to say she's dangerous, Togo. Like they said I was dangerous. And they were right too, I *am* dangerous . . . but only in certain circumstances. And sometimes . . . I just think this system wants people to all be safe and normal and predictable, and not everyone is. And if we cut all those people out of society, and make everyone normal and safe and bland, we'll lose something really important."

"Couldn't agree more," said Togo, looking around at his crazy party.

"And she's just . . . she's *such* a good kid Togo, and . . ."

She was choking up, the sentence left unfinished. Togo was gazing at her, his eyes sparkling.

"Sandy," he said, with the broadest smile and put a gentle hand to her shoulder. "*Wonderful*, Sandy. Wonderful."

Meaning that emotion and what it meant. Sandy smiled sheepishly.

"Not so tough, huh?" she managed.

"Never so tough," he beamed. "Not to me."

Sandy told the cruiser to come and meet them at eleven, which she figured wasn't so late it made her a bad parent. But with Safdajung city crowds, the cruiser was going to take a good twenty minutes to reach them. After they'd said good-bye to new friends and old, with lots of hugs for Svetlana, the cruiser was still stuck in the parking lot traffic. They walked to it, past patrons exiting restaurants and clubs and others wandering in, their evening just beginning. Coloured lights blazed off the puddles of recent rain, as the occasional car hissed by on slow, wet tires.

"Thank you for taking me out," said Svetlana happily. "I had fun."

"Excellent," said Sandy, holding her hand. "You deserve to have fun. We'll find some more fun things for your brothers to come and do as well."

Svetlana giggled. "Danya would have hated that party so much! Changing clothes, I mean, god, it's so pointless!" They both laughed.

"Kiril would have liked it though."

"Yeah, true," said Svetlana. "Let's bring him next time."

"Deal, but only if you think really hard about some fun things we can find Danya to do on his own." Svetlana frowned. "His entire life has been about looking after you guys, and I'm sure he always will. But he also deserves to have some fun for himself, like you had tonight, don't you think?"

"Yes!" said Svetlana, nodding vigorously. "Absolutely." And frowned again, thinking. "But what would Danya like to do on his own?"

"Think about it," Sandy repeated. "I need your advice with that, you know him better than anyone."

Svetlana thought for a moment, shoes splashing in puddles. "This is because I killed those people, isn't it?" Sandy looked at her in concern. "I mean, in the interview the other day, they were asking me about it. Danya and Kiril never killed anyone, but I did."

"Killing is a very serious thing, Svet. It's the most serious thing."

"You do it."

"I'm an adult. And I work in security, and sometimes it can't be helped. But you're a child, and people here find it hard to conceive that a child might kill someone."

"I didn't have a choice!" Crossly. "They were going to take Danya!"

"Hush, Svet." She put a hand on her head. "I know. I think you did the right thing. I'm certain of it." Hell of a thing to tell a child. Tanusha's psychologists were going to be horrified at *her* now. *What are you trying to do, encourage her?* But it was the truth. "And you know what? I've killed a lot of people. Most of them deserved it. With none of them did I really have a choice. It was my job, you see, and . . . well, you know what I am, and what I was designed to do."

"I know," said the girl, looking up at her with big eyes. "You were made for it; you didn't have a choice."

"Right. But you listen to this." She stopped and crouched with her back to the wall so she could look Svetlana in the eyes. "I killed some people when I first arrived on Callay. They were working for a big federal agency back then, this was before Callay was the central world of the Federation. And . . . and they did terrible things to me. They cut me up." Svetlana looked horrified. "I don't want to tell you that story now, it's not the time, and to tell the truth, I don't like talking about it. But I healed up, and with some good friends—this was when I met Vanessa—we went after some of these people, and I ended up killing some of them."

"Good!" said Svetlana hotly.

Sandy nodded, licking dry lips. "Yes. They killed a lot of innocent people; it wasn't just that they hurt me. If anyone deserved it, they did. But later, I was looking at some of their personnel files, those are things that tell who they are and where they're from . . . and I saw that each of these people had families. They had brothers and sisters, just like you have Danya and Kiril. And they had mothers and fathers, who presumably loved them . . ."

"That doesn't give them the right to take other people away from *their* mothers and fathers!"

"No, I agree completely. But everyone was a child once . . . or everyone who's not a GI, anyway . . ." She looked Svetlana very closely in the eyes. "And those men you killed were all children once, like you are now. Like Danya and Kiril." Svetlana looked uncomfortable, trying to look away. Sandy drew her attention back. "And maybe . . . who knows, if things had turned out differently, maybe they'd be nice. But Droze was really nasty the last five years, and people had to do all kinds of things to survive . . . I mean, you saw it, right? You saw people you thought were good, who ended up doing bad things? Working for bad people?"

Svetlana was getting upset now and not knowing what to do about it. Obviously she did know plenty of people who were basically good but had done bad things. She herself had stolen plenty of times. And she knew none of them deserved to die for it. Half-hating herself, Sandy pressed on, knowing it had to be done.

"And people can change, right? Maybe some of those men were just doing what they were doing to Danya for money? Maybe they'd change their minds later, if they had a chance. Maybe if they weren't working for Janu, you'd have liked them, and they'd have been kind." She squeezed her arm tight. "It doesn't mean you did the wrong thing, Svet. Wars have been fought that desperately needed to be won, and it's good that they were won, but that doesn't mean that all the people on the other side were bad and deserved to die, it just means that their *cause* was bad. Sometimes there's no choice in killing, but the really sad part, the thing that keeps even me awake at night, is that even when you really have to, and when it's absolutely right, sometimes the person you kill is really pretty good. Or could be good, if things were different. Maybe they'd even be your friend. And maybe they have brothers and sisters who'll be as sad to lose them as you'd be sad to lose Danya or Kiril. And maybe they're crying right now, because of what you did."

Svetlana stood there, blinking back furious tears. She looked so helpless, having this awful thing inside of her and not knowing where to put it. Having this conviction that she'd done everything right and not knowing why it still hurt so much. And already beginning down that dangerous path of covering the pain by getting angry, defiantly, to try and convince herself that she could do the same thing over and over again, and it didn't bother her.

Only it did. It broke Sandy's heart to look at her. She'd lived with this most of her life. She knew exactly how it felt, and she wouldn't wish it on anyone, least of all a confused and frightened little girl.

Svetlana collapsed into Sandy's arms. "I didn't want to!" she sobbed. "I didn't want to shoot anyone, I was just so scared and I didn't want them to take away Danya and I didn't want to be alone . . . !"

Her words trailed off into incoherent sobs against Sandy's shoulder. Sandy held her close, her own cheeks wet with tears.

CHAPTER TWELVE

Vanessa walked into the FSA medbay with a customary cup of coffee in hand, finding Sandy on the central table, sitting topless save the receptor vest, with various other electrics strapped over that and big sensor paddles surrounding the table. Several doctors with VR eyewear assisted or gave instructions, sometimes just presenting Sandy with an open hand to press her fist into and push against.

"Jeez," said Vanessa, "how long does a lube job take?"

"You leave my personal life out of this."

"Eww," said Svetlana as Vanessa gave Danya a one-armed hug and kiss on the cheek. Danya was surprised by it, but Vanessa remembered when Sandy had been surprised by it too. Vanessa had forced it upon her then and was even more determined to do so with the kids, who needed it more.

"You guys all think we don't know what it means, gross."

"You know," said Vanessa, not at all apologetic, "I was so looking forward to corrupting them." And hugged Svetlana too.

"Too late," said Danya. He was reading again, AR glasses on, sitting on a bunk in the rough denim and plain shirt he preferred to the more trendy stuff Tanushan kids typically wore.

Vanessa hugged Kiril last, he was sitting on a chair right next to Sandy so he could watch the doctors' displays. She recalled he'd helped a lot in the Chancelry med ward on Droze and found all this stuff interesting.

"How's your head, Kiri?"

"It's okay. I don't see colours and lights and stuff now." Vanessa saw Sandy's displeased glance and decided to leave that alone.

The scars on Sandy's arm were nearly gone, nanos repaired scar tissue as well as underlying tears and separations. The blast that had done it had been a big one, probably a DX grenade. In some reflexive modes Sandy could nearly shoot those from the air. Certainly she'd have seen the muzzle flash and known the firepower was there in the first place—DX mounts weren't fast to operate, GIs moved fast; whoever'd been wielding the DX would have been in support fire position quite deep in defensive formation so it didn't get taken out in the opening exchange . . . it was how you slowed a GI advance: soak up the initial pressure with mines, then grenade and fixed fire, slow them down, then hit them with the heavy stuff from farther back.

With few "go around" options, even Sandy would have typically backed off faced with that, used some tricks, taken some time. But this time, she'd gone straight in and gotten hammered. Not as bad as the defenders, of course, but it was something rare indeed. And no prizes for guessing why she'd done it.

"How's your mobility?" Vanessa asked. Sandy showed her—she couldn't lift the arm much over her head and couldn't extend the elbow from any position save straight by her side. "That'll extend though, right?"

"Another two weeks," said one of the doctors. "The muscles were completely severed, beyond their capacity to independently regenerate. It's only once she got back here to proper facilities she's been able to heal fully."

"You'd think they'd have made me modular," Sandy complained, gesturing for some of Vanessa's coffee. Vanessa lent it, and she sipped and gave it back.

"At least your face is okay. Eyes and ears don't heal fast like muscles and tendons."

"I dunno. Maybe an eyepatch, Svet?"

"That would look wicked on you!" Svetlana agreed. "You'd be like a blonde pirate."

"What's a pirate?" Kiril asked.

"You haven't given him any pirate stories?" Vanessa was very disappointed.

"Huh," said Sandy. "Another of those things not nearly as glamorous in real life. In the war we used to shoot them on sight, good thing too."

"*Must* you always be so literal?"

"What's a pirate?" Kiril complained.

"Pirates used to sail around on the oceans on old Earth in big sailing ships!" Vanessa told the wide-eyed little boy. "And they had big swords, or old pistols called blunderbusses, and they had big hats, and they were always looking for treasure!"

"What's treasure?" asked Kiril.

"Gold and jewels and stuff, Kiri!" said Svetlana, joining the enthusiasm. She was wearing denim overalls, but with girly pink and blue stitching patterns and colourful socks. And could that be the tiniest smudge of eyeliner? "Stuff that makes you rich!"

"And pirate captains had peg legs," said Vanessa, "and talking parrots, and they were always drinking lots of rum, and they laughed like this! Har har har har, Ar Ar! Can you laugh like that?"

And there followed a lot of pirate laughing with Vanessa, Kiril, and Svetlana. The doctors worked on, getting more readings as Sandy rotated her shoulder in a new direction, and pushed for gentle pressure. Probably thinking that if they had a private practise, they wouldn't have to put up with this shit . . . but working for the FSA or CSA, you didn't just tell their combat spec ops to shut up, nor their kids. And you got to work with bio-synthetic wonders like Sandy, which for most of the payroll doctors made up for a hell of a lot.

"I'll get you some pirate stories," said Vanessa, "my nieces and nephews have some great ones, pirates are cool."

"'Cept when they board innocent traders, murder the crew, and rape the female passengers before stealing all their stuff," said Danya, still reading. "Guess the stories forgot that bit."

"Thank you, Danya," Sandy deadpanned with an approving look. Danya might have smiled a little.

"Yeah, well, that was a long time ago," Vanessa said brightly. "Sandy, now that you're duty rostered again, got some people you should meet soon as you're finished here."

"Five more minutes," said one of the doctors. "Almost done."

The kids went home with an FSA driver, which would doubtless include a stop somewhere exciting to look around and buy a few things, usually food and clothes. Tanusha was very safe, the kids weren't uplinked and so couldn't be traced, and Danya was smarter and more cautious than most adult child-minders. But still Sandy didn't like it much, even as she knew she couldn't and shouldn't stop it. Now she knew why parents worried.

"It's just that they're mine now," she explained to Vanessa, still rotating the shoulder in her jacket as they walked FSA HQ corridors. "Anyone who doesn't like me might go after them."

"And they're network protected so openly publishing images or names is illegal and violations get scrubbed, plus you've got the underground on side with them just like with you, so the people most likely to break the protection barrier are actually helping it. And there's sixty-two million people in Tanusha, what are the odds?"

"Get your own damn kids," said Sandy, "then start talking to me about odds."

Vanessa laughed, determinedly upbeat as usual. "So you brought them to see a medical procedure, huh?"

"They were worried. Well," she corrected, "Danya and Svet were worried, Kiril just likes it, all that medical tech. You'd think with all the injuries he saw he'd be put off hospitals for life."

"That boy knows what he's interested in; he won't get put off easily."

"Besides," Sandy added, "it's good for them to see it. I mean, they know what I am, they're the least naive kids ever. But it's still good for them to be reminded now and then."

"I guess," said Vanessa. "Any luck on next of kin?" That search had gone nowhere. League records were incomplete; they knew who the kids' mother was, Lidya Seravitch, but that name had no matches on existing records. Of course, League was currently expelled from Callay in what some were calling a post-war trough in relations, and others were calling a new cold war . . . whatever it was, it made requests for further access to League citizen and migration records impossible. They just had to go with what the intel agencies had access to. Or had stolen.

"Lots of Pantala migrants had dodgy pasts," said Sandy, "Seravitch might have changed her name, might have changed her face too, even gene switches aren't illegal in the League."

"And boy, are they going to regret that when the shit hits the fan in a few years," said Vanessa. "I wouldn't worry about it, the odds that someone of the Seravitch clan in the League is going to pop up and claim parental custody seems pretty slim, and Federation adoption law supports existing relations more than past heritage."

"I know," said Sandy. "That doesn't worry me. League dirty tricks do. I showed them they shouldn't come after me or the kids with force, but their legal crap is another matter. Like with the war crimes stuff."

The war crimes stuff was still pending. It was all bullshit too, but it had never been the moral currency of such cases that gave them life, when aimed at Sandy.

She never even bothered to query where Vanessa was taking her. They just arrived in a very secure room in the heart of headquarters. Sandy half-expected to see a senior Fleet officer or maybe even a politician with a famous face. Instead, there were two men and a woman in suits whom she did not recognise.

She glanced at Vanessa. Vanessa nodded to the suits and then the full security suite activated, jammers, net barriers, sonic white noise. Several of the walls transformed into pleasant green grass and trees, a fake view from fake upper-level windows. A university campus, perhaps, buildings with nice old brickwork, students wandering the pretty grounds.

"Sandy," said Vanessa, "these are some cool folks I know. I'd tell you who they work for, but they don't actually have a name."

"No name?" said Sandy drily. This game of "our organisation is more secret than yours" was becoming a little silly. Usually it was just silly acronyms and pseudonyms. "Good heavens, you must be important."

The young man who extended his hand to her grinned. "No, actually. We're only as important as people think we are. I'm Steven. These are Reggi and Abraham." At the woman and man with him. "Please, I understand you've been injured, have a seat."

There were tea and biscuits waiting for them on the table. Neatly arranged. Sandy sat, increasingly suspicious. But if Vanessa had pointed her into a room containing the devil, she'd still have gone inside.

"Now, Commander," said Steven, as they all took seats, "we basically run some interesting software programs. Social sciences, predictive routines, I'm sure you know the stuff."

Again, if it had been for anyone other than Vanessa, she'd have politely, or less politely, excused herself. "Poli-sci cubed," she said. So called because it was, as some wag had described, political science in a box. "And what's your success rate running at lately?"

Steven's face fell. He was very young, no more than early twenties, blond and small and earnest.

"Sandy," said Vanessa with an assertive smile. "Be nice."

"That's not the nature of our software," said Abraham, a tall man with a goatee, skullcap, and a gentle Bengali accent. "We've no interest in predicting the future of broad events. As your scepticism suggests, there is little productive sense in such a path. We only try to analyse trends along specific axes."

"Pyeongwha," Reggi added, a little impatiently, as though she thought the boys weren't getting to the point Sandy needed to hear. She was African, round-faced, with long, girly dreadlocks. "Our research comes from the data on Pyeongwha."

It did get Sandy's attention.

"What about Pyeongwha?" she asked.

"Pyeongwha has been classified as a mass isolated outbreak of Compulsive Narrative Syndrome exacerbated by Neural Cluster Technology, a branch of uplink tech that was supposed to be banned in the Federation for precisely this reason," said Abraham. "The theory has always been that NCT causes this because NCT is a defective technology, leading to defective outcomes."

"Well, I've never bought that," Sandy said cautiously. "NCT isn't defective, it does precisely what it's supposed to do—allow data-sharing across multiple neural levels to create a multi-dimensional neural environment for all members of a society to enjoy a collective emersion experience. Which is safe if the human brain were constant, but it's not, it adapts and develops pathways depending on usage, so if you make it behave like a hive mind, it will eventually grow into one. That's what we see on Pyeongwha. Not defective, just deadly efficient."

The three suits exchanged looks with each other, and with Vanessa. As though just now reassured that they hadn't made a mistake in coming to Sandy.

"Good," said Abraham. "Not defective technology, no, it's an entirely reasonable outcome, if you understand the psychology and wiring. On the larger scale, it creates nightmares."

In Pyeongwha's case, a totalitarian state addicted to NCT and its advantages, creating a collective sense of "we" that labelled anyone not similarly addicted as an enemy, even its own citizens. Six hundred thousand dead over several decades, most of those in the last five years as the terror escalated, before the FSA raid led by Sandy and Vanessa had smashed it. News was still coming out; only now were the more gruesome details becoming public, though not having the impact it should have thanks to a media more obsessed with the "scandal" of the Grand Council's decision to attack in the first place.

"We've come to you because we think a similar phenomenon may be occurring here on Callay," said Reggi. Sandy just looked at her. People who didn't know her often found it intimidating when she did that. And a few who did know her. "At first Intel Chief Naidu found our reports interesting, and they were circulated amongst some CSA people, mostly . . . a few FSA, but it's not really a Federal thing yet. That's how Commander Rice encountered our work, and she recommended you."

Glancing at Vanessa, as though hoping for assistance. Vanessa just looked thoughtful. Measuring. Ah, thought Sandy. Not a fan, no, Vanessa was rarely so simple. Just looking to start an argument, perhaps. But to what ends? Sandy didn't think Vanessa would give her much help either. Vanessa liked arguments. Could chew your ear off for hours, then depart with a hug and a smile, taking none of it personally.

"Go on," said Sandy. "I'm listening."

Relief on surrounding faces. There followed the lecture. It was complicated, social science types always were. There were data inputs, algorithms, collation models, cross-reference systematics, network pattern analytics. Programs that stored and cross-referenced huge volumes of historical and current events, within certain parameters, to try and trace trends. Sandy found it somewhat impressive . . . though with her own network skills, she could immediately see areas where their processing software could benefit from significant upgrade. Unfortunately for them, the programs she had in mind would be largely illegal. Stuff she'd invented herself that could extract personality profiles from construct matrixes.

But her main problem, as always, wasn't with the software, it was with the human operator inputs. Events had to be classified into groups for the software constructs to work. So a Callayan Parliament vote on a particular piece of legislation had to be classified as an "x" type of event, and placed into particular categories . . . but was it really? And if those choices were bad, or misleading, that rendered all data collation pointless.

"So here's where it gets interesting," said Steve, with building excitement. He was the software guy, the young genius who ran all the network stuff. "We have some very interesting network constructs that analyse personal constructs and the interfaces between them and visible network traffic." Opening up a whole new window on the holographic presentation he had hovering above the table. "Now what this enables us to do is gather and collate very rough psychological profiles from visible traffic."

Pause for emphasis. *Crazy voodoo shit, right?* his smile said. It sounded entirely too familiar. Sandy's suspicion, recently suppressed, now resurfaced.

"How?" she asked, cutting off whatever he'd been about to say next.

"We can't say. It's classified."

"You made this stuff yourself?"

"Well . . . no." But he badly wanted to say yes, it was obvious.

"Because I've had success running psych profiles off network traffic by running co-receptive parallax cognitive matrixes off the primary support bands in an echo pattern . . . only I can't say more than that, because *that's* classified." Blank looks. "Looks a bit like this."

She fished out a rough draft of her particular illegal function and showed part of it, just shoved it onto their hologram without asking a passkey, and spun the fancy bundle of intricate, glowing lines around a few times.

"Looks familiar," said Vanessa, with feigned surprise. She'd been in on those meetings too, the ones where several intels had nearly flipped their lids at what Sandy was proposing.

Reggi put a hand to her mouth, eyes wide. "Oh, my God."

Abraham exhaled hard and looked at the ground. Steve looked confused. "You mean it's . . . it's *yours?*"

"Don't worry," said Vanessa, "it doesn't make your research unoriginal, it just makes the parts that processed it unoriginal."

Sandy uplinked to Vanessa. *"Naidu gave it to them, didn't he?"*

"Pay attention," said Vanessa. *"The kid's right, this* is *where it gets interesting."* And hadn't answered her question, Sandy noted. Not Naidu? Ibrahim? *Ari?* Not without permission, surely? The trouble they'd all get into if some outside rights agency discovered they'd been running this stuff on actual profiles, not just dummy tests.

"Okay," said Steve, "I'll do this more quickly then, since you probably understand what we've done better than we do."

"Wouldn't bet on that," said Sandy, "I just write software for a hobby, I'm built for it. Third- and fourth-generation extrapolations aren't my thing."

"Okay, when you look at Pyeongwha network traffic, using this software, what do you see? What makes it different from Tanushan networks?"

Using this software? That she wasn't allowed to have and could be imprisoned for using on unsuspecting folks without their consent? Now she understood the secure room, given what she was being asked to admit to.

"Less deviation," she said. "I've analysed automated traffic from user-generated construct patterns on Pyeongwha from about a month before we hit it. Usually you'd expect pattern deviation thirty to forty percent higher than what I saw."

"Wait," said Vanessa. "Pattern deviation in what?"

"Standard communication. We're talking now. We're speaking words, sentences, grammatical patterns that modern software can run, and analyse things like our degree of intelligence, education, relationship to each other, social structures . . ."

Steve was nodding excitedly as he spoke, following her intently. Clearly this was his *thing*, and he looked like he might be in love. Sandy was used to that.

"And you can verify that for accuracy?" asked Vanessa, frowning in concentration. She was not an expert here, just an interested layman. But the results of this stuff determined how often she got shot at each year.

"Absolutely!" said Steve. "We've blind focus test grouped it, many times, it's amazing how close we get. You add in stuff like voice stress analysis, microsecond pauses between words, then overlay the emotional state onto the words, then back into the broader psychological profile . . . cascade feedback, we call it . . . it's incredibly accurate."

"But between each of us in this room," Sandy continued, "you'll find psychological deviation. Particularly with me, since my background and psychology, I'd hazard a guess, is the most distinctive of any in this room, and the most different from the rest of you. But again, the differences in speech patterns, identifiable psychologies, background influences from racial, religious, gender and other factors, ought to make for a reasonable level of deviation."

"Except between us three," Steve added, pointing to himself and his two colleagues, "because we're in the same field and use the same socialised vocabulary and speech patterns when we talk, group dynamics are hugely important in measuring deviation. At least in this present conversation—if we were talking about football, probably we'd get a standard deviation result."

"So put you with a group of your GIs," Vanessa said thoughtfully, looking at Sandy, "and you'll get a big drop in deviation levels."

Sandy nodded. "Probably even more so than with straight humans. GI psychology is influenced by mass early life formatting and tape teach, we're not as different from each other as you are." Sadly, she thought, recalling the Droze rebellion. And shoved dark thoughts aside.

"Now," she continued, "when you run analytical programs on network traffic like this, you have to adjust for group dynamics and clustering, I mean you can see dramatic drops in deviation just here in Tanusha if all you listen to is people who share the same beliefs, same religion, same politics, etc."

Vanessa nodded. "The isolated mainstream, I know." Every law and security person knew that one, the tendency of networks to bring like-minded people together. Even extremist views could become mainstream in a chat room where everyone was an extremist, and thus the net had always tended to cluster extremists together and make their own little mainstreams where they felt accepted and legitimised. Which could be very bad news, from terrorism to paedophilia.

"But even adjusting for that, deviation on Pyeongwha was way down. NCT just produced a conformity. How much of it was simple fear of being seen to be different from others, and how much of it was the genuine hive mind rewiring that NCT does on people, we can't measure yet . . . or I can't. But on Pyeongwha, prior to the invasion, people were thinking and talking in general public conversation as though they had far more in common with one another, psychologically, than is typically or naturally the case, in human society."

"Makes you wonder what results you'd get if you could run that on a pre-uplink society," said Vanessa. "Free information technology was always supposed to make us more independent and individual, but sometimes I wonder."

Steve smiled, with a glint in his eye. "Have you tried running those communication deviation figures against a full social spectrum analysis like we've compiled here?" Nodding to his holographics.

"That," said Sandy, "would be too far down the rabbit hole, even for me."

"This," said Steve, "is the most illegal thing you'll ever see me do."

He activated a function, and a whole new graphic appeared on the display. A three-dimensional graph with multiple axies. Coloured lines squiggling all over the place. Sandy was good at processing complex three-dimensional imagery, but this took her a whole lot of staring and squinting to begin to make any sense of.

"That's it," he announced. "That's the great, Callayan collective conscience. Or Tanushan, mostly, as Tanushans generate six times more network traffic than other Callayans, the whole echo-response effect."

"It's pretty," said Vanessa, not even trying to analyse it. "What does it say?"

"You've embedded psych signatures," Sandy murmured, still gazing. "Psych profile categories, from network traffic. Holy fuck."

Vanessa looked at her. Sandy didn't swear often . . . or not in response to holodeck presentations, anyhow. It took serious data to impress her that much.

"Psych categories?" Vanessa asked.

"We arrange them in a grid," said Reggi. "Different psychological profiles, they've all got technical terms that mean nothing to laymen, but surely you've read many profile categories dealing with dangerous people in your line of work . . ."

"Right," said Vanessa, "but these are just ordinary people?"

"Chatting or transmitting or accessing VR or whatever," said Sandy, "on private networks with no knowledge their transmissions contained enough data to allow a government agency to scan their brain and make a personality profile."

Silence around the table. Very illegal, yes.

"And you collate all the profiles," said Steve, "and you run them against particular events on the calendar . . ."

"Oh, fuck, you temporised them too," said Sandy, both fascinated and horrified.

"Well, yeah," said Steve. "So about here," and a mark appeared on a running graph line, "is where President Singh won the election." A group of lines, measuring various personality profiles in aggregate tens of thousands . . . and the lines wobbled as graphical waves hit them, moving in temporal simulation. "Those are wave cascades, breaking news, new data, you can check the lower windows to see what . . . this orange one here was the news the finance minister was going to lose his seat . . . and this one was news that Shanti Lal was pregnant."

Vanessa frowned. "The pop star?"

"Hey," said Steve, grinning, "you'd be amazed what affects the graphs. See, look at the reactions, these are people registering active connection to election results, that's verbal conversation, news uplinks, active alerts or seekers, even someone watching a show and the host *mentions* the election . . ."

Sandy swore under her breath. Big Brother didn't even begin to describe it. This was uncomfortable, but astonishing.

". . . and yeah, celebrity pregnancy comes up on the feed too, we get that response as well. Helps to further refine a lot of psych profiles because we get data on alternate axes."

"I don't see anything unusual though," said Sandy, eyes darting quickly over the zagging lines. "Deviation, differentiation, category spread . . . it all looks normal."

"Yes, it does," said Abraham. He was the organisational theory guy, the one who dealt with institutions rather than people. Reggi was the psych. "But break it down by the key axies known to compulsive narrative syndrome . . . race, religion, political party affiliation, political philosophy, regional location, and others."

The graph separated into squares and displays. Still the lines danced and spun.

"No change," said Sandy. "Tanusha's very stable like that, even within the warning groups there's enormous diversity. Diversity across all axies remains the best indicator of stability, that's why the education department runs anti-polarisation routines through its tape teach education kits each year."

"That was last year," said Abraham. "Now go to this year."

Steve made the adjustment, and now some of the lines were running noticeably in parallel. Following each other. Clusters, locked in tandem.

"Same individuals?" Sandy asked.

Abraham nodded. "See where they work."

Sandy looked, as new colour codings appeared to let her do that. There were lots and lots . . . but here were general categories, health, education, big business, small business, law. Aggregates still in tens of thousands. Mostly the spread was quite broad . . . but there were hotspots. Specific institutions, where the lines ran very close together.

"It's not just the deviation, or lack thereof," Reggi said somberly. "It's the speed at which deviation disappeared, given recent events, in certain institutions. Hiring practises can't account for much, their turnover isn't that large. It *looks* like site- and time-specific Compulsive Narrative Syndrome, at a speed that can only be accounted for by some kind of faulty uplink acceleration. Bad technology, like NCT."

"Only they don't use NCT," said Sandy, "they use the same stuff everyone uses."

Reggi nodded. "But it's happening nonetheless. Balance in those institutions and areas, and deviation appears to be fading, we haven't yet made an exact profile of what the balance is changing *to*, but we're working on it."

"With Chandi's permission."

No reply to that. They weren't about to say, but then, it went without saying. Director Chandrasekar was not known to be the moral paragon that Ibrahim was. Which raised the next question . . .

"Does Ibrahim know?" Sandy pressed.

They didn't answer that either. "Name one serious thing in this city that Ibrahim doesn't know," Vanessa answered for them. But that wasn't the same as agreeing with it, it just meant it was out of his immediate jurisdiction now that he was a Fed, and not a Callayan. Technically.

Next question. "*Which* institutions?"

Abraham took a deep breath. "Elements of the legal profession. Elements of the police force. A significant chunk of the news media."

"They all borrow the same brain anyway," Vanessa said dismissively.

"Special Investigations Bureau."

"Big surprise," said Sandy. "You've *no* idea where this is headed?"

"We didn't say that," Abraham replied. "We're uncertain. But based on this research we've a list of individuals we think should be placed under special surveillance, given the high statistical likelihood of trouble in the sensitive institutions they head."

"Because they're showing statistically low levels of psych deviation within their institutions," Sandy deadpanned, "as revealed by a secret network program that's illegal and shouldn't exist."

"Levels of deviation unseen since Pyeongwha," said Reggi, deadly serious. "We saw what happened there. This borders on institutional psychosis. It's not there yet, but it's headed there. If this happens in any institution, in my opinion it should be treated like at termination signal. Shut it down before anything bad happens."

"Christ," Sandy muttered with feeling.

"People disagree," Reggi continued with determination. "Naturally. In these institutions, something is bringing them all into line. History, and especially recent history, tells us that when that happens, balance disappears, trouble follows."

"I'm going to formalise this," said Director Chandrasekar. "Given it's based on technology you created, Sandy, I was going to call it Project CK, your initials."

"I'm sorry, sir," said Sandy, "but over my dead body."

This time it was CSA HQ. The old briefing room, well familiar to Sandy from her time here before the Federal apparatus moved to Callay and began dividing everyone's place of employment. But not, one hoped, their loyalties. Here were the top CSA officials, Naidu most prominent after Chandrasekar, with Vanessa active SWAT Commander, and Sandy the top FSA spec ops but still holding a liaison CSA rank, as most FSA troops also filled in with CSA SWAT for the practise. CSA both loved that arrangement, for the top-line troops and technology it granted them, and hated it, because if the FSA, god forbid, actually needed to use its troops, CSA SWAT dramatically shrank by thirty percent. It joined the two institutions together at the hip, which had both good effects and not so good ones.

"I can't deny that they have some interesting data," Sandy told the various faces turned her way, "and it's probably worth exploring further. But if you formalise a project like this, you institutionalise it. You make it permanent. I think that's extremely dangerous in itself, and more, I don't trust their findings.

"Fact is, we don't have anything to compare it to. Because, obviously enough, we don't know what these psych profile graphics did before uplinks and modern neural interface networks, because we need that stuff to create the psych profiles in the first place. If we had a model of stuff that happened well before neural uplinks, I'm sure you'd find results much more alarming than this."

"Like?" asked Chandrasekar.

"Well, go back to the Pacific Crisis, 2170, infotech was becoming pretty advanced then, but it was still long before uplinks, and a lot of really extreme institutional and psych behaviour patterns were observed. Or way back further, Second World War, people killing each other left, right, and center. You don't need defective uplink tech to make human societies act crazy in portions or in total, we do that naturally."

"Men think in herds and go mad in herds," said Naidu. "They only recover their senses one by one. Charles MacKay, 1841."

Sandy nodded. "Exactly. We can't start jumping at shadows now and thinking every strange phenomenon we observe is a net-tech driven social breakdown. Because if major security institutions like this one start implementing cures for diseases not yet proven to exist . . . well, I for one would rather the disease."

"The Pyeongwha situation is a lethal wrong turn in the co-development of human technology with human biology," said Chandrasekar, quoting from some uplink visual. "All such situations should be tackled like cancers, and the misgrowth cut out before it can endanger the larger organism. Cassandra Kresnov, 2549." Sandy's look was unimpressed. "You were advocating the assault on Pyeongwha at the time."

Sandy frowned at him. "There's a parallel between this and Pyeongwha? Pyeongwha was an entire planet. This, if it is anything, is just a few institutions. Pyeongwha involved the confirmed state-sponsored murders of thousands of Federation citizens. This has produced a few wiggly lines on a graph."

"You were extremely concerned about the nexus between uplink technology and human sociology running off the rails," said Chandrasekar. "I recall it very clearly. You said every precautionary step should be taken. You're not a psychologist, but being what you are, you have insights into the possible manipulation of mainstream society using advanced network and uplink technologies. I've seen those insights at work, and I've come to take them very seriously. Are you now stepping back from those concerns?"

"Not at all," said Sandy, and leaned an elbow on the table to make sure the point was understood. She was not given to demonstrative gestures, and people noticed. "I'm placing an even larger concern in front of them. The concern that people like us will become so worried at the perceived threat that we'll start presuming every dodgy social phenomenon is an outbreak of technologically induced CNS.

"Compulsive Narrative Syndrome isn't just a technologically induced problem, it's the way our brains work, since millions of years. It's not even a bad thing, it's mostly a good thing, our brains couldn't function without it. We're going to keep seeing it in this society, and dealing with it as we've always done. To outlaw it would be to lock up half the population. All the population. Starting with us, since all of us are experiencing it right now to varying degrees."

"Normally I'd be inclined to agree with Cassandra," said Naidu, grimly rubbing his broad nose. "But we've all seen those simulations. Pyeongwha has shaken everyone, and now our best neurologists and social scientists are telling us there is a very clear possibility that neurological and social response patterns may be altered by rapidly evolving uplink technology in ways that they did not predict. And I think that in the light of this danger, and what we've seen it do to Pyeongwha, and now in the League . . ."

"What else are they going to say?" Sandy interrupted. "These scientists? They failed to predict the phenomenon or see its extent while it was unfolding, and then all these security types arrive on their doorsteps asking them threatening questions about why they didn't, and what else they might have missed, and they don't want to incriminate themselves again by ruling anything out, so they say sure, anything's possible."

"Cassandra," Chandrasekar warned her.

"And you take that as an admission that the sky's about to fall in," Sandy finished.

"Commander," Chandrasekar tried again, "just because you are what you are, that does not give you the right to interrupt everyone else's statements."

"How about being right?" Sandy replied, eyes dead level. Chandrasekar knew her well enough not to flinch. "Does that give me the right?"

CHAPTER THIRTEEN

Sandy got in a full hour of surfing before the alert call came in. She sat on her board beyond the break, in the glow of early light, and looked at the preliminary reports, the unfolding tacnet graphics, and considered whether the situation looked like it needed her.

"Vanessa, you on it?" she asked, sending audio that way on the secure setup.

"*I can take point for now,*" Vanessa replied, "*anything more than a four unit cover is probably overkill. Keep surfing another half hour at least, if you like.*"

Sandy considered it, chewing her lip. It was her first surf in the week since she'd returned. Normally it would have been the first thing she'd do, but lately her priorities had become all mixed up.

"Intel was warning of overlapping cells," she said finally, riding up a new swell. "If we put the heat on this one, and they activate everything in response, we'll need everything up. I'll be there when I can, let's get it rolling."

"*Gotcha,*" and Vanessa disconnected to do that. In truth, Sandy didn't mind too much. She'd been lucky with the schedule so far, her injuries and the kindness of understanding superiors giving her more time than they might in different circumstances. When everyone started going full time again, things would get interesting. And by full time, she wasn't just thinking of the good guys. It took a while for the ramifications of New Torah to ripple their way back to Callay, and she found this new disturbance suspicious, in timing at least.

She caught an average wave back in, dropped to her stomach to catch the wash through the shallows, then emerged in full wetsuit, as the currents were cold this time of year. There was Danya, sitting knees drawn up on the higher sand, AR glasses allowing magnification—he'd been watching her and the few others out on this pretty, pale morning. And his position allowed him to see Kiril and Svetlana, beachcombing farther up the flat, wet sands. None of them were allowed farther than knee deep, as none of them could swim—another thing Sandy intended to see rectified. Plus there was an automated lifeguard post with multiple feeds crisscrossing the sands, the central post would know within ten seconds if a kid was in trouble, and drones would zoom to that location in another twenty. But still Danya perched and watched, showing no intention of getting his feet wet. Though he had at least taken his shoes off to feel the sand between his toes.

"Whatcha think?" Sandy asked him, driving the board end-first into the sand.

"Amazing," said Danya, gazing across the pounding surf to the hazy horizon. It was a different kind of awe in his voice than when he talked of the city. His awe of Tanusha was that of excitement and wonder, the closest that Sandy had yet seen him come to being a child. But this was darker. The recognition of something wild and powerful that could not be tamed. Something dangerous. The look in Danya's eyes was not only awe, but fear. "What's it like to be out there?"

"A very different experience for me than for non-GIs," said Sandy, crouching beside him. "It can't really hurt me. I can just enjoy it. But these other guys out there . . ." she nodded to the several others amidst the plunging surf. "It's pretty safe, they've life alert vests and trackers, but I guess the fear must add to the sensation. It's pretty big today."

"Is that why they do it?" Danya asked, as a big curler crashed and exploded a hundred meters offshore. "To be afraid?"

"A little bit, maybe. Fear in a controlled environment. Or relatively controlled. To face it, and beat it, one wave at a time."

"And why do *you* do it?"

Sandy smiled. "It's beautiful. These rhythms make me calm. Remind me of my place in things."

Danya nodded, gazing outward. "I want to learn. Teach me?"

Sandy gazed at him, surprise fading as she realised it wasn't really surprising at all. If one knew Danya. And damn, if she loved this kid any more, her heart would explode.

"Absolutely," she said. "We'd start on much smaller stuff than this. But if you liked it, we could come out together. Svet and Kiril too, when they're a bit older."

"Can't see Svet liking it," said Danya. "Too much work." Along the beach, Kiril had found something slimy and showed it to Svetlana. Svetlana jumped back, not game to touch it. Kiril ran after her. "Kiril might, but at his age, who can tell?" Sandy nodded thoughtfully. Danya glanced at her. "Besides, about time I got a hobby of my very own, don't you think?"

Sandy grinned. Svetlana had told him about that conversation, obviously. It was something to remember with these three—never tell one something you didn't want all of them to hear. She yanked the back strap to unzip her wetsuit and began pulling it off.

"You've finished?" Danya asked.

"Not by choice. In five minutes a big CSA flyer is going to come to a combat hover on the sand and I'm going to jump on and go to work. Sorry I can't tell you what, it's a classified situation. We get those quite a lot."

"So how do we get home?"

Sandy pointed to her bag, which contained the flyer control. "Remember what I showed you about the automated sequence? Just let it know it's you three, the system will do the rest, you just need to climb in and it will take you back to TZ3, where Canas security will have a groundcar to take you back inside the walls."

Danya blinked. "We can fly back ourselves?"

"With these systems all automated, sure. The flyer runs direct on CSA traffic control links, and if you have any doubts or questions at all, you just talk to central, someone will be monitoring you directly anyhow, now that I'm leaving. I'm much more concerned about any of you going in the water."

"No chance of that," said Danya, looking back at the waves. "No chance at all. We'd better call Svet and Kiri over then."

"Better where they are," said Sandy, "the flyer kicks up sand everywhere, it's a little scary up close."

"Not as scary as you leaving without personally telling them why," said Danya, standing up and waving at Svetlana. It was a light reprimand, Sandy realised. Sometimes she didn't quite realise how kids younger than Danya thought. Lucky she had Danya to set her straight when her utter lack of parenting knowledge showed.

The VR matrix was not large. Ragi accessed, allowing the functions to propagate, and saw that it described . . . a small room. With detail. He resolved the detail and found floorboards, an old carpet, a chandelier. Creaking walls. He'd never seen an old house before. If VR could qualify as "seeing."

There was a bed, occupied. Beside the bed sat Agent Ariel Ruben, as though waiting for him.

"Ragi," said Ruben expectantly. Perhaps expecting some comment on the VR. Ragi didn't see that there was anything to comment on, technically. But . . .

"I like the house," he offered, looking around. And at the girl in the bed. "Who's she?"

"This is Allison. She's not very well."

Ragi frowned. How could you be not well in a VR matrix? The matrix only accessed brain function; if you were physically unwell it shouldn't . . . ah. Perhaps that was his answer. A brief analysis of the VR circulation showed him that Allison's feed was limited. A fully functioning adult brain should manage a much higher transfer rate.

"What's wrong with her?" he asked, coming over to look. The representation in the bed was perhaps fifteen, pale, brown hair. Frail.

"She has a rare condition," said Ruben. "It's called Milner's Disease, it's a mental degenerative thing. This is a fair representation of her state in the real world, but without the life support, she can't breathe on her own. She has almost no motor control, and the neural wiring makes uplinks very difficult also."

Ragi sat in an old chair by the bedside. "What is her condition psychologically?"

"She's fine," said Ruben. "At lower state uplinks she's conversational and very intelligent, really nice girl. Would you like to talk to her?"

Ragi looked at the frail girl in the old bed for a long moment. "No," he said then. "No, I don't think I would."

Agent Ruben looked surprised and a little troubled. "No? Why not?"

Ragi smiled faintly. "Because I'm guessing this is a test. I'm locked in my room because everyone's worried about my network capability. You're giving me a chance to show what I can do within this limited construct. You'd also like to see how I respond emotionally to this unfortunate girl.

"But if I'm going to try to help her, I'd rather not have any emotional attachment at all. That is what you'd like of me, yes?" A glance at Ruben. Ruben smiled quizzically. "The same way that doctors aren't allowed to operate on those they care about, emotion can compromise results. Please tell Allison yourself that I'll do what I can, but I can't promise anything; I've never tried something like this before, that I can recall. Besides which, it shouldn't really matter if I like her or not, should it? Civilised people will help regardless."

"Civilised," Ruben repeated. "Huh. I like that word, it's one of my favourites."

"Everyone's favourites, surely?"

Ruben shook his head. "It's fashionable to be critical of civilisation, to yearn for our evolutionary roots. But when these 'free spirit' movements inevitably degenerate into spitting and biting and raping and shitting on the sidewalk, everyone's so surprised." He activated some function, and the space above Allison's bed illuminated. Graphical lines resolved to show a construct, complex, multi-partite. Upon the side was an access key.

"She's physically located within this building network," Ragi observed. "Which means she's actually here. In the building."

"Yeah. She'd actually like to meet you, she doesn't get out much."

"A friend of yours?"

Ruben nodded. "Her condition's a big puzzle for us net jockeys; we've all had a go at it from time to time. Even our most advanced local GIs. But so far nothing. She's the first thing I thought of when I heard of you."

"It's brave of her. I mean, assuming you all think I'm a safety risk. She'll be completely vulnerable to me."

Ruben made a dismissive gesture. "We have you profiled for a potential security risk, not a psychopath. I don't think anyone's ever seen a GI who hurts innocent girls for fun, and if you're a security risk you'd be more likely to help and gain our trust, only to betray us later."

Ragi smiled. "But you don't think that, do you, Agent Ruben? I think you're one of these technophile types who likes GIs. Who thinks that maybe by studying us we can teach you something important about the nature of humanity."

Ruben smiled back. "Don't profile me. Get to work."

The CSA's condition red was over by mid-afternoon, and after filing the usual reports Vanessa was astonished to discover she had free time. If she wanted it, of course—had she not, she could have easily found another few hours to complete performance reviews and read red-marked intelligence reports, even to review the latest status on a disagreeable misconduct charge that was making its way through lower ranks. As FSA spec ops Executive Officer to Sandy's Commanding Officer, personnel was her specialty, meaning training, recruitment, and maintenance of standards. People skills, Sandy said with a wry smile, implying that Vanessa had more of those than her.

But after seven hours in the air on emergency standby, tracking the possibility of armed League cells whose warned-about action never took place, she'd logged all the hours today she needed to and could finish the reviews tonight. In the meantime, Phillippe had a concert this evening, and as always, she'd promised him she'd be there if she could. More often than not, she couldn't. But tonight, well, even Executive Officers were allowed to bend their schedules to fit in valuable private time if possible.

Even more surprising, Rhian was free too.

"It's the city zone expansion out in Kuta District," she explained to Vanessa as they flew to Ranchi, where the concert was. She was wearing a nice blue dress she'd kept in her FSA locker just in case of unscheduled engagements without the time to go home and change, and now fitted earrings in the passenger seat and applied some makeup in a mirror. Vanessa was still amazed how *civilian* Rhian had become in such a short time. Well, seven years wasn't that short, but it was a lifetime of relative tranquillity for a former League spec ops GI. Rhian no longer played the part, she *was* the part—a young Tanushan working mum, busy, devoted, and fashionable. Given where she'd come from, it was quite beautiful to see. "They need Rakesh to supervise on the design work for the transportation instructure, he's so much better at that than anyone else, so they keep working him late because his boss screwed up the schedule and didn't give him enough headway, even though Rakesh warned him it would happen. He says they just don't appreciate how hard his job is, they never give him enough time."

"Maybe he should work for someone who appreciates him more," Vanessa suggested.

"Well, funny you should say," said Rhian, with a conspiratorial look. Smacked her lips to make the rouge stick. "He's been talking to someone else; I'm not really supposed to say. The gist of it is fewer holidays, but better daily hours, so more time with the kids. More money too."

"Huh, well, who actually takes holidays anyway?"

"Most people," said Rhian, matter of fact. Civilianised she might be, but

Rhian had never understood rhetorical questions and probably never would. "Just not us because we're security. We forget what most people get."

"So the kids are with the oldies tonight?"

"No, aunties." Rakesh had a huge family, his parents off the ship from Nagpur had taken colonial exhortations to propagate very seriously, and had fourteen children. Most of those now had their own children, and there were no shortage of child minders. "That reminds me, it's six, when's the concert?"

"Eight."

"I'd better call Salman now to say goodnight."

She did that, while Vanessa accepted the cruiser's landing course ahead and wondered wistfully what life with her own children would be like. Not long ago it had been Sandy worried that her friends were settling down faster than her—and now Sandy had three kids to look after, and Vanessa was the one left out. But Sandy's life was now officially crazy, and Rhian was always rushed. How would the FSA's spec ops Executive Officer find time for *anything* with kids? And then Phillippe, while insisting it was all her decision to make, was hinting how nice it would be for them to share a natural pregnancy, even though that was crazy and she just didn't have nine spare months to gestate . . .

They found a nice outdoor restaurant near the concert hall and were just about to order when Ari called.

"*Is Rhian there too?*" he asked, obviously knowing she was. How he knew such things when both she and Rhian used the highest security uplinks, Vanessa didn't particularly want to know. "*Put her on.*"

Vanessa linked him to them both, a three-way conversation. "Hi, Ari," said Rhian. "Where are you?"

"*Nearby. You guys should come over, there's something you have to see.*"

"What's that?"

"*I . . . I really can't say, but it's a secure address, there's . . . look, I just wanted to share this with someone.*" Vanessa and Rhian exchanged an odd look. Was Ari . . . emotional? "*I was going to ask Sandy, but of course that's impossible right now . . . this is just one of the most beautiful things I've ever seen, there's a young girl here who's just been given a whole new life, look, you'll love it, you'll be so glad you came and saw, I looked to see who was nearby with the security clearance and found you two.*"

"Well, Ari," said Vanessa, with all sincerity, "that sounds amazing, and

I'd love to come . . ." Rhian nodded vigorously, looking intrigued, ". . . we'd both love to come, but we're about to eat before Phillippe's concert and I get to see him play so rarely these days . . ."

"Trust me, this is worth skipping a meal. I'll feed you a sandwich while you're here, better than a sandwich, Ami's a great cook. Shouldn't take more than ninety minutes round trip from where you are, you'll make the concert easy."

The autocab from the restaurant only took fifteen minutes, a groundcar on busy roads.

"Obviously he's at Denpasar," said Rhian, looking up for a glimpse of the tower above. "And he mentioned Ami, that's Amirah Togales."

"Oh, that's right, the 45 series," Vanessa remembered. "You were impressed with her, yes?"

"She's amazing," said Rhian. "I'm not sure why, but Tanusha is attracting some very impressive female GIs."

Vanessa smiled. It wasn't arrogance from Rhian. Just fact, stated Rhian-style. "Can't argue with that."

"Not that the men aren't impressive too. They just seem to lack a little dynamism. They don't integrate as much, socially."

Vanessa thought of Poole. "There's a theory that female GIs are more aesthetically activated. Femininity in Tanusha is certainly more aesthetic."

"Aesthetic?"

"Colourful. Decorative."

Rhian made a considering face. "That might be true. Sandy's theory is that female orgasms are so much more powerful, which generates brain development." Vanessa laughed. And laughed some more. Rhian looked a little surprised Vanessa thought it so funny. "It's actually not a stupid theory. Female orgasms are internal, and GIs have them from early stages of life when brains are still growing, unlike children. GI muscles are so powerful, when they contract, like in orgasm, it's a full body experience."

"Trust me, you're not alone there, girl."

"I know, but compared to men. I'm sure male GIs have great ones, but speaking for the females . . . I mean, when my stomach muscles contract like that, that's literally like steel, right through my core."

Vanessa laughed some more. "I know. Poor Rakesh, Sandy was always scared shitless of sex with Ari."

"I'm much more controlled than Sandy, Rakesh is completely safe," Rhian replied with a knowing smile. Of course, those two had served together League side, so Rhian had actually seen her do it. "But those intense feedback mechanisms in early-stage development for GIs actually contribute a lot, so it's not a dumb theory."

"Sure, but it's also just Sandy being Sandy, finding a way to tie everything back to sex. I think she was pulling your leg, Rhi." Rhian still sometimes missed that.

The taxi turned a corner, its nav screen projecting a stop ahead at the base of the HDM tower. "Poor Sandy," said Rhian with a grin. "Three kids. Has she had *any* sex lately, do you know?"

They giggled. Vanessa sighed. "We shouldn't laugh. The poor girl, it'll be so hard for her."

"She'll explode," Rhian suggested. They giggled again.

They got out onto the busy sidewalk of downtown Denpasar. HDM tower was ninety floors, nothing super big, the neighbouring mega-rise was half as tall again. Here around the tower bases was all typical Tanushan retail, like anywhere with maximum footfalls. The shopping, high glass, and dazzle extended into the tower foyer, with lots of people. Interesting place to put a CSA secure facility, but so long as access was tightly controlled it wasn't any less secure for all the activity, and its main occupants, HDM, were an insurance company whose interest in high security meant they were quite happy to coordinate theirs with the CSA offices on the top floor.

And upon thinking it, walking across the foyer to the elevators, she got the oddest chill. It started from somewhere back between her shoulder blades and worked its way down her spine and up to her scalp, an unpleasant tingle.

"*Ricey,*" said Rhian, formulating internally, sounding alarmed. Vanessa glanced at her and saw her walking on edge, looking around.

"*Don't look,*" Vanessa told her. "*I know, I feel it too, keep walking.*"

They stopped before the concierge to the hotel that occupied the tower's lower third. There was a queue for luggage facilities, and they stopped in it and looked around. The thing with running so many combat sims and having seen quite a bit of actual combat, with a head full of augments trained to process suspicious patterns, was that you couldn't always tell what triggered it. A particular set of frequencies you hadn't realised you'd been receiving, a deployment of certain kinds of people in different positions about the floor of an open space. Sometimes the subconscious recognised the pattern before the conscious had figured out what was going on.

"*By the elevators,*" said Rhian. "*Two pretty girls. They're GIs or I'm a bunbun.*"

Vanessa looked without really looking. Sure enough, two well-dressed young women waited by the elevators. They wore pants, not dresses, and their shoes were relatively sensible. An elevator came and went, and neither got on.

"*Well, that's active cover,*" said Vanessa. "*Where's passive?*"

"*There,*" said Rhian. "*In the lounge, reading a slate with a suitcase at his feet. Two chairs over from the piano.*"

One-third of the foyer was a lounge, soft chairs, and potted plants, drinks served while a piano played. Rhian's mark was in a suit, neat haircut, young, handsome. Reading slate not raised quite high enough to block his eyeline. Between the three of them, they had the entire foyer covered.

"*You think they've spotted us?*" Rhian wondered.

"*I'm sure they have. This is rearguard, the main action must be ahead of us. I'm going to warn Ari.*"

She tried Ari's link. Nothing. One of the girls by the elevators flicked a quiet glance in their direction, then away again, as though realising she'd made a mistake by looking.

"*Shit,*" said Vanessa.

"*Jammed?*"

"*Yeah, and they saw my attempt. I could go outside and get a clear signal, they've wired the building.*"

"*You wouldn't get out the doors,*" said Rhian. "*Look, their main purpose now they know they've been blown is to buy time. If they start shooting, SWAT will be here in six minutes. If they delay, they can still do their mission.*"

Vanessa looked around at the foyer. About fifty people, sitting in the lounge, attending the hotel desk, shopping at the perfume counter. Coming, going. Starting a shootout would stop this whatever-it-was, but they just couldn't with all these civilians here.

"*Stairs,*" Vanessa decided. "*They haven't guarded the stairs.*"

"*That's because it's a ninety-floor building and stairwells can be intercepted by elevator.*"

"*We can get an elevator on the fifth floor.*"

"They'll respond."

"I know. You with me, Rhi?" No simple question. Firefights against human opponents always came with margin for error. Against GIs any mistake, or split-second delay, was death. Or even no mistake.

"Didn't join the CSA for nothing," said Rhian. *"Stairs, thirty-nine?"*

"Stairs."

They walked for the stairs, behind the concierge and to the side. It was a small, enclosed staircase, rarely used, the atrium was all ground floor and little else. Civilised Tanushans would take the big open-glass elevators. Out of sight from the atrium, they ran up four at a time, spinning corners wide to avoid unlikely collisions. At the fifth floor they exited to a hotel hallway, rows of room doors, a cleaning bot crawling, humanoid room bots plugged to it and recharging.

Vanessa pulled the pistol from her jacket as she ran, and Rhian the small caliber from her handbag, which she left on the cleaning bot as they passed. It beeped a query, then a protest: lost item, lost item. Vanessa stopped at the corner and peered around. Clear but for a few walking guests.

Vanessa gave Rhian's gun a scathing look. "A girly gun? Seriously?"

"Nothing else would fit in my purse."

"Rhi, there's such a thing as *too* civilianised."

"So Sandy tells me. It's good enough if I'm accurate." The point being that GIs always were. At least her dress was barely knee length . . . though she'd already kicked off her shoes on the stairs. "They're not going to let us have the elevators."

"I know. Let's bust the network, see if Ari notices." With any luck he'd already have noticed, net wiz that he was. But if this was the League, it was ISO, and ISO did nothing without preparation.

Rhian closed her eyes briefly and leaned against the wall—not as natural a net jockey as Sandy, but significantly smoother than Vanessa. And without opening her eyes, promptly keeled over, straight onto the floor.

"Rhi!" Vanessa crouched, panicked, shaking her shoulder. Uplinked, *"Rhi, you there?"*

"I'm here," Rhian replied quite calmly. And quite motionless. *"What the fuck is this? I can't move."*

"Looks like the League learned some new tricks . . . hang on." She grabbed Rhian

up, and her gun, held her one-handed (a much easier thing than it had been without her augments) and kicked in a hotel door. The room was unoccupied, and she dragged and dropped Rhian on the freshly made bed. Sat on her and slapped her cheek. "*Feel that?*"

"*Ow, I said I can't move, not I can't feel.*"

"*Should I try the network myself?*"

"*Probably not. I mean you're not a GI, you'll be much harder to disable like this, but if they've this trick, likely they'll have other tricks.*"

"*They're not the only ones with tricks.*"

Vanessa rolled off the bed at the big wall-to-ceiling window, wound up and kicked it. It was reinforced, so instead of shattering it, she punched a hole through to her ankle. Stuck her gun out the hole and fired a volley at the road below, aiming carefully for tarmac between moving cars. By the last shot she could see them slowing and wavering as traffic central realised something was wrong from various sensors and sent the road into emergency pattern. A cross sweep of other sensors in this part of town would confirm gunshots, and their location, and send red alarms howling all the way back to CSA HQ. Cops in three minutes, but they'd not do much. SWAT in maybe ten.

"*Sorry about that,*" she said, scrambling back to the bedside to cover the room's door. "*They might want to remove us now.*"

"*Throw me out,*" said Rhian. "*Out the window. I'll be fine, it's only five stories.*"

"*I'm not throwing you out the fucking window,*" Vanessa muttered.

"*I'm slowing you down, you should move.*"

"*Shut up.*"

"*Vanessa, it's Ari!*" New signal, new voice, crackling through static. "*Wherever you are now, MOVE!*"

Vanessa threw Rhian over her shoulder and rushed the door. Then the room exploded. They rolled in the hallway amidst smoke and shattered bits of door, Vanessa bruised and stung by debris, her ears ringing but maintaining enough sense to get her gun up on the hallway. Still no attacking GIs. That had been a guided round, someone higher up had put a mini rocket through their window; Ari must have pinged its guidance signal.

"*Ari, sitrep!*"

"*They're coming through the secure floor!*" He was audibling, she could hear gunfire in the background. *"Can't tell how many, we're trying to get the network locked back down . . ."*

"SWAT's on its way, Ari! Hang on a few minutes!"

"Ami!" she heard him yelling. *"Ami, kitchen floor! There's a breach!"*

Rhian was moving, just a little. Rolling onto her back amidst debris and smoke, now rolling her eyes to look up at Vanessa. "Go," she whispered. "It's coming back. I'll be fine."

Some hotel guests were in the halls now, shocked, as emergency announcements told them to return to their rooms. "Look after her!" Vanessa yelled at them, pointing at Rhian. "She's CSA, look after her!"

And took off toward the elevators, dodging people on the way. A figure emerged from the elevator doors, weapon raised. Vanessa stepped into a flying aim, the only way to attain stability while running, firing as she fell, saw the figure kick backward into the elevator doorway and fall. She hit and rolled, came up, and arrived at the elevator. Blocking the doorway was one of the girls from the lobby, no longer so pretty, heavy caliber rounds through the face. Still she was moving, only stunned, and Vanessa put another three in her temple to be sure.

A quick peer into the glass elevator and ducked back as rounds from across the lobby smashed the glass. Step one, draw fire, identify source. Step two, hit target. Yeah, sure. She dragged the dead GI from the doorway, then accessed the elevator by network, found the building network open to her, whatever had restricted traffic now released. CSA overrides were good enough to get the elevator moving upward at speed. Whoever was shooting at it across the lobby kept shooting, not knowing if she was in it. And that gave her a location, shots echoing above the screams and shouts in the atrium below. And if she concentrated, she could feel the augments kick in, the armscomp calculating all she'd seen of the atrium, the width of it, the sound of shots travelling across it, traversing up the side wall as the elevator accelerated away.

She took a deep breath and stepped side-on about the edge of the elevator shaft, aiming across the atrium in the sure knowledge that a high-designation GI over there had just seen her and was reacquiring. She glimpsed a figure, fifth floor like her, crouched . . . she fired and ducked back, but drew no fire. Surely that must have been a hit, or she'd have at least been grazed or most likely killed.

And ducked back as shots did take the corner of the shaft but from a lower angle, and now a man in a suit was sailing up over the exposed railing from the floor below, weapon tracking onto a point-blank shot . . . and was hit from behind even before he landed, multiple times, body lurching as he spun and tried to return fire, only to take five rounds in the back of the head from Vanessa, flat on her back.

He fell, revealing Rhian, standing propped against a corridor wall, small pistol in hand. "Told you it works!" she yelled at Vanessa, evidently much stronger. "Go, that's all three of them, I'll follow when my legs are working!"

Vanessa's links had stopped another elevator, and she scrambled in. Doors closed and the car hummed upward, leaving the atrium behind in a gathering rush. Then a long, quiet ride, only not so quiet because her heart was hammering in her ears, and now that she noticed, her hands were flexing in time with her pulse. In fact, she was buzzing, her ears were buzzing, her hair tingling and prickling, colours and sensations surreal. The elevator car seemed impossibly large, as though the distance from one side to the other was a yawning canyon. Her augments felt a little like this in training, but in the real deal they made her a completely different creature. It was awe inspiring. And it was disorienting. Even her emotional responses felt odd, whereas normally this degree of awareness in a deadly fight would evoke some degree of fear, of concern, of desperately pumping herself up, urging herself on . . . here, it was absent. Not that the danger was obscured, she knew it only too well, could see it staring her in the face, teeth bared. But past the buzzing in her ears and the pounding of her heart, she felt she could almost step aside and consider it objectively. Consider her own death, if necessary, and watch calmly as it happened. These were not her thoughts, surely? Her brain didn't work like this. She barely recognised herself.

Seventieth floor. There was elevator music playing. *Four Seasons*, Vivaldi, but played just horribly, by someone who sounded bored. Phillippe hated what these "limp-wristed tarts" did to poor Vivaldi, it was music to be played "like you wanted to punch or kiss or fuck someone." She wondered if she could still make the concert. Probably not with this synthetic blood all over her.

This elevator wouldn't go beyond the 85th floor, and she reckoned the attack had originated from the 89th, so she got off at 84 and went for the stairs. She couldn't reach Ari, hadn't heard anything from this level the whole ride up.

Objectively she knew what that probably meant, but she was CSA, and there were other Agents up here, a good friend of hers among them. She moved fast up the stairs to level 89, paused at the staircase opening, no stairwell doors here; god, how she and every other spec ops agent hated stairwell doors.

This level was offices, all abandoned at this hour. In the ceiling here was a gaping hole, debris blasted down over desks and partitions, all ruined. Shaped charges, Vanessa knew this entry technique well, had done it herself . . . only the CSA secure level would have extra-reinforced floors. An attacker would have to know the weak spots, CSA didn't have architectural permission to just armour plate an entire floor; it could upset structural characteristics. Detailed analysis would show the weak spots. Planning again.

She moved fast, weapon ready. Saw a weapon abandoned in a corridor, then some civvie jackets tossed over some desks. Then some equipment webbing. GIs moving fast through this level, she and Rhian must have rushed them with their unexpected arrival. They'd cast off things they hadn't needed. But they might have had time to booby trap their approach, so she kept a careful eye out.

And reached a big ceiling hole, above the central corridor. And jumped straight up through it, having the augments to do that now, and not daring to announce herself first. The charge had blown through a big room, scorching the ceiling. Adjoining it was a security/surveillance room, its door was busted open; she caught a glimpse of bodies inside, blood spatter and broken glass screens, all limp. CSA Agents, but she couldn't check on them, not until she knew it was secure.

Down a short hall into another room, surveillance glass looking onto a secure apartment with a big, heavy, locked door. The door was open. It looked like the kind of apartment they'd kept Sandy in when she'd first arrived in Tanusha and no one knew if they could trust her or not. Or rather, most were certain they couldn't. There'd been rumours of high-des GIs kept in secret facilities, and it figured that Ari would be in on that . . . had that been what he was doing here? Evidently it wasn't *that* big a secret if he'd been about to let her and Rhian in on it . . . but where was the GI now? Was he in on this? Was that how things had gone down so smoothly? An inside job? What the hell was this new GI anyway?

There were no signs of shooting in the secure apartment. She checked it quickly, saw food in the kitchen for more than one person. Ari had said he'd feed her and Rhian when they got here.

Vanessa left the secure door, down the adjoining hall, and immediately here were bodies, GI bodies, two felled by precise gunfire, two more by powerful blows that could only have been from another GI. And here were more rooms, an office torn apart, bullets and blood everywhere, three human agents down and all far too messy to still be alive. Here a living room, for more agents to pass time while guarding whoever-it-was, two more dead, one decapitated. And now she could hear talking, someone talking fast, and someone crying. A voice sounded like Ari's.

"CSA!" she yelled, pretty sure she'd covered the whole floor; the building wasn't very wide this high up. "I'm clear out here! Is that you Ari?"

"Vanessa!" He sounded relieved, and genuine. "Good god, get in here."

It could have been duress, but Ari would never, not that earnestly, not even with a gun to his head. She entered carefully and found their last stand—the other big penthouse lounge at this level, one semi-circular wall all glass and spectacular view, fractured in places by bullet holes. Ari was holding a girl, slender, long dark hair, who was on her back and covered in blood. She was crying.

"I don't want to die, I don't want to die," she was repeating.

"You're not going to die, Ami," Ari soothed her. "I've seen GIs take much worse than this, this is nothing, you'll be fine."

"I only just got here," said Amirah, blood mixing with tears on her cheeks. "And I like it here so much, I was gonna do so much, I don't wanna die now . . ." She coughed, and blood came up.

There were another two CSA Agents, one wounded, tending to an unconscious girl, a frail teenager, lying on a sofa.

And there was a slender black man, sitting opposite another three individuals and staring at them. Those individuals looked like . . . and Vanessa raised her gun again in a rush.

"What the fuck?" They were GIs, and from their battered civvie clothes and bloodstains, they could only be League GIs. The ones who'd attacked. They appeared mostly unharmed and just sat there, looking vacantly into space. Vanessa stared.

"Ricey!" called Ari. "That's Ragi. We were holding him here, he saved us. He's got them locked."

"Locked? What the fuck is 'locked'?"

"Here, let me show you," said Ragi.

And suddenly she wasn't standing there anymore.

It was cyberspace, pale and indistinct. Her gun was missing. There were a lot of glowing constructs surrounding her, massively intricate. And nearby, some smaller ones, combinations of familiar pieces all joined together in neat, barriered little bundles. Those were people.

"This is them," said Ragi, and she spun to find him standing before her. A pleasant-looking man, round-faced, calm, with intelligent little eyes. "League GIs, ISO, I imagine. They tried to kill me."

"They succeeded with a lot of others."

Ragi nodded sadly. "I'm very sorry. But I didn't ask to be locked up here. I'm certain I would have been safer if I'd been free to venture out and make my own defences. This tower is really a big gleaming target."

Vanessa stared at the three constructs he was pointing to. Massively barriered, GIs always were. They needed to be, as entirely synthetic they were so much more vulnerable to network infiltration. Normally to immobilise a GI you needed a direct connection, a cable, GIs like anyone had hardware that filtered wireless, made it harmless.

And he'd just barrier hacked her as well, transported her instantly to a VR network. It wasn't technologically possible, of course, though she had recently met one man who could do it. But he'd been the representative of a massively advanced alien species.

"You're Talee?" she asked him.

"It's possible," said Ragi. "I don't recall. That's been rather the problem, I don't know who or what I am, and your CSA can't let me out until they're sure. Meantime the League wanted me dead, unless you can think of some other target in this tower they were after."

Vanessa thought about it. "Who's the girl?" And recalled even as she said it the reason Ari had invited her and Rhian there in the first place—a girl, he'd insisted, emotion in his voice. Her life restored.

Ragi smiled. "I can show you that too."

The scene changed with an effortless fade of colours and textures. Suddenly she was in an old bedroom with wooden floorboards in a creaking old house. In the four-poster bed lay a girl, who sat up bright-eyed and smiled at her.

"Hello!" she said with delight. "Ragi, have you brought me a friend? Who are you?"

"*I haven't told her what just happened,*" came Ragi's voice in her inner ear. "*Please don't tell her, the poor girl deserves more joy.*"

"Allison, this is Commander Vanessa Rice," Ragi said audibly. "She's a good friend of Ari's. Vanessa, this is Allison."

"Hello, Vanessa!" said Allison. "Isn't this amazing? I can sit up now, and I can talk properly!"

The pale girl in the room. Vanessa recalled Ari talking a few times over the years, of a girl with a rare disease who couldn't move and couldn't uplink properly to VR either. He hadn't been able to make VR work for her, the usual "cure" for incurable vegetables, and so she was unable to have a life in either world. Until now, evidently Ragi had fixed it so she could.

And then the League had come with advanced GIs to kill him, and once he'd been released from his network restraints, Ragi had brain-hacked them fast as you like and held them in their own externally-imposed vegetative state. If he could do that to the best the League had to offer . . . no wonder he'd been kept in isolation.

"Hello, Allison," said Vanessa. Her voice sounded far away to her own ears. Coming down off the combat high, the brain did funny things. "How long have you known Ari?"

"I think about four years," said Allison. "Are you really a friend of his? He's been absolutely wonderful, I mean, he's introduced me to so many others? You know, hackers and network experts, and they've all been so amazing, I've made so many friends and they've all tried to help me. And they helped a lot, I've been able to access libraries and live shows, I've even made friends with AIs who've helped me to see all across the city, attend concerts and parades, everything's covered somewhere on the net! But I couldn't, you know, actually move. In a VR construct, not like this!"

She swung her legs carefully off the bed.

"I think you'd better wait, Allison," Ragi said gently. "You still need to know how to stand, even in here."

"I know!" she beamed. "But it's wonderful just to sit up."

Even in post-combat shaky wind-down, Vanessa could still see why Ari had invited her here. This was truly something.

"Allison," said Vanessa, "we'll have lots of people here to visit you soon. I have to go right now, but now that you're moving, I'm sure your family can come."

"Can I hug them?" Allison asked, tearing up at the prospect.

"Of course you can."

"I've never hugged my family before." Crying for joy. "Thank you, thank everyone in the CSA for me."

The VR disappeared, and Vanessa stood in the lounge. A CSA flyer roared outside the tall glass windows, lights flashing, while other cruisers hovered nearby. The one healthy CSA Agent was telling them on another channel to break the glass, they had to get Amirah out immediately. That was a new thing, everyone so concerned about the dying GI. She'd saved their necks, it was obvious from the dead attackers Vanessa had seen on the way in.

"Don't kill them," Vanessa said to Ragi, as Ragi sat and watched his captive GIs. God knew where they were now, mentally. Frozen in some VR world they couldn't escape? Unconscious? Writhing in Ragi-induced agony? "I'm sure you can kill them. But we need their information . . . and for God's sakes don't let them or anyone else access their killswitches."

"Believe me," said Ragi, "I want to know what they know even more than you do." And looked at her oddly. "Commander Rice, are you okay?"

Okay? Why shouldn't she be okay? It was her last thought before her legs folded and she hit the ground.

CHAPTER FOURTEEN

D anya was quite pleased at how good he was getting at moving around. He'd been worried Tanusha would become like a golden cage, especially with Sandy as a guardian. They'd end up stuck in Canas, surrounded by high security and unable to move, but increasingly as he was learning the basic protocols, and when and who to contact in CSA just to let them know they were moving, he was discovering they could go pretty much anywhere—so long as he cleared it with Sandy first, of course.

And so they went from a self-organised trip to Ranarid to get some school supplies, back home for dinner with Sandy's apologies for having to work late, then to CSA HQ thirty Ks away, after word that something bad had happened. They just took the maglev and light rail like any other Tanushan, on transit passes they'd bought. Sandy had of course wanted to send them a cruiser, but that would take a while as the CSA were busy, and Danya said they didn't need a chaperone anyway. And walked them to the HQ public entrance off the rail stop, prepared for all the security checks, but a man in a suit took them straight through with minimal fuss, just the obligatory body scans and visitors' passes, then a hand-off to some junior staffer to escort across to medical.

Sandy was there in the hallway, in civvie off-duty clothes. She was talking to several others who looked like they might be SWAT. Danya was learning to recognise the type, tougher and leaner than most, all short-haired, some with the sides shaved for a better helmet fit. They rang alarm bells to look at, like seeing augmented toughs in the street outside a club on Droze . . . but these were Sandy's friends and turned to look as Sandy saw them, and beckoned them over.

Sandy introduced them, and the SWATs all seemed friendly enough, with smiles and handshakes for Danya and Svetlana and ruffled hair for Kiril. And departed, as Danya gazed through the window they were all standing before and saw Vanessa lying in that medical bed, hooked up to various machines and unmoving. There was a tube in her mouth. Danya knew Vanessa as fun and lively, always with a smile or a joke. It didn't look right for her to just be lying there, small and silent. Her husband Phillippe was in the room with her, seated beside the bed, holding her hand and just looking at her.

Sandy knelt and hugged Danya, which startled him because he didn't need the hug . . . then he realised that the hug wasn't for him. He held her back. She was shaking. That scared him. Svetlana joined the hug, seeing she was upset, then Kiril, and Danya broke away to gaze through the window. After a moment, Sandy joined him, hand on his shoulder.

"How is she hurt?" he asked.

"We don't know," Sandy said quietly. "It's like before, at Antibe station, only much worse. It's like her body just shut down, if it weren't for the life support she'd be gone."

"So she's not injured?"

"No. No, she got three fucking GIs in a row, low forties, barely a scratch on her." She took a deep breath. "The doctors think it might be a kind of augmentation overload. She's so fast these days, and so strong. They think when she really pushes herself, the augmentations are too much for her body and it just shuts down."

"I'd thought . . . I mean, didn't they know that would happen before they did the augmentations?"

"It's all so new, Danya. Since the war ended and the restrictions got relaxed, the technology's just gone flying ahead. We're still learning what it does at this level, and SWAT gets the highest tech there is. We're guinea pigs. And I *told* her, I told her it was risky, that the meds didn't know half as much as they thought they did, but she was so excited at getting better, at getting closer to my level. And she just *can't* get to my level, none of them can, we're just made from different stuff and there are limits, and if you exceed those limits, things start breaking."

"Sandy." Danya put his hand on hers, on his shoulder. "Your hand's too tight, you're hurting me."

"Oh, shit!" She removed her hand like she'd been shot, and bent, examining him with concern. "Did I hurt you? Where?"

"No no no!" Danya shook his head, smiling. "It was just a little tight, you could never hurt me properly. Look, there's not even a bruise."

She looked unsteady in her relief. Like she might burst into tears. Danya took the opportunity of her proximity to put both hands on her shoulders, like he sometimes did to Svetlana or Kiril when they got overwhelmed by things.

"Look," he said firmly, "Vanessa's going to be fine. She's incredibly tough, and you've got the best medical care in the galaxy here. It'll be just like last time; she'll wake up and be fine."

Sandy smiled at him and put a hand to his face. The last time Danya had seen any adult look at him with such love in her eyes, they'd been Mama's eyes. So long ago. She hugged him again, and Danya was glad, because he didn't want anyone to see him cry.

"I love you," she said simply. "All of you." And straightened, suddenly calm business again. "Now, I have to go to a debriefing, do you think you guys can hang around here? There's food at the cafeteria, all you need to do is ask . . ."

"Sandy," said Danya, with reprimand. "I think we can manage. We'll try not to burn the place down."

"Right," said Sandy, suitably chastened. "Of course. Oh, and Kiril, Doctor Kishore might want to come by since you're here, do some more tests . . . now if you want me to be present, just tell him to wait until after the debriefing."

"Sandy, go!" Kiril told her, copying his brother's exasperation. "We'll be fine!" Sandy laughed and left with a wave.

"She really loves Vanessa, doesn't she?" Svetlana said as they watched her leave down the hall. Svetlana might find the notion challenging, Danya knew. For her, three was family. Expanding that number to four had been a challenge, but she'd managed it. Now to discover, to *really* discover, that one of those four loved someone else just as much as she loved them . . . that made the number five. And then there was Phillippe, sitting at Vanessa's bedside and looking completely immovable until she woke up . . . and they didn't know Phillippe as well, but they liked him a lot. And then there was Sandy's other great friend Rhian, who was around here somewhere . . . and then even Ari, which all got complicated in ways that kids didn't really grasp.

Where they were from, love was something to be rationed in small parcels. Was it possible to spread love around too thinly, like plastic stretched too far, until it snapped? Danya knew it made Svetlana nervous. If he was honest with himself, it made him nervous too. Too many loved ones were a liability. Three was much safer. Four, if the fourth was Sandy. Sandy had gone through fire to prove herself. How could these others possibly do the same?

Debrief was one long frustration and went long into mealtime. The CSA and FSA's finest minds sat around a table, looked over all the evidence, and ate the cafeteria meals that were brought to them, and concluded that it all made very little sense.

An emancipation activist had been shot too, a lawyer named Idi Aba, he'd helped some League GIs pro-bono through their asylum process. That had happened on the other side of the city, point-blank, just outside his apartment. No one had seen a thing, and it looked like a professional hit.

"Well, that's just fucking smart of them," Sandy summarised in frustration, after they'd been reviewing events for half an hour with little to show for it. "If the League wanted to give the emancipation cause a big boost, they couldn't do a better job than murdering an emancipation activist in the Federation capital. And as for trying to kill Ragi, all that does is confirm he's Takawashi's, because if he was Talee they'd never have heard about it, or at least not yet. But this was planned well in advance, they've probably been at it a month or more . . . hell, we haven't *had* Ragi that long."

"It does not appear the smartest couple of moves we've seen the ISO make for a while," FSA Operations Director Hando agreed. They were all here, FSA and CSA, on occasions like this one there wasn't much discernible difference between the two agencies—League involvement automatically put the FSA in play, and local security concerns automatically made it CSA business. The location at CSA HQ was just a matter of convenience, given this was where all the wounded were taken, CSA's medical facilities being superior.

"And they've given us prisoners," Ibrahim added, on the holoscreen, still back in FSA offices. "How long until we have actionable intelligence from them?"

"Interrogating GIs is hard," said Naidu. "They're impervious to most stress-inducing techniques and have more patience than regular humans. They're more susceptible to uplink hacking, but our legal advice on that is cloudy. With recent synthetic rights legislation passing, it could be construed as torture."

"Which is unfortunate," said Chandrasekar. "Given that with Ragi apparently on our side, we've actually got the ability to get right into their heads."

"Gee, you guys really have a record with locking up suspicious advanced GIs, huh?" Sandy said wryly. "Keep them in a small room, debate, equivocate, then wait until someone tries to kill them in some big blowup before realising whose side they're on."

Naidu and Ibrahim repressed smiles. "Thank you, Sandy," said Chandrasekar drily. She was talking about herself, of course. "And we *haven't* decided Ragi's 'on our side,' whatever that means. If his condition is what it appears to be, even he's probably not certain what side he's on."

"You know how I decided?" Sandy asked them. Curious looks came back. "I went with the guys who treated me well. It's not difficult really, when you're lost and alone and don't know where to turn or where you belong, some kind treatment and offers of friendship can go a long way. Ragi might turn out to be ten times the asset I am. Be nice to him. Hell, get him laid if you have to."

"You can arrange that?" Chandrasekar asked unwisely.

"You know I can," Sandy replied. Chandi was too cool to blush and too smart not to have realised his mistake. "And our three prisoners too."

"Who just killed a bunch of our people?" said Hando with disbelief.

"And nearly killed my three best friends in the world," said Sandy. "I know. If they'd gotten to me at the wrong time of my development, that might have been me leading an attack like that."

"And how many moral excuses do we make for GIs?" Hando retorted. "How many atrocities get the pass because oh, they can't be measured on the same moral axis as the rest of us?"

"Sure," said Sandy, "when they break the laws of war they should be punished for it like anyone else, but they didn't kill any civvies this time, every casualty was an enemy agent defending a secure CSA facility. I did stuff *just* like that when I was on that side, but mostly to Fleet. And like you, some of Fleet still haven't forgiven me. But at the time, I hadn't yet realised there *was* a moral choice involved, I just did what I was told like the good drone I was. Good bet these GIs are the same. Don't just interrogate them, give them a choice. Explain it to them. We might have them in custody indefinitely, I doubt League will ask for them back . . . if nothing else, it's a psych experiment for you, how long does it take to turn a League GI, if at all? Put some of our new GI friends onto it, the difference between them and our new prisoners might only be about twelve months of introspection."

Hando took a breath and raised a hand in faint apology. He was angry, and she got that. Sandy shook her head to say it was nothing, she understood. She hadn't even raised her voice at him.

"The most concerning part of what you've just said, Cassandra," said Ibrahim, "is referencing the 'laws of war.' This attack was very much like an act of war from the League, and the one on Idi Aba was at least a very unfriendly gesture."

"Well, we can't be certain of that," Naidu cautioned. "If Vanessa and Rhian hadn't surprised their preparation and rushed them, the Ragi attack would have been very fast and professional too, and then we'd be calling it a covert operation, and not technically warfare." Unimpressed looks came his way. "I did not invent the nomenclature."

"Any way you interpret it," Ibrahim continued, "League are very upset and are becoming increasingly drastic in their actions. What do we do about it?"

When she got out, she strode fast back to medical. An uplink had already informed her that Kiril was having checks with Dr Kishore, so she went there first, but Kiril was happy enough, chatting away and asking Kishore more questions than he was being asked in turn. She stayed long enough to be reassured herself, then went to see Vanessa and found Vanessa's family all there and some of Phillippe's family; it took time for the security clearance to arrive for anyone beyond immediate partner or guardian, so they'd only now been allowed in. She said hi to everyone, especially favourite cousin Yves, and tried to be reassuring. Svetlana was talking to Phillippe at Vanessa's bedside, and Phillippe seemed pleased at the conversation—he was telling her how they'd met, Sandy overheard. Svetlana showed no more sign of needing her there than Kiril had, so she accessed building security to find Danya and found him sitting in Amirah's intensive care ward with Ari, talking. Amirah was going to make it, surprising given the number of holes in her, but not so surprising given how much the girl wanted to live. The docs must have given them permission to sit in there, so it seemed Danya didn't need her at the moment either.

She went to see the one surviving wounded CSA Agent, and to the bodies in the morgue—she'd already paid condolences to the friends of the others who'd died, but hadn't yet had time to see the bodies. She felt it especially incumbent upon her as senior in SWAT, given SWAT were the ones who usually took the casualties and were not shy reminding Investigations, Intel, and other suits of that fact. These nine suits had stood up to high-des GIs with no armour and average weapons and augments, and paid the predictable price.

Had *stood*, review of security tape had shown, and fought, when others better knowing the odds might have run.

SWAT acknowledged now with an honour guard at the morgue door, two troopers in full armour at attention, beside the growing pile of flowers, mementoes, and other symbols of unknown personal value, about the photographs of the nine dead that were propped against the wall. A football, a fancy pen, a gold ring. A necklace. A mouth organ. So many stories, all suddenly ended. In the seven years she'd been on Callay, she'd come to appreciate how non-GIs weren't born soldiers, as she and her kind were. There'd been a time in the League when she'd never really thought about it, just assumed that soldier was a type of life that people just had.

Being here, she'd come to realise it was a choice, and that these agents had once been regular civilians like everyone else, children in the schools, young men and women wondering at their future prospects. No one forced them to choose, and yet they did, even knowing what it might cost them. Sandy had seen similar shrines in the League for dead GIs. No family mourned them, just their squad mates, a photograph on a wall, a few pictures of favourite things. A few messages of affection or loss. From synthetic minds struggling to comprehend what it meant, in the wider scale of things, that a life should be lost that was made to be lost, and should merely have been accepted as such . . . but somehow wasn't. If GIs were made to die, why did it hurt? Why grieve at all?

She recalled the shrine at a briefly empty bunk of a soldier of hers—Tan. John Tan. He'd liked cats, in the way some people liked cats, photographs of funny cats, silly cats, cats hiding in shoes, cats sleeping in odd places. Not that he'd ever actually seen a cat, besides the occasional station master's moggy, the only people of sufficient rank to keep them on stations, certainly no one on a ship was allowed. And so his photograph on the bunk had been joined by pictures of cats, and a stuffed cat of his, a rare personal item with shipboard luggage restrictions. Hell of a summary for a life, a curious affection for an animal he'd barely known. League didn't do religion much among civilians, sure as hell no one in high command had wanted GIs getting religious, fear of what might happen should GIs wonder at the existence of a higher moral power that exceeded even League Command. And so John Tan had passed, like so many others of his kind in that awful fucking war, without really knowing who he was except that he liked cats, and was a very poor chess player, and had a funny laugh—no service, no honour guard, not even a grave because GI bodies were valuable and full of expensive parts that would be recycled.

She stood now before the nine photographs of the CSA's fallen and knew that *this* was what the League had stolen from her and her kind. Dignity. Meaning. Choice. These men and women had made a choice to be here, and in dying here, gained dignity. Their deaths had meaning, because they'd known for what they risked and fought. If she stood for anything, and fought for anything, it was this, signified by these slowly growing shrines against the morgue wall, and the two SWAT troopers at hard attention, weapons angled sharply at the ceiling.

Sandy had never really gone for ceremony, perhaps because she'd always felt the hollowness of it all, back in League. But now she stood before the photos, central to all, and went to full attention and saluted *hard*. And held it with moist eyes. Fellow agents and family around her saw with approval. There's Sandy Kresnov. She's one of us. She put her arm down and nodded to them all. Then she walked back to her life and hoped that she would not need to do this too many more times. It seemed an unlikely wish, but even so, at least here, in this life, even loss made some kind of sense.

When she got back to Vanessa's bedside, a doctor gave good news—all of Vanessa's vitals were continuing to stablise, and she'd likely wake up on her own in an hour or two. Sandy sat with her for a while, with Phillippe and Svetlana, but a doctor wasn't happy with three in the ward, and Phillippe should certainly be here . . . and he and Svetlana seemed to be enjoying each other's company. So Sandy left them to it and went next door to Amirah's ward.

Rhian was there too. She was holding one of her twin girls, Sunita, who was fast asleep—the CSA sometimes relaxed the family attendance policy, especially in med ward, so it would work more like a regular hospital, and employees could spend time with wounded friends without worrying about family left at home. Amirah was asleep too, hooked up to life support, having undergone surgery to remove all the rounds. Sandy could see her jaw was patched and her forehead. One arm above the covers had another three patches. Presumably she was like that all over.

"Wow," she murmured. "How many holes?"

"Fifty-three," said Ari. "We'd all be dead without her, even Ragi; we didn't get the net collar off him fast enough otherwise." Ari seemed particularly affectionate toward this girl, Sandy thought. Certainly she was very pretty. And funny too, and smart, very socialised for a new, young GI.

"There wasn't enough space to fall back in that place," Rhian observed. "She had to hold ground, and that meant taking fire. She did it well."

"And she was hitting them too or else they'd have been more accurate and she'd be dead," Sandy surmised, well knowing that kind of combat, GI to GI. Even she'd have taken hits. But not so many, and half the CSA's dead would still be alive, at least. But that wasn't Amirah's fault, she was the designation she was, and had done magnificently with what she had. Sandy walked to Amirah's bedside and sat on the mattress edge.

"The doctor didn't want us in here," said Danya. He sat with Ari, between the bed and the windows overlooking the compound. "But Rhian said GI brains were different; you don't like peace and quiet."

"No," Sandy agreed, holding the girl's hand. She was drugged, of course, muscle relaxant the only way you could operate on GIs. "I remember waking up after some procedure in the League, I hated the quiet, I couldn't focus, kept slipping away. Asked for some buddies to come in and play movies and music, that was much better."

"GIs are social," said Rhian, gently rocking her little girl. "Odd side effect of so many combat impulses, but there you are. All those impulses have to latch on something, silence drives us crazy. Hopefully if Ami wakes a bit she'll hear us and know she's not alone."

"Did you sleep with her?" Sandy asked Ari. Meaning Amirah.

She could see in Ari's eyes the pause, wondering whether to lie. And concluding, correctly, that it gained him nothing. "Um, yes. She's, um, persuasive."

Sandy smiled. "Good. She's a good girl. And I can personally attest that sleeping with newly arrived GIs is a great way to make them feel at home."

She and Ari gazed at each other for a moment. She was almost hoping for some jealousy, but predictably there wasn't. She'd thought once that jealousy might be a sign of advancing mental maturity, but it seemed that she just really didn't do that . . . so what the hell, why hope for something that everyone said was intensely unpleasant?

She glanced at Danya. She'd almost expected him to be uncomfortable. These were the kinds of life complications he was mostly unfamiliar with. But instead he just smiled a little and put his hands in the air. "I'm thirteen," he said. "No comment."

Sandy's eyes flicked to Rhian. "Danya, would you like to hold Sunita?"

Now there was caution in his eyes. He shook his head. "No."

Rhian looked a little hurt. "No?"

"Babies make me nervous. Kiril was that age when the crash happened. Younger even. Svet was five." The hurt faded from Rhian's eyes. "They both nearly starved. I had to keep them fed. I nearly died trying, so many times. I'd hear him crying because he was hungry, and . . ." He looked down at his hands, twisting and fidgeting between his knees. "I still hear him sometimes. That's when I wake up sweating."

Rhian looked sad. "I had a bad experience with a child once. When I was a League soldier. But it's not the kind of thing you just live with, Danya. It's the kind of thing you overcome."

She got up and held out her sleeping little girl for Danya to hold. His enthusiasm was underwhelming, but Rhian was accepting no refusal. Danya held the girl and still clearly knew what to do, how to cradle her head on his arm. Rhian leaned close, hand on Danya's shoulder.

"This is a different place than where you're from," she said. "She'll never be truly hungry. If she cries it'll be because it's time for her feed, or she's tired, or she's filled her nappy. No one's going to try and kill her, and if they ever did, I and all my friends would kill *everything* in our path to stop it, ourselves as well if necessary." It was imagery that Rhian, unlike most mothers, would find intensely comforting. "Look how peaceful she is."

Danya looked. And still looked awkward. Like the sight of that little sleeping face brought back too many memories, all at once. But evidently not all of them were bad, because he did not give her back.

"Her mother nearly died today," he reminded Rhian.

"She did," said Rhian, nodding. "But her birth mother's already dead, back in the League, and she got a second chance, like you. There's no room for pessimism with family, Danya. You of all people should know that."

Danya said nothing. And looking at him, Sandy knew that that just opened up a *whole* can of worms. Danya didn't do optimism *or* pessimism, he did realism, hard, cold, and nasty. Pessimism was no help, but optimism got you killed, so he went for something in the middle, something that black-

and-white, straightforward Rhian would probably never understand and was not wired to.

"That's great, Rhi," Sandy uplinked to tell her privately. *"You're good with him. But I think that's enough, huh?"*

Rhian looked up at her and smiled, and returned to her chair. Her eyes again fixed on her sleeping child. Trusting or not, Sandy could read GI body language better than anyone, and Rhian was poised to be there in a flash. And go through walls to do it.

"Where's Ragi?" Sandy asked.

"Not sure," said Ari. "Safer that way."

"He's free? With this network?"

"Limited. He's volunteered to some monitoring and controls; he knows we're nervous."

"Cai could shut down traffic control in a minute or two, I'm sure," said Rhian.

"Ragi's not Cai," said Ari. "But he's something similar, no question. Sandy, we could use your help with him."

"Why? He's nothing like me."

"Takawashi made both of you."

Sandy snorted. "Takawashi made me the same way that the president of a nut company makes peanuts. He's an administrator, bureaucrat, and self-promoter. The *system* grows and packages the peanuts."

"Sandy," Ari tried again, "it's kind of important that he comes to like us . . ."

"A point I made very strongly to Ibrahim, Chandi, and company just now. I don't need to be personally involved in every escaped GI's life. You guys are doing fine without me, and if he needs other GI friends, well, I'd think he should feel quite close to Ami after this. It doesn't always need to be me, Ari. I have other priorities."

She glanced at Danya, holding the baby. Ari exhaled and looked skeptical. "Well, speaking of your other priorities," he said, "let me take Danya out some night or even a weekend. He's a self-sufficient guy, he's not going to be happy just being taken care of all the time. I can show him the real Tanusha. My Tanusha."

Most mothers would have been horrified at the thought. Ari's Tanusha was not a place parents willingly let their thirteen-year-old children wander into.

"You'd do that?" she asked. "You have the time?"

"Well, no, technically I never have the time. But I do what we all learn to do, we involve people who matter to us in our work, we make an overlap." With a glance at Rhian, still watching her sleeping child. "He can come on the job with me for a bit, nothing dangerous, just meet some people, see the sights. Call it work experience."

Danya's look was hopeful. Sandy smiled at him. "Don't even need to ask you, do I?"

Danya shrugged. "I'm glad you're my guardian, Sandy," he said. "But we both know that some things I'm not going to ask permission for."

"Well, then thank you for being polite and asking," Sandy said drily. He and Ari had spoken of this already, she was certain, in her absence. "Make a time. Explaining to your brother and sister why you can go and they can't will be *your* job, understand?"

"Been giving them bad news all my life," said Danya, unworried. Sunita stirred in his arms, writhing and shifting. He bounced her a little, with long-remembered reflex, and cooed to her gently. The little girl settled and went on sleeping. Rhian and Sandy exchanged a glance and a smile.

And looked up at the new figure appearing in the doorway. Male, broad-shouldered, head recently shaved. Poole, in a rough shirt and jeans, like he'd been out in the wilds somewhere. Which he had.

"You're back," Rhian observed.

Poole nodded. "Just talking to my buddy Kiril. He's convinced . . . get this, *absolutely* convinced, that Doctor Kishore's green jelly snakes taste better than the yellow ones." He walked to Amirah's bedside.

"I've watched media debates on security policy that contained nothing so profound," Sandy told him.

"My problem is I always found jelly snakes more interesting than security policy," Poole admitted, looking down at Amirah. "She's going to be okay, yeah?"

"Yeah. How was Callay?"

He'd been touring, looking at the wildlife, climbing mountains, and diving reefs. Looking for whatever qualified as inspiration for Poole.

"Callay's pretty. But I'm back now, and I'd like to join the CSA."

Just like that. Rather than sitting at home and playing piano, or wandering the tourist circuit—also on Anita and Pushpa's money. Disassociated, disconnected, disinterested, no one had yet figured Poole out. He just didn't seem to care that much.

Sandy looked at Ari. Ari scratched his jaw. "Any particular reason?" he asked.

Poole made a face, looking down at Amirah. "Oh, you know. Something to do."

"If that's your answer to psych questions," said Sandy, "you'll fail."

Poole smiled. "Well, I'll just have to come up with something better, yeah?" This time Ari looked at Sandy. Sandy rolled her eyes. Poole looked at Danya and Sunita. "One of yours, Rhi?" Rhian nodded. "Can I hold her?"

"Of course."

Danya got up to transfer the sleeping infant very carefully. Sunita looked so much smaller in Poole's arms than in Rhian's or Danya's. The little girl snuggled and slept on.

"Hello, there," Poole murmured. "Hello, little thing. So when do you go and pay the unofficial League embassy a visit?"

"No idea what you mean," said Sandy.

"Sure you don't. Can I come?"

"Can you come where?"

Poole looked at her for a long moment. Sandy gave nothing away. She was the only one qualified to discuss or deny what he was asking. Poole sighed. "Join the CSA?" he suggested.

Sandy nodded. "I can tell you all kinds of things once you join."

"I'll want to fast-track it to the FSA. Like Amirah."

A smile escaped Sandy's control, but she shut it down fast. "Sure. Just make sure you pass CSA prelim psych tests first."

"Piece of cake."

"Why FSA Poole?" asked Danya. "Why not just CSA?"

"Kids interest me," said Poole, looking down at little Sunita in his arms. "Music interests me. Turns out nature and wildlife interest me too, within reason. And killing people from the League interests me considerably. That's mostly a Feddie job." Sunita stirred again. "And you, little bumpkin," he told her, "aren't gonna know nothing about it."

Professor Gao Dan did not expect to find Sandy waiting in her office. She did a fast double-take and recovered herself commendably well.

"Commander Kresnov! I don't believe we've met in person. I wasn't told you were coming."

"There's a reason for that," said Sandy, sitting in the chair beside the professor's desk. The desk sat before a wide window overlooking the grassy grounds of Rao University, one of Tanusha's five most prestigious. Professor Dan was head of League Studies in the InterSystem Relations Department, and had been for three years since she'd arrived from the League. "Please, take a seat."

"Actually I'm expecting a guest. I've a meeting here with the Ambassador to Jade, and . . ."

"That meeting will not be taking place," Sandy said calmly. "I'm here instead."

"Oh," said Dan. Evidently doing fast calculations in her head. She'd had ambassadorial postings herself, back in League, and the procedures were not so different in the Federation. "Well, in that case, can I offer you some refreshment?"

"No, thank you. Please, a seat."

Dan put her briefcase on her desk and sat. A plain woman, dark suit, straight hair, no makeup. Every inch the unremarkable professor of what had once been known as International Relations, until interstellar travel had made planetary systems, not nations, the primary decisive actor on the stage of human affairs.

Sandy had selected dark pants, boots, and a black leather jacket. Suits did not really work on her, but she'd wanted something that said "authority." Black leather somehow worked where shoulder pads did not. For such a formal effect, her still-too-short hair now played the part, neatly combed, a striking blonde contrast to the black.

"Professor Dan," she said, "we have a situation. Your friends in the League's Internal Security Organisation have gone and done something completely unacceptable, launching two attacks within this city, causing the deaths of nine CSA personnel and one Callayan citizen."

"Well," said Dan, taking a breath to prepare herself for argument, "if you would present me with the evidence of your accusation, I could take it to the relevant officials and see if I can get a formal response for you . . ."

"We have League GIs in custody," Sandy interrupted. "Captured alive. I wasn't making an accusation, I was stating a fact."

Dan shifted uncomfortably. "If that is your position."

"Now, it was an act quite similar to this one that led to the League Embassy being shut down on this world," Sandy continued, "and the League losing all official use of diplomatic privileges and contacts with the Federation capital. Federal Security and our elected masters in the Grand Council find it quite disconcerting that this behaviour should continue, despite the Federation's previously clear assertion that we would not tolerate any more acts of this kind."

"I understand your position," said Dan.

"Well, I wonder if you really do." Sandy shifted forward to the edge of her seat, forearms on knees. "You see, Federal Security's position on these matters has become quite tough, as has the CSA's. Callay keeps getting attacked, you see, and just demanding that it stop does not appear to work. So lately, you may be aware, we've been arranging for some of the perpetrators of these attacks to . . . well, to disappear." She kept her gaze quite calm and level. "Not just the actual agents, but the organisers behind them. People who wear comfortable suits and work in nice offices."

She looked around at the Professor's office. Dan was sweating, eyes darting. There was a reason Sandy had been sent to perform this task. She did not particularly enjoy it; she had no quarrel with the professor personally. But then, conflicts between planetary systems, as Dan taught well to her students every day, had little to do with personal feelings.

"I've been aware of several reports, yes," Dan admitted. "Commander Kresnov, please be assured that I have absolutely no contact with the ISO on operational matters, or on most other matters. It's not like I'm running a . . . a fully-fledged embassy here . . ."

"Oh, I know that," Sandy cut her off. "But like I said, I'm not sure that you do understand our position. Our position is that the ISO are clearly not deterred by our previous threats. Now, there are several broad strands of thought as to how to deal with this, in the FSA. Some say that we should retaliate directly against known League operatives here in Tanusha. People like yourself." Dan swallowed. "We know you had nothing to do with it personally, but the ISO organisers themselves are quite proficient at remaining unseen, especially in light of our new measures, and the people who actually organised *these* attacks are doubtless many light-years away in the League. We can hope that by retaliating against people like you, that it may at least upset League government enough that they crack down on the ISO themselves; after all they were quite upset with the ISO last time too, most of them hadn't expected to lose their embassy here so suddenly to ISO activities they hadn't directly authorised.

"But then others make the case that action against just *any* League operatives would be pointless, partly because we here in the Federation pride ourselves on killing the *right* people, not just any people, and partly because after the retaliatory expulsion of *our* embassy in the League, we too have been relying upon unofficial Federation figures in the League to act as our unofficial embassy staff, to maintain contacts between Federation and League. Anything we do to you would just be done in turn to our people in the League, and that would be criminal negligence on our part toward our own people."

Dan nodded nervously. "Not an unreasonable assumption, I'm sad to say."

"So here's what I've been sent to tell you today," said Sandy. "Firstly, be aware that all our local security apparatus are now extremely suspicious. Of course you're aware that we constantly track who you and your colleagues are meeting with. Best that you scale back the scope and sensitivity of your meetings. You're all on very thin ice, and if we suspect even the hint of threat in planning or purpose, we may act suddenly and unexpectedly against any of you. As a new mother myself, I can personally guarantee the safety of your families—should any of our people touch your families, I'll deal with them myself. Our people know that, and they're not that dumb. But everyone else is now on warning. Am I understood?"

Professor Dan nodded shortly. "Very well understood."

"Secondly, please convey this circumstance, and our displeasure with it, to your League masters. Tell them to rein in the ISO before they upset our politicians so much that someone decides to restart the war. Those are the words of Director Ibrahim of the FSA, not mine."

Another nod. "I'll tell them."

"And thirdly, please convey to everyone that these aggressive League actions shall not go unanswered. We in the security agencies are not in the business of table thumping and accusing others of risking wars by their actions—that's what politicians are for. We understand the difference between a covert action and an act of war. But because we understand that difference, we can promise that the League will now be answered in kind. You attacked us twice, and so you have two attacks coming to you."

Professor Dan blinked at her. "Attacks?"

Sandy nodded. "Two attacks. They will be planned at the highest level and will strike somewhere in League space that you least expect. Be reminded that we have assets now that we did not have just a few years ago. We will strike security-related targets only, which is better than you've done in killing an innocent lawyer just now. And we expect that you shall repay us the same courtesy once we're done of not declaring these attacks to be acts of war, as we've restrained ourselves with you. Should there be more attacks on our territory and our people in the meantime, our replies shall increase accordingly."

"I see," said the Professor. "When should I say these attacks are due?"

"Any time," said Sandy. "Also, please inform your masters that we are currently debating whether or not political figures should be considered a part of League security infrastructure."

Professor Dan shook her head. "I'm sorry, are you saying that you're considering assassinating League politicians?"

"No," said Sandy. "The political establishment is large. Security targets are not necessarily elected, in fact, the most significant ones usually are not. Will you tell them?"

CHAPTER FIFTEEN

Ibrahim took off his shoes and walked barefoot in the sand. His job took him to strange places, and beautiful places, but rarely places as beautiful as this. He stood on a long, curling beach, white sands receding down to the cool water, where aqua blue turned to deep ocean green. Above the beach, the land was thick with palms and other trees. The bay ended just nearby at a headland, a rocky outcrop upon which nested various birds and batwings. Beyond the headland, another long beach. And it was all nearly deserted, save for the recent descent of a hypersonic VTOL onto a small clearing in the trees behind the headland.

His entourage this trip was small—two pilots, Ambassador Ballan and one trusted member of his staff, Agent Ruben, and Commander Rice. And her husband Phillippe. Curious choice that was. The two pilots were both GIs, highly trusted and valued members of the Federal Security Agency for several years now. The indigenous synthetics had to be represented by someone, and of their two seniors, Captain Chu was too busy, and Commander Kresnov had been given the choice and had declined to come.

"Better not tell the rest of the galaxy about the Callayan relocation program," Agent Ruben suggested, sunglasses on, looking around. "They'll all sign up."

Ibrahim smiled. Ruben looked as out of place as he did, in his city suit, shoes in hand. Only Ibrahim was perhaps a little more comfortable shoeless, and the sand reminded him of hot pavings at the mosque. That same sensation of needing to hurry, yet that given the surroundings, one should take one's time.

"I do hope they like it," he admitted. "You have no idea the difficulties obtaining environmental clearance for a secret facility."

"Right," said Ruben, frowning. "How do those pointy-headed little bureaucrats approve environmental clearance for something they're not allowed to see or know the purpose of?"

"I'm afraid that shall have to remain a great mystery."

"You didn't get a clearance did you? You just built it." Ibrahim only smiled. "We've got to be a hundred kilometers from the nearest settlement. Who's gonna know?"

"Someone, eventually," said Ibrahim. "It's only temporary, to buy us some time. And there's the question of orbital surveillance and lone adventurers touring these islands. If it buys us six months we'll be happy." Though of course, orbital surveillance could be altered, if one were the FSA. And lone adventurers spotted in advance and diverted.

Commander Rice's presence was not entirely formal, though it was certainly of use to have the FSA combat arm represented. More than that, she was here on doctor's orders and had been told to stay on a few days and relax. But Vanessa Rice being Vanessa Rice, she was already in her swimsuit and now swam out upon the reef in the mid-shallows with snorkel and fins. Her husband was with her, a necessity if she were to be gone for more than twelve hours, and now swam with her, duck-diving for a closer look at the reef below. He'd been involved in the major security incident four months ago that had led to the closure of the League Embassy and had acquired a security clearance by necessity from that incident plus his relationship to Commander Rice. The psychs said he was little risk so long as he and she were together. Hopefully the relationship would last.

"So how is Chandi?" he asked Ruben. He'd been working on the flight down and hadn't really had time to talk to his old friend. He'd recruited Ruben a little over ten years ago now, when Ruben was a young kid making trouble and getting rich in the Tanushan underground. Such young kids needed choices, Ibrahim had been certain, and were far from lost to notions of civic virtue. With guidance, they could become civic assets. It was a policy he'd continued until his final day as CSA Director—one that his successor was now, word had it, contemplating to change.

"You know, he's handling the pressures very well," said Ruben in that familiar, offhanded drawl of his. "I mean, for a while there it was looking like he was losing control of the left side here, just above the ear?" He gestured to that part of his hair. "But then he attacked it aggressively with conditioner and some truly impressive comb work, and it's settled down nicely since."

Ibrahim smiled broadly. There were those who'd never warmed to Ruben's humour, often he tugged the prophet's beard quite hard. But Ibrahim had always enjoyed it, even when, second-hand, he'd heard it aimed at himself.

"And is there a symmetry between Chandi's hairstyles and his management techniques?"

Ruben sighed. "I wish. Maybe I'm just biased. It was better with you."

"I hear he makes fast decisions."

"*Oh*, yeah," Ruben agreed drily. "He's an administrative chainsaw. Doesn't like too much deliberation."

"He was quite recently a field agent. An excellent one. He was always outspoken against too much delay and deliberation."

"A man of action."

Ibrahim nodded. "Quite so."

"It's not causing too much trouble now," said Ruben. "But it will. It's probability theory again, you flip a coin a hundred times, the odds say most likely you'll get a pretty even spread of heads and tails, within 55-45. Anything more than sixty-forty is statistically unlikely. But a guy like Chandi comes in with fixed opinions and won't deliberate, and he's tough and he won't let go once he's latched onto something. A man of action won't just wait for feedback from his policies, he'll double down every chance."

"He'll flip a head every time," Ibrahim surmised.

"Exactly. And so you get a probability spread like 80-20, or 90-10, and the balance is gone. And that's how institutions get themselves into trouble."

"On some matters, firmness works," Ibrahim disagreed. "What distinguishes human institutions from random nature is that we *make* things happen. A doctor in a hospital does not leave patient survival to random chance, he stacks the odds. That's the thing that has freed human civilisation from the tyranny of natural randomness."

"Sure, when the question is 'would you rather granny lived or died?' that's easy," Ruben replied. "But the stuff we deal with is never that simple."

Ibrahim glanced at the younger man. "If you're unhappy in the CSA, I'm certain a place could be found for you in the FSA."

Ruben sighed. "Well, that's . . . that's nice, seriously. But you know me, I'm a Tanushan, my skills are best where they are, and civil security just isn't the FSA's field."

"Your work in Anjula was superb. Commendation worthy, if we were allowed to admit what you were doing."

"And I was *so* glad to come home," said Ruben. "No offence, but if you want to recruit me to do more jobs like Anjula, I pass. Tanusha's my city, it's where I belong."

"We'll see," said Ibrahim, gazing across the cool green ocean. "We'll see just where the FSA's capabilities and interests expand. This current institutional overlap may have interesting consequences."

Ruben looked suspicious. "You're planning something."

"Not planning. Anticipating."

"There's a difference?"

"Yes," said Ibrahim. "I anticipate rain but cannot plan for it. Rain will do what it does."

"Speaking of anticipating, sir, have you seen these crazy sociologist predictives Chandi's authorised?"

Ibrahim nodded. "I have."

"Excuse my language, but this stuff is all fucked up."

"I'm aware of your objections."

Ruben gazed at him. "You read my reports? My CSA reports?"

"I still keep tabs on the organisation. On matters concerning."

Ruben exhaled in relief. "Thank God! You don't like it either."

"Not liking it, and finding it within one's authority to act against it, are two different things. My jurisdiction is the Federation; Callayan local matters are out of my hands."

"You don't think some bright spark in Psych will start pushing to take the program Federal? Sir, this is some of the scariest stuff I've seen in all my time above ground. They've got it figured so they're convinced uplinks are causing dangerous sociological phenomena everywhere, and they're only looking for evidence that proves it because we're a security organisation, not an objective think tank, and results that aren't dangerous don't interest us. So surprise surprise, that's what they find—it's a structurally self-proving theory."

"They may yet be proven right, there are turning out to be far greater sociological implications of all uplink technology than we had previously figured."

"But they don't *know*! They're interpreting data without the tools to analyse what they're seeing, so *every* phenomena may be perceived as dangerous. And once you get into that mindset, every phenomena can become any excuse to crack down, to lock up, hell, maybe to knock off anyone who's acting funny . . . because like Chandi always tells me, we're a security organisation, Ari, it's what we *do*." With great sarcasm.

Ibrahim nodded slowly, thinking. It was nothing he hadn't thought himself at length. But there were alternatives to consider. To *deliberate*, that thing that Chandrasekar hated to do, though perhaps not quite as much as Ruben accused. And, the fact that he simply didn't have the influence within the CSA that he once had.

"I will consider options," he said. "And observe outcomes."

"You could declare this network psych profiling a Federal security risk and shut it down."

"I could. But that would have consequences too, some of them possibly worse. All we can do is watch and be ready. But know that if you have vital information and find all other doors shut, mine will always be open." He shifted his sunglasses down his long nose for a meaningful stare at Ruben. Quietly, he meant. Ruben nodded with evident relief.

"Yes. Good." He ran hands through short, wavy hair. "Thank you, sir." Only Ruben, Ibrahim mused, would express such relief at being asked to spy on his own organisation against a vital secret program. But then, Ruben had loyalty to principles, more even than institutions, places, or people. Ibrahim had nurtured Ruben as long as he had, and put up with all of his irregularities, because he felt that loyalty to principles, in this work, was the single most important thing there was.

If only he could tell Ruben what he one day hoped the younger man might become. But he knew that if Ruben saw a destiny being planned for him by others, he'd run from it as fast as he could.

The flyers arrived with little warning, two big military models, CSA registered. They roared overhead and circled, aiming back to the hypersonic jet in the clearing amidst the trees. Ibrahim and Ruben walked back, a slow trudge through soft white sand.

When they arrived, both flyers were down and the blowing sand already clearing, engines winding down and cargo doors open at the back. Ambassador Ballan, his aide, and the two GI-pilots were already waiting, as new arrivals walked from the flyers in old military jumpsuits or greens with the duffle bags and backpacks that were probably all they owned in the world. With weapons and other military equipment banned, they weren't left with much.

The first of them reached Ballan's group before Ibrahim and Ruben arrived. With any other arrivals, that breach of protocol might have alarmed Ibrahim, but with these he didn't think it mattered. And it gave him longer to look them over, as Ballan talked and the rest of the arrivals assembled behind. An equal mix of men and women, no great variation in stature, an equal racial spread and collage of skin colours. All apparently young and attractive, with athletic builds and erect postures. They might have been a team of athletes on their way to a sporting competition.

He arrived, and Ballan turned to introduce him. "Director Ibrahim, these are Kiet and Rishi. Kiet, Rishi, this is Director Shan Ibrahim of the Federal Security Agency. And Agent Ariel Ruben, an investigator with the Callayan Security Agency."

They shook hands with both. Kiet was East Asian–featured, with a sour twist to his mouth. He'd shot himself, Ibrahim had read in Cassandra's report, after leading the failed assault to free the remaining corporate GIs on Droze. Rishi looked South Asian, attractive like all combat GIs, wide cheekbones, short hair. She was Chancelry, high designation but young, had led the revolt that freed the Chancelry GIs. Kiet was a lower but still high designation, and much older, a former League soldier abandoned by the League withdrawal that preceded the crash. That experience meant he ought to be the smarter, like Rhian Chu had become smart, "only" a 39 series but now surpassing most young mid-40s. But Cassandra mistrusted Kiet's judgement, with apparent good reason.

"You're Kresnov's friend," said Rishi to Ruben. "You were in orbit; you came to help."

Ruben nodded. "But actually, we're both Cassandra's friends." With a nod at Ibrahim. "It's just that he's a *Director*, you see, of some big organisation whose name I forget, and he has to pretend to be impartial to everyone."

Rishi looked a little puzzled but saw them both smiling, and began to smile herself. As though slowly working through the joke. Young GIs were like that.

"And where is Cassandra?" asked Kiet. He spoke as though he had a mouth full of cotton wool, but clear enough.

"She's busy," said Ibrahim. "We thought that a personal greeting by the Director of the Federation's primary security agency, and by the President of the Grand Council's Intelligence Committee should be sufficient."

Kiet smiled drily. "Most appreciative." He didn't look all that happy. Intel had prepared them for that, too. He looked around. "It's hot here."

"After Pantala I imagine that must be a shock," said Ballan, a tall, enigmatic former-Brazilian, his parents had emigrated to Nova Esperenza when he was a child. "Don't worry, it turns out heat is better for GI physiology than cold, and heat means you have to drink more—the fruit drinks here have to be tasted to be believed, they're delicious. Would you like a tour?"

There were thirty GIs in total, they'd come down at a high-security Fleet airbase at Denver on the southern continent of Argasuto, four hundred kilometers south of this, the Maldari archipelago. This first thirty would soon be followed by two hundred and six others, once Kiet and Rishi established that the Feds had kept their end of the deal.

Ballan and Ibrahim led them on a walk up the sandy main road, where packed earth foundations were already surrounded by piles of precisely cut timber and pre-fab fittings. Lots of trees had been left, making lots of shade, and in several places were imported recyclers to keep the surroundings pristine and provide all the water they needed. Power in this weather was solar all year long.

"How long does it take to build a house?" Rishi wondered, eyeing the deconstructed kits.

"Inexperienced builders might take sixty days for ten people to build one house," said Ballan. Much of the organisation for this had taken place amongst his personal staff, so he was intimately informed. "Experienced builders, probably less than thirty. So each house can take eight people, so thirty-five houses for all of you . . . the whole lot shouldn't take you much more than two months. GI strengths being what they are, probably less."

"One month," said Kiet. "We learn fast. And it doesn't take us as long to move heavy things."

"No," Ballan agreed with pleasure, walking with a slight limp from the assassination attempt by Pyeongwha radicals four months ago. "I'm sure you'll develop your own methods for doing it faster. I'll be intrigued to see updates as you progress."

Ballan brought them around a corner of thick trees and flowering bushes, to a house that had been built earlier by the military contractors who'd done the work so far. Mostly timber, it stood off the ground on stilts, storage and generator below, a wide balcony above, nice timber floors, big windows, and a second storey for three total. Tasteful and homely, it reminded Ibrahim of holiday bungalows he'd stayed in with Radha and the children, when they'd all been much younger. The GIs looked mostly very pleased, no doubt it was a significant upgrade from their previous accommodation. And the surroundings even more so. They'd be in tents for as long as it took them to build, and then this. For pure material advancement, it seemed a good deal . . . if material advancement was all one was seeking.

Most GIs remained behind with the pilots, Ruben, and Ballan's assistant, while Ballan and Ibrahim walked on with Kiet and Rishi to the pagoda and the Krishna temple that had preceded any development here. Priests in saffron robes greeted them—there were many in these wilds, happy in contemplative isolation. These included former senior CSA Agent Rohit Gupta, to whom they now introduced both GIs, grey now with a long beard, well more than a century old and still fit and lean with a combination of technological assistance and sparse, healthy living. It was not an uncommon thing for elderly Callayans to spend their final years in spiritual contemplation, and Gupta had been very pleased at the prospect of sharing that contemplation with a new flock of innocents, however it interfered with his isolation. He and his priests would stay long enough to impart as much enlightenment as possible on the new arrivals, and then any who wished for isolation once more could always move on to one of Callay's countless other deserted islands, coastlines, or mountains.

"Nice touch," said Kiet, as they sat beneath the pagoda and sipped delicious, cool fruit drinks the priests gave them. "Having us make the houses ourselves. Gives us a sense of ownership and control."

"And simplified our logistics considerably," Ballan reminded him with a finger raised against cynicism. "Finding reliable contractors who were not a security risk was hard. Having them hang around for months longer building houses would increase the risk."

"Who else knows?" asked Rishi.

"As few as possible," said Ibrahim. "We'll keep it that way for as long as possible."

"And then what?" Kiet asked tiredly. "How long do we sit in this . . . very attractive prison cell we're assisting you to build around us with our own hands?"

"The sentence is a short one," Ballan said reasonably. "We needed a window to manage relations with the League, and you were in the way. Respectfully. Now we have the Chancelry data on League's various sociological dysfunctions that you were sitting on, and we can attempt further negotiations on their collective resolution. League don't want events on Pantala advertised widely; they'd take that as a hostile position, so for their sake and ours, we need to keep you quiet for a while. And so this." He gestured around. "Your attractive prison cell. But be assured, the situation with the League is fluid and fast moving. The circumstances that force you to be here are constantly changing. It's possible you may be free to leave sooner than you think."

"And then asylum?" Rishi asked. "Should we want it?"

"Asylum for three hundred would cause a large stir," Ballan said cautiously. "But yes, it's the logical next step."

"And our hospital cases? You can guarantee their security in Tanusha?"

"They'll receive the best care at secure facilities, yes," said Ballan. "We can fly you up yourself personally, if you want, on a covert trip to see Tanusha and see that their facilities are what we say." He looked at Kiet, whose mood seemed unimproved. "Kiet. Your concerns?"

"We gave up a lot for this," said Kiet. "Not physically. But we didn't do this to have nice houses on a beach. It was a revolution, and we were fighting our fight. We'd done them damage, we'd gained control over the means of our own production, in Chancelry at least. And then we gave it up. To be comfortable."

"You had the illusion of power and control," said Ballan with a directness that Ibrahim found impressive. "The Federation's arrival was the only thing keeping you alive. League tried to nuke you. If we weren't there, you and all the inhabitants of Droze would be dead, your rebellion a cloud of radioactive dust."

Kiet gazed away, past the temple and into the trees.

"The powerful have control," Ballan continued. "You may not like it, but that is how it is. The Federation controlled that situation and held your lives and the fate of your rebellion in our hand. We found value in a deal with you, and we shall keep our end of that bargain—you have many friends here who will ensure we do. You fought the impossible fight, and you survived and gained a strategic advantage with the greatest human power. You sit now speaking directly to the head of its preeminent security agency, and the third in total rank in the Grand Council. This is not nothing.

"Your mistake is that you presume that your battle is over. Do not view this as an ending, Kiet. This is a beginning. There lie many moves ahead of you, depending on what you choose as your path. What is your path?"

"Emancipation," said Kiet, eyes burning. "Total. Unconditional."

"You have it here," said Ballan. "The Federation allows you to be whatever you choose."

"Not just for me. For all of us, all GIs. All synthetics. Most of them remain in the League."

"Alas, we do not have jurisdiction over the League. And we will not fight a war for emancipation in foreign territories, however much we may wish it."

"Then like I said, I feel I'm in the wrong place."

Ballan gazed at him for a long moment. This, Ibrahim thought, was the crux of the emerging game. The only force in human space that could bring about synthetic emancipation was the Federation Grand Council. Those who supported using that force for emancipation would welcome Kiet and Rishi's presence here. Those who did not, would not. And this game, he knew well, could easily become far more dangerous than just a contest of political number counting. Those who did not want to renew tensions with the League would prevent it at any cost.

The gravity of the moment was interrupted by a small, attractive woman in a swimsuit, dripping wet and carrying her fins and mask. "Rishi!" she said brightly, and went to the GI and hugged her.

They'd talked a little over coms while Vanessa was in orbit over Pantala, Ibrahim recalled. Rishi looked surprised at the embrace, which was also making her clothes wet. Vanessa repeated it with Kiet, even though their relations, Ibrahim guessed, would be significantly less.

"You have to come and look at the coral!" Vanessa continued. "It's amazing; there's so many fish, and it's so close to the surface the colours are so bright!"

"Coral?" asked Rishi. "In the water?"

"You've never swam in the ocean?"

Rishi blinked. "I've never swam at all. And I've no equipment."

Vanessa waved a dismissive hand. "You're a GI, you don't need equipment. Just wear your underwear, hold your breath, and open your eyes underwater . . . you do *wear* underwear, don't you? Not that that would matter either, but you're pretty hot and I don't want my husband getting ideas."

Rishi blinked at the men. Ballan waved his arm toward the ocean. "Go!" he announced. "A great adventure. I envy you being able to do these things for the first time."

Vanessa put an arm around Rishi's shoulders and led her down the steps toward the beach. "You ever heard a real violinist before? Phillippe's a professional musician. He brought his violin and we're staying a few days, so he'll play you some things too, all of you."

"It would be so seductive, wouldn't it?" said Kiet, watching them go. "To live a good life, to forget that there are any other people in the universe but yourself? But they suffer even now. Even Kresnov, with her three new children. Does she recall how many poor street children are *left* in Droze? All just as sweet and deserving as her three."

"And so she should have left her three behind?" asked Ibrahim. "Forget her life's duty to care for those dear to her and dissolve all purpose in guilt because those few are not many?"

"She has a duty to her kind," Kiet said stubbornly. "All synthetics are bound by a common fate, whether she accepts it or not."

"She has argued precisely that in high Federation councils for longer than the concept has occurred to you," Ibrahim said coolly.

"And yet now she abandons us."

"Only in your imagination. She exhorts you not to lean on her so much and frees herself from the burdens of a leadership that you have already once rejected." Kiet's nostrils flared. "And she follows her own duty to care for those she loves. If that does not currently include *you*, Kiet, then I suggest that that is more your problem than hers."

CHAPTER SIXTEEN

"I saw the Education Department PACs for all three of you," said Ari. "Hope you don't mind, Sandy let me look."

"That's okay, she asked us first," said Danya. "Seemed like a good idea."

They were walking from a small suburban parking spot, one Danya suspected was reserved for apartment dwellers, but Ari had hacked it and made the system park his cruiser, something about not trusting the main city grids. Now they were walking across a small bridge, the river gleaming in the light of towers beyond, a tourist barge churning slowly below.

"The first thing you need to know," said Ari, "is that the Tanushan Education Department's a bunch of fascist thugs who'd brain wipe every child into a mindless little automaton if they could get away with it. So if you don't like their action report, you don't have to implement it. Tell them to go fuck themselves."

Danya knew there was a reason he'd been looking forward to hanging out with Ari. Sandy had told him much the same thing but without the direct personal experience to back it up. Ari had actually been a child once, had been through this system, and was very clear on what he didn't like and why. The Education Department's Psych Active Construct was one of those things.

"The department guy said not taking the tape could limit our opportunities to get an education," Danya said.

"Look, every child in Tanusha's got a right to an education, the department can't stop that though I'm sure they'd like to, and whatever the active construct tells them of a kid's defective personality, they can't order corrective tape if you don't want it. Even guardians are limited in what they can order their kids to take; kids have rights too."

"Is the construct right?"

Ari made a face, hands in pockets, looking up at the towers that loomed above. "Right in what? Right in defining distinct tendencies in certain personality types? Sure, but the construct's just a tool, it can say this person has a tendency for violence in certain situations, this person gets claustrophobic in crowds, this person struggles to tell the truth . . . but so what? The real problem is how institutions interpret that data, I mean, do we go about neutralising every off-center personality to the point that we lose the advantages of social diversity? I mean, shit, look at me, I'm a paranoid little fuck and a screwup in relationships, but I'd say those qualities are a large part of my success. Maybe if they'd tape-corrected my personality flaws at an early age I'd be some fucking drone in a bank somewhere who gets a hard-on from currency fluctuation predictive constructs."

Danya thought about it, looking at the reflections on the river. A cluster of pretty girls walked by, all legs, heels, and giggles. Ari walked backward to look a bit longer. "The construct predictives say I've got borderline post-traumatic stress disorder. Svet too."

"Well, CSA runs a dozen routines that take the edge off without doing the complete unbuttoning the department's recommending."

"I don't know that I even want to take the edge off," said Danya. "I mean, sure, I wake up sometimes in the middle of the night sweating. And I get nightmares and stuff. But a few times in Droze I woke up for no real reason and found we really did have to move, that something dangerous was happening and if I hadn't woken up, we might not have moved in time."

Ari frowned. "Look, I'm sure we can get rid of the nightmares without you losing your edge."

"But what if I get the tape, and then it's too late? I mean, they can't predict exactly what it'll do, right?"

"Deep reflex is hard to bury," said Ari, shaking his head. "You grow up with something, you take light corrective tape, it'll smooth it over for a week or two, but then the old reflexes will come back. Light tape's just for recent events, formative events get into structural memory, even the stuff the department wants you to take won't erase it."

"But it'll make it weaker."

Ari nodded. "Yeah. A lot weaker."

"Well, fuck that," said Danya. "Those reflexes have kept me alive the last five years. If I can't panic anymore, I'll panic."

Ari shook his head, smiling. And grasped Danya's shoulder. "You're completely screwed up, kid. Knew there was a reason I liked you."

"Sandy says it's not the trigger reflexes they should be worried about anyway," Danya added. "It's people. She said the biggest problem the department would have with us wasn't that we might get angry and hit someone, but that our . . . our collective survival instincts overrode any respect for authority. She said . . . what was it? She said the thing with us was that we had attitude, and corrective tape couldn't change an attitude."

"Well, shit, she's walking proof of that. She's the most dangerous collection of hair-trigger reflexes ever assembled, attitude's what holds it all together."

"Guy like you must reckon she'd make an awesome girlfriend," Danya suggested.

"Umm . . . yeah. Sure."

"So why'd you leave her?"

Ari smiled. "You get me drunk one night, I might tell you."

"How can I get you drunk? I can't buy alcohol for years."

"Exactly."

Ari took him to the Harihan hardware market, a collection of stalls in display-lit alleys where people who knew their stuff bought and assembled their electronics. Ari had spent a lot of time here as a kid, he explained, once he discovered how much more fun customisation was. And if you knew where to ask, you could get non-civilian parts too, for all kinds of stuff, largely illegal, but there were basement labs where Tanushan techs reverse-engineered everything up to Fleet military processors and micro-nets.

"It's a good place to start for investigators," he told Danya, ducking through open stalls of interlocking holographics that fed the images of passing shoppers back at them, to disorienting effect. "People up to no good usually need customised hardware. You know the right people, get them in your little black book, you can trace down all kinds of stuff."

"The smart ones only tell you ninety percent though," said Danya, looking over a row of wearable opti-cam vests, edging past the steady stream of customers. Volume from nearby entertainment units boomed and crashed. "Droze didn't make stuff like this; we had shitty civilian tech, but the military stuff was good and there was lots of it. The arms markets guys were all informing to the corporations on ninety percent of their customers but made the real money off the top ten percent, those they didn't inform on. Home Guard and big Rimtown bosses, usually."

Ari nodded, looking at him thoughtfully. "Here it's more like five percent

". . . but yeah, they run like double agents, they pretend to inform but let the big fish slip through. So you have to know who the big fish are."

"Then you catch your informant dealers lying to you and they'll owe you, or else you can charge them." Danya picked some acti-gloves that went with a vest, tried one on.

"Exactly. Christ, a thirteen-year-old who knows this stuff better than most cops."

"Not really. I mean, I'm only guessing about what happens when you charge people. In Droze an informant caught out just turned up dead." He made shapes with the acti-glove, and a opti-cam vest's display activated, changing shape and colour like a chameleon. "What did you do here as a civilian kid?"

"Oh, all kinds of stuff."

"What kinds of stuff?"

"Well . . . as a young kid I got kicks making surveillance stuff, bugs, drones, that kind of thing."

Danya looked up at him. "You made surveillance drones?"

Ari scratched his jaw and glanced around. "Um, yeah . . . you know the little micros, buzz through windows, up drainpipes."

"I hate those."

"Come on." Ari kept him moving, putting the glove back. Danya wondered how many people around here knew him on sight, and how fast that word would spread. But then again, Ari wouldn't have so many friends in these places if being his friend wasn't valuable. "So that caught a few people's attention, and I made some money on that."

"How old were you?"

"Maybe twelve. Don't get any ideas, kid, Sandy would kill me."

"I'm not the tech, that's Kiril." The shelves of product, displays, sound and visuals were nearly overwhelming. But with Ari here, his nerves were holding fine, and he didn't jump at every new distraction. Ari knew this place and would know if anything was wrong. Besides, everyone seemed to be having so much fun, gangs of techno-buffs oohing and aahing over the latest gear. "What else did you make?"

"Oh, I got bored with making stuff; I'm not much of a tech either. But selling to a few of these people made me realise what's really valuable in Tanusha—information. And for that you need the net, and net access . . . which you're not legal for until you're eighteen."

"When did you get yours?"

"Fifteen."

"What did your parents say?"

"After I started making monthly deposits into their accounts of about half their annual salary, not a lot."

Next, Ari took Danya to the Doha District main maglev station. That was surprising, Danya hadn't thought a transit hub would be a great hangout for Tanusha's techno underground, but Ari got them a table at an upper-level café beneath the massive open atrium with retail and walkways on all sides, where they watched the flowing streams of thousands, tens of thousands of people, up and down the travelators, flowing in and streaming out, from the maglev line below to the underground metro lines beneath that, to the adjoining light monorail lines, the auto-taxi ranks, and up to the cruiser ranks above.

"Any place like this on Droze?" Ari asked as they drank coffee, and Danya looked down into the artificial canyon, then above to the transparent ceiling and night sky, all alive with light and motion. Cruisers were leaving off the rank one level above, beyond glass walls, engines thrumming, people queuing to climb in, others climbing out. Shops everywhere up and down the multiple levels, restaurants, cafés like this one, and the constant roar of a thousand conversations above the hum of departing trains, the electronic chime of announcements, the clatter of footsteps, and the clink of nearby cups.

"Fuck no," said Danya. "It's amazing."

Ari studied his face, a glint in his eyes. "You love it, yeah? All this stuff?" Danya repressed a smile, but denying it wouldn't work. Ari saw. "There's nothing like a great city, Danya. Nothing in all the universe. People think I'm a tech head or a net geek or whatever they want to call it, but I'm not really. Mostly I just love this." He nodded to the great artificial construction before them. "Cities. This one in particular. I just want to dive into it and bury myself in it. Always have."

Danya nodded to himself, sipping coffee. Looking around. A level below them, the entire side walkway was casino entry, a big glass front with inbuilt water features reflecting hyper-colourful displays showing all the excitement within.

"The tower above us is a casino, yeah?" he asked.

Ari nodded. "First five floors. The rest is a five-star hotel, lots of casino guests stay there."

"I don't know why you've brought me here, but I'm guessing it's got something to do with the casino." Ari smiled, encouragement for him to continue. "Lots of people passing through, this would be a major info hub, lots of signal IDs, lots of constructs on the net."

"And?"

"Casinos would have massive net barriers. I mean . . . with all these net hackers like you in this city, the potential for them to lose money to fraud is just . . ."

"Huge, yes. Though just quietly, they used to pay guys like me as additional security too. Do you think a high-traffic place like this would be safer or more dangerous? If someone was after you?"

Danya thought about it. Hiding in plain sight? That sometimes worked in Droze . . . but rarely, because kids got noticed just for being kids. It would be nice to think you could lose yourself in a crowd like this, but . . . "More dangerous," he said.

"Why?"

"I just reckon that if everyone's after information, places like this would be where you'd get it. And that casino would be keeping tabs on everyone who passes by or monitors the traffic."

Ari nodded "Yep. I can't show you because you need uplinks to see it, but the casinos run intercepts on every passerby, just a precaution. But anyone transitioning from the casino matrix to the main grid leaves an imprint; there's a government intermediary program that traces everyone because individuals can ID switch behind the casino barriers, they're that powerful, and all these shady characters getting tailed by cops or government agents go up to casinos, switch IDs, and come out again as someone else. So with that many handoffs between different grids, different systems, if you're a clever little observer like me, places like this are great to run programs that leech off one or another barrier system, you can pick up all kinds of traces of ID imprints from constructs moving between grids."

"No idea what any of that means," Danya told him.

"Doesn't matter. Just know that if you're ever in trouble, stay away from places like this. Crowds won't hide you, they'll amplify any signal you make into an echo that can be heard across the city."

"How could I make a signal? I'm not uplinked."

"AR glasses." Ari pointed, Danya had them in his pocket. "Anything that interfaces with the net, even if you don't think it's active, there's programs that can query it, make it respond even if it's turned off. I'll show you how to make it run silent. One signal here can multiply a thousand times off all these query programs."

"I know why you guys come here," said Danya, watching the passing human streams. "You come here to steal IDs. I mean, look, if you can get imprints of net constructs, and I remember Sandy said visual ID was still hard, it wasn't published on most net constructs so even if you take over someone's construct you still don't know what they look like . . ."

"That's the basic security measure, yeah," Ari agreed.

"But here, with good vision or a minicam, you can match the person's location off the net from their transmissions, see their face, eye colour, height, race, everything. Run a high-intensity laser scan from the right spot you could probably even get a fingerprint. And then with all the biometric stuff to go with the net constructs, you've got everything to take over someone's life completely."

Ari sighed and sat back in his chair with a smile. "Wow. You're a natural, you're either going to become the hottest CSA agent since me or the biggest crime kingpin this city's ever seen. Either way I'll be so proud."

Danya had never thought about joining the CSA. A security agency? Security agencies meant authority over ordinary people, and that made them scary in ways only someone who'd been on the other end could appreciate. But Sandy worked for them, and Ari, and Vanessa. And it would be the obvious way to protect everyone he cared about. Although joining would mean he had to protect *everyone*, not just the few that really mattered. It seemed a hell of a leap.

"I'm beginning to think uplinks are overrated," he said. "I'm glad we're not on the net yet."

"Well, it's only a problem if you can't defend your connection, which most civvies can only do a little, but security and underground do really well."

Danya shook his head. "If I was ever in trouble, I'd stay well off the net. I know other ways to get by."

"Yeah? Like what?"

"Follow the money," said Danya. "Get paid in cash or trade. No one in Tanusha would suspect a kid of working under the radar, 'cause no kids here have those skills, or not many. We could fill a niche for some shady person who needed jobs done, we'd survive off the grid indefinitely without any net contact, and in a city this size no one would have a clue. We'd disappear."

Ari considered him for a moment. Then grinned. "And if your survival depended on offing someone in power, how would you go about that?"

"Well, you've gotta recon the situation first," said Danya, all seriousness. Ari's grin faded. "With basement manufacturing here, I imagine weapons are easy to get, and if you saved money you could probably pay someone else to do the net recon so we wouldn't need to, no need to tell them what it's for. And being kids, you know, we can get in places with no suspicion."

"You know I was kidding, right?" Ari looked a little worried.

Danya just looked at him. "There's no kidding where I'm from," he said.

The man on top of her could have been anyone, Sandy wasn't really in the mood for faces. Dark skin, for whatever subconscious reason she'd selected that, muscular and hard and lean, because bulk, as she'd told her grunts often enough, was not the same as fit . . . and he moved like he had a purpose, and some skill, and had some concept of what his actions felt like on the other end.

That wasn't her problem. Her problem was that the sensation receptors went out of balance as soon as the data spike began, and with her the data spike was pretty big. The primary sensation was good enough, and very real, but then as she grabbed him, and he thrust into her, the sweaty skin sensation on her hands fuzzed up, like static reception on her palms. Making realtime corrections in this state wasn't easy, but she readjusted the receptor flows and saw where the feed balances weren't regulating properly and patched it. But then the sheets against her back felt too smooth, slippery without texture, so she adjusted that, but now it felt like sandpaper. And now she could feel her actual sex drive kicking back against the VR, and the VR struggling to compensate as the serious sensation built up, and she gasped and arched her back . . . but dammit, now his breathing in her ear sounded like some dumb animal, and she *liked* that bit, the feel of a man gasping in her ear, but now she felt no lips, no chin-stubble, no sweet scent of aftershave . . .

She flipped him over and tried again. That minimised conflicting sensation receptors, her being on top, but now the mechanics of it meant she had to look him in the face . . . and he didn't really have one. Generic, maybe an athlete, maybe a rock star . . . she cycled through a range of possibilities, but while anonymous sex worked sometimes, she just liked it so much better with someone she knew and liked, only these days most of them were at work and ranked well below her, so she couldn't touch them. Unless they were GIs, where different fraternisation rules applied, but that now came with baggage all of its own . . .

Frustrated she tried it on hands and knees, and that worked well for a bit, but the thing she loved doing it this way, apart from the obvious, was the feel of his hands, grasping her waist, running up her back, grabbing her breast . . . and here, the fingers didn't bite, it was like being held by a corpse, and no amount of adjusting the data flows was helping. Even so, she was still getting somewhere, and when she braced herself and pushed back in rhythm, she figured this was going to be the one that worked best for her . . .

. . . and then her real visual pulled her out, the VR collapsing as suddenly she was back in her room, and Svetlana was running in.

"Sandy! Are you doing VR?"

She was sitting cross-legged on her bed and now unfolded herself with a sigh. "Yeah. What's up, Svet?" It was morning, pre-breakfast, and she was dressed and alone. VR never consumed enough of her brain space to let her forget that. Subconsciously, it was a killer.

"Danya called! He says he's on his way back, he said he had a great time and Ari got them a hotel room, but Ari didn't use it much, Danya says he only slept a bit himself then Ari took him out again this morning to see some stuff."

Sandy stretched. "That sounds great."

"He'll be back in ten minutes, he's on his way now . . . Sandy, can you ask Ari if he'd let me come out with him soon too?"

"Well, I might be Danya's guardian, Svet, but Danya's kind of yours and Kiri's. That's why I wanted him to go, think of it like a scouting mission."

"Sure, but I want to go too!"

"Ari's very busy with serious stuff, but I'm sure Danya's learned a lot, he could take you around." Plus, Danya could be shown this stuff and be relied upon to make sensible judgements on what to do with it. Sandy still worried that one day in this retail paradise, Svetlana would just see something she liked and take it, certainly she had the skills. But she'd spoken to Danya about it, and Danya wouldn't allow it, and Svetlana, happily, would never defy him. She held out a hand. "Come here, I want a cuddle."

Svetlana's cuddle, and then Danya's arrival home, cheered her up until she got out of the house, then the frustration came back. She was short and borderline irritable with people all morning at the CSA, where she checked out the expanded SWAT training facilities, which now included GIs, Poole among them. GIs mostly did combat training on their own, certainly there were no other trainees and precious few veteran SWATs who could match them. But non-combat was integrated, including SWAT's famous out-of-time techniques, which crammed a student with so many things to do within such a limited time, it was known to bring some to the point of nervous collapse. Particularly as there were no drill sergeants, no instructions, no one telling them what to do next—everything was self-motivated, and if you didn't check to see the ever-changing class times, or the next piece of schedule, or when the tests were due, you'd miss them and fail.

SWAT had no time for people who only functioned when others told them what to do. SWAT wanted people who could think independently and who never just assumed the predictability of routines. And lately, word had it, out-of-time had gotten even harder, because the inclusion of GIs with regular students was making it too easy.

She still found some minutes to borrow a trainer's office to have a brief word with Poole and see how he was doing. He seemed happy. "It's not so hard," he said. "You just have to pay attention. How about you, you look like crap. No sex?"

Sometimes she loved being a GI with other GIs. They just knew and didn't dance around it for fear of embarrassment. Vanessa was the only non-GI who did the same. "I'll be okay," she sighed. "It's not your problem."

"Well, you set the standard for all us synths, so it kind of is. Here, let me help." Just like that, reaching for her pants button.

"Help?" Incredulously, stopping him. This was Poole, so distracted from other people's mental states he'd barely notice if they were crying. "Help how?"

"I'll show you, look, don't waste time, I've only got a few minutes." Which bewildered her, but she *had* to see this if only to see Poole's definition of "help." And in a few seconds with the door locked, he had her pants off and with a *very* effective use of fingers and tongue . . . oh, *God*, where the *Hell* had he learned to do *This*?

It only took a few minutes, but she had orgasms so big he had to drag her into the middle of the room so she wouldn't smash the furniture as she thrashed. She convulsed and strained in a way that turned all her muscles to the literal density of steel and was probably quite unattractive, and certainly would have severely injured any non-GI partner, but Poole just wrestled her like a man wrestling a crocodile and kept going. It was all she could do to clamp a hand over her mouth to stop from screaming and bringing unwanted attention running.

And then, after number six or so, he stopped and grinned at her. "Sorry, that's it, I'm late." And dragged her to her feet, while she sank shakily against the desk, muscles slowly dissolving, and helped her back into her pants. "Look, Sandy, your brain isn't wired like any other GI alive, so you being abstinent for your kids and all, that's real sweet of you, but it's seriously not healthy . . ." he pointed to what they'd been doing on the floor. "That's not normal, even for you, and if you keep carrying that much tension around, with the structural damage you have in your past, I can tell you as a part-time medic you will do yourself an injury, core tension in GIs is nothing to mess with. So from now on, if you need a fuck, ask me, ask anyone, they won't mind, honest."

Sandy recovered enough to start laughing.

"What?" he asked.

"You. You're such a samaritan."

"What's a samaritan?"

"Look it up." She gave him a big hug. "Thank you, you're a true friend. Now go and try out that technique on your squad buddies, great way to make friends with fifty percent."

"Where do you think I learned it?" Poole told her, and departed with a wink. Sandy laughed all the way back to her cruiser, feeling completely awesome, and not just because of the orgasms.

"He's right, you know," said Vanessa, as they took a brief lunch break at FSA HQ's training facilities. This part was an office building simulation, five floors of it, realistic down to the potplants beside the office partitions. They sat in a particularly troublesome stairwell, in full armour, eating sandwiches amidst the plastic remains of simulated booby-trap covers. All urban troops hated stairwells, bottleneck deathtraps that they were, and the two of them were reinforcing that hatred in those under their command. The enclosed space smelled like explosive and burned rubber. "I'm technically an athlete, so I get a pretty decent sex drive, but I've only got half what you do. And GI muscles are so powerful, tension will be much worse too, you gotta let it out, and I know doing it yourself doesn't really do it for you, nor VR, so . . ."

"Fucking high maintenance," said Sandy around a mouthful, exasperated. "I can't have GI boys marching in and out of my bedroom all day, what would the kids think?"

"I don't know, they've seen some pretty far-out stuff, why would they care?"

"Vanessa, they need *normal*. Single parent, fine; single parent who runs FSA spec ops, fine; single parent who's a GI . . . bit weird, but okay. Single parent and cock addict? Seriously."

Vanessa laughed. "Get yourself a steady guy."

"None of the GIs do steady. And after four years with Ari I'm pretty sure I don't want a straight."

"I know, we don't fuck like GIs do . . ."

"*Not* just that," Sandy reprimanded, "I just . . . I don't know. I'm up to my neck in complicated. Relationships between GIs and straights are complicated. GIs and GIs are simple, I need that right now."

"Rhian and Rakesh aren't complicated."

"That's because Rhi's so gorgeously simple, and she picked a guy to match. They're not me."

"Jeez," said Vanessa, laughing around a mouthful of sandwich. "*Aren't* you such a problem."

"I know, right?"

"So what'd Poole do?" Vanessa pressed, all amusement, armoured boot up against the stairwell wall. She wasn't actually participating, the doctors hadn't given clearance for that. But she was supervising, and if you supervised in the assault run-throughs, you had to wear armour, even firing blanks. "Special moves?"

"Fingers and tongue," said Sandy, demonstrating quite crudely.

"Oh, I love that." With a nostalgic smile. "Used to be quite good at it myself."

"And you know how fast GI fingers can move."

"Good for Poole, nice to see him learning new skills. Though it's nothing I haven't wanted to do to you myself."

Sandy put her sandwich down from her mouth with emphasised displeasure and gave her friend a very long, hard look. Vanessa didn't quite meet her gaze, chuckling to herself. Then looked increasingly embarrassed.

"Good," said Sandy accusingly. "Well may you blush. Your poor husband, what would he think."

"Oh, he knows," said Vanessa dismissively. "He thinks it's hot."

"It's always hot in theory. I've learned among you straights that it doesn't always stay hot once put into practise."

"Oh, don't be such a moralising wench," Vanessa complained. "You know I'm kidding around, it's just fun."

But it wasn't . . . or not *just* fun, anyway. It had always been there, or for quite a while. Vanessa had gotten over it once, and had fallen in love again, this time with someone capable of reciprocating the same way. But the old feeling had never entirely gone away, just . . . displaced. Or translated, into new form. Sandy would have preferred it if Vanessa wouldn't keep prodding, but she knew her too well, and like a kitten at a passing butterfly, she just had to take a swat. Ignoring it wouldn't work, because Vanessa never ignored anything, and it drove some less patient people up the wall. Better to wear her down, strike first and control the conversation.

"If I were even five percent lesbian," Sandy told her, "I'd have done you so well you'd be walking funny for a week."

"Oh, come on, every woman's at least five percent."

"I recall your theory was twenty percent."

"Depends how much I've had to drink."

"You should be pleased I'm not," Sandy joked. "I might have killed you."

"You wouldn't have," Vanessa retorted. "And I'm not."

Sandy gave her a properly reproachful look now. Vanessa grinned at her, an apology of sorts, and took another bite of her sandwich.

"Sorry," she said. "Just a near brush with death. Gets you thinking."

Right, thought Sandy. She was asking for it. "Vanessa," she said, very hard, very blunt. Vanessa blinked at her, paused in mid-chew. "If you desperately want to fuck with me before you die, I'll do it, I'll fucking close my eyes and make Poole's effort on me look like light petting, I'm sure I could. But it'll damage us forever, because you'll feel guilty, and I'll be resentful because I won't enjoy it, because believe it or not, when you're *not* bisexual, it's actually not that much fun to have someone twisting your arm to do gay sex because gay sex is actually pretty disgusting."

Vanessa looked offended.

"I'm your best friend forever," Sandy said shortly. "That should be enough."

"You don't think it's disgusting," Vanessa accused her, mischief unquenched. And poked her with a boot. "You're making that up as you pretend to be angry." And held up her hands in defence, laughing, as Sandy threatened to hit her. "I'm sorry." Somewhat sincerely this time. "I know you're right. I've just felt like poking at things lately."

"I've noticed." Another bite. "Entirely too much talk about poking, I think."

Vanessa gave her another friendly push with an armoured boot, this time at her head. Dangerous in armour against anyone not a GI. Sandy head-pushed her off with a glare. Vanessa sighed, just smiling.

A com link opened. *"Cassandra, there's a meeting in the Director's office in ten minutes, all senior officers will be present."* That was Angelis, Ibrahim's secretary.

"I can't be there in ten minutes, but I'll be there," she replied aloud.

"The Director requires you to be there in ten minutes."

"Son, I'm on the combat course, and unless the Director wants me to blow holes in walls, it's not possible to get there in ten minutes."

"Cassandra, it's very important that you be here on time."

Sandy disconnected and finished her sandwich, still seated.

"Something important?" Vanessa wondered, not privy to that secure message.

"Some fucking secretary with no sense of time or geospatial relationships," said Sandy. "You were saying?"

She got there seventeen minutes later, in full armour. Angelis gave her a reproachful look behind his desk outside Ibrahim's door on the way in. Inside, as she'd suspected, everyone was gathered on the broad carpet before Ibrahim's desk, watching the wall display—ten minutes' notice usually meant some political announcement, and while those could be important, they did *not* require her to rush like a lunatic from the combat course to the Director's office. If it had been more important, someone would have said, but some overzealous secretaries whose only concern was ensuring punctuality didn't see things that way.

Ibrahim was half-sitting against his desk rather than seated, so it was moderately serious, whatever it was. Hando was here, head of FSA operations, technically second-in-command. All three Branch Chiefs, Cassillas, Shin, and Boyle. Admiral Vernier too, Fleet Liaison.

On the screen were politicians, standing in the Grand Council foyer before the main chamber, a suitably grand setting for professional show-offs, with high ceiling, patterned tiles, and busts of important dead people. That in itself was somewhat alarming—all the people standing before the journalists' cameras were Grand Council representatives, ambassadors from their various worlds and systems. A majority of those were selected indirectly by parliaments and leaders, not directly by their populations. That usually made them less prone to populist theatrics, being technocrats rather than baby-kissing politicians, and a long way from their support base anyhow. So what were they all doing standing together before the cameras, making this announcement?

"They're forming a party," said Chief Shin of FedInt.

"A party," Sandy repeated distastefully. And toned down her armour reception so the actuators wouldn't hum while everyone was trying to listen. "In the Grand Council?"

There were no parties in the Grand Council. Ambassadors were beholden to their worlds, and those worlds had typically divided politics. Ambassadors displaying a preference for one or another line of politics in the Grand Council would usually find themselves replaced when the other side won power back home. Most long-serving ambassadors, and most had aspirations to be long serving, studied a bland neutrality on most things, only daring to venture a strident pronouncement when they were absolutely certain that a majority back home would agree.

"They're called the Party of 2389," said Hando. "We've seen them coming for a while. Which you'd know if you'd read the political reports."

"Some of us work for a living," said Sandy. She *had* read some reports, but this seemed premature. The Federation was founded in the year 2389. The original language of the Federation constitution excluded the possible use of force by the center against its member systems, language since considerably altered by an entire war's worth of constitutional amendments. Many factions were agitating loudly for systems' rights against the center in light of the recent Federal attack on Pyeongwha, demanding a return to the original language of 2389. Thus, this party. "Do they have the numbers to block the amendments?"

"No," said Ibrahim, stroking his goatee, watching the screen with lidded eyes. "Constitutional amendments take a two-thirds majority. They've got 21 out of 57. But this creates a pressure group that can agitate for more, and they'll get them."

Thus denying any Federal arm of power, be it FSA, Fleet, or otherwise, the right to mount further operations like the one against Pyeongwha.

"Wonderful," said Sandy. "They could call it the genocidal murderer restoration movement. Pyeongwha would have loved that a year ago, they'd still be dissecting people."

"My sources indicate they'll push for a trade," said Shin. Shin Chung-Kwan ran FedInt, the largest spy organisation in the history of spying. He was an Earth native, a top Chinese operative from Beijing, and was reputed to have an IQ off the charts. He looked the part, deadly serious, slicked hair, elegant black suit, and expensive, old-fashioned wristwatch. "Repeal amendments 14, 19, and 20, or 16, 22, and 23. It's a package deal, swap one for the other."

Sandy recalled her constitutional amendments. "You mean they'll give the choice of repealing local security powers or foreign ones?"

"We'll have the choice of using force against the likes of Pyeongwha," Hando said heavily, "or against the League. But not both."

"That's not a bargaining position," said Sandy. "That's a suicide pact."

"And this is their moment," Ibrahim added, "because they never had a chance at a majority before. But right now there's a lot of folks upset at what we did on Pyeongwha, and a lot more folks very jittery as tensions come back up against the League. Combine the two groups, and suddenly they might have the numbers for at least one repeal, as Mr Shin says."

"Which casts recent League activity here in Tanusha in a different light completely," said Shin.

"Shit, yes," said Sandy. There had been a lot of alarmed talk on the news nets after those attacks, people scared that League was serious, and League was crazy, and League was really prepared to fight. The last thing anyone wanted was another war against the League. Now League ratcheted up the local populist fears, helping to create this rift in the Grand Council. "They hit us just when Federal military action is least popular, inside the Federation or out. They know the only way we'll lose a war is if we defeat ourselves before firing a shot. Clever."

"Indeed," said Shin. "But two can play at this game. Our plan for reciprocal covert attacks is in play, and not a moment too soon." With an appreciative nod at Sandy. That one had been her and Shin's plan together; he'd come to her the morning after the attacks seeking her League knowledge and found her about to propose something very similar to him. They'd combined the two plans over a long afternoon with reports, charts, and lots of green tea, and presented it together. Ibrahim had approved, and now the details were in motion through the bowels of FedInt.

"I still don't like it," said Boyle. Boyle was head of the FSA's League Department. Many of his assets were actually Shin's, but LD provided an overarching network of specialised intelligence gathering that pooled all the data and talked endlessly to Fleet about it. Some dismissed LD as just a glorified networking function with no real assets or power, but Sandy had found some of their data and contacts quite useful. "The most important thing we know about the League right now is how much we don't know. The last thing we need over there is to be creating more instability."

"As a security agency, it is our responsibility to create an adequate deterrent to known threats," Ibrahim replied. "League attacked us, now we privately promise them attacks of our own—the threat will be far more useful than the actual action should we genuinely choose to follow through with it, the fear of covert attack with our new GI assets may alter their decision making in useful ways. It was my call and I'll stand by it.

"What truly concerns me about the Party of 2389 are the forces behind it. These Ambassadors are barely the tip of the iceberg. I want full reports from all of our system bureaus, I want to know how the announcement is being met on all the worlds. So much here depends upon public reaction. There aren't many issues that have the potential to destabilise the Federation from within, but this is one of them."

CHAPTER SEVENTEEN

Picking the kids up from school was the most incongruously, weirdly, surreally civilian thing she'd ever done. She had to rush there from FSA HQ, with special dispensation to skip the mid-afternoon's crush thanks to a rescheduled meeting and a delayed review of ongoing Pyeongwha operations, which kept a couple of field agents waiting who'd travelled all the way back to Callay to make their reports. But she'd said she just wanted to walk her kids home from their first day, and people had smiled and said "aww" and made the arrangements.

All the kids at Canas School were high-security kids. Sandy had considered putting them elsewhere, but they were all from Droze, couldn't be asked to pretend otherwise given their ages and accents, and while news media weren't allowed to show their faces or names, they did know their ages and genders. With all three in the one school for mutual support, with matching ages and genders to the "Kresnov kids," people would put two and two together as even in a city the size of Tanusha the odds weren't great they'd be anyone else. And once people knew what school they were at, outside a secure zone, travelling back and forth on their own became genuinely unsafe, which meant armed escorts, and guards at the school, and comments from the other students, the whole mess.

And so they were here, with pretty, old brick buildings, green playing fields, and big trees, looking about eight hundred years older than it actually was, like the rest of Canas. She waited by the playing fields with the rest of the parents or private minders or nannies; no car pickups in Canas, the district wasn't big enough, nor the streets wide enough, and you could walk across it in fifteen minutes—not that that would have stopped some of them from driving if they'd been allowed, but the school deliberately had a no-parking policy. If you attended, you walked or cycled, teachers and students alike.

Other parents politely avoided eye contact while she waited, the way people did who were accustomed to the presence of "big names" and were often "big names" themselves . . . but this time it was different, everyone desperately curious to see her *here*, of all places, and looking while pretending not to. Especially given that it meant that her kids, the three they'd heard about from the war zone, were also here, mixing with *their* kids.

Danya, Svetlana, and Kiril emerged amidst the stream of other kids leaving across the grass and down the paths, and were delighted and surprised to see Sandy waiting, and ran to her. She hugged Kiril, then Svetlana, then even Danya, who hadn't invited it but didn't protest at a kiss on the cheek. There were other parents watching, and now lots of other kids too, looking to see if what they'd been told about these three new kids was true. Sandy listened to them talking, hearing tuned to those farther frequencies even as she listened to Kiril and Svetlana talking eagerly about their first day—"Look, that's Kresnov!" "Hey, look, there she is!" and the ever-predictable, "I thought she was bigger." And their parents, reprimanding them not to stare and point, even though it was nothing the parents hadn't just been doing, only kids were more honest about it.

"I'm sorry I couldn't be there this morning," she told them as they walked home along the winding footpaths, decorative walls and gardens of Canas. "I had to go in at four."

"Why?" Kiril asked, genuinely curious. "Was it an emergency?"

"She can't talk about it, Kiri!" Svetlana reminded him cheerfully. They hadn't quite gotten him to grasp the concept of "confidential" yet. Or rather, that "confidential" also applied to him, even with her. "It's to keep you safe too, remember? Otherwise people will think you know important stuff and try to kidnap you!"

"Svet!" Sandy scolded.

"Well, they would," said Svetlana defensively.

"No one's going to kidnap any of you," said Sandy. And because it was the simplest, most comforting explanation they knew, "If they tried, I'd kill them." And glanced around to see if any parents were close enough to hear that, but the only others walking this road were too far away to hear.

"Yeah, that's right," Kiril agreed far too loudly, "if anyone tried to kidnap me, Sandy would kill *all* of them!"

"So how were all the other kids, Danya?" she asked him. It was the thing that really concerned her, partly for her kids' welfare, and partly for the other children's. She'd made certain the principal was very clear that bullying was simply not on, not just because she'd get upset, but mostly because her little darlings would lure the bully into a bathroom, put a bag over the bully's head and a knife to his or her throat. Not that she thought they'd actually *cut*, but then they'd all be in serious shit with the Education Department, various psychs, and eventually, inevitably, the scandal media, as someone found a loophole excuse within which to reveal those events.

"They're okay," said Danya with a faint smile. She'd discussed her concerns with him, and he'd promised to bring any such problem to her and the principal, in that order, rather than take matters into his own hands as he was accustomed. She still didn't trust his promise; Danya didn't outsource immediate self-defence willingly, but she was at least confident she'd get enough warning in most circumstances to head off anything drastic. She was still astonished to learn how nasty kids could be amongst themselves. And was thus convinced it was better if they all knew exactly where her own kids came from, so they might refrain from nastiness, from simple fear. "They know we're your kids, all day it was Kresnov Kresnov Kresnov. Got a bit boring."

"Some of the girls are really dumb," Svetlana complained. "A few of them were really rude, asking what it was like having a GI for a mum. One of them asked if you'd killed my real mum, and they laughed, like it was *so* funny." Sandy felt her heart skip a beat with worry. "I said no, but you'd kill their mums if they didn't shut up, because you were FSA and you knew where they lived. They shut up pretty fast."

Sandy didn't know what to say. Svetlana had de-escalated the situation, which was good, but done it in a pretty shocking way, which wasn't so good. Danya saw her confusion. "Svet made some friends," he said. "She was hanging with a couple of the popular girls after lunch. They came up and talked to all three of us when we were sitting together."

"They just liked Danya!" Svetlana teased. "All the girlfriends I ever made were just girls chasing after Danya!" Grabbing his arm as they walked. Danya swatted her off, smiling.

"No," he said reasonably, "they like Svet because Svet's such a bitch." His sister gaped at him. Sandy laughed, seeing it was safe to do so. "Well, she is, she's tough and pretty nasty when she's pushed; I think they heard her put those other girls down. And you know, she can pass herself off as pretty when she has to . . ."

"Hey!" Svetlana pushed him into the neighbouring wall, which Danya bounced off and kept walking faster to escape her.

". . . and you put that together," he continued, "she's got popular written all over her."

Sandy hadn't really thought of that. Svetlana as one of the cool kids?

"Sandy, you don't need to worry about us," Danya explained to her further, seeing she was a little slow in getting it. "We've seen people get killed. We've seen war. We're not scared of what other kids our age think of us. The worst that can happen is that they don't want to be our friends, but we don't care because we only need each other, and you."

"And the worst they can do to us," Svetlana finished, "is say bad things, because they don't know what *really* bad things are, not like we do. Danya already gave us this talk, Sandy. Some of them are kind of scared of us; you can see it. We're fine."

Somewhat astonishingly, another possibility occurred to Sandy. She'd gotten this all wrong. She'd been so accustomed to seeing her kids as frail victims walking on eggshells, she hadn't considered the possibility that let loose in the typical Tanushan playground, *they'd* be at the top of the pyramid. Because they weren't alone, they had their usual support network of three, plus her, and they were accustomed to an environment of constant and ruthless competition. Faced with a serious threat, sure, they'd get jumpy . . . but against Tanushan kids their age? Kids who'd never faced real danger in their lives? It wasn't like they weren't socialised with other kids, they'd mixed with plenty of other street kids in Droze, though not always in a friendly and cooperative manner.

"Okay, guys," she said, "here's the thing. I was worried you might have trouble fitting in, that you might get bullied. But it seems that was stupid, you're way tougher than any Tanushan bullies and they'll know it."

"Absolutely!" said Svetlana with ferocious satisfaction.

"So here's the next thing. Kids who've always been kicked around and frightened might suddenly discover they're in a place where *they* can be at the top of the stack. And how much fun would that be, to be able to push *other* people around for a change?"

Danya frowned. "I don't think we'd do that."

"You don't think so now, but if they were nasty, or stupid, or you just lost patience, you could, right? So let me tell you this now—if I find out that any of you have actually been bullies *yourselves*? That you've pushed around or hurt or said nasty things to some other kid just because you could, or because they annoyed you without meaning to? Or maybe they're just weird? I'd be *so* upset with you. I'll always love you, but I'd be *so* upset. So promise me you'll never do it, promise me you'll only ever be nasty to kids when you need to defend yourselves."

"We promise," said Danya quite seriously. "We promise, don't we, guys?"

"We promise," Svetlana and Kiril echoed. Sandy repressed a smile at the thought of Kiril bullying someone. Surely never.

"You know the reason I'm really serious about this?" Sandy pressed. "Think about it. Think about what I am, and what I could do to people if I wanted."

"You could kill anyone," Kiril announced. For such a sweet boy, he was very pleased to pronounce that at any time.

"That's right. I'm the toughest GI ever, I could be the *ultimate* bully if I wanted to. But I don't, because the way I see it, this is like one of your stories, Kiril. In the story there are good guys and bad guys. Now I know it's not always that simple in real life, but we should try to make it simple, like pretend, right? So in this story, I choose to be the good guy, and try to do good things. Bullies are *always* the bad guys, no exceptions. Got it?"

Danya didn't need the lecture, but Svetlana and Kiril were suitably thoughtful. Danya was a trouble avoider, and there was simply no percentage in bullying because bullying made trouble. Especially when Danya's biggest fear was trouble with Tanusha's authorities and getting kicked off Callay . . . which couldn't actually happen legally, but in Danya's imagination big authorities in big cities were always bad people just waiting to do bad things, and never mind that one of the biggest of those authorities was Sandy herself.

Kiril didn't need the lecture *yet*, but with young kids it was never too early to start and get them fixed on the right path from an early age.

The real worry, of course, was Svetlana. Because Svet was both confident and insecure, happy and angry, more easily provoked and less likely to be merciful. And if she did become one of the popular girls, it didn't take much imagination to see her in a few years' time, a teenager, beautiful, giddy with attention from boys and girls alike, and with a famous guardian who was cool to teenagers because she scared people . . . it would be natural for such a girl, having experienced so many bad things, to revel in this new and expanded self-confidence, and to love being on the top of the stack for a change. And in the psychology of insecure teenagers, the best way to make sure you were on top of the stack was to tread on the faces of others beneath you.

Sandy didn't really know what else she could do about it, other than to try and function as a handbrake, and to diminish those teenage insecurities by loving her to bits and providing a good example in how to treat people well, especially those you didn't need to. At which thought she put an arm around Svetlana's shoulders as they walked and took Kiril's hand in the other, while Danya took Kiril's other hand and swung him happily between them while they talked about lessons, teachers, and sports.

Kiril thought Danya should play football, but Danya wasn't interested. He'd have to join the school team, Sandy reckoned, and the only team that interested him was right here. Svetlana wasn't much interested in sports or teams either, but she wanted to try dancing, the school arranged classes. Terrific, Sandy told her. Do it. And since she'd enjoyed swimming, the last time they went to the public pool, maybe she could try the swim team too . . . with a scheming look at Danya, because as she'd told him, he had to learn to swim before he could surf.

Kiril wanted to swim too and also wanted to play the piano, because his friend Poole played the piano, and pianos were really interesting with all their internal hammers and strings and stuff. So maybe, she said to them, if they wanted to try these other things, they could arrange their schedules so they could do stuff after school together. And since she didn't need too much sleep, if they didn't mind her being gone in the mornings, she'd try to work her long-hour days early when she got them, and be home for all the evenings?

"I want to know martial arts too," said Danya.

"Oh, me too!" Svetlana and Kiril chorused together.

"I mean, we picked up some stuff on the streets," Danya continued, "but just tricks really. Teach us?"

"Sure," Sandy said cautiously. "I know stuff you can use for starters. But real martial arts for non-GIs is a different thing completely from what I use, so if you get onto the more advanced stuff, you'll need another instructor."

"I want proper tape teach." Very seriously. "Top-level stuff. SWAT stuff."

"I don't know if it's safe to use that on kids."

"But you can ask someone who knows."

"I can," she agreed. "I'll look into it."

They were approaching the house when one of Sandy's network seekers fed her back something it thought she should see—a visual came through, shaky and hand-held, and she watched on internal vision as Svetlana and Kiril ran to her across the school playground, then Danya bringing up the rear, then hugs and kisses and talking. A rapid process of the image location found the file relaying off one of the circumference hubs, where node blockers should have shut it down, given it was featuring her image and had "Kresnov" in the title heading.

It was rare but happened sometimes, so she sent to the usual blockers . . . and got a bounce back from half of them, unable to link in. Which snapped her into full emersion visual with the construct ahead of her so she could hack in quickly and disable some of the barriers, but that took time and each node was different, and the codes embedded in this visual feed were propagating to new nodes faster than she could hack the old ones.

"Dammit," she said, as they crossed the road to the house, interrupting whatever Svetlana had been saying. "Sorry, guys, I need to net talk for a moment."

"Problem?" asked Danya.

"Maybe, there's a visual just now from the school, when we met to walk home. Someone was recording us and now the feed's on the net and propagating, it shouldn't be, it should all be blocked."

She tried CSA protective intel, who were alert to it and making inquiries. Then some underground friends, a few of whom were unreachable, then finally up to Anita, who said she'd look into it, but sounded slightly . . . evasive? Or was she imagining things?

Now she was sitting on the sofa while Kiril and Svetlana played a noisy vid game, and Danya put an ice coffee in her hand, strong, the way she liked it. And sat beside her, waiting patiently. Ari got back to her.

"Yeah, Sandy, I think I know who that is . . . can't tell you, it'll violate an investigation I've got running."

"You mean you know someone compromising Canas network security?"

"Yeah." Reluctantly. Like Anita had sounded reluctant. What was going on?

"Can't be many people with the expertise to penetrate Canas net?" she pressed.

"Yeah, it's kind of the point of confidentiality to, you know, hide the identity of the person being investigated?"

"Sorry. If you can't tell me who, how about why?"

A pause. *"Sandy, you might have noticed . . . you're not quite as popular as you were amongst the underground."*

"I actually had noticed that. I'm the authority, they're anti-authority, it was bound to happen."

"It's more than that. 2389 hits a nerve with a lot of folks. A lot of the underground seriously don't like Federal power used to assault member worlds."

"Sure, and a lot more of them who know about Compulsive Narrative Syndrome and are heavily into tech-induced mass psychology thought what we did on Pyeongwha was awesome because Pyeongwha scared the shit out of them."

"Right," said Ari, *"and so there's a crisis of ideology and politics right through the Tanushan underground right now, a lot of people who thought they were anti-authority find themselves cheering the attack on Pyeongwha, and a lot more say no matter how awful Pyeongwha was, the precedent established by using Federal force to attack it was even worse."*

"The thing is, you've been relying on these people for a long time now to stop a lot of the chatter about you, they're naturally pro-biotech, pro-technology generally, often pro-League, and so almost always pro-GI and GI rights, and lucky for you, they're the ones who pretty much control the flow of covert information through the net's back channels. They've been helping with the CSA's filters to stop the information flows that make your life unsafe, but I think it's a pretty safe bet a lot of that assistance will start to break down now. Could be a concern, now you've got the kids."

"Yeah." She thought about it for a moment. *"Shit."*

"Sandy," Ari ventured, still cautiously, *"I was waiting for the right moment to talk to you about this, but this seems as good as any. I think it could get a lot worse. The FSA's fine because the FSA serves the Grand Council, but the CSA serves the Callayan government. And President Singh is all over 2389 like a rash."*

"Noticed that too. I've considered it, Ari."

"Sandy, a lot of your security rests with the CSA, whatever the FSA being your main employer now. Now . . . I don't want to do this thing where I outline my usual paranoid theories, and then you tell me I'm a lunatic, and I accuse you of lacking imagination, etc., etc. I mean, we've had that fight before, right?"

Sandy smiled. *"About a hundred times. But Ari, on this one, I'd appreciate having a friend inside the CSA who could keep tabs on this for me. A paranoid friend who didn't just assume that the Singh government wouldn't come after me through the CSA would be perfect."*

"I can do that." Not even joking. That was serious.

"The real question is, if such a thing were to happen, in any form, what should the FSA do about it? Because Callayan security IS Federal security, to a large degree, given all Federal institutions are based here. If the CSA and FSA ever started to work at odds . . ."

"Sandy, they're already at odds." He sounded quite unhappy. *"It's just they haven't realised it yet. The Singh government's completely at odds with pro-Federalist politics; they're for member rights all the way. They see the FSA as an accomplice in pushing dangerous pro-Federal policies, and they control the CSA, which with recent close ties is the FSA's soft underbelly right now. But the FSA can't change any of this without letting Singh know that they know."*

Crap, thought Sandy. *"If you're talking like this, that means Ibrahim knows."*

"Of course."

"Ari, Chandi doesn't like you nearly as much as Ibrahim does."

"Noticed that, thanks."

"Chandi doesn't like people who are more loyal to others outside the CSA than to those inside it. Chandi might want to teach those people a lesson."

"You do realise that you might fall into that category at least as much as I do. And Chandi won't do worse than fire me, at which point Ibrahim's already offered me a job, and I'm betting Chandi knows it. Chandi doesn't give a stuff about crossing me, but crossing Ibrahim's another matter."

"I think he might give a stuff about crossing me as well, Ari. We're friends, but this is moving well beyond friendship."

"Chandi has this way of defining his friendships by their usefulness to his work. I stopped being particularly useful to him a while back, as he sees it. Sandy, I was thinking we should get a trusted little group together, all friends, and have a good long talk about this. I know I don't want to get caught with my pants down."

It was all very, very preliminary. But they'd both seen enough of this stuff up close to know they didn't want it getting out of hand before they had plans in place.

"Good thought. The good news is that I think we can get most of the guns on our side. Always good to have all the firepower together, and my network through SWAT and FSA spec ops is a group with more loyalty to each other than to either."

"Sandy . . ." she could almost see the familiar grimace, facing an unpleasant thought. *"Speaking as a native Callayan who's been here all his life, and a lot longer*

than you, don't underestimate the power of a local nationalism. I'm Federation too, but I'm mostly Callayan."

"Tanushan," Sandy corrected. *"A wise man told me there's no snob like an urban snob."*

"Naidu?"

"Justice Rosa. But I accept your warning. I just want to head this off before it goes anywhere, let the manipulators know they face a brick wall and there's nothing to manipulate, because we all stand together."

"That's . . . that's very . . . rousing, Sandy." With dry cynicism.

"We could use some rousing. I'll talk to my people, you talk to yours, then let's have our meeting, okay?"

"Good. See you there."

Disconnect. And she just sat there, heart thumping a little too hard, and wondering what the hell had just happened. It wasn't that dangerous yet, it was just annoying as hell to discover this cleavage that ran straight through the center of what had until recently been a very cozy little setup, Callayan government, CSA, Grand Council, and FSA together. With any luck they could stop it from getting messy before it even started, that was the nice thing about having so many trusted friends in high places: those connections could hold things together against the best attempts of the most determined saboteurs. But still, 2389 was being driven by the Grand Council, and the Grand Council represented forces far, far larger than what could be found just on Callay.

Danya was looking at her with a frown that told her he hadn't missed the concern on her face. "Trouble?" he asked.

It was all speculation, nothing real, all in the future. Danya was a sometimes troubled kid who had difficulty sleeping. She should really just say it was nothing and save them both the alarm.

But the pact she'd made with Danya hadn't included her keeping him in the dark. Adults and children didn't make pacts. Pacts existed between equals, and if Danya discovered she'd lied to him, the bond could be broken. And that scared her worst of all the possibilities that emerged on this sunny afternoon.

She took a deep breath. "Okay," she said. "This is what we know."

Ari was sitting at his table at the upstairs lounge of the Happy Song Club with Ruiz when the police raid hit. Ruiz had been charged on more than twenty counts of permit forgery related to illegal augmentation, but only convicted on one for a suspended sentence. At the next table along, some wealthy customers were discussing full illegal gene mods for their yet-to-be-born blue-eyed baby girl, and how the charges would be disguised as "consultation," which, if handled by the wife's business, were actually tax deductible. At a table beyond that, consultants for a transport company were discussing government-mandated biometrics, required for government contracts, and could they by any chance be falsified? Across from that, with copious amounts of vodka, cards, singing, and the occasional arm wrestle, a big corporate who was a personal friend of Mr Song was "negotiating" with Song's son and cousin about the price of virtual (read false) net identities and the scrubbing of past records from network memory so that new business clients wouldn't find out about that previous graft conviction. Overhearing the nature of that job, and the money involved, Ari was nearly tempted to offer his own services. Some GIs he knew could do that in a few days; the Song family were proposing to take a month.

And then here came the cops, kicking down the doors and yelling at everyone to freeze, guns drawn and angry looking. Ruiz just rolled his eyes and raised his hands, while the Songs all had world-weary chuckles with their client, a big Punjabi with a gold watch and a custom gold pistol big enough to blow his head off, turban and all. He said so to the cops that levelled guns on them, that it was licensed, e-monitored, and unloaded, just to show to his drinking buddies . . . smirk smirk, another sip of vodka.

And here came the detective in charge, and whoa! Ari blinked, thinking he'd stepped into one of those noir detective mysteries Sandy had gotten him into—not that she was a fan, but she thought *he* would be—a dame with long legs, black hair, and eyes straight out of some Ramprakash Road song and dance blockbuster.

"My my," said Ruiz, grinning as the two men watched her weave between the tables with purpose. "Another victory for Tanushan random genetics."

It was an in-joke in these circles, the Federation laws and their local variants designed to protect the "necessity" of the randomly determined gene pool. Because if everyone got what they wanted—long legs, smouldering eyes, perfect breasts—the gene pool would be robbed of diversity, and, presumably, the universe would end in a frenzy of sobbing self-flagellation. But in Tanusha, these things were easier to talk about than to enforce, thanks largely to places like this one, and people like Ruiz and the Song family. They'd created what the underground called "Tanushan random genetics," which they'd laugh about whenever one of Tanusha's multitudes of smoking-hot babes sauntered by, multitudes that any half-serious analysis of random Tanushan faces would tell you were statistically impossible, given how much all the "looks" indices had changed in the last fifty years.

"Best-looking city in the Federation, my friend," said Ari. "Must be the water."

She was collecting IDs now, showing her warrant. Ruiz was stood up and searched. Then Ari, who gave the cop doing it a "seriously?" look. The cop avoided meeting Ari's eyes. Ari sighed. That meant . . .

"This way please," said the cop, indicating for Ari to step out, no attempt to remove his gun, or double-check the CSA badge. Ari went, glumly, but it wasn't all a lost cause because Detective Legs followed him. Out in the hall she beckoned him to follow, down the stairs, then past the restaurant still full of dining patrons, but now with Song's other employees clustered at the bottom of the stairs looking askance upwards for further news.

Then out onto the side road, where police vehicles sat with flashing lights, cops waiting for arrests to emerge. A police van's rear door was open, and the detective gestured Ari inside and followed.

"Sinta," she said, closing the door. "Homicide, Lagosa District. Need to talk to you."

Ari blinked at her for a moment. Even prettier at this range, hair tied back, typically Indian gold stud in the nose against milk-chocolate skin. She wasn't *trying* to look smoking hot, he conceded—she was dressed like a plain-clothes cop, jeans, jacket, tied-back hair, minimal makeup. But poor girl, she just couldn't help it, and Ari could see situations, amongst the kinds of men cops had to deal with (and sometimes were) where that would make her life much more difficult than if her genetics were toned down several notches. "So you're leading this raid?" No disagreement. "And you're sitting here talking to me instead? Dear God, you didn't do this whole thing just to talk to me?"

Frustration flashed in her eyes. "Listen, do you have any idea how hard it is for a cop to get a hold of some bigshot CSA Intel? You put in a request through channels and it just disappears, you talk to guys in the field and they won't give you a straight answer . . ."

"Look, lady . . ." he struggled to control a grin. "I'm not that hard to find, honestly. You held up the Songs for this? Oh, boy, they'll be pissed."

Her eyes hardened. "So what were you doing in there anyway? A bit of that 'legal experimentation' we know you shadowy types like to get up to?"

"Talking to contacts," he said, still amused. Sinta got even hotter when she was angry. "They don't hang out in coffee shops."

"Talking about what?"

"Join the CSA and I'll be allowed to tell you." He leaned back against the bench seat, amidst spare vests and tactical headgear hanging on the ready rack behind. "So tell me, what's a stunner like you doing in the cops? I mean, surely mom and dad didn't pay all those genetic extras so their darling daughter could get paid like robot maintenance to hustle the Song family for scraps?"

He was surprised, and even a little impressed, when that didn't make her more angry. She just gave him a "look," probably having heard all that before. "I did law and hated it. But I grew up on crime fiction, decided to take a pay cut and enjoy my life more."

"Ah." Even more impressed. "Friend of mine did something similar, good for you."

"Look . . . I don't know if I have anything. But I've got a very weird case, and it's not going anywhere with my superiors. I think they're getting leaned on."

Ari frowned. "Homicide, you said? Whose homicide?"

"Idi Aba."

"The emancipation activist lawyer? The one the League killed?"

"Well, that's just the thing," said Sinta carefully. "I don't think they did."

Ari knew just the place to take a hot girl for some alone time. A private booth at Tickler, one of the hotter clubs in Patna, three blocks from The Happy Song. From the completely cool way Sinta accepted his choice, with expensive holographics, thumping music, and three multi-level bars around the dance floor serving all kinds of probably spiked and VR-interactive things, he had to fantasize that she'd been a patron in these kinds of places before. Maybe like one of these scantily clad girls they walked past on the floor to get to the booth. Or maybe she was just a cop and busted these kinds of places regularly. But that idea wasn't as much fun.

"I know the guy who set up these booths," said Ari as they settled in, "and I've a passkey to their inner network, so these booths are pretty unbuggable. Drink?"

"Don't suppose they do a cappuccino?" she asked wryly.

"No, but a hell of a cinzano-flavoured lassi, tastes like it'll blow your head off, but zero alcohol."

She raised her eyebrows. "Sure, but you're paying. Me on the salary of robot maintenance and all." Ari grinned and ordered. Cops weren't actually paid *that* badly, they just complained a lot, especially to the CSA.

The drinks came in no time. "The owner knows you?" Sinta said tiredly.

"Sure. Good contacts here."

"And you won't bust him in the process. You know how many clubs like this are involved in really bad stuff that CSA guys like you just let go?"

Ari cleared his throat. "Well, firstly, there aren't any CSA 'guys like me,' just me. And secondly, if you cops knew half the stuff I chase down in places like this, you'd wet yourselves."

"Sure, let me adjust my sanitary pad." Sipped her drink. "You're right, that does taste like alcohol."

"I'm getting you drunk," said Ari. And, "Kidding, kidding," at the look she gave him. "So, your case."

"Okay. I can't reveal any files, can't show you electronic, VR, paper, anything, it's been classified secure and I have to file paperwork up to the highest level to share it. If they saw your name on it, they'd can it and I'd be in trouble."

Ari frowned. "Some reason they don't want the CSA looking?"

"Not just the CSA, anyone not from our precinct," Sinta explained. "Organisational barriers, once it gets out you can't control it. They've been instructed to control it, or that's what it looks like. But just because I can't show you actual stuff doesn't mean I can't talk about it. So long as no one else knows."

With a wary look. She was serious, at least. A mere detective could get into serious shit with this kind of thing.

"I didn't get this well connected by just repeating every sensitive thing I was told," Ari reassured her, sipping his drink. The leather booth seats vibrated beneath them, boom boom boom, lights from outside flashing against the curtains.

"Okay, Idi Aba was shot close range, outside his apartment, almost exact same time as the attack on the HDM tower took place." The very mention made Ari feel far more serious than he wanted in such entertaining company. He remembered that attack very well. Remembered thinking it his last moment alive. "Building security has no record of an entry or exit, we've looked at all the hacking tricks, counted the numbers of people coming in and out in case the attacker used someone else's face, you name it. But we've still no idea, which tells you it's a pro.

"Idi Aba was shot in the back as he walked from his door, one in the back, two in the head on the ground. Gun was an 8 mil, no one heard anything, so figure something quiet, probably a mag shooter. Only two other doors on that apartment level, he had a nice place, big apartments, not much risk of being surprised. Hallway camera shows nothing, empty corridor."

"Security system?" asked Ari.

"Zaphira Tech."

"Good," Ari affirmed. "Not that good, but good as they go. You'd think serious pro to do it that clean, maybe ISO."

"Here's the thing," said Sinta. "For all the security, this big apartment building has external glass elevators. Facing them is a sniper's paradise, buildings, cover points everywhere. If it's ISO, League GIs, why not just shoot him from range? Rather than penetrate all those levels of security to get into the building and get out again? It's a two-person job for a real pro, one to keep lookout, the other to do the hit, right?"

Ari frowned. Thinking of several things he could offer at this point, but Sinta was good and on a roll. "Keep going."

"And again, an open-air parking lot at a lower level. So even if the glass elevator makes a tough moving target, again doubtful for GIs but possible, they could get him while he goes to his car. I didn't want to run the sim because I didn't want to have to explain what I was doing to my captain, but just standing there in that parking lot, I counted maybe thirty spots for a good sniper. Including a couple of mega-rise where you park up top and bring the sniper rifle in from there, that's much easier security to breach than coming up from the bottom.

"And I don't reckon there's any way this was GIs, because ISO GIs are fighters not sneakers, and there's talk going around that League don't like training their own GIs with these kinds of covert skills in case they start using it against League, they prefer their GIs as spec ops combatants, not spies. So if this other attack is GIs, Idi Aba's murder isn't, must have been regular humans.

"But League lost their diplomatic access to Tanusha three months ago when the embassy was closed. They can't get people in through those channels anymore. Now, it could be sleeper agents, people who've been here a while . . . but deep cover in Tanusha's hard to get, you'd blow that for, what, an emancipation activist? We know they can sneak stealth ships into the system and make capsule drops into the atmosphere, but the Gs they pull are hard for regular humans, GIs do much better. It's just a lot of work for such a small target."

"Doesn't mean they didn't do it," said Ari. "Trying to guess the how and why of ISO is best left until three years after they've done it. They play long-term chess; short-term analysis never makes sense."

"Right," said Sinta, nodding. Ari liked the way her eyes became all animated as she followed her train of thought. "So it looks open and shut, right? Two League operations, against two League enemies, an emancipation activist and the CSA, both at the same time, using each other for cover. And with pros like that, we're not going to find any evidence, so when we've such an obvious explanation, why bother looking further? Blame it all on the League and do the paperwork. Very convenient. I hate convenient.

"So I figure if the shooter's this good, he's not going to screw up and I'm not going to catch him that way. So I look at the victim instead. Idi Aba was acting very strangely up to his death. I got access to his data files, only they've crashed, they had a delete function that saw he was dead and erased everything."

"Well, some of these emancipation guys are paranoid," said Ari. "They think all the anti-GI crazies will come after them."

"I couldn't see what was in his files," Sinta continued, "but he put the delete function there last week. The same time he started taking *lots* of network calls. I talked to his colleagues, lately he'd been net talking all the time, normally on business he'd just shrug them off like anyone does, but he was stopping in the middle of briefings to take urgent calls, missing the beginning of trial preps because of calls . . . some thought he was having woman trouble, only he wasn't married and wasn't seeing anyone, that anyone knew, and his financials seem to confirm that.

"I couldn't get any message content or where it came from, but a buddy of mine who works off-grid . . . a bit like your buddies here . . ." with a glance around, ". . . managed to salvage a bit of the encryption whoever was calling him used."

"Just one caller?" Ari asked.

Fast nod. "Yep. Government encryption. Grand Council. Top security."

Ari's eyes were wide. "Oh, fuck."

Another fast nod. "It's not supposed to survive a recording, but my network guy knows some serious tricks."

"Look," Ari said urgently, "do you still have a copy of that encryption pattern? Because I know some people who can place that even more specifically than . . ."

"Already done," said Sinta, a gleam in her eye. "My guy put me onto some other guys . . . the same guys who put me onto you. They'd broken the fucking Grand Council encryption seals, can you believe that? Just for fun. They still don't know what the messages say, but they know who's saying it. This one's coming from Ambassador Ballan's office."

"All of those calls?"

"Yes. He's got a big staff though, narrowing it down would be hard even if I had access, which I can't get without telling my Captain I suspect it's not League GIs, and him getting all ratty on me."

Ari stared at her for a long time. Normally that would be very distracting, but now his thoughts raced unimpeded. Sandy called him paranoid, but even she would be thinking nasty thoughts at this point, surely. Sinta finally got tired of him staring at her, and made a "so?" expression and a little shrug, challenging him.

"That's it?" asked Ari.

"That's it. I was kind of hoping you could do some digging yourself with Ballan, I understand you know him."

"Well, not really." That was Sandy's friend, and he didn't want to bring her into this right now. "But I'm real good buddies with a fellow named Ibrahim you might have heard of."

A wide-eyed nod.

"Look," he said, "you said you like crime fiction . . . when I read it, I'm terrible, I turn to the last page first."

"Barbarian," she said.

Ari nodded. "What's your last page here? What do you think it is?"

Sinta shook her head. "My working theory is someone in the Grand Council. Probably not even one of Ballan's staff, probably that's a cover used to throw any investigations off. Beyond that, I'm not prepared to guess. What's your last page?"

Ari shook his head. "You're not thinking anywhere near big enough. First, ask yourself a couple of questions. If someone in the Grand Council used the League attack on HDM tower to cover the murder of Idi Aba, how did they know League was going to attack?"

Sinta blinked at him. "I hadn't really thought of that," she confessed. "You think they knew in advance?"

"If they did," said Ari, "then we're looking at a traitor. They won't see it that way, of course, but working in conjunction with League agents attacking Federation agents is treason, and the last I checked the war may be over but the statutes are still on the books for treason, and the punishment is death. Now if the person to be put to death is a high-ranking member of the Grand Council . . ."

Sinta's face paled. She really hadn't thought it through that far. Some people were micro-focused, their brains were brilliant at small details, but they missed the larger picture. Such people might make good detectives, paying attention to every tiny clue but never looking up long enough to see where they were headed. The macro-focus people might be better suited to CSA Intel.

"Secondly, ISO don't just let slip their plans to people in the GC by accident. So either they approve, or they're using someone there for another purpose. What would make the League really, really happy right now? Concerning Federation policy?"

"Well, if we started . . ." Sinta blinked rapidly, and she looked up at him with dawning concern. ". . . fighting ourselves," she concluded.

"And stayed out of their business," Ari added. "There's a new political party in the GC advocating pretty much that."

"Oh, no," Sinta breathed. "You think those calls from Ballan's office to Idi Aba were someone warning him to drop whatever he was onto?"

"Could be. And when he didn't, it got passed onto someone higher who did more than just threaten. 2389's been attacking emancipation activists left and right lately, verbally at least, saying they'll provoke the League and what we all need right now is a kinder, gentler Federation that doesn't go around upsetting people. You get what I'm thinking now?"

Sinta nodded.

"Good," said Ari. "So if you want to work with me on this, here's my deal. I'll dig as much as I can into the Grand Council and all the places you can't access. You do all the legwork on Idi Aba that cops are much better at than CSA, tell me what he was organising, what he was into, why he might have upset someone in 2389 or anywhere else. And also, I don't know what your personal security situation is like, but take all precautions and if you don't think you're secure enough, call me and I'll put someone onto it. We've got systems cops don't get, and your superiors don't need to know."

Sinta was staring at the tabletop, a knuckle in her teeth. "God damn it," she muttered.

"Ah, yes," said Ari. "They all think it's such a great idea to come and bother Ari with their cases and their problems. Then they change their minds. Hey, are you single?"

CHAPTER EIGHTEEN

R ishi watched a debate on the flight up. It was between a woman, who was spokesperson for the new Grand Council Party 2389, and a man, who spoke for the present Federalist position. It was the big political news story, everyone was watching it . . . except of course for the ninety percent of the Callayan population who, when they weren't working, were watching anything but.

"*. . . no one is arguing that what happened on Pyeongwha wasn't the most tragic, awful thing,*" the 2389 woman was saying. She was older, white-haired, and elegant. "*But what Federal Constitutionalists like myself are arguing is that the precedent unleashed by Federal intervention on Pyeongwha, whatever short-term gains might be apparent, will ultimately be much worse. And look, even now we see guerilla war commencing against the new Pyeongwha provisional government and its Federal backers, a few hundred dead so far and that number will surely escalate before long, so the short-term gains would appear illusory also.*"

The FSA jet bumped a little through the troposphere, nearly Mach Four and the five-thousand-kilometer flight would take barely an hour and a half all told. Rishi ate a small bowl of fruit salad and sipped a glass of red wine provided by the stewardess—it was just her, Rishi, and the apparently junior female FSA officer accompanying her in the cabin, seating for up to twenty others left empty. The FSA were certainly being very nice to go to all this trouble just for her.

"*But you are saying exactly that,*" the spokesman countered. Spokesman for what, Rishi hadn't entirely figured—2389 was the only party in the Grand Council. Spokesman for all the others, she supposed. Not an ambassador but senior staff. "*You're saying exactly that Pyeongwha wasn't a bad enough situation to warrant interfering, and I'm sorry, maybe it's just me, but the vision of all those people being gruesomely murdered by the lunatics who ran the place tells me otherwise. Pyeongwha is not a foreign state, it's a MEMBER state, and member states of the Federation only enjoy their rights as Federation members so long as they abide by their obligations, foremost of which is that they can't massacre their own citizens. Pyeongwha abrogated that right, and so is denied all rights as a Federation member as well—*

membership should and does have conditions, otherwise what's the point of having a Federation at all?"

And from there it degenerated into a series of increasingly personal arguments about what the founders of the Federal constitution truly envisioned, and whether that vision was relevant any longer. Rishi didn't know what to make of it. She was a new arrival and lived now on a mostly deserted island archipelago a third of the planet's circumference from Tanusha. They didn't get a lot of news there, though she tried to watch some, during breaks in construction work. It all seemed so distant there.

The jet circled around Tanusha at altitude, coming in to a gradual hover at a district where the city sprawl abruptly ended at virgin forests and rivers. Building there was illegal until authorised, the bored junior agent informed her when she asked—every centimeter of Tanusha was planned. Certainly it looked every bit as impressive as Sandy had described it, and as she'd seen herself, briefly, on a very impressive VR Sandy had shown her some months back. A hell of a long way to come from Droze, that was certain.

They landed vertically on a pad between officious-looking buildings, then walked to one of them, across pleasant grassy gardens, trees everywhere. The FSA building was nice too, air-conditioned with lots of glass and wide spaces. She barely had to check through any security, the agent accompanying her just handed her off to another agent, who walked her though various halls and offices, then across an air bridge to an adjoining building that she immediately recognised as medical, because it looked like Chancelry medical back on Droze, only way more advanced and pleasant.

There she was handed off again to a couple of doctors, and the guard disappeared completely. That surprised her. No security at all. Though of course they'd be monitoring her, and probably there were FSA-employed GIs nearby, just in case, little good a non-GI agent could do if she suddenly did decide to turn on them. As if she would, now of all times, when she had nowhere else to go.

The doctors took her to the new floor of the medical wing, which she was told had been deserted until just recently, FSA HQ having been built several sizes too large with the intention to grow into it. Here in the first ward was Stezy, female GI, a 42 series. She was completely immobile here, which was good, because back in Chancelry she'd occasionally convulsed when they reduced the drug dosage, damaging equipment and requiring restraints. She had a mask on her face and a tube in her mouth, and advanced equipment monitored every function.

"We've tried to make contact through VR," Doctor Singh explained to her, "but though her uplinks seem to be functioning, we just don't think there's very much going on." He seemed very nice, and quite sad at the fate of this Chancelry GI he'd never known. And he wore a red turban, which Rishi thought was odd; people didn't wear stuff like that on Droze, or not that she'd seen. Certainly they hadn't around GIs in Chancelry Corporation. "We'll keep trying until we can establish what degree of mental function she has, and what if anything we can do to increase that function. I must warn you that our best estimate is that we can't really do anything, but we'll try. And then, if she's adjudged to be mentally nonfunctional to even the primary degree required, then we'll have to discuss with you appointing someone to act as the guarantor of her legal rights. When it comes to making the decision on whether to turn off her life support, you understand."

Rishi nodded, not really having expected anything else. "You don't want to keep her alive to study her?"

"That would be illegal under Federation law," said Doctor Singh. "Certainly we can keep her alive longer to study her if we can demonstrate material benefit to the lives of these other GIs in our care, but if we can't establish that, we're not allowed to keep a brain-dead body alive for reasons of any other profit. But we'll need someone to be appointed her official guardian. If that person is you, then you can meet with Stezy's lawyer while you're here to make sure you understand how all the legal clauses work in her case, and in others. And then if you wish you can talk about it with your other friends down in Malina, whatever you choose, just so long as you understand that by Callayan law, where we can't establish the wishes of the patient, the guardian holds most of the cards and we have to do what you say, within reason."

Rishi felt dazed. Rights, he said. Sandy had told her about this too—in the Federation, GIs had the same rights as everyone else. Lawyers, clauses . . . it was confusing, but it was good too. Director Ibrahim had assured her that the Chancelry medical cases would be well looked after, and it seemed he'd kept his word. Cassandra had assured her the same, back on Droze, and it looked like she'd been right too.

In the next ward was Melvin, similarly restrained, but with less life support. He drooled and stared blankly at a wall. Dr Singh explained that he was just as brain damaged as previously feared, but that with time they might be able to restore some more pathways and improve cognitive function, since he was still so young. But most likely he'd be little more than a vegetable for life. Despite the expense, someone in the government would keep him on and look after him; euthanasia was only legal on Callay for the brain-dead and irre-coverable, with technology these days no one was prepared to pull the plug on hopeless medical conditions that in thirty years turned out to be changeable. And with biosynth moving as it was . . . Singh shrugged, maybe in thirty years Melvin's life would change for the better as well, he said.

There were seven more, nine in total, most similarly hopeless. Down in Malina, twenty-six others could probably be classified as "damaged" to varying degrees but not in need of hospitalisation. All of those preferred to sit in the sun anyhow, and many were able to help in daily things even if not in construction, like making food. A few had taken to meditation with the Krishna priests, and one of those had shown remarkable improvement since he'd started doing so. FSA doctors were keeping tabs on them, too.

The last patient was Pongsit, similarly restrained and immobile like the others. But unlike the others, Dr Singh was smiling when they entered his ward.

"I've something to show you with Pongsit," he said. "I think it would be better to wait until we go downstairs."

Downstairs was a private lounge, glass windows fronting onto the broader FSA compound, gardens, and glass buildings, Tanusha's towers rising beyond. Here in comfortable chairs sat Cassandra Kresnov and little Kiril, who had his AR glasses on once more.

"Rishi!" he shouted, jumped off the chair and ran to her. Rishi was accus-tomed enough to Kiril that it didn't surprise her, and she bent for the hug. More surprising was that Cassandra followed and gave her a hug of her own. She looked a lot better than when Rishi had last seen her upon returning from the Droze spaceport, face cut up and one arm dangling. Also interesting was that Cassandra seemed quite pleased to see her. Which was quite different from Kiet's talk of how she'd abandoned them and didn't care to be involved anymore.

"Rishi," she said, "this is Ragi." Indicating the other person in the lounge, a slender black man who'd been sitting directly opposite Kiril. "Ragi's a non-combat GI from the League."

"Really?" Rishi went to shake Ragi's hand, having learned how those manners worked. "Did you defect?"

"Not so much defect as abandon, I think," said Ragi. Immediately, from the way that he spoke, Rishi could tell he was very high designation. "I was wondering for a while what side I should be on, but then League tried to kill me, so that seems to have solved that problem, yes?"

"League do that a lot," Rishi agreed.

"Ragi's helping me to use my uplinks," said Kiril, returning to his chair and his glasses, which he was controlling in turn with a hand slate. Rishi supposed that children needed that extra control function. "They're not supposed to be working yet, but Ragi makes them work."

"No, they're still not working, Kiril," Cassandra said sternly, returning to his side. Ragi smiled patiently, also resuming his seat. "It's just a preemptive activation, they won't be working properly for a long time yet."

"I don't care," said Kiril defiantly, readjusting manual settings on his slate. "I can get a basic colour pattern now, I can actually *see* it."

Rishi noted Cassandra looking at Ragi, not looking very pleased. "It's entirely harmless at this point," he said. "Or rather, it won't make anything worse."

"Shouldn't mess with this stuff," Cassandra said shortly. Rishi thought it was an argument they'd had before. "You activate it, you stimulate it, it grows more."

"It's already activated, at a very low level," Ragi said calmly. "Your doctors have it crawling with nanos that repress further propagation and keep it at a very low rate. By testing function I can get a better picture of what's working and what isn't.

"But Rishi, I imagine you'd like to see Pongsit?"

Rishi frowned. "See him? I just saw him lying upstairs."

"Oh, we can do better than that. Take a seat."

Rishi looked at Cassandra and Kiril, who was preoccupied again with his slate. Cassandra nodded encouragingly toward a vacant seat. She sat and . . .

. . . was suddenly somewhere else. A large outdoor balcony beneath a blue sky. It was a restaurant, high up on a valley side. The valley was green with thick forest, mountain peaks soaring high above. At tables across the balcony, people sat, ate, drank, talked, and laughed. They wore clothes and had bags by their tables that looked like they might be good for walking long distances. A little way down the valley, an old village, made of grey stone, with little bridges across a sparkling stream.

"Hello! Is your name Rishi?" Rishi looked and saw a girl, no more than fourteen, sitting at a table with a jaw-dropping view of the valley below. She had a book in front of her, a real paper thing with white pages that glared in the sun, and was now pushing sunglasses up onto her head. "Please have a seat, Ragi told me you might be coming."

It was VR; Rishi had done VR before, but the only other time it had been this intense was with Cassandra. Cassandra had required a direct cord link to do that, and she'd been her prisoner at the time; Cassandra had had to forcibly break defensive barriers to access her construct. Ragi did it now with no cord at all, and no warning. She hadn't even realised her barriers had been bypassed.

She took a seat opposite the girl and noticed the man sitting beside her. Brown, Asian features, sitting serenely in the sun, and looking over the valley. "Pongsit?"

Pongsit looked at her. He seemed to recognise her, because he smiled at her. Then he resumed looking at the view. Rishi stared at him, amazed. She'd never seen Pongsit actually *look* at anything. Had never known him capable, until now.

"He loves it here," said the girl. "I'm Allison, by the way. I'm a friend of Ragi's and Cassandra's. I have a medical condition; in the real world I can't move or speak at all. But here I can sit in the sun and read my book. Ragi's been expanding on the VR for me, it's actually a tourist simulation provided by the government of France, back on Earth. These are the Pyrenees mountains, aren't they beautiful? But Pongsit and I can't access a public VR, so Ragi's cloned it into his own format, no one still knows how he does it, but he's got a special construct worked up that allows me to be here, and now he's done the same for Pongsit, even though we've got completely different conditions."

"Does he speak at all?" Rishi asked, gazing curiously at Pongsit. He had no book in front of him, nor anything else. But he looked perfectly content.

"No," said Allison. "But I've been spending some time with him here for about a week, and he's been more animated each time. At first he was just dull and lifeless, but look at him now. I'm hoping he'll join me for a walk up the valley soon. I think the more he experiences, the more animated he'll become."

The VR was very good, Rishi thought. Besides the view, the contrasting sensations of warm sun and cool mountain breeze were quite amazing.

"Well, thank you for spending time with him," said Rishi. "I'm a friend of his; we're about the same age. I always thought that if he was awake and alert in there, it must be so depressing for him not to be able to move and enjoy things. It's nice to see he can enjoy a place like this."

"Oh, we go other places too," Allison said cheerfully. "We've got a beach simulation . . . oh, and Ragi's even got me a flight simulator; I'm leaning to fly, can you believe that? I wanted to bring Pongsit too, but Ragi says motion sickness might not be the best introduction to real-world sensations! I'm not that good yet."

Rishi talked to Allison for a while, marvelling at the girl's good humour. For all the beauty of this place, it was still VR, a limited world with limiting choices. And if she moved too fast, or her hand brushed the wooden tabletop, the sensation wasn't quite the same, or a sound could crackle rather than flow, or a lovely outline of tree-lined ridge would pixelate momentarily or freeze before evening out once more. But it was a *lot* better than what she'd had, and besides, she hadn't given up hope that new technologies would get her walking soon.

They were interrupted by a circular portal that appeared in mid-air before Allison, who gasped with excitement reading it, and said that her brother was going to uplink to go walking up the valley with her. Rishi wasn't supposed to meet anyone non-FSA approved, but Allison understood, and they said good-bye, which, as Rishi was only now coming to anticipate, included a hug and a kiss on the cheek with people you liked, especially if you were a woman.

Back in the real world, she was still sitting with Ragi, Cassandra, and Kiril. Ragi was talking Kiril through different responses to signals he was being sent. Ragi had established some kind of network Kiril could receive on at a very basic level. Watching them, Rishi thought she understood.

"You're the same tech, aren't you?" she said. "Talee tech. Like what they were working on at Chancelry."

Ragi gave her a sideways glance, away from whatever he was doing with Kiril. "It seems so. Though I've no idea what they were working on in Chancelry."

Rishi made a face. "Some stuff just experimental. That's the stuff that made Melvin a vegetable. They'd just throw stuff at a wall and see what stuck, some of us did, some of us didn't. I was lucky. But there was other stuff they didn't have the facilities to do themselves. We figured that after you left," and she looked at Cassandra, "we found piles of new data, experimental biosynth models, new brain structure, stuff we haven't seen before."

Cassandra blinked at her. "Where did you find that?"

"Hidden compartment. Not even on the main computer, just physically hidden, like they knew their mainframes might be compromised one day."

"You wouldn't happen to have saved any of that?" Ragi wondered.

Rishi nodded. "We brought it with us. Wasn't allowed to say anything until now; we were waiting to see if you guys followed through on your side of the bargain." Cassandra and Rishi exchanged glances. "Another thing, remember Margaritte Karavitis?"

Cassandra nodded. "The neural biosynth expert, yes?"

"Cai said she's League. Dalia System. It's well hidden, he says, but he overheard her talking while on uplink, said her accent is definitely Dalia . . . though how he knows what a Dalia accent sounds like, I don't know."

"I'm sure a Talee agent would know a lot of things about humans from lying offworld and listening," said Cassandra.

Rishi nodded. "Sure. Cai said she probably hadn't been on Pantala long. So she's League, she knows Takawashi, or so she said, and Chancelry are working on super-high-tech GIs with massive network capability using Talee neural biosynth techniques no one's seen before but don't have the capability to produce themselves. And now I find a GI with exactly those abilities who doesn't know who he is, appears to be very young, and was probably made by Takawashi and dropped off here for reasons that only Takawashi knows."

Both Cassandra and Ragi were staring at her. "Karavitis was Takawashi's spy!" Cassandra exclaimed. "That's how Takawashi suddenly acquired the technology to make you!" Looking at Ragi.

Ragi was frowning intently. "And he gave me to the Federation to prevent a strategic imbalance. We think."

"Shit, I bet she's behind Eduardo suddenly appearing here in Tanusha too. We never did discover why, we assumed he was sent to assassinate someone . . . but that just put us onto New Torah as a threat, so it's pretty dumb if they did it. Maybe Karavitis was trying to give Eduardo to us, only her superiors got onto it and killed him first. Maybe it was a warning of what was going on, but once the killswitch had been used, we just didn't have the technology here to sort through the mess that was left and make sense of it. Damn, I have to tell someone to exhume that body and take another look . . . excuse me a moment. Kiril, will you . . . ?"

"Go!" Kiril sang, pointing to the door like it was some private joke. Sandy grinned and kissed him, then left.

A few hours later, Sandy and Kiril were in the cruiser flying home with Danya and Svetlana, who had gone to a nearby public swimming pool while Kiril was having his tests. Sandy was pleased Kiril's tests had become at least that routine for them, and now, following some instructional tape, both Danya and Svetlana were becoming reasonable swimmers. She was also quietly pleased, and not at all guilty, that her little manipulation had seemed to work so well—insisting to Danya that he couldn't truly keep everyone safe unless he and they were physically fit, not just tape-skilled. Since then they'd been exercising a *lot*, not only relieving her fears that they'd inflate like balloons from all this unaccustomed food and relative inactivity, but also encouraging them to act more like kids. But she couldn't say that to Danya, or she'd put him off.

"And we took the waterslide too!" Svetlana said now from the rear seat with Kiril, her hair still wet and spikey. "The waterslide's huge; it was like a hundred meters long!"

"Sixty," said Danya.

"You went down it too?" Sandy asked hopefully.

Danya shrugged. "She insisted." Sandy smothered a smile.

"We go so much faster together than on our own!" Svetlana insisted. "And then I bet Danya he wouldn't jump off the top diving platform!" Laughing at him. Danya looked a little annoyed. "And he told me I shouldn't because it was really high, but all these other kids were jumping . . ."

"Kids older and more experienced than you," Danya added.

"Yes, but I'm awesome," said Svetlana. Danya laughed. He and Kiril had found and bought her a "Little Miss Awesome" T-shirt on one of their shopping trips, and she loved it. "So I jumped off and it hurt a bit, but it was so cool and wasn't dangerous or anything, so I told Danya he had to go now, because he couldn't be shown up like that by his *little sister* . . ."

Danya rolled his eyes at Sandy. Sandy gave him a sympathetic look. Poor Danya. Svetlana loved him to death, but neither would she give him an even break. In her mind it was the greatest compliment.

"So did you jump?" Kiril asked.

"Sure I did," said Danya.

"But he didn't like it," Svetlana teased. "I could see he was all wobbly up there." And just when Sandy was about to tell her that maybe she should show her big brother a little more respect, given that she owed absolutely everything to him including her life, Svetlana removed her restraint and scrambled in the gap between front seats to give Danya a cheerful hug, cheek to cheek. Danya smiled and ruffled her wet hair, no hard feelings. As though they were telepathic, and Svetlana just instinctively knew she might have gone too far. Not that that would stop her doing it again in a moment.

"Besides," said Danya, "she's so skinny she doesn't feel anything when she hits the water. Wait until you get a bit bigger, Svet."

"Hey, Sandy!" said Kiril in the backseat, gazing out the window at passing towers and traffic with his AR glasses. "That building's called the Providence Tower, it's got a hundred and five storeys and it's . . . 512 meters tall!"

Svetlana leaned over to look where he was pointing. "Wow, Kiri, how many people are in it?"

"Umm . . ." scanning on his glasses, "it doesn't say."

"Well," Svetlana reasoned, "let's say there are forty people on each floor. Now there are a hundred and five floors, so how many people are there?"

"Four thousand two hundred!" Kiril exclaimed almost immediately.

It was also impossible to get angry with Svetlana after seeing how good she was with Kiril, entertaining his enthusiasms no matter how non sequitur.

"Now I wish I'd gone swimming with you," said Sandy. "That sounds like fun."

"You can't disguise yourself with hat and sunglasses at the swimming pool," said Danya.

"And you wearing a swimsuit in public isn't like the best way to not draw attention," Svetlana added mischievously.

"Well, thank you," said Sandy, "but I'm not really Tanusha-sexy; I've got shoulders and muscles. In Tanusha they go for lean and leggy—you'll be Tanusha-sexy in a few years, Svet, Danya will have to beat the boys off you with a stick."

Another girl might have blushed. Svetlana just grinned.

"Why bother?" said Danya. "Just expose them to her charming personality."

"Hey!" Svetlana unbuckled herself again to try and hit him, as Danya laughed and fended off.

"No fighting in the cruiser!" Sandy told them. "Svet, put your belt back on!"

A call light blinked, from Ari. Sandy put it on speaker. "What's up, Ari?"

"Hi, Sandy, small favour, I see you're in the air near Turin? Could you just head across to Dalhousie and give Detective Sinta a ride?"

"Why does she need a ride?" Ari had told her about Detective Sinta, and her suspicion that the lawyer Idi Aba hadn't actually been murdered by the League.

"She thinks someone's following her. Actually she's certain. Given who that might be I don't want to send the whole cavalry or they'll get suspicious about just how important we think her case is, but if I send just one person I need that person to be, well, capable."

"Ari, I have the kids with me."

"Ah. Well, surely you can just pick her up?"

"Ari, you know damn well you're not just asking me to pick up some random friend. These are my kids."

"Can you drop them off?"

"Now that you've called me, the folks who might be watching Sinta are now watching me, no matter what your fancy encryption. If I drop them off they're exposed."

"Well, talk to us," said Danya. "Who's Detective Sinta and what's her case?" Suddenly sounding calm and sober and twice his actual age.

"Very classified, Danya," said Sandy. "Can't really say."

"Sandy, this is a damn good cop," Ari insisted. *"She sounded scared. I asked around earlier, no one thinks she's the type to scare easily. Any trouble she's in is most likely network trouble, and you're perfect because you're immune . . ."*

"Is it important?" Danya asked. "If it's important, we should do it." Sandy gave him a distracted, surprised look. Danya was usually so cautious with Svetlana and Kiril's safety. "Sandy, the main reason we're safe with you is people are scared of you. But if you stop doing your job because of us, the bad guys will notice and then we're all in more danger. If they're watching us like you say, they'll notice if you don't help."

"Like I said, that's a damn smart kid."

"Fuck," said Sandy, laying in a new course and turning. "If it gets at all hairy, Detective Sinta will have to find someone else. And get me some fucking backup."

"I've got you three units, CSA plainclothes."

"That's no good, get me a GI."

"There's no one available. One of the plainclothes is Kazuma."

"Okay," Sandy muttered, "I guess that'll do." She disconnected. And announced to the others, "Double belt, please, I'm putting us into performance mode."

"You mean we can go even faster?" Kiril asked with excitement.

"Yes, Kiril. Much faster. But not right now because we don't want to alarm anyone." They were holding to a standard skylane, traffic ahead and behind, holding the pattern like any other vehicle. Dalhousie was twelve kilometers away, getting there wouldn't take longer than three minutes.

"Who's Detective Sinta?" Svetlana asked.

"Homicide Detective," said Sandy, flashing an overview file onto the cruiser's screens. "Friend of Ari's, I've never met her."

"This is her?" asked Svetlana, looking at the photograph on file. "She's hot."

Danya looked too. "Wow," he said.

"I bet you knew she looked this good," Svetlana accused him. "That's why you wanted to help her."

"How could I have known that?" Danya replied.

"I bet Ari showed you a photo. Boys are like that with each other."

"Nice theory," said Danya. "But no."

Sandy wondered what would happen when Danya got his first Tanushan girlfriend. That Danya could get such a girlfriend, Sandy had no doubt. That Svetlana would let her live was the bigger question.

Sandy established personal tacnet off independent FSA servers and quietly established a backup on local servers. Sinta's investigations were into the Grand Council, which in turn controlled the FSA. It wasn't inconceivable that if Sinta really was being tailed, that person had GC connections and could use GC codes to get into FSA networks, perhaps even knock down tacnet once she'd established it. That was what Ari meant about needing someone who could handle network problems—someone like Vanessa, or a dozen Vanessas, couldn't run tacnet on local servers without FSA backup. But Sandy could, plus other tricks besides.

Once in tacnet, she used the com functions to establish new links to Sinta, via Ari's links. "Detective, this is Sandy Kresnov, if you talk to me for a few moments FSA tacnet will integrate your construct and we can coordinate from there. What's your situation?"

"Wow, they weren't kidding when they said Ari knew people, were they?" Making light of it, but the tone was strained. *"I was running down a lead. I called my car to come get me halfway, only some traffic emergency function intercepted it and parked it on a corner a block from me. I walked there and it just* looked *wrong, you know? A blind corner, few people around, perfect ambush spot.*

"So I pretended like I'd forgotten something and walked away, but I don't think I'm fooling anyone, I've spotted three solid tails, there's some creepy network interference that's static delaying my calls, even Ari can't pinpoint it, and if I can't trust traffic net because these are Feds and they can access everything and I can't . . ."

Damn right she sounded a little panicked. Sandy's heart thumped a little harder, vision swimming into combat mode as she listened. A good cop would be right to be scared getting into stuff like this.

"I mean, I'd ask my guys in my precinct to come get me, or some random cops on the street for a lift, but an emergency call to the precinct will mean telling my captain everything I've been investigating, and I can't ask anyone out here without an emergency call because if I'm right about this they could be walking into some real shit—same with local cops, plus some Feds might just drop in and tell them to hand me over, no questions."

What the hell did she think she was into, Sandy wondered?

"Detective, where are you currently?" Sandy had her on speaker so the kids could hear, it was policy for her that no matter who you were, if you were in a situation, you got to hear all of it, or as much as possible. And these kids were not to be patronised with ignorance.

"I'm in a little gift shop off Manfred, I'm pretending like I've forgotten to buy presents. Then I was going to go and get my first manicure in about a year, there's a place across the road with a good view and lots of people, should be safe enough there."

"Okay, hold the manicure, I'm going to bring it down on the street, they won't risk anything with so many people around."

"Yeah, there's no transition zones where I am, you'll have to go . . ."

"Don't need them, I can override without declaring emergency."

"Okay, good, I'll be here."

"Two minutes. Buy yourself a nice bottle of something, you might need it afterward." Soft disconnect, tacnet still registering the active connection.

"What does that mean about transition zones?" Danya asked.

"TZs are where you can land a cruiser and merge with ground traffic," Sandy replied. "Security or emergency services can override that and land anywhere, but it has to be an emergency. Except for FSA and CSA, we can land anywhere if we have to, without declaring emergency."

"So you don't let anyone hooked into the network know that you're coming," Danya surmised.

"Exactly. But if we misuse it we'll be in the shit afterward . . . guys, be a bit careful with me the next few minutes. I'm half in combat mode, just don't grab me unless you have to, okay?"

In the rear seat Svetlana was checking Kiril's straps, all business. She saw Sandy looking in the mirror. "You got another weapon in here?"

"Under your seat. Too cramped to use it in here."

"But would save time if I had it out and ready, just in case." She loosened straps to find the seat controls, a panel popped and she reached in past her legs.

"Svet . . ." Sandy started, but the girl was already pulling out the gun, a compact, snub-nosed thing not too big for a kid to handle. "Yeah, just . . . careful with that, don't forget the . . ." As Svetlana quickly popped the mag in and out, checked the rounds, chambered one, set the safety and held it correctly, across her body with both hands.

"I got it," she said innocently. "Just in case."

"Hold it real tight in case we have to manoeuver," Danya added, then squinted up ahead to where their flightplan ended. Ahead, a business hub of many buildings, a few of them enormous, on a delta between two gleaming rivers. "That's Dalhousie?"

"Yeah, Sinta's on the other side, let's come around."

Finally she broke lanes on FSA privilege, projecting a decelerating curl around central Dalhousie to come in low over Sinta's position on the far side. Sandy was now watching traffic central carefully, also an FSA function, for anyone else breaking lanes or acting suspiciously. If the people tailing Sinta were what Sinta thought they were, they were now seeing *her*, and though her flightplan was not registered with central, they'd now be certain where she was headed.

"Detective, ETA forty-five seconds." As they passed between towers, unbothered by the passing buzz of air traffic, safe in their lanes. "Detective?"

Silence.

"Crap, Ari, I lost her, do you have anything?" Abruptly overriding the previous flightplan and accelerating, cutting corners, and dodging beneath a pair of intersecting lanes as traffic central bleeped red warnings at her.

"Negative, what happened?"

"I don't know, she's not replying, she's not linked on tacnet. I'm going to try for a visual." Braking hard now as the road appeared ahead and below, a moderately busy urban road on the edge of the business hub, a large park nearby, beside which tacnet was identifying Sinta's vehicle. The cruiser had scanners, now sweeping the road as she mentally configured parameters to look for at least two people moving close together, though if they'd bundled her into a waiting vehicle she wasn't going to see much.

"Guys, look for her," Danya told Svetlana and Kiril, craning to look down out the window. "There'll be at least one guy with her, probably with a gun in her ribs, walking with an arm around her."

"Unless there was a back way out of the gift store," said Svetlana, also looking, rifle pressed against the door as Sandy refrained from warning her.

"I can't see!" Kiril complained, too short for the straps to let him reach.

Sandy crabbed them sideways above the street, only ten meters high and a few folks now stopping to look up. That narrowed it further, Sinta's captors would be amongst those not looking.

"Sandy, this is Kazuma, we'll set up a search perimeter and watch for escaping vehicles." Sandy saw the three other cruisers on tacnet, coming in close to help.

"Good," she said, "keep your spacing, don't get bunched up down here. If something happens we could run out of space."

Traffic central abruptly blew out, a cascade of disintegrating code. *"Fuck, watch it!"* someone yelled.

"FSA priority," Sandy sent direct on full emergency, "Detective abducted in Dalhousie District. Perpetrators just blew traffic central in this district. Their capture is priority." As her backup called warnings about vehicles straying from lanes as central attempted to reestablish and emergency protocols kicked in.

"Whoa, Sandy!" Kiril exclaimed, seeing something on AR glasses, and Sandy shoved them hard at the ground, yelps from the back as the restraints stopped them from hitting the ceiling. A cruiser zoomed straight through where they'd been, innocent occupants no doubt astonished at where the auto-control was sending them.

"That one was aimed at us," Sandy muttered, pulling them out barely three meters over the road, which was now filling with jammed traffic, crossroad lights on red as automatic precaution in case of central failure, pedestrians staring about in bewilderment. "That does it—central, I'm gonna nuke them."

She broke into all Federal frequencies at once, a rush of data that nearly overloaded her vision, but her data backups jumped to life and she caught a familiar jolt of shapes, repeating patterns, Federal codes in predictable repetitions and construct shapes immediately protesting her intrusion. Normally she'd have worked her way through it and tried not to break anything, but as a combat GI the main design function of her net access was to smash and grab, and in her time in Tanusha she'd improved the effectiveness of those functions too.

Pattern seekers ID'd likely anomalous structures. She flashed through them, shredded several friendly structures in the process for data, matched codes, and sorted . . . and here was a primary encoded function, looked like some version of Fed-level tacnet. She hit it with everything she had, and its local supports, a massive service attack with barrier breakers and nearby servers flooding giga-tonnes of data into processors that couldn't handle it.

Pandemonium on the net turned to panic as portions of local Federal network well beyond traffic functions began to melt down. Now in some buildings, the power was going out and basic communications dissolving to static. And on a nearby TZ several blocks away, a rising cruiser let out a squawk of alarm on a completely different coms function entirely.

"Got you, you fucker." Her own tacnet was flickering, but she put it onto main servers further out, howling sideways around intervening buildings to acquire a visual. Got one, locked the cruiser scanners on a low-altitude cruiser, and put a target lock on it. "Kazuma, get this fucker for me."

However they'd been aiming innocent civvies to crash into her, that function was now gone too, but there were lots of vehicles hovering aimlessly, meandering, climbing on independent initiative to rejoin some higher lane and get out of the mess in Dalhousie District . . . she wove between them, headed back to the street where Sinta had disappeared.

"If they've lost control of traffic central then they've lost their escape route," said Danya, gripping handholds tightly against the unexpected Gs. "They're stuck down there."

"Not if they get a cruiser," said Sandy, seeing Kazuma's cruiser on tacnet coming about to intercept the one she'd targeted. "Dammit, Sinta, give me a sign."

Suddenly she was taking fire, rounds cracking into the rear gens as she spun the cruiser about and up.

"Everyone down!" she yelled, crabbing up the street to get an angle on the location it was coming from, dropping the window and firing one-handed, a cluster of shots into the lip and railing about a short building's rooftop, behind which the shooter was covering.

"Sandy, gun?" Svetlana offered.

A new shooter opened up below, but Sandy was ready and hauling sideways, nose missing a glass building front by a meter, spinning about to get a good angle down on that first rooftop, the first gunman running even now . . . and diving for cover just as she got a shot out the window, putting a dozen holes into a parked cruiser, determined to frighten if she couldn't hit him.

"Gun!" she said to Svetlana, holstering the pistol and reaching back for the rifle—it smacked precisely in her hand, G-forces and all. There were buildings all about, the next gunman with a good vantage could get a shot *down* at them, where the cruiser had more glass and less protection . . . but surely all this shooting was to make a distraction for an escape?

Something bleeped on tacnet—her seekers picked up Sinta's com function, just a single pulse, and tracked it to . . . cruiser! On another shorter tower rooftop, ten floors, now lifting as it built power.

"Everyone *hold on!*"

Sandy fell once more, got beneath rooftop level as she built speed down the road and across a block, then slowed quickly and flared, rising above rooftop level at the last moment, hurtling sideways and slowing, straight at the cruiser. They hit side-on-side, hard, alloy crunching and shrieking, their target spinning once as it lost attitude atop its lift axis and fell off it sideways . . . straight into the neighbouring building front. It was glass, and the cruiser smashed through and lodged there.

Leaving Sandy's cruiser hovering just off their side, Sandy with the rifle out the window, now flicking coms to external speaker, volume high. "*THIS IS SANDY KRESNOV. RELEASE THE DETECTIVE NOW OR I'LL FUCKING KILL ALL OF YOU!*"

It had the desired effect; she could see them bailing fast, out of the windows into the office building . . . and just as well, because firing into a cruiser was imprecise with ricochets and tumblers. And she had no desire to mow down a car full of people in front of the kids.

The rear window smashed from the inside, fracturing white, then boots kicking it out—in an impact the glass went from aeroplane tough to children's-safety-glass-tough. Then Sinta was crawling out atop the rear gens.

"Guys, right door open—Kiril! Scoot across, Svet, help him!"

The right gull door clanked open on emergency overrides, red lights flashing until Sandy killed them, wind and noise howling in as she brought them right up against the rear of the wall-embedded cruiser. Sinta looked okay, crouched, hair blown . . . and now jumped a simple two meters with a cop's respectable augments, grabbing the rear gen supports. And astonished to be assisted inside by a ten-year-old girl swapping places with her little brother.

"We're going!" Sandy was off even now, door closing, full acceleration and keeping low to deter shooters, weaving between towers over streets filled with crazy traffic jams. She put the safety back on the rifle and handed it back to Svetlana, with a quick glance back to Sinta. "Detective, you okay?"

"Yeah, what the . . ." distractedly, holding onto things rather than strapping in. "You've got kids in here!"

"She's observant!" Svetlana said brightly, getting her own straps on, clutching the rifle. "She must be a detective!"

"I bit my lip," said Kiril.

Sinta blinked. "Why do you have kids in here?"

"Ask Ari," Sandy muttered, setting course to FSA HQ and not slowing down for anything. Not game to even send word that she had Sinta safe, in case someone with access to FSA coms intercepted it. The combat vision was fading now, normal colours reasserting. Damn, she'd insisted she'd be out of there as soon as shooting started . . . but as always with combat reflex once she was in it she couldn't pull out. All her combat instincts were dangerous, and attack wasn't her best defence, it was her raison d'être.

"I think 'thank you' would work," said Danya, looking around his chair at Sinta. Sinta stared at him, still gasping.

Unexpectedly, Sandy found herself grinning. "That's okay, Danya, she's a bit rattled. This kind of thing's new to her."

Even more unexpectedly, Danya grinned back. "Well, I don't know about you guys," he said loudly, "but I heard a *lot* of interesting words just now." Svetlana shrieked with laughter. "Around *children*, Sandy, how could you?"

She blinked at him. "What did I say?"

"Sandy's favourite word is fuck!" Svetlana sang. "Sandy's favourite word is fuck!"

"Oh, you poor precious things," she retorted. "Damaged for life."

Danya laughed so hard he nearly hurt himself.

CHAPTER NINETEEN

Sandy offered to help the kids get their dinner at the FSA cafeteria, but Kiril said quite loudly that they ate there all the time, they knew where everything was. It was the closest Sandy had felt in her life to being embarrassed.

In the Director's office were Ibrahim, Hando, and Shin, along with Sandy and Sinta. They all sat in various chairs, as they did in an informal meeting, save for Ibrahim, who half-sat on the edge of his desk as usual. Sinta looked dazed, hair disorganised, hands gripping a cup of strong coffee, one wrist bandaged where she'd had it twisted when the anonymous Feds had grabbed her in the gift store. When she sipped from the cup, her hands trembled, just a little.

"You didn't get any?" she asked now, as Hando brought them that news.

"They disappeared," said Hando, settling long limbs into his seat with a displeased frown. Rubbed his chin with a gold-ringed finger. "We'll get DNA from their cruiser, but if they are who we think they might be, we're not going to get any matches."

Sinta blinked. "I'm sorry, who do you think they might be?"

"Every world has intelligence agencies, Detective," said Hando. "Including a branch of the FSA, on every world, but others are independent, run by those local governments just as the CSA is run by the Callayan government. They're quite proficient in forging identification, and while they're not supposed to show up here, that doesn't always stop them."

"And they'll have access to Federal and Grand Council codes and networks through their world's ambassadorial links with the Grand Council," Sinta finished. "Just great." Muttering that last into her cup as she took another sip.

"Your file shows that you are single with no children," said Shin. "I must ask if you have a boyfriend, or other close family, for our protective detail."

"Oh, come on," said Sinta with a forced smile, "I'm sure you guys know all about me by now."

"We are the Federal Security Agency," said Shin quite seriously. "Were you a League citizen or a Federal employee, we would know all about you. But you are a Callayan citizen working for the Callayan government, so more likely the CSA knows something about you. This agency does not overstep its bounds, Detective."

"No, right," Sinta agreed, placating. "No boyfriend. Very single. My parents live in Brookside, you don't think that . . ."

"These operatives are focused, not vindictive," said Shin. "Co-habiting family may be useful to them because of information you may inadvertently share with them. Your parents should be safe as they know nothing. Presumably." Sinta nodded again, still worried. "We'll watch them all the same. Just to be sure."

"Detective," said Ibrahim, and Sinta looked up at him. "I hear you found something." Of course he'd heard, Sandy thought. On this, Ari was reporting to him. Looking at Sinta, she wondered if the detective was thinking the same thing.

"Yeah," she said, and gulped a mouthful of coffee. "As you've heard, my theory was that Idi Aba wasn't killed by League GIs at all. I figured that since whoever did it are clearly pros, and I was pretty stretched for resources, I wasn't going to find the assassins by any screwup they might have made. So I looked into the victim instead, to try and find what he might be into.

"I won't bore you with the detective trail, though if you doubt me I can provide you with the full write-up later. But the short version is that Idi Aba had been going to a 'massage parlour' in Patna and seeing one masseur in particular, a guy—Idi Aba's gay—named Pon. Pon in turn is mixed in with a Christian group who provide cover for a network of emancipation activists, Freedom Rail . . . the name's partly inspired by the Underground Railroad in the USA in the eighteen hundreds that moved slaves from the slave-owning South to the free North. These guys have been helping to move GIs from League to Federation, or specifically Callay . . ."

"We know the group," Shin interrupted. "A lot of those people are former Intelligence themselves. They're very well hidden; we've been looking for their Callayan contacts and only found whispers. That's very good work, Detective."

"Anyhow, get this." Sinta was leaning forward now, hands calmer, eyes intent. Maybe Ari really hadn't just been thinking with his dick, Sandy considered. "Pon's disappeared. No one knows where. No one in the Christian Group would talk, but some leads got me to an external drive, which stored personal communications between Idi Aba and a guy you'll certainly know—Ravi Das. Head of Abraham's Children, leading emancipation organisation in the League."

Nods around the room. "And wanted by the League on charges of sabotage and treason," Hando added.

"They were discussing a deal," Sinta continued. "They didn't say what, they were being discreet, but it sounded big. Maybe an exchange of information. Ravi Das said it would blow the Federation opponents of emancipation out of the water. Said it would change the whole game; the Federation would find it very hard to oppose emancipation afterwards."

Everyone looked at Sandy. Sandy felt very cold. "They must have found something," she said quietly. "Maybe the kind of thing about GI development in the League that I have nightmares about. If they were going to release that information *here* . . ."

"League would have a big interest in stopping it," Hando suggested.

"Not as big as 2389," said Sandy. "Supporting emancipation could get the Federation into another war, or that's the fear. Sinta mentioned the USA Civil War in the eighteen hundreds . . . that was about slavery. The Northern president then, Lincoln, his name was, declared emancipation in the middle of that war to strengthen his cause. Abraham Lincoln. Where Abraham's Children got their name, I think."

"North and South then were already at war before emancipation was declared," Ibrahim countered. "Declaration did not cause the war."

"And yet the war was always about emancipation whether the participants admitted it or not," said Sandy. "The idea of emancipation was the catalyst, because freeing the slaves would destroy the Southern economy, just as freeing GIs will destroy the League's strategic advantage. Northerners begged Lincoln not to declare emancipation. Before the war, many hoped that stopping him would stop the war, in vain as it turned out. Now we have 2389 doing everything they can to rein in 'out of control' Federal power, and . . ."

"They're more interested in keeping the Feds from their own backyards," Hando interrupted. "Like Pyeongwha. Threatening to strip warmaking powers is just a ploy."

"And that ploy got all the pacifists, and all the political groups who just want to avoid another war at any costs, on board with 2389," Sandy replied.

"And that gives them the numbers in the GC to be as powerful as they are. Possibly a majority, if they keep building like this. And at that point, which cause controls which?"

Ibrahim gazed at her for a long moment, with heavy-lidded eyes. He knew. She'd read a lot about this, the American Civil War and the slaves in particular. Lincoln and emancipation. He'd suggested it once, long ago, saying that it intrigued him how closely some of the parallels ran between the situation of the slaves then and GIs today. Perhaps he was now wondering if his suggesting it had been wise.

"The question," said Ibrahim, "is whether the release of this information from Ravi Das, through the channels Detective Sinta has uncovered could possibly reverse that sentiment? If large-scale abuses of synthetic rights, or should I say *human* rights, have been committed in the production of GIs elsewhere in the League, as Cassandra has feared for many years, then it's conceivable it could swing popular support in favour of emancipation here in the Federation."

Sandy nodded. "As I see it, the Federation general public isn't the problem, most of them are reasonable, and reasonable people don't want another war, but neither do they want to see atrocities. The problem lies with those groups that have all come together in 2389 to try and control the general public opinion, whether it's corporations, political parties, NGOs, whatever. They claim to be representative of the people, but of course they're not, no institution is, because popular opinion can change. So they try to control it. And it looks like controlling popular opinion, in this case, meant silencing Idi Aba by any means necessary."

"So who?" said Shin thoughtfully, unfolding himself from his chair and heading for the small table where a secretary had left a tea set, gently steaming. "Detective Sinta. As I understand your work, you look for motive, means, and opportunity. But this is the Grand Council. Motive will not narrow anything down, motive will include every declared member of 2389, and many of the non-declareds as well. Thousands of individuals and tens of thousands of associated sympathisers on this world alone."

He looked around for fellow tea drinkers. Ibrahim and Hando declined. Sandy nodded. "Means will of course determine opportunity," Shin continued, pouring tea, his movements precise, graceful. "Only a few in the Grand Council can command such means officially, but unofficially the possibilities are vast.

If our controlling agent were acting as a parasite within the GC system, using offworld operators and GC codes and networks to keep it all obscure."

"They're too good," said Sandy, accepting the teacup he handed to her. Green tea, and fragrant. Sipped. "There were too many command codes in what they were using. I can see them stealing a few and leeching minor operations off the system. But what I ran into today wasn't that. And after I left, they all disappeared. That capability can only come from someone very well placed, with access to the highest-level functions."

"You have people in the Grand Council now?" Sinta asked. "Tracing where those operations were coming from?"

"It's nearly untraceable," said Ibrahim with distaste. "I tried to change this when the Council was relocated to Callay, but as in many things I was overruled in favour of retaining old systems and status quo. Grand Council security protocols remain opaque, they call it secrecy, but in truth it's obfuscation. Too many people in that building do not want anyone on the outside to know what they do, with our current predicament the inevitable result."

Sinta stared at him. Not stunned, just . . . wondering at the surrealness of it all, Sandy reckoned, having such cynical matters explained to her by the FSA Director himself. Like the kind of tales Detective Sinta might herself tell some ordinary citizen over a drink one night, about the kind of thing a cop might hear on the job regarding some extremely famous person and how their sparkly public image did not match with the sordid things they'd been doing out of the public gaze. One might suspect such a thing, in general cynicism, but to hear it from the mouth of authority was still a shock.

"Thus my conjecture," said Shin, settling gracefully back into his chair, tea in hand. "We may yet still catch the perpetrators by works of cunning, but first we must narrow the pool of suspects."

"You mean *you* may still catch the perpetrator," Hando said sourly. "Official investigations into the GC are a waste of time, for the same reasons the Director explains. Which leaves us with unofficial investigations. Mr Shin's specialty."

Spymaster Shin sipped tea and ventured no comment.

Kiril was asleep when they got home. She carried him upstairs to his bed in his and Danya's room and tucked him in in his clothes. And sat there on his bedside for a moment gazing at him, knowing she had no right for him to be this good to her. She'd gotten him into a dangerous situation, a scary situation, then kept him waiting in the FSA cafeteria, then offices while she attended important meetings, and to hear it told, he hadn't complained once. Or maybe just once, when he didn't like what the FSA cafeteria had optimistically called sausages. And again when his AR glasses wouldn't penetrate FSA security and he couldn't see outside the building.

Her heart was beating just a little too hard sitting there, looking at him, and she didn't want to leave him, even asleep. Funny that she didn't seem to do "love" emotionally, as straight humans understood it—that monogamous, brain-meltingly intense thing that all the songs were about. That was a thing between adults, and while she loved certain adults as intensely as anyone could love anything, it had nothing to do with that poetic sex-love stuff. That part of human experience, which all other humans seemed to have, was missing in her. And so she'd just expected that this part also, the motherhood part, would also be missing . . . because what were the odds that a walking killing machine would feel this kind of love anyway? Presumably she was missing that other kind for a reason, the same reason she'd probably be missing this kind too.

But here it was. And its discovery was at once confounding, exhilarating, and terrifying.

Despite it being so late, she sat with Danya and Svetlana for an hour after they'd washed and just talked, about what had happened, and about as much of the case with Sinta as she could considering it was classified, but the kids had seen some of it now and could know a little more, she'd cleared that with the relevant people. It was hard for kids to keep a secret if they didn't know exactly what it was, and an incomplete story would only get them asking more questions, and posing a greater risk than if they knew more.

And she apologised for getting them into a situation where they could have been hurt. Or worse. Only her brain just wouldn't accept "worse" when she tried to confront it rationally.

"Oh, that was *nothing*," said Svetlana, curled against Sandy's side in her pyjamas. "This one time, this real scary guy followed me through some deserted buildings. I was alone. I tried every sneaky trick I knew, but I took nearly an hour to lose him. *That* was scary, today was fun compared to that."

"She's right," said Danya. "The two months we've been here have been by far the least dangerous two months we've had. Since the last five years, anyway."

"It's still not right," Sandy insisted. Danya was sitting in the next chair across. He didn't do pyjamas, wouldn't take to them like Svetlana had, and wore tracksuit pants instead. Sandy wished he'd come and snuggle up like Svetlana but knew better than to suggest it. "Kids shouldn't be put in danger at all. I was wrong to do it, and I'm going to kick Ari's butt when I see him."

"Not for real, right?" said Svetlana.

Sandy smiled down at her. Concern for someone outside of her immediate little circle. That was good. "No, Svet, of course not for real. I love Ari. But he still needs to be told when I'm pissed, because Ari doesn't always look at things from other people's perspectives. Sometimes he needs it shoved in his face."

"I don't know," said Danya, sitting sideways in the chair, knees up. Looking thoughtful. "I mean, what are we going to be doing once we're grown adults anyway? I can't see myself sitting in some peaceful office job."

"Yet I kind of wish you would," said Sandy sadly.

"I don't know what I'll do, but I'm so caught up in this security stuff anyway, I figure I may as well do it for a profession. It's not like I could leave it alone now even if I wanted to."

"I know."

"Which means it wasn't the first time I've been shot at and won't be the last," Danya reasoned. "Think of today as work experience." Sandy gave him an unimpressed look. Danya looked almost amused. Which both alarmed and pleased her. Having kids seemed to do that to her a lot—scared and happy, all at once.

"Well, I'm going to be a supermodel," said Svetlana. "In the daytime, that is."

"And at night?" Sandy wondered.

"An assassin!"

Sandy sighed. "Of course you will."

An uplink registered. Local Canas services, a delivery. Sandy frowned. "There's a delivery coming, did either of you order anything?"

Head shakes. It was very late, but the house was probably registering that she was still up and informing the delivery service. Uplinks showed a car arrive out front, then the gate opened, and a delivery bot entered, holding a box. Danya was right, it *did* look a little creepy, she thought, with its projecting eyes and awkward gait. Or maybe she was just learning to see things from a child's perspective.

She went to the door and took the box—uplinks showed it was an outside delivery, checked by hand at Canas gate two, and passed through so many sensors she had no concerns of danger. Besides, she could faintly smell the contents, and they smelled delicious. She put the box on the kitchen cabinet and opened it. It was a cheesecake, with berries and a dusting of chocolate.

"Cheesecake!" Svetlana exclaimed. "I'm suddenly hungry, can I have a midnight snack?"

"Me too," said Danya. "We got shot at today, I think we deserve some cheesecake. Who's it from?"

There was a card, hand written. "For the kids," it said. "Hope their well. AR." She knew two ARs, but only one of them liked cheesecake.

"Arron Reichardt," said Sandy. "It's from the Captain. He must have sent an order electronically, and they laser copied this card and his signature." She'd learned from Vanessa and Rhian's weddings that some cake shops worked late in Tanusha. Wedding orders could rush in and keep them working all night, the deliveries could come any hour if you let them.

"And he misspelled 'they're,'" said Svetlana, peering at it. "Don't they teach spelling to fleet captains?"

"That's odd," Sandy agreed. "It's his handwriting; it's not possible the machine made an error, it's a facsimile not a translation."

"Actually that's grammar, Svet, not spelling," said Danya, taking a knife from the drawer and cutting. "He hasn't spelt it wrong, he's just used the wrong form. He's in the middle of those negotiations out at Pantala, he's probably under some stress."

"No, not there, here!" Svetlana demanded, seeing his next cut and pointing to where she thought it should be.

"It's eighths, Svet," Danya retorted. "Four people, two slices each, this is eighths."

"Yeah, but you'll mess it up! Do quarters first, then you can judge eighths better between the quarters!"

Because if they'd ever been so lucky as to encounter a cheesecake on Droze, the precise sharing of every last millimeter would have become a matter of monumental concern.

Danya's knife hit something. He frowned. "There's something in here." He cut over it, carefully pulled out a slice onto the plate Svetlana provided, then pulled out the metal object inside. It was as long as Danya's hand, and slim. He cleaned the cake off one side with a finger.

"Hey!" said Svetlana before he could clean off the other side, and did that herself, then sucked her finger. And looked at the thing in Danya's hand. "What is it?"

"It's a handfile," said Sandy, taking it from Danya. "An antique, though I imagine some old-style woodworkers might still use them."

"Why would Captain Reichardt put an old woodwork tool in a cake?" Danya wondered, not sufficiently preoccupied with the mystery to keep him from eating. "I suppose Canas security saw it wasn't dangerous and let it through. Maybe the cake maker lets people do that for a joke or something."

It gave Sandy a very odd feeling. And she suddenly remembered a story Vanessa told her, five years ago, in the conclusion of the Battle of Nehru Station. She and Reichardt had finally secured the Nehru Station bridge against Fifth Fleet marines. Reichardt had suggested he'd probably end up in prison for the rest of his life, at the least. Vanessa had joked that she'd send him a cake with a GI baked inside, and had had to explain to Sandy what that meant—in the old days, when prisons had been made out of concrete, iron and other things that crumbled, prisoners had tried to smuggle things into prison, in gifts and the like, that would allow them to tunnel walls or break bars over a long period and escape. The oldest cliché was something baked in a cake, Vanessa had said. Something like a file.

Reichardt sent her a cake with a file in it, from negotiations into the future of Federation-League relations. A warning, perhaps, that someone was going to prison. After the Battle of Nehru Station, Reichardt had been concerned it would be him, for fighting against elements of the Fleet, and never mind that that Fleet element had started it by violating basic Federation law about the rights of worlds. If there was trouble again in Fleet over negotiations out in New Torah, Reichardt would be the one who'd know.

But he sent this warning to her. With a misspelled card—Reichardt was a well-read man, and like all captains a stickler for detail. "They're watching us," he said. "I can't tell you what's going on. But one of us is in trouble." And the card expressed concern for her kids.

"Danya," she said quietly. "Go and wake Kiril. Then all of you pack a bag of things you think you might need."

Silence as they stared at her, but only for a moment. "For how long?" asked Danya.

"I don't know. Probably I'm just being paranoid and we'll be back tomorrow. Probably. But take more, just in case."

Danya took his and Svetlana's half-eaten cake to the fridge. Svetlana just stood, looking upset.

"Svet?" Sandy asked. "What's wrong?"

"I like it here!" she said, lip trembling. "I like living here with you; I don't want to leave!"

Sandy put hands on her shoulders. "Svet, it's just a precaution. You know if we live this life, we all have to take precautions sometimes. No one's going to make you leave. If we ever leave, it will be because we've chosen to leave for somewhere even better. If someone tries to *make* us leave, they'll have to come through me first. You understand?" Svetlana nodded. "Now go with Danya and get ready."

She went, following Danya up the stairs. Canas security would see them leaving. That could be accessed. It no longer felt safe, not after Detective Sinta's run-in with anonymous Feds today. If there were enemies in the Grand Council, then there weren't very many places that were safe. Nowhere on the official network anyway.

Click. "*Sandy, what's up?*" Vanessa's voice.

"Reichardt just sent me a warning, something's not right. I think Fleet trouble."

"*The negotiations. Fuck.*" Waking up fast. "*What did he say?*"

"Nothing, he can't risk it, that's the point. We know there's Feds in town we can't account for. We know an internal push within the GC could tip us all out. Too many variables, I'm shifting house with the kids. Say we're visiting with friends if anyone asks."

They'd talked about this, her, Vanessa, Ari, Rhian, and some of their FSA/CSA comrades, people who'd had each other's back under fire and could be trusted absolutely. FSA spec ops only existed on the GC Security Committee approval, and their other employer, the CSA, was run by a Callayan government administration that currently disliked everything Federal. If the squeeze came, they'd agreed, it would be political, aimed at shutting down the perpetrators of the Pyeongwha action. If it happened, Sandy wanted herself and, most importantly, her kids to be on ground that couldn't be pulled out from under them by any administration. Canas security barriers were Callayan government–controlled and could turn from a shield to a noose.

"*Dammit, we didn't figure on Fleet. You've checked who's in town?*"

"Yeah, they'll never tell us, not even Ibrahim knows ship movements if Fleet doesn't want them known. Only Shin might know."

"*Who carried that message back from Reichardt, do you think?*"

"More likely some freighter, so Fleet couldn't touch it. Hasn't the best relationship with his fellow captains, Reichardt."

"*Well, thanks for the heads up, I'll spread the word with the others, you just look after the kids.*"

"Thanks, I appreciate it. What about you?"

"*I'll stay here. I understand you wanting to get out of Canas, but this is a more normal neighbourhood. They couldn't detain me without detaining Phillippe, he's a public figure, it's awkward for them. No political stunt they might pull will work if they start upsetting the general public, and Phillippe's friends are all on their side right now. They piss the Tanushan arts community off, next thing all the actors and singers turn on them, etc.*"

"That's a nice theory Phillippe's been peddling," Sandy warned. "Don't rely on it."

"*I won't. Talk to Ibrahim, huh? You're the only person he'll listen to more than Ari.*"

They drove out the Canas gate in the replacement cruiser, the old one in an FSA shop getting repairs to dents and two bullet holes. Canas security scanned them leaving, but once they were airborne Sandy activated her self-designed functions and disappeared from the grid. It wasn't strictly legal even for an FSA agent, because she'd disappeared from their grid too, and HQ liked to know where all its vehicles were. She landed at a deserted TZ in a quiet neighbourhood, then lifted off once more with a false ID on the traffic net, and no one would know without a closer look.

She explained the situation to Ibrahim as they flew.

"*I've not heard anything myself,*" he said. "*But as you suggest, if there were moves afoot in the Grand Council they'd be careful not to let me know. Mr Shin is another question.*"

"Director, if they decide to shut down FSA spec ops, that's one thing. They'll find an excuse, like League did six months ago with the war crimes charges. My main worry is the CSA, because most of us FSA spec ops are also CSA SWAT. If the Callayan government goes after SWAT as well, not only are all we agents in some difficulty, but Callay is left relatively defenceless."

"I'm not certain President Singh is quite that pig-headed . . ."

"I myself have no doubt of it," Sandy cut in.

". . . but I'm keeping an eye on him. Or Chandi is."

"And who keeps an eye on Chandi? If you were still CSA Director, I'd have no doubts of your support. Chandi remains very vague on this."

"Cassandra, Director Chandrasekar answers directly to the President of Callay. Should Singh give him an order, he'll follow it."

"Yes, but you see how precarious this whole thing becomes. We rely upon one person who relies on another and so on. 2389 is struggling for the majority in the GC to make constitutional amendments, and people like me, like FSA spec ops, we get in the way. There's a lot of desperate people who seriously think we're headed for another war, or Federal disintegration, if they don't pass those amendments. And now Detective Sinta has evidence they've already killed one person who got in their way."

"We should not taint an entire groundswell movement because of the actions of a few extreme operatives," Ibrahim reminded her. *"We've no evidence so far that it's anything else. But your concerns are justified, and the FSA will stand by its own people."*

"Some elements of the FSA will be happier to hear that than others," Sandy replied. FedInt, she meant. The broad remains of the old FIA, before it had been disbanded. Or rather, central command had been disbanded, back on Earth, but the tentacles lived on, though somewhat reformed, as Federal Intelligence. When the FSA had been constituted under Director Diez, FedInt had been folded back into the structure—suddenly the FSA, previously just some fancy offices in Tanusha, had a body that spanned the Federation. But there were many who speculated that the body had never entirely accepted its new brain.

"I'm onto it, Cassandra," said Ibrahim. *"I cannot put the FSA on alert without our potential enemies being aware of it, but I'll do what I can off the grid."*

The kids were very impressed with a hotel room on the sixty-third floor. There were two adjoining rooms, four beds and two bathrooms. For most even advanced net hackers, passing a famous person through hotel biometrics with intent to hide was a difficult thing. But Sandy simply took over the whole hotel construct and told it what it saw. VR matrixes of the kind Cai had used made it possible, no longer was it a matter of hacking through barriers the old way and hoping the different portions didn't notice the sudden lack of symmetry, rather a matter of enveloping portions of the construct in another construct, which fed its inputs a constructed world—like VR for non-sentient AIs. She'd given this hotel a face, biometrics, stride pattern, everything, while the kids had gone straight to the room.

Tanusha's network and functions were evolving, but not nearly as fast as hers were. She was becoming so accomplished lately, utilising new construct tools, shredders, and environmentals like VR, it was nearly alarming. And still she'd never be nearly as capable as Ragi, let alone Cai. Suddenly the horizons of those possibilities seemed so much further away.

She'd barely closed the door when an uplink com link blinked, an advanced function, relaying through FSA secure systems to find her. Steven Harren, network expert extraordinaire, lately running the K project, as it was being called—something so obscure and bland that no one could possibly guess its origins, if any.

"*Hello, Cassandra, you should really see this.*" Earnestly alarmed. Like a teenager with his first uplinks, who found them doing something weird and wanted to show an expert before he knew how worried to be. Sandy gestured to the kids that she was uplinked and sat on one of the beds as they noisily sorted out whose was whose.

"*Concerning what?*" she formulated.

"*Look, I know you're skeptical about my work, but this concerns your personal safety among other things, and it's just easier if you take a look.*"

"*I'm not skeptical whether it works, Steve,*" she said. "*Just whether using it constitutes selling our soul to the devil. Would VR suit you?*"

"*Um . . . I can't do a secure VR from where I am, and I don't think something that bandwidth would be too smart where you are.*"

He'd heard then. "*Plug in on the hardline, I'll show you something.*" A techie like him wouldn't be able to resist Sandy Kresnov volunteering to "show him something." She found the construct, access gates, cleared a path on massive encryption, and sent him the link. And announced to the room,

"Guys, I'm on VR for a moment, if you need anything just give me a whack."

It opened, and she still had to consciously relax, taking her various resistant net functions out of play, toning them down so they didn't disrupt the VR formation as it slowly wrapped around her main construct . . .

. . . and she was sitting at an outdoor restaurant halfway up a mountain in the French Pyrenees. Ragi's copy of public VR space; Allison wasn't here at the moment, she had a number of different spaces she liked to spend her time now. And here seated opposite, in a slow rush of materialising data, was Steven Harren, a look of astonishment even now on his unresolved gridform face.

"Wow," he said as the last textures of skin, hair, and clothing resolved themselves, grinning and looking around. "This is Allison Roundtree's space isn't it, the one Ragi made for her? I heard about this."

"The Pyrenees were my idea," Sandy admitted. "My biographer comes here to cycle, he rigs his bike on a feedback stand, then pedals in VR like he's actually climbing mountains. Crazy pretty place. What's up?"

"Well, I ran our infamous little software analysis package on the Grand Council."

Sandy stared at him. She wasn't often left speechless. Then, "How and why?" she said.

"How doesn't matter," said Steven. "Let's just say I got permission. Why, well, I'd think that was obvious. To figure out what they're up to. Look at this."

He drew a square space above the table with his fingers, activating that space, then uploaded his data to it with a fluency that Sandy had to find impressive. A 3D graphic of the Grand Council building appeared. Sandy knew it well enough to identify various offices and sections, from central Grand Chamber to basement parking and security, to the Committees with their permanent staff. Building staff, security, she'd helped review those setups, knowing more about how they might be broken by League GIs than most.

"Now obviously," said Steven, "the sample sizes are far too small to come up with any meaningful sociological analysis. Deviation levels are about what you'd expect considering staff tend to favour offices according to their own ideological preferences, not much to be learned there either."

Graphics emerged from the different offices and sections, 3D lines and indices. He must have had access to all Grand Council network traffic, Sandy thought, to run through these software filters. Who the hell had the authority to order something like that? She doubted even Ibrahim did.

". . . but," Steven continued, "if we stop running broad scale analysis like we've been accustomed to, and start using the truly freaky capabilities of the psych analysis stuff that you wrote, over a week's worth of data we can get things like stress, anger, general anxiety."

More graphical lines appeared, spectruming through various colours. Percentages indicated, changing levels, all time stamped. If only the average person knew how much net traffic their uplinks generated, and that personality and states-of-mind were imprinted onto most of it, if one had the tools to decipher it. It would scare the shit out of people, to know governments could learn this stuff so easily.

"Hold it," said Sandy, eyes wide as it occurred to her. "Can you run for matches in chronology?"

Steven smiled, making more changes with little indications of his hands in mid-air. "I knew you'd see that." The graphs all shifted, running over the last week, shifts in anxiety, anger, progressions of disturbance. "Within the Grand Council, nothing."

"Hmm." Sandy gnawed a thumbnail, staring at the display. A little guilty for finding it this compelling, but in these circumstances she wasn't about to miss an opportunity.

"But," Steven added with a glint in his eye, "you cross-reference this with the profiles I ran of the Callayan Parliament and President's Office . . ."

"Crap," said Sandy. "Chandi gave you permission to run this stuff on the Government of Callay?"

"Sure," said Steven. Evasively? Or was that just her imagination? Who else would he be answerable to, if not Chandi? The whole project was CSA, Ibrahim didn't like it . . . "Look at this, this is the last week's worth of traffic."

He ran it. Sandy could see changes, sudden spikes in anxiety and stress readings, coinciding with various events over the past week, all while the timecode unwound, first twelve hours, then twenty-four, then more. But they diverged too. Different departments in different parts of the government were concerned with different issues, the things that might make tempers boil in the Education Committee may not concern anyone in Communications or

Biotech. The big events effected everyone, but the software could recognise those "universals," factor them out, and search for underlying variances . . .

"There," said Steven, as the program found two increasingly synchronous matches and put them together. Sure enough, the highlighted timelines were running at a statistically significant parallel.

"It's still within the margin of error," said Sandy, still gnawing her nail. GI nails were hard to cut with scissors, sometimes teeth were easier. Now the habit was translating to VR. "Why won't it show what those two timelines are from?"

"So we won't be swayed by personal prejudices and leap to conclusions," said Steven. "Now look at this . . . these major spikes, across the last seven days?" As the timelines ceased running. "I discard most of the data, just look for similar spikes at those exact date lines, this is the stress/anxiety line here. And I get . . ." more data flashed up in the space above the tabletop, ". . . these additional matches, a couple of them just individuals, but very strong readings, matching those times down to the minute."

Another wave of the fingers, and names appeared. Sandy stared and felt herself drop almost immediately into combat mode. VR nearly broke up completely, she had to consciously force the reflex down, disabling interface functions so she didn't lose the link. VR never worked in combat reflex, her brain tried to break down code, not build it up and be manipulated by it.

"Son of a bitch," she murmured. One of the highlights originated from the Intelligence Committee staff, no more than two or three people. Another came from the office of Ambassador Kitimara, from the Argell System, appointed leader of the Federation political party most commonly known as 2389. Another came from Ambassador Ballan's office, Sandy's old friend, head of the Intelligence Committee and highest-ranking security rep in the GC. Another came from President Singh's office, Callayan Government. And one more, a spike less convincing than all of them but still a temporal match, came from the office of Chief Shin of FedInt, FSA.

"The system matches them all up because on these specific dates, all generated network interface that the system reads as high on the stress/anxiety indicators," Steven explained, his usual excitement with the tech now tempered with worry. "This first date matches with only one notable event— on Wednesday the 18th, the Intelligence Committee met, and broke up at

1:22pm, this first spike peaks at 1:25, so just after whoever was in the meeting gets out of the com shielding and starts talking to people.

"The second spike was on Thursday, and we don't know what it was, there are no matches I can find, but it was at 4:16 in the morning, and again, all of these offices registered an anxiety spike between then and 4:30."

"Early morning and no record, that's probably a ship," said Sandy. And if it was a ship, could be it Fleet? She thought of Reichardt's cake, and the file inside.

"And the third spike was here." Steven pointed to the spot, hovering in mid-air. But he was looking at Sandy, not at where his finger was pointing. "Sunday, today. Or yesterday rather. Just following your little tangle with the Feds who were after Detective Sinta."

Sandy's mind was racing. But there were too many possibilities and not enough firm information.

"The question," said Steven, "is what could there be that connects all these individuals to either be talking to each other, or to be simultaneously responding to the same event, in a way that generates a stress/anxiety response? One event can be statistically explained, sure, but all three? And all quite different—an Intel Committee meeting indicating forethought and planning, something that might have been a call from a ship, and your rescue of a homicide detective tracking down some leads that could embarrass the Feds? It's nearly statistically impossible that there isn't some specific connection."

And now Reichardt sent her a warning, which meant that whatever it was, it was connected to League-Federation negotiations. Negotiations on how to handle the biggest crisis in League-Federation relations since the war, and some very powerful people with great incentive to sweep all the League's nasty little secrets under the carpet in the name of not rocking the boat.

She'd thought the move when it came would be political only, perhaps the disbandment of FSA spec-ops for starters, perhaps legal proceedings to follow. But would something technical like that require this much coordination between this many different groups? Of course, just because an office was implicated did not mean that the head of that office was involved—she'd have bet her house Ballan was not involved with such schemes, 2389 was anathema to him, he'd helped plan and mobilise the Pyeongwha operation after all. But Ballan's office was large, as was the Intel Committee staff, as were all of these highlighted offices and institutions. If there were spikes emerging on this software directly following an Intel Committee meeting, then someone *very* high must be involved, because most of those even she wasn't allowed into. But there was one person she trusted who the Committee weren't allowed to keep out.

"Ibrahim," she said. "I have to talk to Ibrahim. Now."

CHAPTER TWENTY

Sandy had only visited Ibrahim's home a few times—Ibrahim scheduled no official functions, parties, or gatherings there of any kind, believing in the strict segregation of work and home life. She set a course there now, only telling traffic central she was heading nearby, not game to let it know her destination until she was right on top of it.

Hypothetically Ibrahim would have some of the best network security in Tanusha, yet he was Federal. All security at the Federal government level was now suspect, and she had to suspect that any direct contact would be traced back to her. It was face to face or nothing.

"Vanessa," she said as the cruiser left the hotel vicinity, building up speed on a main skylane amidst a smattering of 3am traffic. "Go red please. No time for more, just go red and tell everyone, thanks."

"*Gotcha,*" came the terse reply. "*Take care.*"

That would set the ball rolling, at worst if she was wrong it would cost them all some sleep. But now all their personal security plans would be activated, and there weren't many operatives in Tanusha, legally or otherwise, who would confidently tangle with FSA spec ops, even alone and just out of bed.

"*Sandy, what's up?*" came Ari's voice.

"Code red, Ari, best not talk to me, if this is Feds, we don't know what codes they can break and trace."

"*Sandy, I don't know what you're tracking, but good authority just told me there's RFM in orbit, you understand?*" Random Fleet Movement. Which was usually nothing, unless it wasn't. "*This good authority also tells me that . . .*"

Sandy registered a combat track and dropped into combat mode so hard it hurt, a physical jarring. Two warheads, twelve Ks out, accelerating past Mach One, and very fixed on her. "Ari, I have incoming! This is a war, if they come at you, shoot back!"

And disconnected, tacnet establishing fast, complete 3D visual as time slowed and trajectories displayed. Ten Ks, fired from two-K altitude, war indeed. FSA weren't allowed to do that over Tanusha no matter who the target, no one was. Acceleration profile showed her what she'd suspected; they were military tech, nothing her little FSA cruiser was equipped to dodge, dividing even now in case she tried to hide behind a tower, the first would force her stationary, where the second would nail her. Her only chance was to hack them, but they were running full autistic, independent warheads that not even their owners could call back, save a simple termination signal.

Four Ks and still accelerating, if she stayed here she had seconds to live. She broke her restraints, smashed the window, and pulled herself out. And fell. The cruiser exploded with a deafening thump that sent her spinning as she fell, twisting in the howl of wind to reorient herself on the ground for a landing. Suburban streets, some high-rise residential, otherwise two and three storeys, lots of trees. If she angled herself and caught the wind like a skydiver, she had just enough altitude left to aim for that road over . . .

Fire cracked past her, detonated on proximity charges, then more, hailing shrapnel. Long-range fire, inaccurate but getting closer, and she spread-eagled to catch the wind, saw her chance at the road disappear, then curled into a ball, super-tensed her muscles, and smashed into rooftops at a forty-five-degree angle like a cannon ball. Blacked out briefly at the force of it . . .

. . . and came to as she spun off a wall and onto gardens, digging a furrow. Unwrapped her limbs with difficulty, a rippling sensation as tightly lodged synth-alloy muscles at first refused to move. Her clothes were torn but still serviceable, the very reason she liked jeans and leather. Back the way she'd come, she could see a hole torn through the top of a tiled roof, branches missing from a large tree, and now a big dent in the wall she'd glanced off. At least two house alarms were blaring, and several dogs barking. And surely no one would shoot at her down here, sleeping families on all sides.

New missile tracks registered even as she thought it, and she was up fast, uncooperative muscles pushing hard for speed. She leapt a fence, turned hard left, jumped for a rooftop as a round blew up half the garden behind her, sending her spinning, crashing off the tiles, but recovering as she sprang for a roadside tree, kicked off a branch, smashed another that got in her way, and landed on the road with barely a hand down to steady herself.

And accelerated. Overhead trees made some cover but couldn't hide her. A house could, but she had no guarantee they wouldn't just blow the whole thing, family and all. Whoever "they" were, they were playing for keeps; she was senior FSA, and the legal penalty for killing her was death. Unless "they" were planning to upend the entire foundation upon which that legality rested. A family's life might not count for much against that, and God knew where her cruiser's wreckage had landed.

Claremont business district was only a K away. She sprinted down the avenue, overstriding as GIs would with far more power than a human stride pattern could contain, leaping ahead in ever-increasing bounds. Whatever was shooting at her was not registering on her uplinks. In fact, nothing was. Tacnet was there, but it was a tacnet of one person, connected to nothing, like an empty shell. To draw such a complete blank, they'd had to have shut down nearly everything. But she still had basic mapping, which told her a right turn ahead took her to Claremont District . . . she cut the corner by leaping a couple of rooves and caught the first glimpse of something dark hovering, out of lanes, perhaps a K behind.

And firing now, sonofabitch, they weren't kidding. Micro-munitions, highly strung enough to target fast-moving GIs as most missiles couldn't, and she kicked off the last rooftop for a moment's extra airtime, spun, pulled both pistols, and fired. Kept spinning, hit the road she was aiming for and kept running as one missile dropped abruptly short, the other spinning off into the night . . . thankfully neither exploded, those warheads were very stable, even her pistol fire wouldn't set them off. This asshole was too far away and apparently poorly informed of her abilities—big missiles would leave craters all over Tanusha, little ones she could shoot down, and his gun wasn't accurate enough against her mobility in this environment from that range. He had to get in close and use it where she couldn't dodge. Perhaps now he was realising.

She hurdled light traffic on the road to Claremont, reaching nearly 100 kph as the bridge across a river approached ahead . . . and suddenly the flyer was descending over it, everything aimed her way. It was big for a combat flyer, broad-shouldered, entirely jet-powered rather than rotor nacelles, and foreign to any Callayan service. An A-12 gunship, mostly they were Fleet marines and Federal Army. They'd shot at her before in the war, but she'd rarely seen them. They were typically long-range, airbourne artillery largely immune to counterstrike.

She leapt left, hit the wall of an apartment building at 100 kph, and stopped hard, concrete shattering and falling, leaving her a hole in the outer wall. And she waited, because blowing up a civvie house was one thing, an entire apartment building something else. A strategic victory, if it claimed her as well, but surely a political disaster.

Then she saw the second flyer, coming around from the side. *Two* of them. She dropped into cover between buildings and ran for the river. It was forty meters wide at this point, far enough that a simple, arcing trajectory across it would get her killed, predictable as armscomp would find it. But her uplink map showed that here, moored by the riverbank was a pleasureboat, a tourist ferry.

She leaped down the road between taller apartment buildings that over-looked the river, a few astonished pedestrians looking, some not even noticing, her singular, bounding footfalls made little sound, and the engines of nearby hovering gunships made a distinct shrieking that covered everything else. Sandy took off between buildings, flying low, cleared the riverside walk, saw the ferry rooftop rushing at her ahead, planted both feet and shoved as hard as pre-tensed combat myomer could shove, a force that rocked the whole boat.

And flew, low and hard as office towers loomed ahead. Gunfire from the right, proximity rounds thudding a string of fireworks across the river in her wake, adjusting now for her riverside course change and plotting ahead until . . . she made herself thin like a diver and hit the office windows opposite, curling again into a ball as the glass smashed. Another impact, less hard than the last, and found herself lying amidst panels in an office hallway having punched straight through a partition wall. She got up and ran, away from the river—putting missiles into expensive office buildings would be drastic, but unlike suburbia, at three in the morning these were all deserted.

BOOM! as the concussion blew her off her feet down the hallway, flames and debris ripping about, clattering off the walls. But now she was at the con-crete core, and the storm of high-explosive cannon fire that followed could not penetrate concrete, as she pressed herself into an elevator alcove and watched the walls disintegrate around her. The occasional shrapnel chunk tore her skin and stuck hard, thumping impacts like hailstones and about as dangerous . . . unless one took an eye, which she covered beneath an arm.

Then, after she'd ensured he'd wasted a good chunk of his ammo, she yanked open the elevator doors and slid down the central cable, past the ground floor to underground parking. Hauled those doors open and found herself in a large underground car park that was certainly immune from anything those flyers could throw at her. Which gave her time to think, so she walked to the center of a driving lane, holstered both pistols, and stretched armour-tense limbs and back. Shrapnel caught at her left arm, she felt and yanked it out. Another protruded from her neck, right where the jugular would be on a straight. A third she felt, then pulled from her buttock. There was always one in the butt; back in Dark Star it had been Sandy's immutable law of shrapnel.

Stay here? To pull this off, whoever was behind it must have pulled some serious legal move through the Grand Council. More than just declaring her and her colleagues disbanded, more like illegal. Probably they'd fabricated something, a plot she was supposedly hatching. A coup would be perfect. Thus giving these attackers full legal authority to "save" the Federation from nefarious traitors. But with all uplinks down she had no idea what else was going on . . . how the hell were they doing that?

Tacnet! She abandoned it, empty shell that it was—it left her more exposed, but suddenly the city was crashing in, various seekers feeding her news reports, breaking news, crisis news, great alarm at the Grand Council, reporters hurrying in the dead of night, big announcements, breathless reportage. And reports of shooting in Claremont District. She wound back her profile, kept all functions passive, her attackers would be watching here as well, and if she operated in combat mode in the open city network without tacnet to organise and shield everything, she'd stand out like a beacon. A beacon that announced "Shoot me!" at the top of its voice, complete with targeting coordinates.

A few smaller shrapnel pieces removed, she stretched once more, trying to get the stiffness out. From somewhere outside, she could hear the howl of hovering engines. No one would be dumb enough to send troops into a closed space to get her face to face. But if this was now political, every poor foot soldier she had to kill to get out of this was a PR victory for the other side. And God forbid they had enough strings and levers to pull to send Callayans after her, maybe even people she knew.

Plus it was a bad look—caught in a basement car park surrounded by authorities, like a common fugitive. Negotiating for her emergence, no doubt in full media view. It would look like she'd done something wrong, and as of now, this was all about power at the highest level. Ultimate power in any democracy came from popular opinion. She could no more do anything to hurt popular opinion toward her now than expose herself to deadly fire.

So. That made it easy.

She selected a car park exit, waited for the engine noises to fade a little, then kicked the security roller door off its side hinges. She could have just hacked the system, but it was too dangerous now; she was a deadly net operator, but the powers currently arrayed against her, all knowing she was trapped in the one location, were not something even she wanted to tackle. Ever since she'd discovered her own killswitch nearly six years ago, she'd been very cautious of open-grid net access, especially where shadowy conspiracies prepared long-gestation plots against her. Her killswitch was far too well shielded to be accessed, everyone said so . . . but she hadn't lived this long by just accepting what people said.

She slid through the gap and onto the car ramp, crouched low. The sidewalks were as close to deserted as she'd ever seen in any Tanusha high-rise center, but this was a business center, offices only open in work hours, very little residential or nightlife. Down by one intersection she could see people gathering to stare and point upward, no doubt at the smoke rising from the tower above, wondering what all the shooting was. Damn fools should go inside, the firepower on an A-12 could level city blocks. Accessing the map now was risky, but she did it anyway . . . and got a good 3D visual of the Claremont CBD skyline. There. That was a good spot, just around the corner. If her attackers wanted to finish her here, they'd have to try it.

She took off running toward the little crowd on the intersection, pistols still in holsters, and took a fast right. Away from the river the towers got taller, glass canyons rising sheer on both sides. Not even micro-munitions could turn right angles, and cannon would require *very* close range . . .

The howl of engines abruptly doubled, as directly ahead a flyer crabbed down the cross street directly in front of her. And levelled cannon.

Sandy sprang, not straight up, nor ahead, but for the left wall. Hit, and bounced hard off for the right wall, the cannon traversing rapidly to follow. Then left, then right, careful not to push so hard she broke the glass, an ever ascending zigzag. A final bounce, straight at the flyer cockpit. Smashed the canopy, then the pilot's head, and yanked the frame off with a bang! of snapping alloy. Broke the pilot's straps, determined to throw the body out and repeat the trick she'd first used on Droze a few months ago, as the weapons officer struggled against straps to try and draw a personal weapon and twist around to shoot her . . .

Only now there were missiles heading in. Sandy jumped well clear, a ten-storey fall to a bounce on barely bended knees, and watched as the flyer was hit once, then twice, explosions tearing out all windows within fifty meters, flaming wreckage crashing to the road amidst a hail of falling glass. And burned, an orange glow reflected in the foyer glass of intersection buildings. One nacelle had flattened a parked car, and Sandy peered inside—it looked empty, thank God, an auto-park overnight. The only visible pedestrians were running away.

The second flyer emerged, hovering perhaps six hundred meters off, with a clear line of sight down this road. Deadly serious he was, if he had orders to shoot down his buddy rather than let her commandeer his flyer. Sandy stood amidst the flaming wreckage of his wingman and stared up at the second flyer. Smiled at him and beckoned. Certainly he'd see her on armscomp, full magni-fication. Come on, you still want me? Here I am. Surrounded by towers your missiles can't turn fast enough to get in among. You'll have to use your gun at such close range that you'll have towers on either side, and I can ping-pong off the walls and bring down your multi-million-dollar machine with a single fist. Fire now, and I'll see the barrels spinning a half second before the bullets fly, and will be up the side road before they reach me.

She pointed her fingers at him, in the shape of a gun, cocky as all hell. They wanted to know they'd rattled her. Scared her even. She smiled and pulled the trigger with gangsta-style exaggeration. Boom. This is just me having fun, and I'm gonna kill every last one of you fuckers, just watch. The flyer turned and flew away.

Phillippe was playing Kubayashi when armoured troops smashed in through doors and windows. Alone in the living room, wearing just the clothes he'd dragged on when Vanessa had grabbed her things and left with a kiss. Kubayashi was quite loud, fast, and required concentration that he much preferred to spend on his instrument than watching armoured goons trash his lovely house.

One of them finally stood in front of him, while several others covered, and addressed him through tinny helmet speakers. "Where is she?"

"You think she's stupid enough to tell me?" The allegro fourth verse was a real bitch, now the distraction made him miss his fingering. "By the way, you're being recorded."

"Your house net is jammed."

"The wireless boosters aren't." Which set off a new round of scurrying, stomping footsteps, *all* enforcement types hated being recorded when they stormed a house, and Vanessa had considered this possibility long ago. Jamming big signal boosters would shut down entire neighbourhoods, not the low profile this operation was targeting, and the house feed was currently going straight to the net, with an emergency signal to get people's attention. Vanessa thought it would make things safer for him and more embarrassing for everyone else.

Finally the man who'd addressed him reappeared. "Stop playing and get up, you're under arrest."

Phillippe stopped playing. "On what charge?"

"Federal emergency, we don't need charges."

"What emergency?" He got up and put his violin back in its case. It was one of his cheap practise instruments, not the replica Stradivarius. That was safely locked away; he'd been unsure the goons wouldn't smash it.

"None of your business." Phillippe didn't recognise the armour, and there were no insignia, nothing to identify an organisation. The accent sounded foreign though.

"What kind of facist smashes into the home of a law-abiding citizen and tells him the reason he's being arrested is 'none of his business'?"

"Quit your posturing," said the armoured man. "We found the signal booster, you're not being broadcast anymore."

"All of them?" asked Phillippe. And smiled as they went scurrying again.

Ibrahim arrived at the rooftop HQ pad to find Agent Teo waiting for him. Nearby the engines of A-12 flyers keened. Over by the looming Grand Council building, a steady stream of VIP cruisers approached, flowing into secure parking. Ground defences covered them on hair trigger, ready to remove anything unauthorised from the night sky with violent precision. Outside the ground defence perimeter, the A-12s were authorised to do the same. The Federation capitol had been woken early this morning, and now everyone rushed for their offices. Before the gates, the media were gathering, cars, vans and cameras in swarms.

"Sir, the official word is a coup," said Teo, terse and worried. They walked for the entrance, flanked by armed agents. "Office of the Intelligence Directorate, they say FSA spec ops were plotting a coup against the Grand Council; they're taking steps to arrest and neutralise."

"Utilising what resources?" They entered the main hall off the pads, people were rushing, shouting across offices. Checking data, finding weapons, asking after colleagues.

"We're not sure yet, though they came down on assault ships, so we know that Fleet brought them. We think their ground forces are mostly non-Callayan Federal assets from other worlds, but the A-12s are using army codes. Sir, we're technically suspended, emergency order from the Office of Intelligence Directorate countersigned by Council Chair, FSA is ordered to stand down and await further instruction."

"I know." Silence was Ibrahim's greatest professional strength. Silence of mouth and silence of mind, save what was absolutely necessary. He could have thought and worried and demanded a thousand things, yet none of that would help him here. "Which of our people have they gone after?"

They arrived at Ibrahim's office, and here at the doors waited Fleet Liaison Admiral Vernier, grey and grim. "Shan, I'm sorry, I didn't know." Ibrahim nodded and walked past, finding Hando inside in furious conversation with someone on uplink.

"Mostly they seem to be going after the GIs," said Teo, hurrying to keep up. The big office screens showed live feeds from various sources, crowds before the GC gates, fires burning in some unidentified part of the city, news camera shots of A-12s cruising the Tanushan skylanes, ominous foreign silhouettes. "They seem to have most of them in custody, we've instructed them not to resist. Some of our senior spec ops aren't responding. We think a small group of them centered around Commander Kresnov saw something like this coming and were ready for it. We know foreign assault teams went in hard at both Commander Rice and Captain Chu's homes and found no one. But they don't seem to have shared those preparations with many others, probably they didn't want to be discovered.

"Sir, there's some confusion over Commander Kresnov's whereabouts." With great concern, as Ibrahim sat on the edge of his desk, and others filed into the office behind. Like a conductor preparing to lead his orchestra into musical battle. "She went off-grid more than an hour before the emergency was declared, it's like she was tipped off. Twenty minutes ago we received an emergency signal from her cruiser, and now there are reports of a cruiser crashed in Claremont District. It hit a house and killed several occupants. It seems to have been shot down."

Teo indicated a display, pictures showed a house on fire, emergency vehicles responding, a chaos of strobing lights and flames. "And just nearby in Claremont District an A-12 has crashed, and there are reports of shooting preceding that crash. We've queried Intelligence Directorate but received no reply." Another screen showed wreckage that looked to have once been a flyer, sprawled and burning across a high-rise city intersection, more emergency vehicles and gawking civilians surrounding.

"If an A-12 shot down her cruiser, then was itself destroyed, chances seem likely Kresnov was in the cruiser at the time," Ibrahim observed, watching the screens with narrowed eyes. "Cassandra is very hard to kill; attempts usually backfire."

"How does she shoot down an A-12 with pistols?" Hando asked, ending his uplink conversation.

"Bare-handed," Vernier replied. "Her action report from Droze was an eye-opener. Those towers give her access and cover."

"No wonder they went after the GIs first," said Hando, hands on bald head.

"Sir," Teo added anxiously, "can I also remind you that the Office of Intelligence Directorate has summonsed you to appear before them immediately, Ambassador Ballan himself."

"I know," said Ibrahim. "I was supposed to go straight there." No one asked why he hadn't. "I want assessments. Is Ballan leading this?"

"Who else could it be?" Hando replied. "Even the Council Chair doesn't have the authority to tell the FSA to stand down, they need Intelligence Directorate approval. OID are the only ones with unilateral authority to run something like this and keep it quiet."

"Ballan ordered Kresnov killed?" Admiral Vernier asked. "Aren't they friends?"

The room gave him faintly pitying looks. Military people were sometimes slow to understand how the politics worked. The brutal pressures of popularly elected billions. All forces collided here, like continental plates, creating both mountains and earthquakes. Some military people believed in old-fashioned concepts like honour that those forces contrived to destroy.

"Next assessment," said Ibrahim. "What are the chances that the coup plot was real?"

"Led by Kresnov?" asked Hando. "Unlikely. She wouldn't do anything without Rice, Chu, probably Ruben. I can't imagine any psych profile pegging that group as plotting to overthrow the Federal government."

"Difficult to tell until we've heard the allegation in entirety," said FedInt Chief Shin. He'd drifted into the room and now stood by a wall, watching unobtrusively. Of all the worried, grim faces in the room, he was the only one besides Ibrahim to look calm. "There may be illuminating details. No possibility should be ruled out so early. Kresnov is known to be dissatisfied with current Grand Council policy in many respects, and sees constitutional amendments about to pass Council that would cripple all her hopes of pursuing emancipation for her fellow GIs. Her capabilities appear to be increasing fast beyond their already impressive levels; she has many fellow GI friends to help her."

"And then do what?" Hando replied. "A small team of GIs taking over the Grand Council, what possible support base could they have?"

"The same support base that OID now create by declaring it was a coup," Shin said calmly. "The support of outraged citizens, rising up against wrongdoing. Certainly it may be a fabrication, a tactic. Kresnov may have had a tactic in mind as well. Note this Detective Sinta, purportedly pursuing inquiry that could conclusively discredit 2389's primary political operatives. What if *that* was the fabrication? Certainly that evidence would hurt 2389's public credibility just as a coup hurts Kresnov's."

"And Compulsive Narrative Syndrome dictates that the public will be most compelled not by the evidence," Ibrahim concluded, "but by whichever ideology they supported in the first place, irrespective of the evidence. I'm not sure that evidence matters at our present juncture as much as power, and currently all power rests in the hands of 2389 and the OID. Perhaps that will change, but only after a time.

"I expect that 2389 will use these events to demand a vote on the amendments and ride that wave of popular anti-Federal sentiment to get them passed. The FSA's duty is not to take sides in this, even though some of us may feel that we ourselves have been placed on one side or another by OID's actions. We will look after our own, preserve operational integrity to the greatest degree possible, and await further developments."

He could have said more. Currently, he did not know if it was safe to. In the CSA, he had been relatively certain of the loyalty of all departments beneath him. But the FSA was a different animal entirely, its different parts far larger and with far less in common. Individual units, organisational theory said, pursued not individual power but autonomy. Autonomy to make decisions, to control events, determine outcomes. Sometimes, within a large enough system, with diverse enough conflicting interests, autonomies came into competition.

"Sir," said Teo, "OID have also requested our assistance in locating our officers whom they cannot locate themselves. Commander Rice and Captain Chu primarily."

Not Kresnov, thought Ibrahim. Either they'd killed her or did not wish to admit that they'd tried. Such actions were best presented as fait accompli, after the fact. "No. We'll not obstruct their operations, but neither will we assist. Besides which, I'm quite sure those individuals can take care of themselves.

"Two people I do want, as a matter of top priority, are Ragi and Detective Sinta, and all of her case details. If OID is correct about a coup, Sinta's information will be crucial. If they're not correct about the coup, even more so. In the latter instance, I expect someone will try to have her eliminated. I will accept *any* action, no matter how violent, and no matter who against or who it upsets, to prevent this eventuality. Am I understood?" Grim nods. Cautious ones. "The FSA will not take sides, but we will protect the truth, whichever side it supports."

"And how do we find and protect Ragi and Detective Sinta if OID have ordered us to stand down?" Hando asked. "I understand she's gone to ground as well, no surprise. Ragi we lost contact with almost immediately when it went down."

"Quietly," said Ibrahim, with a very direct, dry stare.

Hando nodded. "I understand."

"Now," said Ibrahim, pushing off the table, "I must go and speak to Ambassador Ballan in person. I'd like some protection. Is Agent Trainee Togales still in medical? I heard she was in for final checks."

Agent Trainee Amirah Togales was the only GI in FSA HQ not in an otherwise incapacitated state. As such, she had a pair of armed guards outside her ward, and a second pair inside as well. Ibrahim gave the guards a long look as he passed them, learning nothing. All were armoured and helmed, with no identification marks and, he'd been informed, were silent when spoken to. All his people were certain of was that they weren't Callayans.

Unprejudiced as he fancied himself, even Ibrahim sometimes found female GIs a surprise. Cassandra often looked the part, strongly built and ice cool . . . when she wasn't laughing or otherwise ruining a perfectly good GI stereotype. Even Rhian Chu, lean and pretty, had that unworried calm of a synthetic mind raised on foundational tape, that sometimes-deadly focus. But Togales at first glance was mild and utterly unthreatening, slender with an incongruously large nose, pretty eyes, a self-effacing smile, and what was lately becoming a mop of long dark hair. She wore it tied now, sitting cross-legged on her bed with promising poise for one still recovering from enough gunshot wounds to have killed a regular human ten times over.

"Agent Togales," said Ibrahim, as she regarded him with cautious astonishment. "You're aware of events?"

"Yes, sir." Tapping behind her ear to indicate uplinks and pointing to the display screen in the ward.

"I find myself in need of personal protection. Do you think you're up to it?"

Togales blinked. "Yes, sir. The latest tests were just precautionary, I was in for observation overnight but nothing's been observed, so . . ." She shrugged.

"Director," said one of the guards. Ibrahim turned to him. "Our orders from OID are that she is not to leave this ward."

"We stand on FSA administrative territory," said Ibrahim. "There is no institution in the Federation constitutionally empowered to exercise overriding authority here."

"My orders are clear."

"The FSA's founding charter is even clearer," said Ibrahim. "Listen well, soldier. Outside of this compound, your authority stands. But defy me here, I will have you killed. Do you understand?" An uplinked pause, as the soldier called for advice. "Within the next thirty seconds," Ibrahim added, with clear pronunciation.

Togales must have moved to stand behind him, because both soldiers raised weapons. She was thoughtfully standing to one side, taking him out of their line of fire. Ibrahim deliberately stepped across, placing himself in that line.

"Agent Togales," he said, "I find myself personally threatened by these soldiers. "Will you require a firearm?"

"No sir," she said. "Probably not even both hands."

The other shoe dropped when Ibrahim was on his way to the Grand Council building by groundcar. A live announcement on all news channels, from Callayan President Singh. The gist of it, Ibrahim heard while perusing three active uplinks and two handheld display slates simultaneously, and listening to a field agent describe the last known whereabouts of Detective Sinta, was that FSA spec ops had been caught doing something very bad, that Singh had personally been shown incontrovertible intelligence proving the coup plot, and that CSA SWAT, given its operational links and sharing of personnel with FSA spec ops, was now stood down indefinitely pending further investigation.

"This means Callay is effectively defenceless against all foreign forces," Agent Teo suggested from the driver's seat. Ibrahim was mildly surprised that he'd care. Teo was Earth Chinese like his boss Shin, a personal recruit of Shin's, to hear the reports. As rising star of FedInt, he was doing his stint as Director's Assistant—and, Ibrahim had no doubt, keeping an eye on him for his boss. As always with FedInt, Ibrahim had no illusions who the spies thought their *real* boss was. "That's ironic given Singh's anti-Federal stance. Surely it puts his public standing in danger."

"Singh has no choice, he's nailed his colours to this particular mast," said Ibrahim, still scrolling over fast-moving data. "CSA has always been more pro-Federal than him; this is his chance to purge the CSA, and so he cuts off Callay's nose to spite its face."

In an odd way, the current situation proved Singh's political point—moving the Federation capitol to Callay hadn't strengthened Callay's autonomy, it had weakened it by creating Federal jurisdiction here. And now look at Callay, no CSA, no local firepower at all, foreign A-12s cruising the skylanes bristling with weapons and foreign troopers raiding private Tanushan homes, and all answerable to the Grand Council's Office of Intelligence Directorate, backed by the Council Chair. Cassandra had predicted something like this would happen, that Singh would leave Callay defenceless in the name of protecting Callay's rights. Ibrahim had always agreed with her assessment of Singh's wisdom but was quite happy for others to take the credit for being proven right. Silence was his weapon, not Cassandra's.

He spared the briefest moment to hope she was well. Surely she was. Surely.

"Gosh, look at this checkpoint," said Agent Togales from the rear seat. "Ludicrous deployment." The checkpoint marked the separation between Grand Council grounds and FSA grounds, the two buildings in Federal secure land but still with a wall between.

"Why is it ludicrous?" Teo asked, slowing the car as the checkpoint flashed lights at them, bristling with heavily armed soldiers and built-in sensors.

"No spacing, no real cover, one good fire position would get all of them." Togales wore standard light combat armour, quickly fitted in HQ's armoury, and carried a modest arsenal besides. Nothing too frightening for GC security but befitting the situation. "I wonder if the rest of the GC's security deployments are like that."

"Cassandra thinks so," said Ibrahim. They stopped at the checkpoint and were swarmed by sensor barriers, sniffers, scanners, lasers. Then biometrics, windows rolled down, verifying identifies.

"Very interesting," said Togales, peering up at the GC building walls ahead and at the gardens and layout surrounding. Like an expert mountaineer contemplating a juicy slope. Or a combat GI wondering how she could peel the Federation's most important institution like an orange.

Ibrahim said nothing and wondered if that in itself was traitorous. No, he decided. He owed the Grand Council nothing. He owed the Federation everything. The two were not the same. He would do his job and let historians decide what to call his actions afterward.

Teo drove them to the downramp and into underground parking. A central drop-off manned by GC security brought them to elevators, where security once more intervened as they left the car.

"Sir, we cannot allow the GI to proceed inside." With weapons pointed not directly at Togales but in her general direction.

"As I understand it," Ibrahim replied, "FSA spec ops is suspended from operations, as is CSA SWAT. Agent Togales is neither, she is a CSA agent-in-training, and I have utilised my discretionary authority to appropriate her for the role of personal security in this emergency, according to the personnel sharing agreements between FSA and CSA."

"Sir, our orders are specific, straight from OID."

"They may be specific to you, soldier, but they are not specific to me. OID has no authority to give this order, and I am under no obligation to follow it."

The security man straightened. "I'm sorry, sir. She cannot be allowed to enter the Grand Council. You are free to enter without her."

"Unacceptable," said Ibrahim. "Agent Teo, please communicate this impasse to Ambassador Ballan, and tell him I refuse to proceed without my security. I will be in the vehicle awaiting his reply."

"Sir," Teo acknowledged, and turned away to concentrate on his uplink. Togales stood at easy guard by the car as Ibrahim climbed back into the passenger seat and worked various data links, as new vehicles came in and their occupants entered the elevators, with concerned looks at the FSA Director sitting in his car with the door open.

After a few minutes, Teo leaned in. "Sir, we're clear."

Ibrahim got out, and he, Teo, and Togales walked to the nearest elevator. Security said and did nothing. A short ride up, and they got out in a main hallway, heading for Ballan's office.

"Sir?" asked Togales as they walked. "Are you really that concerned for your safety?"

"Yes," said Ibrahim, as activity hurried past them, aides running, others standing in conversation, the occasional ambassador or other VIP striding quickly amidst an entourage on their way somewhere important. "But that's not the main point. The main point is that OID is attempting to exceed its authority, as powerful institutions will do in crises. If surrounding institutions do not push back, they will be swamped. We must hold our ground at all costs, Ms Togales, the balance of Federal powers depends on it."

"I understand."

"And," Ibrahim added, "I sense a potentially nasty anti-GI trend in OID's current actions. Naturally they fear GIs as their most capable potential opponents, but the politics lines up too neatly with the anti-emancipation people, who in turn attract the support of bigots and fearmongers. I do not wish this to become an anti-synthetics pogrom. A stand must be taken."

"Yes, sir," said Togales, striding perhaps a little taller. "Thank you, sir."

"No thanks required. I stand on principle or not at all."

Togales smiled. "Sure. But thank you anyway." Ibrahim's lips twisted, just a little.

Ambassador Ballan's front office was crowded, people talking loudly, working uplinks and slates, watching screens. Several were clearly waiting their turn to enter the main office. Ibrahim walked straight past them all and opened the door to the main office, neither guards nor secretaries moving to stop him. Teo went with him, and Togales took up guard outside the door.

The several people in Ballan's office finished up quickly when they saw him and quietly retreated. Beyond the windows, a view of the GC building's central bowl, gardens about a glass roof at the base, offices arrayed in the sur-rounding walls, like an arena. Typically at night it would not look so impres-sive, but tonight all the lights were ablaze.

Ballan rose from behind his desk, harried but looking not at all tired despite the hour. Too much adrenaline, no doubt. "Shan, I'm so sorry for the circumstances. I'm as shocked by this as you are, I'm sure."

Ibrahim shook the offered hand and sat, offering no comment. Crossed his legs, adjusted the suit jacket, meticulously, and settled his gaze upon the head of the Grand Council's Office of Intelligence Directorate. Ballan looked a little concerned at that, taking his own seat. Good.

"I'd like to see your evidence," said Ibrahim.

Ballan sighed. "Shan, the FSA is under investigation. Its Callayan head-quarters anyhow. That includes you. I'm afraid our operating procedures won't allow it."

"Who *has* seen the evidence?"

"I have. President Singh has. The Council Chair has. That's all." So Li Shifu, head of the Federation's central committee, had seen the evidence before signing off on it. Was Li just playing along, or was this in fact a conspiracy that went all the way to the very top?

"When did President Singh see this evidence?"

"I'm sorry, Shan, that's above your level."

"Mr Ambassador, there's no such thing."

Ballan's expression hardened. "Shan, he's the President of Callay. I'm head of OID. And your agency is under investigation."

"And by what authority, and upon what evidence, my agency is under investigation shall remain firmly suspect in my mind until I have seen that evidence. I am an Intelligence Director, Mr Ambassador. I believe nothing unless proven. If one does not understand that, one should not investigate my agency without being prepared to show me the evidence."

"My rank and office are authority enough," Ballan retorted.

Ibrahim barely blinked. "Not while I'm Director of the FSA they aren't."

Ballan took a deep breath and readjusted his jacket. Looked unsettled. Ibrahim watched him, mercilessly curious. "Shan, I'm sorry to have to do this to you, but you're not leaving me much choice. Either you cooperate with this operation, or I'll have you removed as Director. I can do that too, you know."

"I'll be happy to cooperate fully with this operation," Ibrahim replied. "Just as soon as I am presented with evidence of its legality."

"Its *legality*?" Ballan looked incredulous. "For God's sake, Shan, you speak of legality? Just who do you think you are?"

"Failing such evidence," Ibrahim continued, "I shall be forced to keep a very open mind on the matter. Furthermore, if you move to have me removed, I will file appeal to the High Court. That is my constitutional recourse. The High Court could take weeks to decide. Those weeks' delay shall not serve the purposes of Federal security at this time."

"Shan," Ballan said firmly, recovering his balance somewhat. This was not an inconsiderable man to be pushed around even by the likes of Shan Ibrahim. "There is a reason beyond rank and procedure why you are not being presented with the evidence. Some of that evidence speaks to your own complicity. Now, there are wheels turning here. I don't need to explain to you."

"No," said Ibrahim with faint amusement. "You don't."

"It would not be in your interest, or anyone's interest, for you to be furthering that impression now. We need your cooperation to find several of your agents, Commander Rice and Captain Chu in particular. They shall not be harmed, merely detained, for the duration of independent investigations."

"Why was this arrangement not considered for Commander Kresnov?"

A faint evasion in Ballan's eyes. A sideways flick. "My latest reports are unclear on Commander Kresnov's status. I don't know what our operatives did when they tried to detain her."

"They appear to have shot her down," said Ibrahim. "With no attempt at detention. This appears rather the targeted assassination of one my most valuable people, on evidence that you refuse to share. In such circumstances,

I would be failing in any professional duty were I not intensely skeptical of this action."

Ballan held up his hands, placating. "Shan, I'll look into it. I assure you that whatever happened to Cassandra, it wasn't my idea and I never authorised it. The woman saved my life."

"And is there any particular reason you have not asked me to help with Kresnov's detention? Only with Commander Rice and Captain Chu?" Ballan blinked, not understanding. Or pretending not to. "Kresnov is surely more valuable to you if she still lives, and indications are that she does, given the combat flyer that fired upon her was itself destroyed shortly thereafter. If there was a coup attempt, surely she would be the ringleader? Yet you do not ask for my assistance in finding and detaining her, just her friends?"

"We're hearing reports that she may be dead. Information is very sketchy right now, I'm sure you can guess. If she's still alive, certainly we'd like your help to find her."

"With evidence of her complicity in a coup attempt, I would be happy to do that."

Ballan's stare was very hard. "You'd shelter her? As a fugitive?"

"A fugitive from *what*, exactly?" Ibrahim very rarely injected aggressive sarcasm into his tone. This was calculated. Ballan looked increasingly wary.

"Shan, I'm warning you. You have been an exemplary public servant for Callay and the Federation. But this could end very badly for you."

"I'm quite sure," Ibrahim agreed. "The difference between you and me, Ambassador, is that I don't care. You know how to gain my cooperation with this operation. Failing that, you shall not have it. Further, the FSA shall retain full operational independence and conduct operations of its own according to the best interests of the Federation as I see them. If some external power attempts to close down those operations in a manner that I perceive to be unconstitutional, I will resist that external power with every weapon at hand. Even if it should cost me my job. Even if it should cost me my life. Or your life. Do you understand?"

The Grand Council hallways were not safe to speak in, so Ibrahim waited until they were back in the car.

"Spec ops remains suspended," he told Teo, opening an uplink channel so the other FSA Chiefs could hear. "Half our people are arrested anyway, more than half if you count those who were at SWAT when the CSA locked them down. That's a command authority, if I ignored it they really could come in shooting.

"The rest of the FSA's technical suspension I'm ignoring. If anyone is sent to arrest me for that decision, I told Ballan I'll have them shot. All FSA personnel shall be armed from this moment, and no one will return home. We'll sleep on floors and sofas, all of us."

"Yes, sir," said Teo, adrenaline obvious in his voice. The situation was intense. Any young agent would feel both fear and excitement. And older agents might wonder why they hadn't brought forward their retirement.

"I do not discount the possibility of a genuine coup plot against the Grand Council," Ibrahim continued. "But given the OID's behaviour, I have no choice but to treat such claims with great suspicion. I'm seeing the systematic elimination by arrest or assassination of individuals potentially embarrassing to the cause of 2389 and the constitutional amendments. The FSA will regard these actions as illegal until proven otherwise."

"*Sir, begging your pardon,*" came Hando's voice on uplink, broadcast through the car, "*but spec ops are suspended, CSA SWAT is suspended, and something like half the serving combat GIs in Tanusha are in detention. We've lost most of our shooters, while OID has brought in combat teams from 2389-friendly worlds, we're guessing at least a thousand individuals from what we've seen, plus A-12s, we're seeing recon and combat drones, all operating under the authorisation of the President of Callay. We can regard them as illegal all we like, what can we actually do about it?*"

"Answering that question is our next step," said Ibrahim, as Teo steered the car onto the offramp, tunnel lights flashing by. "Let's finish this step first.

"Mr Hando, I would like our legal experts to investigate the possibility of approaching the High Court. And I would like a secure communication arranged with Director Chandrasekar of the CSA ASAP."

"*Sir, we've already heard from Chandi, or from his assistant . . . he said President Singh has ordered him directly to have no contact with the FSA. He intends to obey the order.*"

Ibrahim recalled Agent Ruben's jokes about Chandrasekar's perfect hair. The humour had not been superficial; Ruben had been making fun of precisely this—the instincts of a man for whom appearances mattered sometimes more than substance, and who thus obeyed the chain of command above his institution's constitutional requirement to serve and protect all the people of Callay. A good Director should know that they were not always the same thing.

"*Sir, Council Chair Li is making his announcement.*"

Li Shifu appeared on car displays, projected before the windows. Grey-streaked, a serious, pale-faced man, though capable of kindly expression.

"*This morning at 1:16am,*" he said to the array of waiting reporters and cameras, hands upon his podium, "*I received confirmation of previous disturbing reports, that senior members of the Federal Security Agency's Special Operations Group were preparing the final stages of an armed coup against the Federation Grand Council. Acting upon advice from senior intelligence and military personnel, I have ordered preventative security action to eliminate the threat, and to protect the security and integrity of the people's representative body of the entire Federation.*"

A slight pause, perhaps caused by a dry mouth or a racing heart. Ibrahim could hear the reporters shuffling, scribbling, straining to hear each syllable, desperate for question time that they would surely not be granted.

"*Central in these intelligence reports was the discovery of a secret base of combat GIs, down in the Maldari Islands, thirteen thousand kilometers from Tanusha. These reports conclusively established that this group of several hundred GIs was being secretly armed and equipped to assist in the coup. Such a force of GIs would have proven formidable for even the brave Tanushan security forces. To eliminate this danger, at slightly after 2am this morning, I ordered the elimination of this base by means of an orbital artillery strike from a Fleet warship. Surveillance indicates there were no survivors.*"

The gasp from Togales in the backseat was clearly audible above the thrum of tires on tarmac. Then the faint squeal that might be tears. Ibrahim stared stony-faced at the approaching guard post between Grand Council and CSA HQ.

"*That little cunt Ballan!*" Hando seethed over the rest of Chairman Li's announcement. "*Secret base my ass, he put them there! He set the whole thing up, then he uses them as proof of a coup and kills them all!*"

"And so the game changes again," Ibrahim said quietly, as the car pulled to a stop before the security gate. "A 'secret' base of League GIs will convince many of the public that the coup threat was real."

"*Yeah, but we know what Ballan did. We could leak it.*"

"The FSA does not play petty games through the media," Ibrahim said firmly. The security search heading back the other way to HQ was nowhere near as thorough, just a brief skim. "We would cheapen our image, and thus our authority to our detriment, and we would also harm any genuine public dissidents, providing their enemies with ammunition to discredit them as FSA stooges. We may consider the use of that information later, but not now."

"*And,*" came the cool consideration of Chief Shin, "*the coup may still be very real. Those accused of it certainly have motive, those now withholding the evidence of it have solid reason for doing so if they believe Director Ibrahim somehow involved, and if it were being planned, two hundred battle-hardened combat GIs based in a remote location would be the logical way to do it. Absence of evidence is not evidence of absence, and I would counsel that we do not treat it as such.*"

"Quite so, Mr Shin. However, OID's refusal to share evidence with the FSA is a procedural breach, perhaps explainable in extraordinary circumstances, but a breach nonetheless. I am confident that of our two institutions, my actions are the more procedurally correct."

Going head to head against the Grand Council itself, they'd need to be.

CHAPTER TWENTY-ONE

"**T**he Owl" was an old-fashioned bar on Ramprakash Road that never closed. Sinta had loved coming to places like this in her teenage theatre days, when she'd still harboured some dreams of stage and lights. Her younger sister Lakshmi continued to live in and out of places like this, up and down the Big R, a solid two kilometers of theatres, concert halls, and other stages, plus all the diners, bars, and fancy restaurants that catered to audiences, performers, and stagehands at all hours, dawn to dusk and round again. But this very early morning, the Big R's lights still ablaze before the sun, she was not here to meet Lakshmi and friends after an encore performance. This morning, she was looking for someone else.

She walked the bar, looking at booths by the windows. Only one in three were occupied. Some dancing girls with painted hands and faces under off-duty clothes, sharing coffee and complaining about their choreography. A couple of drunk young men in tuxedos, all that remained of a wedding party, sprawled and giggling into their coffees as they reminisced about events just hours old. A man alone, slumped in a dark corner, shades on, face twitching as the VR kicked in.

Around the bar corner, beneath signed photographs on the wall of famous performers, sat another man, watching the booth's holo. News, images of recent events, Chairman Li speaking at the podium, scrums of journalists, other important people making announcements. An Indian man, but with a gold ring on the fourth finger, like a Christian wedding ring.

Sinta slipped into the seat opposite, with an easy smile and clasp of the hand, like she was meeting an old friend. "Sinta," she introduced herself quietly. "We can talk. This place is clean, I scoped it just a week ago tailing someone."

The man deactivated the holo, giving her a clear look at him. The beard was probably fake, but good work. Solidly built with thick arms, he worked out, was possibly a fighter. An old scar on one cheek.

"How the hell did you find me?" he asked. Clearly he was surprised, and unhappy. She could see the tension, the sideways dart of the eyes.

"I'm a detective," she said. "I detect. I know you've something to tell me."

"I've something to tell someone," the man replied edgily.

"You don't have the luxury of waiting any longer. Half your contacts have gone to ground, there's at least two I think the Feds have grabbed . . ."

"They're dead." Sinta stared at him. "If we're talking about the same two. I found one in his apartment two hours ago, looked like a VR assistant overdose. I was supposed to meet him."

"Ravi Das sent you from the League?" He nodded. "To meet Idi Aba?"

"Him too. Only I get here, find everyone dead or missing. And now you've come to me, and we're probably going to die too."

"I wasn't tailed," said Sinta.

"Sure." The bearded man sipped coffee. "They always think that."

"I have contacts," said Sinta, leaning forward, holding eye contact. She had advantages there, with heterosexual men. "Big contacts. People you can't reach now that everyone's out to get you. People who need to hear what you know, if they're going to stop 2389 reshaping the GC to pass any damn amendments they like. *They're* the ones doing the coup, you get that? And if those amendments pass, there won't be a damn thing anyone can do legally in the Federation to help your cause, FSA, Kresnov, hell, they'll even be able to rule that underground Federation groups with the same cause as yours are in constitutional violation and thus outlawed."

The man grimaced and looked at big hands on the tabletop. Cracked a knuckle. "It's a fight the Federation could win," he muttered. "Should win. Fucking cowards."

Sinta shook her head. "No one is going to war against the League to emancipate the GIs. You guys have to understand that, no matter how bad the atrocities, it's not going to happen."

The man rubbed his brow. "We didn't find atrocities. Or not beyond the usual." Sinta frowned at him. He looked up at her warily. "I was hoping to speak to Kresnov. Kresnov cares about GIs. You're a brave cop, but at the end of the day you're just another Fed."

"Kresnov was nearly killed. No one knows where she is. I'm all you've got, and if you don't give me and my friends something fast, not only are you going to lose your only potential allies in the Federation, I'm going to lose even basic democracy in the Federation. Damn right I won't die for your cause, but right now our causes are the same."

The man looked out the window, at the blazing lights and displays of the neighbouring theatre. A couple of beat cops were moving on some wanderers—sleep walkers, the street called them, high on AR assistant drugs, wandering the night in an augmented parallel universe of simultaneous drug and uplink realities.

"I was League marines," he said. Sinta wasn't surprised. "We never worked with GIs directly; they had their own units. Most of us didn't think much about them; they got the toughest assignments, we were glad it was them and not us.

"Then one day . . . eleven years ago now . . . we were sharing a ride with a Dark Star team. Dark Star are smart, I even talked with a few of them, a few were smarter than me." A self-deprecating smile. "But that's not so hard."

Sinta nodded. "Kresnov was Dark Star. And Captain Chu."

"And then," the ex-grunt continued, "we got hit. No idea what did it, marines never do. One minute we were playing cards, the next it's emergency manoeuvering . . . a couple of my guys couldn't make the acceleration slings in time, they got plastered on the walls, except for two of them, GIs grabbed them, held on all through the manoeuvers, GIs handle ten-Gs fine. Saved their lives.

"And then we were spinning and power-out, half the environmentals went, maybe half the crew died slowly, suffocated or decompressed. The rest of us were crammed into airtight compartments, trying to jury-rig what was left of the air and temperature controls to give us a few more days to live. Some of us were GIs, these Dark Star guys. They were just . . . just great."

His voice was a little tight. He sipped coffee to cover it. Sinta listened, wide-eyed.

"Helpful, you know? No selfishness, no wigging out. Helped with the technical stuff, volunteered to risk airlocks into airless compartments, since they last longer without air than the rest of us. And the rest of the time, we just talked. And they were scared just like the rest of us. I'd never figured that, you know?" Looking up at her. "GIs, being scared? I mean, they're killing machines. But you get locked in a closet with someone for forty-eight hours, running out of air and slowly freezing to death, you get to know them.

"Anyhow, ship found us, we were okay. But I kept in contact with some of these GIs, forty-eight hours of hell and we were like, best buddies. Six of them, three guys, three girls. Girls real pretty too, you know?" A faint smile, remembering. "Even met up with one of the girls a year later, happened to be on the same station, she showed me a good time. Could have snapped me in half with the back of her hand, but she was gentle.

"Two years later, five of them were KIA, including that girl. Jade was her name. They just got sent into the toughest shit; command spent them like toilet paper. And then a year after that, my last buddy, Roh, just stops replying to my messages. I asked after him, but there's this blackout on Dark Star, he's disappeared, no one knows a thing about him or anyone from Dark Star. It's only after Kresnov appears here, and makes waves in the Federation, that everyone back in the League learns about what command did to Dark Star, got rid of them all. I mean, command were never allowed to build GIs that smart in the first place. All us normals who met them, we knew. But we all liked them, so we didn't want to get them in trouble. Should have guessed that would happen.

"I'm not some crazy bleeding heart, Detective, not like some of this group. I still love the League. But the League can't be what I want it to be unless we stop treating GIs like shit. And until we apologise for what we did to those others. Can't blame Kresnov for leaving. Couldn't blame any of them."

He reached into an inside pocket and pulled a chip. Sinta took it on the table top, covering with her hand. "What's on it?" she asked. Making an uplink connection wasn't safe. In a city of sixty million she could stay undetected indefinitely so long as she resisted the Tanushan compulsion to stay permanently uplinked. Autistic, she was safe.

"Inside footage," he said. "A new production facility. We still don't know where; it's an inside job. But the vision is real."

Sinta frowned. "A production facility? For GIs?" The man nodded. "New GI production is outlawed by the Five Junctions Treaty."

"That it is." Another sip of coffee.

"How big a facility?"

"Production maybe ten thousand a year. Mostly high-des." Sinta nearly gasped, hand to her mouth. "New tech. Rumour is there's a way to make GIs that don't think as much but are still high-designation. Keep them loyal."

"Ten thousand high-designation wouldn't violate the treaty," Sinta breathed. "It would smash it."

"And if the Federation's still serious about anything, restart the war."

"Only 2389's trying to stop us from ever fighting another war unless we get attacked first. And you guys come along with this info at the worst possible moment, Idi Aba's preparing to go public, so they kill him. Only maybe it *was* the League, League would want him dead as badly as 2389 . . ."

"No." Her company shook his head. "Internal Federation politics is too far away, local League operatives might have helped plan it, tell them when that other attack would take place so they can use it as cover. But League Gov's never going to authorise that themselves on such short notice, how can they? Takes two months each way for a message, Idi Aba was killed on short notice."

"And ISO's lost their main operatives and facilities when the League embassy closed," Sinta finished. "Much easier to plan long-term hits on orders from League Gov than short-term reactive ops, their decision-making processes aren't there anymore. Dammit, if you guys had only gone straight to the FSA, Ibrahim would have heard before any of this happened. He'd have stopped it."

"Detective, I understand you're normally dealing with gang bangers, jealous spouses, and drug addicts, so this Federal-level stuff isn't really your go. But think for a moment. Who does the FSA answer to?"

Sinta blinked. "The Office of Intelligence Directorate. Shit."

"Who are probably behind this whole fucking thing."

"But Ibrahim doesn't have to tell OID everything, does he? He can operate alone if he wants?"

"Sometimes, sure. But how does Ibrahim get his information? Especially from the League?"

"Federal Intelligence."

"And FedInt is run by Chief Shin, who is very likely in on this as well."

"How do you know?"

"Shin's the real power in the Federation. The thing with interstellar civilisation, there's this communication gap between worlds. In the old days, with just one world, easy, communications lasted seconds. Here it's months. Messages don't hit with the same force, getting a month-old recording isn't the same as being yelled at real time by your superior. And foreign events can't be monitored real time, you just see them in bursts, like trying to watch a football game from the cheap seats as people keep walking in front of you, you see bits and pieces, but it's hard to put it all together, figure out what's really going on.

"But, Shin." Another sip, finger raised for emphasis. "Shin's job is ferrying those messages, all through the Federation. He controls appearances. And he knows exactly what's going on, because he's the only guy with the whole picture. He's the guy who controls what Ibrahim sees and doesn't see. And he's the guy who knows what goes on in Fleet, because Fleet ferry a lot of the most sensitive data. You think Fleet could land a bunch of foreign troops on the Federation capitol to fight this 'coup' without Shin knowing? Hell, he probably made it happen."

Sinta knew enough war stories to know the entire League were paranoid about FedInt, and thought they caused everything from cricket scores to nosebleeds. Yet in parts, it sounded all too plausible.

Someone was walking toward them along the bar, calm as you like. Sinta looked . . . and stared. It was Agent Ruben, smart jacket, cool stride. Dark shades, even before sunrise . . . but not uncommon for the Big R. The ex-grunt reached into his jacket, looking alarmed, but Sinta raised a placating hand. Ruben stopped at the booth and leaned in.

"We have to go," he said. "Now."

"Who the hell are you?" Then an accusing look at Sinta. "Not tailed, you say?"

"I was tailing the Feds who were tailing *you*," Ruben replied. "They're close, we have to leave."

"Agent Ruben, he's CSA," Sinta explained, climbing from her seat. And saw two men had followed Ruben in, both in suits, following him around the L-curve of the bar. At the rear entrance, another two, pushing through the door. Her heart hammered. She wasn't trained or equipped for this. She didn't have these men's augments, nor their weaponry and backup. Panic threatened.

"Come on," said Ruben, straightening his jacket and walking back the way he'd come quite calmly. Sinta followed, eyeing the men behind, hand itching for her pistol but knowing that as soon as she drew it, the others would draw faster, and be far more numerous. Her contact hesitated, as though sizing up the situation.

One of the two men approaching Ruben lunged as he came around the L-bend. Ruben countered with both arms, blocking and driving an elbow, smashing that man aside. The other came at him hard, Sinta missed it as the first bounced off barstools and landed at her feet, where she proceeded to kick the shit out of him.

Turned on the two behind, saw their guns out, seeking targets without hitting their own guy. She dropped low, pressed hard against the bar, fumbling for her pistol, was suddenly hit from behind by a huge weight as Ruben's opponent fell over her, struggling to bounce back up, but finding that hard with his face split open and ribs broken. But he gave her more cover to scramble around the L-bend, as Ruben's fire sent the other two diving low.

Back to the bar, Sinta found herself staring at the booth opposite, the dancing girls cowering and screaming as the big window behind them blew out . . . an exit! She scrambled up for it, but Ruben grabbed her collar and slammed her back, whack! as she hit her head on the bar. Ruben dragged her instead for the entry door, doubled low for cover, dazed and seeing stars and trying to turn in case the men behind rounded the L-curve behind . . . and where the hell was her contact?

The roar of an engine, tires squealing, then a car smashed through the front door, taking much of the wall with it, and the man covering behind the doorframe.

"Go!" Ruben yelled at her, shoving her past, shooting behind as one of their two pursuers tried the L-curve . . . Sinta ran, skidding under collapsed door frame and ceiling, scrambling low as she kept the carside for cover . . . the car was empty, Ruben must have uplinked it, crazy trick in mid-firefight.

Random street traffic was stopped on the road, some reversing as traffic central tried to get civilians out of the danger zone, light pedestrian traffic rapidly taking cover. A cruiser hovered low, coming closer, turning side-on, window down . . . and Sinta ducked back hard and rolled as bullets punched through the car body.

A flash, and the shooting stopped . . . Sinta popped up in time to see the cruiser going sideways, all aflame, hit a building side, flip, fall, and pancake into the road with horrid force.

"Ayako!" Ruben exclaimed with pleasure, leaping out beside Sinta, as another cruiser appeared, higher and behind the one just killed. "Bitchin' girl!" As a groundcar roared up, high performance, lights blazing and doors up. "This one's ours, go go!"

Firing behind as Sinta ran from cover, flinching against the expected blaze of agony as bullets would surely find her. Reached the car and dove in with such force she nearly broke her arm, scrambling into the driver's seat. Ruben followed, gunfire now crackling overhead from the newly arrived cruiser, into the bar doorway, keeping heads down behind.

He hit the seat and saw she was preparing to drive. "Hey! Move out!"

"No way, buddy." She put the doors down and skidded off in a 270-degree howl of power, reverse-steered out of the slide, darting neatly between two immobilised cars up a crossroad. "This, I can do."

Ruben stared, then shrugged. "Cool. Take the L35, please. Let's go south."

Sinta put them squarely in the middle of the road, wheels dividing the centerline, making it easier for traffic central to avoid them, saw cars ahead sliding across to avoid. "Dammit, they're going to track us on central, central's got us pinged as off-grid." Slid around a corner with suicidal confidence, trusting central to keep obstacles aside. "That your friend up there?"

"Ayako Kazuma, old buddy." And paused, receiving something on uplink that Sinta couldn't hear. And laughed hysterically, gripping door handle and dash as Sinta's driving slammed him around. "You just watch your cute ass, you hear?" And to Sinta, "Doesn't care she might go to jail, just wants to shoot stuff, as usual."

"You got a plan?" Sinta asked, taking another corner even faster as her rhythm kicked in. "We'll have air support on us any second, and even you can't get net superiority against these guys."

"Get the chip your friend gave you to FSA HQ."

"That's thirty Ks, we'll never make it."

"Help's coming, no choice but to try." Wincing at something unseen. "They've got us fucking net bracketed, I can barely make connection. I'd send the fucking chip data to someone else, but they'd just trace it and nail them . . . can't even *see* HQ, they're completely cut off."

"Hard job without your net tricks, huh?" Sinta said edgily, howling around a wide bend, holding the difference between over and understeer with little flicks of wheel and accelerator, just missing several vehicles.

"Holy crap, where'd you learn to drive?"

"Racing sims, loved 'em since I was little. Ruben, they're not just going to let us get there, if that chip has what the guy said it did, it blows them out of the water . . ."

"Lemme guess, ramp up GI production again? Restart the war?"

"How'd you know?" Hard braking, crazy right turn past a bus, leaping a low median, twitch to miss overpass pylons accelerating back past 170 kph.

"Holy fu . . ." as Ruben held on for dear life. "Nice. Just a guess." And received something on uplinks and grinned. "Ayako, quote, says you drive like a motherfucker. Compliment from her. If we get on the L35 we've got a chance; it goes nearly straight there, at those speeds it's only a few minutes and there's always a fair bit of traffic, they'll not risk shooting up the freeway."

"Huh," said Sinta, unimpressed. "You reckon?" The upramp was ahead, on the far side of a commercial district, more big towers. Sinta indicated right so central knew she was diverting to the ring road, slowed approaching cars and gave her a free shot up the road past green parks and a blur of low rise commercial at 200 plus.

"Ayako, still there?" Ruben twisted around in his seat to try to see her, up and behind somewhere, keeping an eye on them. "Watch those towers, huh? Good cover spot."

Sinta saw the road drop to an underpass ahead, gunned it hard through the tunnel that followed, then up the exit ramp to the surface, squeezing past a truck with centimeters to spare, and here ahead with towers on either side was the L35 elevated expressway. Leaped all four wheels in the air as the road levelled off, bounced, then swung wide left without slowing, timing that arc neatly across wildly avoiding oncoming traffic and directly onto the onramp.

Ari laughed. "Ayako says she wants you on her team the next sim challenge night . . ." And his eyes widened as ahead, coming just into view as they rose up the ramp, hung an A-12 combat flyer, full missile racks deployed, hiding behind the overpass. "Ayako, watch front!"

It fired, and behind them, something blew up. Sinta howled onto the expressway, fishtailing as they straightened out and accelerated. Ruben was fully turned around in his seat, staring out the rear window. Sinta did not have time to look, but her rearvision display glimpsed something flaming, falling from the air like a comet. Then out of view.

Ruben turned back around, pale and silent. Wiping his eyes. Sinta accelerated in the right lane past 300 kph and kept going, a wide open lane ahead as central moved all traffic left, only the gentlest bend to negotiate. Nav said they still had twenty Ks to go.

"If you want to surrender," said Ruben, voice tight and strained, "we can do that. That thing'll be onto us any minute."

"No chance." And she was astonished at herself. She was terrified, and she was far too young to die. But the fury astonished her even more. This was her city, and her world, and her Federation, and no, damned if she'd stop. Fuck them all.

"We gotta send that chip data somewhere they won't expect and can't trace," Ruben muttered. "I can't get through to anyone properly, just audio. We gotta keep moving; if we stop they'll bracket us completely and shut down all local net receptors. If we keep moving we've got a shot."

"Moving, I can do." Eyes flicking fast from the road to the rear display, searching for the black machine that had killed Ruben's friend. "I can't see it, where is it?"

"It's coming wide, figuring the next attack. They won't want to blow holes in an expressway, makes them look bad." Ruben could see so much more on the net than she could, with her uplinks Sinta had to stop everything and concentrate, freaks like Ruben did it simultaneously.

"Shouldn't we get off the expressway and get some cover?" They were awfully exposed up here, towers and smaller buildings whipping by, exits and glowing signs with them. "I can still go plenty fast with cover."

"It's not fast enough." Ruben had his shades down, concentrating hard. "They've got some . . . freaking huge net controller locking us out. It's shutting down whole sections of network reception that we're in, the only thing it struggles with is rapid transition from one region to the next. We need at least 300 kph."

They were nudging 350; Tanushan groundcars routinely did 180 up here, perfectly safe under central control, but at 350 even huge, gentle corners seemed to come up awfully fast, and the steering translated even the faintest little nudge into a life-threatening event. She'd done sims like this where she'd made mistakes and crashed. It was quite an experience to know that a similar mistake here would end her life for real.

"Dammit," Ruben muttered at something he saw on uplinks, "not now!" Pause, Sinta concentrating as hard as she'd ever concentrated in her life around a wide left, jaw clenching at every little slide of tires. "It's coming around on us. Give me the chip."

"Left inside pocket," said Sinta, not daring to use a hand. Ruben reached, removed it, pulled a small reader from a pocket and placed it in.

"Ten seconds," he said. "I've got a connection, ten seconds and we can take the next offramp. Get ready to dodge."

"I can't fucking dodge at this speed, we'll die."

"Well, then find the next exit. Five seconds." Slower cars ahead were blocking the left lane approach to the exit, Sinta hit the left indicator and watched as central slowed them dramatically, clearing a way.

"Coming up!" She began to shift left, easing onto the brakes with increasing weight, if she hit the ramp at 350 they'd leave the road and bury themselves in the fifth floor of a neighbouring building.

"Got it!" he said triumphantly. "Missile lock, hang . . . !" Something blew them sideways. Then upside down, the world slowly turning, then a screech of metal, sparks, and a freeway barrier racing at them faster than fear.

Danya looked across from his perch watching the rising dawn by the hotel window, as Kiril woke up, looking puzzled. He put a hand to his head, then waved it in front of his eyes.

"Kiri?" Danya asked. "What's wrong?"

"I think my uplinks are working," said Kiril. "I can see things, it's weird."

Danya went quickly over to Kiril's bed and sat. "What can you see, Kiri?" It wasn't the first time Kiril had had strange flashes on his uplinks. Maybe this was just another one.

"I don't know." He sat up, blinking. "Funny things. Shapes."

"Does it hurt?" Danya asked with concern. "Does it give you a headache?"

"No. It's just weird. I feel a bit dizzy."

Danya's heart was thumping. He didn't like this at all. He could defend Kiril from ordinary dangers, but he had no idea what to do about the uplinks except to take the doctors' advice that they'd done everything possible to freeze their further propagation, and report anything further to them. But he couldn't contact the FSA's doctors now, not with all the stuff going on he'd been watching on his AR glasses.

Svetlana raised her head from the other bed's pillows, where she'd been sleeping in her clothes, bleary-eyed and hair messed up. "Danya? What else happened?" She'd been awake periodically, as Danya told her about the coup.

"Um, they released a bunch of stuff about the coup to the media, and the media treat it all like it's true. Sandy always said the media were full of shit."

"Did Sandy call?" Hopefully.

"No, she can't call us Svet, she doesn't want anyone to track us here. Kiril's uplinks are acting up again."

"Oh, Kiri, not again." Svetlana was less than impressed. "You want those things to be turned on so badly you think they're working all the time."

"I can see writing," said Kiril, putting a hand over his eyes. "It's like someone wrote me a message."

"Really?" Danya didn't know what to think. Svetlana was right, plenty of times he'd thought they were working when they weren't. "What does the message say?"

"And why would someone write you a message?" Svetlana asked tiredly, head back on the pillows. "They're uplinks, why not just talk to you?"

"Because Dr Kishore says my eyes are more connected than my ears," said Kiril, putting a hand over his eyes to block visible light. "It says . . . wait a minute . . ."

"It says wait a minute?" Svetlana grinned.

"Leave him alone, Svet," said Danya. "Go on, Kiri."

"Hello, Kiril." Danya looked at him blankly. "That's what it says," Kiril explained. "Hello, Kiril, this is Ari Ruben."

Danya stared at him. "Ari! Go on!"

"I'm so sorry to do this to you, and Sandy's going to kill me." Kiril was a very good reader, even by Tanushan standards. His teachers had been very impressed. "But I had to send this info . . . information to someone, and you're the only person I can reach . . . reach? Yes, reach, whose uplinks won't be traced, except for Ragi, and I don't know where he is."

Kiril looked up at Ari. "Who's Ragi?"

"I don't know," said Danya. "Sandy never mentioned him. What else does he say?"

"There's a file with this message that the memory por . . . portion? Portion of your uplinks will store. It's very important that you don't get caught. Try to get this information to Director Ibrahim of the FSA. He's the only one you can trust, except for Sandy and Sandy's friends, but they can't contact you without putting you in danger. Be safe, and listen to Danya, he'll know what to do."

Kiril gazed up at Danya expectantly. So did Svetlana, now bolt-upright on her bed, wide-eyed. He'd know what to do? He didn't. How the hell would *anyone* know what to do in a situation like this? Let alone a thirteen-year-old boy who'd only been here a few months?

He got up and went to the windows. The sunrise was beautiful, across the enormous cityscape, guidance lights blinking on the towers, warning to the slowly increasing air traffic, busy on this day like any other day, political crisis or not. Panic was not an option. He'd been in dangerous situations before. He just had to think his way through the process like he had then. And then . . . well, the first thing was to realise that you didn't need to know everything. Kids usually couldn't. But kids could be very good at seeing what was immediately in front of them. Deal with that, let the rest sort itself out.

"Well," he said, and took a deep breath. "It must be really important. I mean *no one* uses Kiril's uplinks; I didn't even know Ari could activate them. And he's right, Sandy will kill him."

"Maybe he had no choice," Svetlana said urgently. "Maybe he's in trouble."

Well, stating the obvious, Svet. But he didn't say it. "And he wants us to go to Director Ibrahim. But we can't just call him because Ari would have done that himself if he could . . . and Ari's so good at everything network, if *he* can't get through, no one can."

Except maybe this Ragi person. Whoever that was. But it made sense, because as he understood it, what was happening was a takeover of the Federal government. Not the local Callayan government, that was big enough . . . but the *Federal* government, the Grand Council. The place that ran *everything.* And if you controlled that, surely you could control the network in ways that even someone like Ari couldn't. Ari was like a car on the road or a cruiser on a skylane, but the Feds controlled the roads and skylanes. And could deny access however and to whomever they wanted.

"So how do we get to Ibrahim?" Svetlana wondered. "I mean, we can't just catch an air taxi, right?"

"No one can land at FSA HQ without clearance," said Danya. "I mean, we could probably get it if we asked, being Sandy's kids, but they're after Sandy . . . they're saying she was leading the coup."

"Yeah, right!" Svetlana snorted.

"No, the Feds will grab us before we get halfway there." Or shoot us down, was the less pleasant version. "We could try to sneak in, but security will be everywhere, and we kind of stand out. I mean, they know there's three of us, they know our ages and genders, they see us three together they'll figure it out."

"But why do they want us?" Kiril asked. "We're just kids. And Ari said they can't trace that message." Smart Kiril, always understanding just enough to get him into trouble.

"We're Sandy's kids, Kiril. They've accused her of leading a coup. We know that's bullshit, they won't want us telling anyone, they need to prove she did it."

"But she didn't!"

That Kiril and Svetlana were so certain was predictable. Danya wasn't so sure. He loved Sandy, but loving someone didn't mean you trusted they'd do everything right. And he hadn't known her that long, really. But voicing those doubts here served no purpose.

"They're liars, Kiril," he explained. "They need everyone to believe they're not liars. We know they are, so they won't want us talking to anyone."

"Maybe we could go to the media?" Svetlana wondered.

Danya shook his head. "None of the media like Sandy, they wouldn't believe us." And they'd make us into the story, he thought. Sandy was always worried about that, it was why the media knew so little about them. Poor little brainwashed kids, believing their GI foster mother was a good person when she was really a monster.

"So if we can't go to any of the HQs ourselves," Svetlana said slowly, thinking as hard as Danya had ever seen her think. "But we can't use the net at all because the Feds will find us." And she brightened. "We have to find Ari! Ari can find anyone, right?"

Danya shook his head, gnawing a nail. "If he could find us, he wouldn't have sent that message. Like you said, I think he's in trouble. In fact, I think maybe he's . . ." but he didn't know that. And wouldn't say it, not just for his siblings' sake, but for his own. And Sandy's. But sending vital information to Kiril seemed like the desperate last act of someone about to run completely out of options. "I think maybe he's gone to ground, so no one can find him," Danya finished.

"Then who?" asked Kiril.

Danya thought hard. Sandy had friends in the underground . . . many of whom she'd lately suspected were becoming less keen to help her. The Feds would be watching all of them, and besides, Danya didn't know them well enough to guess which were real friends. In Droze he'd discovered all too often how people who were friendly when it was safe for them became less so when it wasn't.

Sandy also knew people in civil rights, lawyers and the like, helping on various GI asylum cases . . . but she hadn't been in contact with them since she'd been back, and he'd gathered some of them were kind of upset with her. Ditto various GIs in Tanusha with whom she was always friendly but no longer regarded as "one of the team," as she'd heard Sandy once put it in conversation with someone else.

"There's Poole," he considered aloud. "But he's a CSA-trainee and the CSA are locked down."

"There's Detective Sinta?" Svetlana suggested.

"The Feds were after her even before all this happened," Danya replied. "She'll have gone to ground, if they haven't got her already."

"This sucks!" Svetlana exclaimed in frustration. "This is supposed to be a good place, how can the Grand Council go around grabbing and killing everyone they don't like?"

"They say they're responsible for a coup," Danya explained tiredly, slumping against the wall by the window. "Or an attempted coup. So they get everyone and say they had no choice, the coup was just about to happen. Like that time you punched Hanny Graham in the nose, then said he was just about to hit you so you had no choice."

"Well, he was!" Danya raised a skeptical eyebrow. Svetlana huffed. "I bet you he was. I was sure of it."

"It's called a preemptive strike, Svet. And if you make up a big enough tale about the thing you were preempting, you can excuse pretty much anything, without the other person actually having done anything."

"Hanny *was* going to do something, he was balling up his fists like this, and . . ."

"Hey, look!" Kiril cut her off, pointing to the room display, flashing images with the sound off. There was a picture of Sandy, from back when she'd had longer hair. It was in the corner of a larger image, a house on fire, surrounded by fire trucks. The image divided, back to a studio, a commentator behind a desk.

"*. . . now confirming the sensational news that Commander Kresnov was person-ally piloting this cruiser when it flew into a house in Claremont, killing three occupants, including a small child. Officials will not confirm whether Commander Kresnov has been confirmed killed in the incident, but we've all seen the footage of the A-12 combat flyer crashed in nearby Claremont CBD. Officials will neither confirm the cause of that inci-dent, but eyewitnesses and some emerging security vision indicates at least two gunships chasing and shooting at someone on the ground, followed by one of them being destroyed . . . and again, I'll repeat that this is just speculation at this point, but the speculation is that that gunship was destroyed by Commander Kresnov. No civilians were killed or injured in that shooting, which is quite remarkable given how built up the area is, and how little concerned Commander Kresnov appears to have been about civilian casualties in this firefight, using these populated buildings on the ground for cover.*"

"What the fuck is she supposed to do?" Svetlana yelled at the screen. "Stand in the open and let them kill her?"

"Shush, Svet," said Danya, staring at the screen.

"They make it sound like she started it!" Svetlana protested. "They attacked *her*! And it's not her fault if her cruiser lands on someone after they shoot it down!"

"I know, Svet, quiet!"

"*. . . trying to get an official response from Director Ibrahim of the Federal Security Agency . . . our viewers will of course recall that Shan Ibrahim was previously the Director of the Callayan Security Agency, before being transferred in controversial cir-cumstances to head the Federal body following the abrupt resignation of former Director Diez four months ago . . .*"

"Is anyone here stupid enough not to know that?" Svetlana asked. "I know that and I only just got here."

"Yes, plenty are that stupid," said Danya. "Now quiet."

"*A short time ago a spokeswoman for Ambassador Ballan of the Office of Intelligence Directorate gave this brief statement to the media.*" A woman's face appeared, before many lights and cameras. She spoke. "*It saddens us greatly to learn that Commander Kresnov was behind this despicable plot. We'll be releasing records, intercepted communications between the Commander and various of the other plotters. We're confident they show just how central she was to the entire affair. Given her capabilities, it was with great regret that the OID concluded it had no choice but to eliminate the Commander in the opening moments of Operation Shield. The results of that strike are as yet inconclusive, and we ask you all to be patient as we investigate further into the Commander's status. Thank you."*

And departed, ignoring the shouted questions of reporters at her back.

"Ha!" said Svetlana. "They didn't kill her; if they'd killed her they'd be shouting about it! They know damn well she killed their gunship instead, and now she's going to kill all of them!"

"No, she won't." Svetlana and Kiril looked at Danya in surprise. Danya was nearly surprised himself. But suddenly, he found himself increasingly sure of what was going on . . . or at least, of what he had to do. "Killing people won't change the situation in the GC, Sandy will have to prove this is all a setup. You do that by being smart, not just by killing people."

"I bet she kills a few of them," Svetlana said hopefully.

"Probably a few," Danya agreed. "But whatever Ari sent to Kiril, it's important to help prove this is all a setup. If we're going to help Sandy, we have to get that information to someone who can help."

"Who?"

"I don't know. But I want to start by finding out who this 'Ragi' person is, because if his uplinks are based on the same technology as Kiril's, he might be the only guy who can still talk to everyone on the net."

CHAPTER TWENTY-TWO

Tacnet showed Poole that they were flying very low, and very fast. Which would be interesting for the pilot, because CSA SWAT's emergency lanes privilege couldn't be working, so how they were doing it without crashing into people, Poole didn't know.

Captain Arvid Singh was having a harsh conversation with someone back at HQ, probably Director Chandrasekar himself, but no one could hear exactly what because Singh's faceplate was down, and the conversation wasn't registering on tacnet. The rest of SWAT One were crammed onto bench seats in full armour, fists gripping supports and some standing to make room for four medtechs, their gurneys, and other equipment. Poole was not the only GI—the other was Patrick, a 41 series now a permanent member of SWAT One, having passed all training and acquired citizenship some months back. After hearing what had happened to the base down in the Maldaris, pretty much every GI in SWAT had volunteered, but Singh had selected Poole as his plus-1 and left in a rush. Fair bet that Chandrasekar was not happy, but no one had waited long enough to hear his opinion.

"*Okay,*" said Singh, using tacnet com to be heard above the roaring engines and rattling equipment as they bumped through Tanusha's humid air. "*ETA two minutes. We don't have a feed on the crash site because the Feds aren't sharing and they've banned media overflights. But there's a crash on the L35, two badly injured, we're pretty sure one is Agent Ruben, not sure who the other passenger is.*

"*The CSA charter says we have medical jurisdiction on all of our people, but the chatter from the civvie ambulance that just landed suggests they're taking both to Arora General, where the Feds have cordoned off the top floor to treat all the other people they've shot. Be warned what you're getting into here, legal advice is murky, CSA SWAT has been suspended, so technically we're not supposed to be flying, but then this is an emergency medical rescue, and to the best of my extensive legal training, I can't see how suspending SWAT suspends the CSA charter, given the rest of the CSA is not suspended.*

"*If you don't want to dismount, that's fine, possibly we'll all get arrested at some point. But removing our people from our care is an assault on the CSA charter, and an* assault on the CSA charter is an assault on Callayan security. These guys are Federal security. Fuck Federal security, if they want to step on us, we'll step on them harder. Let's get our people back."

Poole suspected the bit about "extensive legal training" was a joke; there were stories about how Captain Singh had once been considered the SWAT trooper least likely to achieve anything significant, only to prove everyone wrong when the heavy shit started seven years ago. But he couldn't tell if his colleagues were smiling, their faceplates were down, systems tuned into tacnet and hoping the damn thing wouldn't collapse on them once they were down. Probably why Singh wanted him along, Poole thought, gripping his handhold as they jolted through another three-G turn. An independent thinker with few qualms about pulling the trigger, his training reviews were all in agreement. Singh wanted another GI who wouldn't freeze if tacnet crashed, and the fact that he'd chosen Poole suggested he was in no mood for talking nicely.

Then they were slowing. Poole could tell the nacelle pitch was changing by the changing note of the engines, a vibration that made the interior hold rattle and throb.

"*Hello, anonymous Federal authority,*" Singh addressed them. Poole guessed that was humour too, the unfunny kind. "*This is emergency CSA dustoff, we're here to pick up our people according to the constitutionally approved CSA charter, please assist.*"

"*Negative CSA dustoff, we register your vehicle as a SWAT flyer, SWAT is currently suspended by order of OID, return to base or be considered in violation.*"

"*Hello, Federal authority, only a nuclear strike will nullify CSA charter, so unless you're prepared to nuke CSA HQ, I suggest you prepare to assist.*"

No reply, as the flyer flared, Gs pressing them down, a disorientation of inner ear and balance as they swung about and dramatically lost speed.

"*Okay, guys,*" Singh said calmly, "*let's keep it nice and low key. Medics off first with me, Poole and Patrick on the flanks, everyone else defensive perimeter. No aggressive moves, no weapons raised, keep it casual and be prepared to shoot anything that moves on my signal.*"

The rear ramp went down, and the medics were rushing out with their gurneys, with light armour more to help them carry gear and move faster than for combat. Singh, Poole, and Patrick went with them, walking rapidly along the wide expressway in the early dawn, just twenty meters short of where a twisted lump of metal that might once have been a car now lay amidst a rain of debris.

Emergency crews were already there, a fire truck with several firemen in armoured suits not too different from SWAT's, bending and pulling at wreckage with gloved hands, another with cutting tools. Even now one body was being eased out, limp and bloody . . . a woman, and bending in amongst the firemen was a uniformed cop, looking alarmed.

At the approach of CSA medics, Feds made a line between them and the wreck, four armoured, another six plainclothes, weapons ready, several more running in from where their cruisers had just landed farther up the road. Singh held up a hand for his guys to stop short, then gestured at the cops around the perimeter of the wreck. The cops were now in furious conversation, the one who had checked the just-removed woman pointing back to her. And saw Singh gesturing and came walking briskly over. Not running, not with all this twitchy firepower around, and the shrilling howl of an A-12 circling somewhere around the perimeter.

"Brother," said Singh, shaking the cop's hand, faceplate still down. In the noise of flyer engines, cruisers, and cutting tools, no moderate conversation would carry much beyond Poole and Patrick. "Captain Singh, SWAT One."

"That's one of ours," said the cop, with no interest in what Singh was doing here, risking a firefight at an accident scene. Pointing back to the wreck. "That's Detective Sinta. We're getting word the Feds wanted her in connection with the coup, now they just fucking blow her up?"

"Okay, listen," said Singh. "First, cover your mouth when you speak or they'll read your lips. The guy she's with, that's one of ours, Agent Ruben, he's best friends with Ibrahim from Ibrahim's CSA days, got it?" The cop nodded. "Ibrahim wants Sinta, Ibrahim doesn't buy this coup bullshit, that's the word. Sinta knows something that could sink them. You let Sinta go with these guys to Arora General, you might never see her again."

"They're saying they'll arrange access for us . . ."

"Buddy, when I say you'll never see her again, I don't mean some procedure will block you for a week. I mean bullet in the head. You get me?" The cop's stare was fearful. "If we get her, you can come see her immediately. They look badly hurt, we've got no time for some legal pissing contest. Just get ready to hit the deck."

The cop nodded shortly and walked back to his colleagues. His stride was a little shaky, the way untrained straights got when adrenaline overload hit their system. Another few seconds, someone would pick that up and give them away.

Singh beckoned Poole and Patrick closer. "Don't kill anyone; we'll need a couple of hostages so they won't shoot us down on the way back."

Poole shrugged. "Cool." And to Patrick, "One high, one low?"

"You go high," Patrick acknowledged. "Armoured targets first."

Poole nodded and jumped. Powered armour didn't help a GI much, probably slowed him down if anything with weight and mobility restriction, but he didn't want to get higher than four meters, hanging in the air any longer with a totally predictable trajectory would get him shot.

He put down two of the armoured troops with short bursts in the legs, shots clustering to overload and fragment the armour, then switched to single fire as he fell, and the other two armoured troops fell to Patrick, pulling a pistol left-handed and firing with both hands as his feet hit and knees took the impact with barely a jolt. Feds fell everywhere, clutching arms, legs, knocked spinning by the sheer force, others diving for cover, Poole letting them go and running instead to one of the wounded plainclothes, flinging him over a shoulder, then walking backwards.

The CSA medics were running at the wreck, pushing startled firemen and civvie medics aside, wrestling a body off one gurney and onto another. "Go go go!" Singh was yelling, taking the wounded plainclothes off Poole's hands even now. A Fed agent popped out from behind a flyer's undercarriage to fire, Poole put a round through his arm, then put more fire into some grounded cruisers farther off to keep heads down.

And turned to look out at the hovering A-12, now at a full stop with racks extended . . . but what was he going to do, use heavy weapons on a cluster of his own wounded people?

The medics were running back now, heads down, but no fire pursued them, those Feds not shot having seen what happened to anyone who tried. Captain Singh walked, his armoured stride supporting a wounded agent over each shoulder, his two GI troopers retreating backward behind him, weapon in each hand. One wounded man reached for a weapon lying nearby; Patrick shot it away from him.

The defensive perimeter troops pulled in, then Poole and Patrick jumped aboard just as the flyer lifted, ramp closing, nose dropping as it thundered at full power and roared away.

"That A-12's right up our ass," said the pilot, and Poole looked, seeing the ramp hadn't gone up completely, probably Singh figured it was better whoever chased was reminded of the Feds now aboard. Sure enough, the gunship was barely a hundred meters behind, just to one side and above their slipstream, full weapons deployed and unable to use them. Whoever was in charge of this back at OID would be looking through its visuals, real time, fuming at the CSA flyer that had defied their grounding and apparently their expectations, judging from how they'd gotten away with it.

Seated alongside the two gurneys, equipment, and medics treating their patients, now including two wounded Feds, Captain Singh took off his helmet, giving the A-12 a good look at his face, thin beard, patka turban. Popped some gum, handed some to Poole as he removed his helmet too, and accepted, then tossed some more to Patrick who did the same.

"When I was first assigned to Commander Rice's SWAT Four," Singh shouted at Poole over the roar and howl of engines and wind, "back when she was just an LT, she told us that in psychological standoffs, sometimes you just gotta be a bigger pain in the ass than the other guy!"

"Well, she'd know!" said Poole. Singh laughed. "I think that job description suits me! Jason Poole, CSA SWAT, pain in the ass!"

Singh smiled. And pointed to the gunship following them, attracting its attention. Raised a middle finger at it. "Why you think I'm so good at this job?"

Landing at CSA HQ was even more intense. Waiting for them at the edge of the pad was Director Chandrasekar, arms folded, smart jacket and sleek hair blown about by the downdraft, grim as death. The medics wheeled past at a run, gurneys and patients on their way to intensive care and surgery. Singh and SWAT One followed at a walk, their Captain first, helmets off. At Chandrasekar's back were other agents, Investigations, various specialties, all armed and tense.

"Agent Varghese!" Chandrasekar yelled above the declining shrill of engines. "Place Captain Singh under arrest, remove him of armour and weapons, and take him to holding!"

Singh pulled his pistol and chambered a round. But did not raise it. The agents backing Chandrasekar were very reluctant to raise theirs, seeing how outgunned they were. "Sorry Vargie!" he said. "You do that, I'll put you down!"

"Captain Singh!" Chandrasekar fumed. "This is dangerously close to mutiny!"

"Maybe it is!" Singh snarled. "What you going to do about it, hairpiece?"

Chandrasekar stared. Hell of a question. Poole could see him thinking. The agents at his back were good men and women, real professionals, but combat was not their specialty. SWAT's was. And if SWAT rebelled, who in the CSA would stop them? Not only did they lack the will, they lacked the capability.

The pad doors opened once more as Lieutenant Widjojo walked out, a small man in his service jumpsuit, unarmed, cigarette in mouth and a cup of coffee in each hand. Commander of SWAT Six, no less. He walked straight onto the pad, past his primary boss, and up to Singh, his second but more immediate boss. Handed him the coffee, utterly nonchalant.

"Sorry, boss," he told Chandrasekar. "I did a year of constitutional law. CSA charter doesn't get annulled just because chain of command says it does. If chain of command breaks with constitutional practise, chain of command is broken, that makes *you* the top link in the chain. At which point you stand for us, and they can go fuck themselves. Ibrahim wouldn't have made that mistake."

"Ibrahim isn't here," Chandrasekar retorted. "And you break with *this* chain of command, your career is over."

"Which brings me to my second constitutional point," Widjojo added, tapping cigarette ash onto the pad. "Fuck you."

Poole liked that one better. That one, you couldn't argue with.

"Sir," said another agent, a woman whose name Poole hadn't learned, in a calming voice, "it's obvious we're at a serious impasse here. Why don't we go inside and talk about this?"

Singh shrugged, indicating he was willing. But showing no sign of putting his gun away. Chandrasekar calculated furiously. If he'd lost Singh and Widjojo, he'd pretty much lost SWAT. And short of calling in the Feds with A-12s and heavy firepower, there wasn't much he could do about that. If he declared SWAT in open rebellion, the entire CSA became a paralysed laughing stock . . . and who actually arrested SWAT troopers who defied the law? The police? What could the poorly armed cops do about it? And in current circumstances, how many Tanushan cops would be willing? SWAT weren't even openly defying "Operation Shield" yet, just arguing with the way it was implemented where CSA personnel were concerned.

In fact . . . Poole blinked as the connection came clear in his head. SWAT rebellion could become a rallying point in a broader Callayan opposition. Not that most of the Callayan population were yet suspicious of the coup claims, many of them not trusting GIs or FSA spec ops, but that could change. So Chandrasekar now had to find a way to keep it all under wraps before it blew up into something much bigger that could hurt his true master—Callayan President Singh.

Funny how Sandy had always said all this stuff was connected, popular opinion, political forces, and eventual breakouts of shooting and violence. He'd never really seen it before, and never found the prospect that interesting. Funny how all this complicated stuff became much more interesting when the shooting started.

Finally Chandrasekar jerked his head toward the buildings, turned and walked. Relief swept the landing pad, mostly amongst the non-SWATs. Singh de-chambered his pistol round and put it away, walking up to the most notably relieved Agent Varghese.

"Sorry, Vargie," said Singh with an easy grin. "Hairpiece left me no choice. Would have just been a flesh wound, I promise, nice scar to show your grandkids."

Varghese did not look convinced.

Spec ops armoury was walled up tight. Amirah wondered at it, following the Director along the armoury bay floor, past heavy secured door after heavy secured door, electronically locked and sealed. The entire practise range was off limits, full security exclusion activated—it ran on the FSA's private security network; Amirah doubted even Kresnov could have broken into it.

The Director was carrying now, an automatic in a shoulder holster and a backup on his ankle. He'd even put on a light vest under his shirt at Amirah's suggestion when she'd half-expected him to reject it. The Director was not a man to object to sensible things on points of personal pride. Amirah had no idea where all of this was going, but she was glad that her role in it was to protect this man. As a CSA trainee, CSA instructors had spoken privately of their respect for Ibrahim and their uneasiness at his departure. Following him around the past twenty-four hours, she was coming to see what they meant.

In the hall ahead, some spec ops soldiers were gathered in conversation—two GIs and two not. They straightened as Ibrahim approached, almost attention, which was not an FSA thing; FSA were technically civilian, if only in the sense that they were not military.

"Sir," said one of the GIs. "Do you require any further personal protection?" With a glance at Amirah.

Ibrahim stopped, with a faint smile. "You don't think Trainee Togales is up to it?"

"Not that, sir. But wouldn't some more guards be safer?"

Ibrahim considered. "Probably, Sergeant Pinto." Pinto looked pleased the Director knew him—the FSA was a big organisation, and Ibrahim new to the job. Amirah suspected he knew everyone by sight already. "Probably I could have one hundred armed GIs with me at all times and that would be safest of all. But it would be dysfunctional for my current tasks. Should I require more, I'll be sure to ask you."

"Thank you, sir."

"In the meantime, stay patient, and be alert. You may be required to act at a moment's notice, but which moment I cannot say."

Several others came to walk with Ibrahim on his way back up to his office and talk about things. Amirah was locked into the outer layers of his personal construct for security purposes, something of a privilege for a no-rank like her. She could see him monitoring multiple channels simultaneously, with a freedom here in FSA HQ that he would not have anywhere else. From the frequency of those private conversations, the content of which she did not know, she guessed that Ibrahim had a lot of wheels in motion.

Waiting for him outside his office were two distinct groups, one nervous and out of place, the other in busy internal conference on ongoing matters, a tight huddle of chairs in a corner. The head of the nervous group came up to Ibrahim—a woman, youngish, with shoes and bracelets that suggested to Amirah a GC staffer, from across the green canyon, as that division between FSA and GC was now called.

"Director, I'm Norah White, Assistant to the Chief of Staff, Ambassador Ballan's office. Can we have a word?"

Ibrahim seemed to size her up in a split second. Whatever his conclusion, he kept it off his face, as always. "Very well." And stood in the middle of the waiting room.

Norah White looked flustered. "Privately, if you please."

"No," said Ibrahim. "I didn't invite you. I'll only hold private audience with people who can act directly upon what I tell them."

Ms White pulled herself up. "Very well. Ambassador Ballan orders that the FSA shall remove its security detail from the Supreme Court Justices. OID will now take that security under its own jurisdiction."

Ibrahim nodded. "Ambassador Ballan informed me of this himself. My answer remains the same."

White looked quite tense. "You mean you do not intend to comply?"

"No."

Silence in the waiting room. The second group paused in their little huddle of chairs and watched the drama.

"May I ask why?" White ventured.

"You may," said Ibrahim.

White took another deep breath. "Director, I do hope that you fully grasp the gravity of this decision, the OID . . ."

"Has no jurisdiction to overrule the FSA on the matter of security for the Supreme Court and its Justices," Ibrahim cut her off, clean like a sword. "Furthermore, I also hope that Ambassador Ballan recognises that I am not playing at some game of career advancement. I am fulfilling my life's mission. Please tell him so, those exact words. That will be all."

White took her leave with more relief than grace. "Yes, Director." And hurried away, several assistants in tow.

Ibrahim beckoned the other waiting man into his office. As they went, Amirah saw the looks of approval on the faces of surrounding agents, the barely restrained grins at having witnessed something cool. "We'll give you gravity, bitch," she heard one say at the retreating White. Ibrahim, she'd overheard another agent say earlier in the day, was the only person in the FSA who could beat the shit out of someone without touching them.

"Ms Togales," he called over his shoulder, "with me please." Amirah followed the two men in and closed the door behind, surprised at being invited. Usually she waited outside, as personal security would.

The other man was Herman Cassillas, Chief of Domestic Affairs Bureau. That meant the entire Federation civil society, anything that did not include military or paramilitary forces, which were the responsibility of the Strategic Affairs Bureau. Cassillas was responsible for dealing with threats to Federation security coming from everything else, from civil uprisings to lone individuals, political crises to worrying social trends.

Amirah took her stance by the side of Ibrahim's desk, side-on to the two men as they sat, so she could talk if Ibrahim required, while still watching the door and ready to move. Cassillas gave her a sideways look, perhaps curious.

"Ambassador Ballan," Cassillas announced with the air of someone resuming a previous conversation. "My best analysis is fear. The assassination attempt by Pyeongwha radicals gave him post-traumatic stress, the psych reports bear that out . . . tape can cover the immediate effects, but only so much. And then the political scene on Nova Esperenza changed; there are some big local disputes the public there feel the Feds screwed them on, then Pyeongwha attacks happened, the atmosphere has become quite anti-Federal, and thus pro-2389. Ballan is publically identified as the man who orchestrated Pyeongwha, he was hoping to retire home in a few years, take up a prestigious university post, public speaking, etc. All that's in jeopardy now, so when whoever's *really* behind this came leaning on him, he folded like a pack of cards. Possibly more than his career is being threatened, but we've no proof of it."

Ibrahim's mouth may have drawn down a little behind steepled fingers in disgust. "And have we yet any idea who is really behind it?"

"Oh, the usual suspects." With another glance at Amirah.

"One of the many features of GIs that I find admirable," Ibrahim said, "is their general lack of deviousness. Trainee Togales is sworn not to share sensitive information, and I am certain she will not break that oath."

Strange concept that an oath was to any GI, Amirah thought. Was it the very deviousness of normal people that required them to take oaths, like some kind of internal-psychological choke hold?

Cassillas nodded slowly. "It's very high level. And it's definitely coming from the lateral connectivity, the political groupings beneath the actual representative level. I've recommended some of the best readings on this, Choi, Wellsworth, Jayapura."

"I read Jayapura and Wellsworth," said Ibrahim. "And I met Ms Choi personally two years ago when she gave that lecture tour. In the context of recent events, very alarming."

With her degree studies, Amirah had read some of the same. They discussed the process of electing Ambassadors to the Grand Council, and the mechanisms on different worlds to do so. Ambassadors were not popularly elected for the most part, they were appointed by bipartisan political bureaucracies. The problem with bipartisan political bureaucracies was that they lacked accountability. Certain academics had lately been warning that such unaccountable bureaucracies were beginning to deal with each other in ways that created an enormously powerful network of unaccountable people, controlling appointments to the GC, deciding on the fate of the Federation. Previously they had stayed out of deciding policy, but a few had warned that this might change.

Ideologues and media clowns crowed with delight at displays of bipartisanship, but too much bipartisanship was deadly. Autocracies were bipartisan.

"You can layer political power in human civilisation as many times as you like," said Cassillas. "It still functions, so long as each layer is independently accountable and interactive. But the layer that appoints the GC has become an independent entity, and you network all those independent entities together, they start to serve themselves above anyone else."

"Or conflate their own success with the people's success," Ibrahim murmured. "Well, we can't deal with it now, most of them are too far away. We'll have to sweep them up later, but our response window today is too small, the amendments could be voted on in a week on the present schedule."

"Sir . . ." Cassillas winced, as though anticipating Ibrahim's response. "A public revelation, by you . . ."

"Now is not the time," Ibrahim said firmly. "I understand the temptation, but the OID currently control the Grand Council, every opponent of 2389 is too afraid to speak or conveniently will not speak without authorisation from their homeworld. The GC is a soft institution, but this current power wearing the cloak of 2389 is a hard power, a wolf among sheep. They have constructed a web of deceit, and we must position ourselves first to weaken it before moving."

"Yes, sir, but it seems to me that their power increases . . ."

"Herman, I cannot unilaterally declare war against the Federation's ruling authority in the knowledge that one orbital artillery round could make a large smoking crater here just as easily as it did on the GI camp down south." And to that Cassillas said nothing. "Besides which, truth revealed too early runs the very real risk of civil war, as different worlds line up on different sides of the equation, backed by different Fleet captains of different warships. We act when we're certain we can win, not before."

He looked up at Amirah. "Ms Togales, I know how competent GIs are at multi-tasking. In addition to your duties as my bodyguard, do you think you could give me an analysis of possible options for a rescue and acquisition mission?"

"Yes, sir." He was right, she could review schematics and make plans while performing security duties with no loss of concentration. "Who is the target?"

"The Supreme Court Justices. All nine of them."

Just as well she was new here, Amirah thought. Probably if she'd been a Federation citizen for longer, the sheer gravity of that proposal would have knocked her sideways. If a GI of her designation could get knocked sideways.

"Sir, FSA have current jurisdiction over the Supreme Court Justices, yes?"

"And OID are likely to try and take it away. In which case, there are several scenarios that I'm sure you can envisage, in which we will need plans to get the Justices from there, to here, under hostile conditions. The Supreme Court remains the last institutional barrier between the OID and passage of those amendments, thus they become the next center of battle."

"Yes, sir. Why me and not a higher rank?"

"Commanders Kresnov and Rice have assessed your planning ability and judged it superior to all currently serving GIs save Kresnov herself. She's not here, and fortune has delivered you."

"Planning, yes," Amirah warned. "Combat, no. I'm capable, but there are a dozen better than me, at least."

Ibrahim smiled. "Kresnov's assessment also. You are a thinker, Ms Togales. Right now I need thinkers."

"You did better than okay in HDM tower," Cassillas added.

"I got shot full of holes," said Amirah, repressing a shudder. "Kresnov,

Jin, Pinto, Chu, Bujan, Poole, Halloran, all would probably have had barely a scratch."

Ibrahim had put the display screen on while they were talking. Now Amirah looked and saw the lean face of Justice Rosa, the writer who'd been writing Kresnov's biography . . . or limited biography, as Kresnov called it. He sat in a studio, looking serious, opposite an equally serious interviewer. Ibrahim turned the sound up.

". . . *honestly, knowing Commander Kresnov as I do,*" Rosa was saying, "*I think it's bullshit.*"

"What is?" asked the interviewer.

"*The coup plot. I am a very good judge of character, Deepak, and I'd stake my professional reputation on this—Cassandra Kresnov is no plotter of coups. There is only one coup plot at work in Tanusha today, and that is the one currently being perpetrated by the Office of Intelligence Directorate in the Grand Council, against the government of the entire Federation.*"

All three in the Director's office stared at the screen.

"Well," said Cassillas.

"Well indeed," Ibrahim murmured.

They watched in silence for several more minutes as the interviewer harangued Rosa on his accusation, and Rosa replied that his position was not ideological because he was in fact a pacifist and disliked the Federal intervention on Pyeongwha no matter what short-term good it did, but that neither did he like the imposition of draconian emergency powers on evidence that could easily be faked with today's technology. And furthermore, if anyone else felt the same, he'd be leading protests in Russell Square, London District, where other like-minded thinkers would be joining him to advocate civil disobedience against Operation Shield and its backers, which currently included President Singh and the government of Callay.

"Interesting," said Cassillas and got to his feet. "Must get back."

Ibrahim nodded, and Cassillas left. Ibrahim glanced up at Amirah once more.

"I do expect you to ace your political exams now," he told her. "Given this unmatched experience in political function." A joke. Good lord. Amirah suspected that most people who were very good at something enjoyed it on some level, even if they didn't like to admit it. Like Kresnov with killing people.

"Actually, sir, since you brought it up," she said with an offhanded smile, "I've been a little concerned my career track here might lead me straight into combat roles, given that I'm a combat GI. Lately I've been thinking I might enjoy a more administrative track."

Ibrahim raised eyebrows. "The two are not mutually exclusive. And in the Federation, GI or not, you have the perfect right to pursue any career track you prove yourself capable of."

"Yes, sir. Let's just survive the next few days first."

"The next few hours, indeed," Ibrahim agreed, rubbing his face. "As if I did not have enough on my plate, now I find my bodyguard covets my job."

Amirah laughed. "Maybe. Give me forty years." Ibrahim, to her delight, smiled quite broadly.

Chief Shin entered, calm as ever. Shut the door behind him, barely a thread or a hair out of place. "Director. You wished to see me?"

"Latest word from the Pantala negotiations," said Ibrahim without preamble. He did that, Amirah was learning. Launched straight into people, giving them no time to brace. "They're extremely thin. Your explanation?"

"Our sources are tenuous." Shin approached the chair opposing Ibrahim's desk but did not take it. Ibrahim did not offer it to him. Shin tugged a cuff, clasped hands. "OID run a tight ship, the negotiations are mostly theirs and Fleet's. FSA is an extra-governmental agency, and a non-military one, so neither avenue affords us much return."

"Interesting," said Ibrahim. "My days in the CSA give me much direct access to Callayan intelligence sources normally denied to a Federal security operative. As such, I've been talking to some sources very close to Fleet Intelligence."

Shin did not flinch. Amirah did not think the two men unfriendly. Between such men, on such matters, personal relations were not relevant. Yet she could smell the tension.

"Local sources are often best at finding informal routes of contact, as you'll know," Ibrahim continued. "And Fleet Intel will talk to less important local operatives more willingly than the Federal kind. The consensus amongst Fleet Intelligence is that whatever this whole episode is really about, it's about Pantala and lines that the League will go to any lengths to keep us from crossing."

"I had heard similar theories," Shin admitted.

"Yet did not report them."

A pause. Only five words, yet a dagger at Shin's heart. Amirah marvelled at the efficiency.

"There are many theories, Director," said Shin, unruffled. "Were I to report them all, you would have no time to read anything else."

Ibrahim gazed at him for a long moment. Then, "I have a theory of my own. I wanted to run it past you, see if it struck the Federation's chief spy as at least plausible."

Shin nodded. "Director."

"Commander Kresnov reports to us, quite plausibly, that League did not create synthetic neurology as they've always claimed. GIs are in fact a Talee invention, borrowed by the League, as the Talee carelessly left it lying. This, of course, is an enormous can of worms.

"Point one, the League lied about the defining technological breakthrough of their existence. Hugely, and destructively embarrassing, for League's reputation and founding ideology, and thus constitutional stability.

"Point two, League misused this technology in the creation of their own civilian uplink tech, which now threatens mass destabilisation on the psychological and social level, to the point of potential League disintegration.

"Point three, the Talee are known to be quite upset about this, to the point of siding with FSA operatives, against League forces, in military engagements on and around Pantala.

"Point four, a League cruiser tried to destroy Droze with a nuclear weapon and kill a million citizens, rather than let any of this become known.

"Now it doesn't take a great strategic mind to guess what the primary conditions are for the League's acquiescence to any Federation demands for involvement in managing this new crisis. League will want this kept quiet, to the greatest degree possible. Likely they'll demand the neutralisation of those 200 GI refugees from Pantala. And now we see that their Federation interlocutors have achieved just that.

"But most importantly, the faceless powers behind the appointments to the Grand Council get wind of all this and fear another war. Perhaps they are directly contacted by League operatives, a two-track approach by the League to play hardball negotiations at Pantala while intimidating the powers that control the GC on the other. And now, this sudden rush to referendums that will not prevent a League social meltdown but will rather prevent the Federation from intervening in it, curling us into a ball in the vain hope that this shall somehow pass us by if we don't provoke it. Plausible so far, do you think?"

"Quite plausible," Shin agreed. "It appears to fit with most of what we know. But the appearance of a fit is not the same as an actual fit."

"True. And there is one very important piece missing in this theory. How could such a series of machinations be achieved without the Federation's premier security agency finding out? Especially now that it is being headed by a man who is, let us say, known to be disagreeable on matters such as the subverting of democratic process by self-interested and violent parties?

"Well, the FSA has an Achilles heel—it relies overly much upon Federal Intelligence for much of its information, particularly that from infiltration-resistant parties like Fleet, OID, and the like. But if the plotters had a powerful ally onside, say, the Chief of FedInt himself? Most likely that information would never reach the FSA at all."

Shin nodded approvingly. "An excellent theory, Director. It would explain certain things. All too conveniently, in fact."

Ibrahim smiled, conceding that riposte. "Such a theory, were it proven true, would indicate a possible path of advancement. Intelligence blockages are as damaging as intelligence leaks, perhaps more so. Blockages must be unblocked. Eliminated if necessary. I'm sure you agree."

"Completely, Director."

"Excellent," said Ibrahim. "It so happens that in such an eventuality, I am in possession of the superior tools for that job." He glanced calmly to Amirah. And back. "Both in this headquarters and currently unaccounted for on the outside. Very many of those, I understand."

Shin smiled. "It is good to know that the FSA is in possession of such excellent assets. But I urge you not to abandon alternative possibilities quite so early in the piece."

"Never," Ibrahim agreed. "There are always alternatives. Often even less pleasant than the original. That will be all, Chief Shin."

"Director." A faint bow, and he turned for the door. Closed it behind him, leaving the Director and his synthetic bodyguard alone in the office.

"Now do you understand why I wanted you in for this meeting?" Ibrahim asked.

"Yes, sir. I'll have him watched." As Ibrahim's personal bodyguard, she was now in a position to share information and even to suggest new tactics to other combatants, especially GIs. This time, she understood, it would not be so much a suggestion as an instruction, straight from the Director.

Ibrahim nodded, satisfied that she understood. "Do not underestimate them. FedInt assets are not combatants as such, but against GIs the stealthy operative is probably the more effective option."

"Agreed. We'll be ready."

Justice Tado dove into the wide blue pool and swam. Twenty meters, then turn and swim back. Pity it wasn't a twenty-five meter pool; as a regular swimmer Tado knew just how many strokes that took, and how her form was, and if she needed to lift her workrate. It was petty, to complain about the missing five meters; most people didn't have any pool at their workplace. But it was enough that she typically preferred to swim near her home, and not in the Supreme Court block in Montoya. Exceptions she made for days like today, when the stress levels climbed too high, with coups and talk of high-ranking people trying to kill other high-ranking people, and rumours that FSA and OID were squabbling over the Supreme Court's security arrangements.

Fourteen, fifteen, sixteen strokes . . . her hand touched. It took eighteen. That was seventeen. Her concentration was slipping, somehow she'd lost count . . .

She caught the edge and looked about. And nearly died of astonishment. This wasn't the pool she'd jumped into. There were old stone columns, overgrown in places with creepers, stone floors, and a blue sky above. Men and women in robes, a woman carrying a tall urn, pouring wine for several others sitting poolside. They talked and laughed, in what sounded like . . . Latin. Ancient Rome.

It was quite bewildering to be confronted with something impossible. The mind took several turns to figure it out. Either some old fairy tale from her childhood had suddenly come to life, and she'd travelled far back in space and time, or . . . she'd somehow entered a virtual reality space.

She looked about. The water still felt completely real, swirling between her fingers. And here, sitting by the poolside in a simple dress, bare feet in the water, was a familiar face . . . familiar from news reports at least; Tado had never actually met her in person. She took a deep breath, and the feeling of safety she'd recovered upon realising she was in VR receded once more.

"Cassandra Kresnov," she demanded, over-arming her way to the GI's feet. "What the hell are you playing at? Did you put me in VR?"

It was impossible, of course. Only there'd been rumours that it wasn't, that Kresnov had scared the crap out of some very senior people with the extent to which it wasn't. But a Supreme Court Judge wasn't really supposed to know stuff like that, being senior in the scheme of things didn't mean she was anything more than just another judge, completely independent from all the mechanisms that surrounded for her to occasionally pass judgement on.

"It's a better scenario than the alternative," said Kresnov.

"And *what*, please tell me, is the alternative?" Tado put arms on the pool-side and glared up at her.

"I was killed by Operation Shield," said Kresnov innocently. "Because that would make this the afterlife."

"Or you a ghost." She poked at Kresnov's bare foot. It felt quite real, but that was just VR. "Girl, I am one hundred and seven years old. You should show more respect to your elders."

"If I didn't respect you, I wouldn't be here." Tado was certain Kresnov had learned to use this first impression to her advantage among people who'd never met her before. She was very pretty, calm yet animated. The period dress was a nice touch, the VR giving her a chance to dress as she would normally never choose, feminine and just a little revealing. There was a subtlety to her expression, a depth that must surely astonish anyone prejudiced against her kind. Charisma of a very certain type. "I brought you here to warn you."

Tado was too old and wise for that. To let this stripling dictate the conversation, and thus the situation, quite so easily. She heaved herself from the pool and sat beside Kresnov in her swimsuit. The sun felt warm. These baths were half open, one side a wall, the other opening to olive groves. Someone led a donkey by, bags of olives on its saddle.

"You know I'm pretty sure the Romans didn't build them like this," said Tado. "Bathing was a more formal experience. This is more informal. Like someone from our age might reinterpret an ancient scene."

"Probably," Kresnov agreed. "But we put people into 'types' so often, don't we? I get told all the time I don't behave like a normal GI, or like a normal person from the League, as though who we are means we've only one way to do things. I'm sure plenty of Romans built things however they chose, it was a big empire."

"And why do you like the Romans so much?"

Kresnov smiled slightly. "A clever use of the word 'like.' Implying personal bias on my part, yourself apart in wise judgement." Tado only smiled, wondering again how the hell Kresnov had penetrated security to get this far. But she was only an expert in law, not security. "I'm interested in modernity, and how it happens. What we call 'modern' civilisation pretty much started with the Romans."

"Oh, well," Tado made a face. "Now you're opening a whole can of worms."

"I'll rephrase it," said Kresnov. "If you drop the politically correct bullshit from various peoples who are offended by the implication, modern civilisation pretty much began with the Romans."

Tado smiled. She'd known Kresnov was smart, but she'd expected most of that intelligence to be focused on practical matters, security, intel, bureaucracy. And killing people, of course. This was unexpected.

"Commander, security law and regulation are not my forte, but I'm willing to bet that what you've just done in bringing me here is illegal. Why?"

"Because someone's trying to hack your brain."

Tado smiled benignly. "That's not even possible."

Kresnov indicated the baths, end to end. Waters sparkled in the sun. "This is about the length of your pool, wouldn't you say?"

"The Supreme Court pool, sure."

"And how many strokes does that normally take you?"

"Eighteen."

"And how many did it take you just now?"

Tado frowned. "Seventeen. I think. But that was just you pulling me into VR, wasn't it?"

"This pool in VR is of identical length to the one in the Supreme Court. I made it so."

"So what does that mean?"

"There is a technique," said Kresnov. "Some call it value adjustment. And the Justices of most courts are almost continually uplinked with all your case files and readings, so you barely notice it's happening."

"The networks we're linked to are some of the most secure anywhere."

"Made secure by the Federal government, yes, I know." Sardonically. The same Federal government that had just tried to kill her, Tado recalled. "Tell me this, how do you know that something is big?"

"Excuse me?"

"Big," Kresnov pressed. The pretty blue eyes at this range were disconcerting. Never threatening, not like in some B-grade action movie where the eyes glowed with fearsome intensity. They just never lost focus, never wandered, never darted or did any of the multitude of random things a normal person's would. "How do we define big? In a world where there is only one object, how do we know if it's a big object or a small object when there's nothing to compare it to?"

"Yes," Tado said slowly, "most linguistic or psychological concepts are relative, and thus meaningless in isolation. Very basic psychology, so what?"

"So something is only big because it's relatively larger than everything else. If everything else was larger, it wouldn't be big anymore, just average. The size of surrounding objects changes the meaning of 'big.'"

"I understand," Tado said impatiently. Kresnov was smart, but if she thought she was smarter than *her*, Justice Tado would give her a lesson in humility. "What does this . . ."

"Try a more difficult one. Try 'bad.' I kick an innocent puppy, for no reason. That's bad, and I deserve to be punished. I walk into a room full of innocent people and shoot them dead. That's bad. How do we know which is worse?"

"Learned experience that the life of a person is worth more than the life of a puppy."

"Scale has nothing to do with it?" Kresnov pressed.

Tado blinked at her. Then back at the pool. Eighteen strokes. Seventeen. Was Kresnov getting at what she thought she was getting at? "I suppose," Tado said carefully. "We judge the value of life on a hierarchical scale. Humans are at the top. Puppies further down. And the degree of violence inflicted, bullets to the head are at the top, kicks further down."

"I was just in a place where bullets in the head were a common punishment," said Kresnov. "You could get a bullet in the head just for being in someone's way. Value scales can be adjusted."

"Look," Tado said warily. "If you're suggesting that someone is using the court networks to change my value judgements . . . well, that's just crazy."

"Your Honour," said Kresnov quite calmly, "I work for the Federal Security Agency. I've seen it done."

"You, dear girl, have just been accused of planning a coup to overthrow the Grand Council."

"Yes." A small smile. "I heard."

"And if you could do that, why wouldn't you lie to a judge?"

"You don't have to believe me," said Kresnov. "Just remember your figures. Eighteen strokes to swim the pool. Six steps to cross your office. The length of ten hands to cross your desk. Write them down. They start with spatial perception, and that gives them a way in, size affects value judgements, the brain automatically attaches size to facts as a function of memory and internalises them. Used cleverly it can appear to give more weight to some facts than others, affecting judgement. Recall you're not being asked to pass sentence on questions of obvious morality, just constitutional technicality. Should one clause for some unnamable reason appear to all judges together as holding greater weight than the others, in a relative comparison, your conclusions can be arranged without you being aware of it."

Sandy was in the Courts Building bathroom, sitting in a toilet stall. Now she flushed, exited, and washed her hands like any other person. The bathroom was empty, as was much of the building—the Supreme Court Building was hardly a hive of activity, cases were limited, and staff few. Security was primarily remote, and in here, enough of the old Tanushan government security systems still ran that Sandy could access most of the building.

Tapped into building security, she could see other people in the corridors and judge when it was safe to move. She watched herself leave the bathroom, not bothering to fool the system into thinking she was someone else but simply blocking that portion of the security nervous system that processed faces. That in turn required a fairly complex VR overlay that duplicated system functions and fooled it into seeing what she wanted it to see, at least in portions—that thing that Cai and lately Ragi had proven so good at, doing to automated intelligent systems what VR did to the human brain. She wasn't nearly as good at it as they were, but good enough for limited needs like this. But she needed help.

"Rhian, are you there?" Rhian was maintaining the command structure, like a control center for VR function, seeded within the court building's own central matrix. Sandy had infiltrated and put it there, but did not have enough processing power to keep both it running and personal functions at the infiltration level. Once Sandy was inside, Rhian had come in through the front door, the system fooled into thinking she was someone else, and taken a seat in the waiting gallery, shades on, busy on multiple uplinks, all dark suit and no nonsense. Security types often looked the part, and no one bothered her. After all, she'd penetrated building security with no difficulty.

But now, Rhian did not reply. Sandy looked for her on building systems . . . and found her seated in the waiting gallery with various others, mostly press awaiting some announcement by a court clerk scheduled for some time in the next thirty minutes. The connection was working, why wouldn't Rhian reply? She slowed her pace in the corridor. Either she was getting incorrect information as to system function, or Rhian was ignoring her. That wasn't possible. The system function must be down, but she wasn't seeing it. Given that these systems didn't particularly trouble her, that wasn't possible either.

The only option it left was a crazy one. But she didn't see that logical deduction left anything else.

Am I out? Or still in?

She punched the wall, hard. It bounced without breaking. Shit. And began winding back through network functions as fast as she could; this shouldn't be possible, not to her, her brain usually rejected VR, and it was only with recent software adaptations that she'd begun to damp down that reflex . . . so disable the adaptations. She did, and . . .

. . . abruptly found herself atop an impossibly tall mountain. All about was empty space. Below, stretching away into the infinite distance, smaller, lower peaks, themselves snow covered and incredibly high. Clouds formed beneath them, filling valleys. The air was crisp and clear in the way it became at very high altitude. She should have been freezing to death. Suffocating. It happened more slowly with GIs, but it still happened. Instead there was numbness and absence of sensation. This was VR, and the program, unable to give her accurate-to-life sensation, gave her nothing instead.

It could have been Everest, she supposed. The Himalayas on old Earth. Old Earth simulations were most common in the Federation, the most famous of human worlds; the colonists all wanted to see it for themselves. The sun was small and low on the horizon, a bronze coin. The small platform of rock beneath her feet was barely a meter wide. To either side was space to step, trails. Forward or back would send her plunging into empty space.

She had no net access here. Could sense nothing on her uplinks, the kind of total absence you'd have on top of a huge mountain in the middle of nowhere. Hell of a capture program. It was a trap, of course, specifically designed to catch VR hackers. It shouldn't have worked on a GI, let alone a high-designation one like her. A regular human might be stuck up here indefinitely, lacking the skills to climb down or the courage to jump. But she wasn't scared of falling.

She leaped . . . and the VR refused to translate her synthetic power into momentum. She fell rather than flew, saw the rocky cliff face racing up below and flatly refused to brace for it, trusting a lifetime's experience of synthetic strength . . . and hit, the VR attempting to turn impact into pain, which a GI's brain could never accept as real . . .

And snap! she was back in the toilet stall, uplinks down and hearing that others were entering the bathroom. With her unarmed, unable to fool building security into thinking that a gun was anything other than a gun.

She fell and rolled under two neighbouring stalls as gunfire erupted and the partitions above her disintegrated in a hail of exploding panels. Planted a foot on a bowl and shoved just as the gunfire dropped to floor level, shot out through a riddled door with a blow that sent it off its hinges, collided with the armoured soldier on the far side with an elbow smash that caved in his lungs, kicked his neighbour into a third, jumped high, and rebounded off the ceiling at an angle to drop down on a fourth. Used him as a pivot to kick a fifth, removed his weapon to shoot a sixth and seventh, then an armlock on the fourth's retaliation, flipped him, ripped off the helmet and levelled the newly acquired weapon at his nose.

"Who?" she said, standing there covered in dust and debris from shattered stalls but barely a scratch besides, amidst the ruins of armoured bodies.

"Go to hell," said the man. An accent program ran without prompting . . . Nova Esperenza. Ambassador Ballan's homeworld. Big local security agency, locally known as K13, more heavily armed and, some claimed, more kick ass than the CSA.

Her network was back and showed gunfire in the waiting gallery. *"Rhian, we're blown, it's K13!"*

"Yeah, got that!" came Rhian's reply amidst heavy gunfire. Sandy's central feed was no longer working, she couldn't see Rhian's situation. *"Thanks for the head's up!"* Which could have been sarcasm. From Rhian?

Sandy abandoned all caution and hit the building network with everything . . . and found the command setup more easily than she'd hoped. Head Justice's chambers. Dropped her man, hit the door, then out the corridor at a sprint.

"Rhi, you good for three minutes?"

"Take ten," said Rhian. Return fire suggested she too had a weapon of her own now. *"Why should I mind?"* Definitely sarcasm.

Sandy took a corner so fast she ran up the wall to do it, skidded into a controlled collision with another corner, then fell down some stairs, taking the entire flight in a jump. Stopped with another collision in a wide, polished hallway. Ten strides away were the big panelled doors to the Head Justice's chambers. One usually approached them with reverence.

Sandy went through them in a combat dive, bits of wood and mechanism splintering as she did, weapon out and searching . . . and came up on one knee to find the chambers empty of all but two, both Judges. One was Malima Yadav, the Head Justice herself. The other was Sarah Tado.

"So it's true," said Yadav quite sternly. No robes, she wore a simple suit, hair in a braid. A much younger woman than Tado, only in her sixties, a high flier from Romero System. The Federation's senior legal authority. "You won't even respect the sanctity of the Supreme Court."

"Where is he?" Sandy demanded, looking about the room. K13's operational commander had been here, she was sure of it. With court approval. "K13, where is he?"

"So you can do what? Kill him too?"

Sandy did not waste time with disbelief. Yadav was supposed to be neutral. This wasn't neutrality. "You?" she said to Tado instead. "You were playing along?" Tado said nothing. "Using the entire Supreme Court as a trap to help Operation Shield get its most wanted fugitive?"

"When the security agencies that protect us start fighting amongst themselves, and we get caught in the crossfire," Tado explained, "there's not a lot we can do."

"You can do what's right," Sandy suggested. "Shouldn't be a novel thought in this building." No replies. "Last mistake in your legal careers."

Fear, on both their faces. They thought she was going to shoot them. As though they'd learned nothing from her last eight years of service. But these people, she recalled, were Federation, not Callayan. Callayans had become accustomed to her. The Federation, less so.

"*Rhi*," she formulated as she turned and left the chambers. "*I'll be there in thirty seconds.*"

CHAPTER TWENTY-THREE

Svetlana wandered easily across Russell Square, picking her way between milling groups of people. "I think there's about three thousand here," she said.

"*One of the news nets is saying six thousand,*" said Danya in her AR setup's earbud. "*They've got an overhead camera, they can see more than you.*"

That was true enough, Svetlana conceded. And, being from Droze, she'd rarely seen more than a few hundred people together in any one place at a time and wasn't much good at estimating crowds. Russell Square was pretty, like all Tanushan public places. It had grass, trees, and paths, was surrounded on all sides by buildings that were modest by Tanushan standards, and enormous by Droze standards. Over in the northeastern corner, the land dropped to a natural amphitheatre, where public performances were sometimes held. Over that way it was very noisy, with lots of shouting and amplified voices. Here in the middle of the square, it was less crowded.

"If Justice Rosa's going to start some sort of rebellion," she said, "doesn't he need more than six thousand people?"

"*A lot more,*" said Danya. "*I guess most people don't believe him, they think Sandy was plotting a coup.*"

"If they believe that after all she's done for them, maybe she *should* have plotted a stupid coup," Svetlana muttered. "Would serve them all right."

She wasn't wearing much of a disguise; they were all counting on any automated surveillance programs searching for all three of them—surveillance programs were limited, they all knew from experience, especially in crowds. And presumably Cassandra Kresnov's kids wouldn't be a very high priority if Ari was right and the Feds didn't know about the uplink message he'd sent to Kiril. Surveillance programs would narrow the odds by searching for all three of them together in a limited space—three kids of 13, 10, and 6, two boys and a girl, etc. Her alone, wearing the cute beret that her and Sandy's trip to the dress-up party had inspired her to buy, along with her own AR glasses, ought to hide her well enough amongst these people.

And here before her, as she emerged from the cover of a big fig tree to the grassy rim about the amphitheatre . . . "Oh, look," she said cheerfully, not breaking stride. "Surveillance."

Not that there weren't a lot of people overlooking the amphitheatre, there were—office workers come out on their lunch break, some with food in hand, other perhaps tourists, a few genuine attendees . . . but most of those were in pairs or small groups. Only this one woman, in unremarkable civvies, was standing alone and watching not only the ongoing speeches but also the people around her.

"*Careful, Svet*," said Danya. "*Don't get cocky.*"

"They're not looking at little girls after an ice cream," Svetlana replied, breaking into a run toward the ice-cream stall farther around the rim. Her run took her straight past the surveillance agent, close enough to show the little bulge at the back of the belt and a weight in the left pants pocket . . . and probably a gun in that silly handbag too.

Danya and Kiril sat in the southern part of the square, a nice series of playgrounds, including an enormous and well-supervised jungle gym, a crazy water playground, and a go-cart track. They ate some lunch, roti rolls and samosa, and took their time because, as Danya had explained, it would look suspicious for kids to be sitting between all these play spaces and not joining in.

They now watched on AR glasses of their own as Svetlana's vision feed approached the ice-cream stall, peering around taller bodies as she waited impatiently in line.

"I want an ice cream too," said Kiril.

"We've got more important things to worry about than ice cream," Danya replied.

"But she's having one."

"She's using it as cover," his big brother explained. "So she can get close without anyone being suspicious, they'll think she's just another kid with nothing better on her mind than ice cream."

"Like me," said Kiril sullenly.

Danya grinned and ruffled his hair. "Yes, like you."

"So what if she's using it as cover, it's still ice cream."

"Kiril, pay attention and help your sister like you're supposed to, and I'll get you an ice cream later, promise."

Ari had shown Danya how to blank the AR glasses setup so that it ran without ID—a very common thing in Tanusha, where people were techie smart and didn't like governments or advertisers tracing their every move. But most people, Ari said, then ruined it by using Augmented Reality in conjunction with uplinks, which weren't supposed to be easily traceable by communications law, but really were, to governments or security organisations with skills. Kids using ID-less AR, sans uplinks, wouldn't even register. The net monitored cyberspace constructs, but portable devices just bouncing signals off relays like antique phones used to do were anonymous, thanks to legal campaigns long ago by people who cared about stuff like this. People like Ari, Danya thought, whose concern of Feds abusing their power seemed pretty smart right now. And he hoped again that Ari was okay, wherever he was.

It meant that Danya and Kiril could receive Svetlana's live feed, with the standard AR overlay, and break that overlay down into parts. Not that Federal agents would make themselves visible to AR displays, but some others did—even now as Svetlana waited in line and looked around, a nearby person highlighted on the feed, and a close-up on that highlight said that she was a journalist and writer, working for something called Golden Pen Presentations.

"That's a journalist," Kiril observed. "Maybe we could talk to her?"

"No, remember we're not after journalists," said Danya. Svetlana's vision stayed trained on the woman, giving them time to consider her, but unable to speak now that she was in a line with other people. "The media's not on our side, we just want to see if we can talk to Justice Rosa."

"But he's a journalist," Kiril reasoned.

Sometimes Danya wished Kiril still wasn't smart enough to be able to follow this stuff at all. But then he wouldn't be reading, or setting up their AR links, or doing any other useful things either. "Yeah, but he's a different kind."

Journalists, Danya guessed, would light themselves up on AR in places like this in case someone with information wanted to tell them something. Probably this woman would be very upset to know how close she stood to the biggest story of anyone's career. And then, maybe not so upset knowing how likely that knowledge was to kill her.

Svetlana ordered strawberry gelato, a double serve, and walked away licking it all over. *"Oh, Kiri, look!"* she said loudly, examining the ice cream thoroughly on all sides with her glasses feed. *"It's really delicious!"*

Kiril grumbled, and Danya tried not to smile. "Don't be mean, Svet."

Svetlana walked to the edge of the amphitheatre, overlooking the crowd. It was thickest here, several thousand at least. On the platform sat some people in cheap plastic chairs, while one talked into a mini-mike, eliciting the occasional roar from the crowd. Some others stood security, arguing with crowd members around the podium, waving hands in discussion, all concerned and serious. Some cops stood nearby, watching, their cars parked on the nearby road corner, lights flashing. The whole thing looked like a last-minute setup, Danya thought.

AR lit up the people on the stage. "Intel . . ." tried Kiril, reading the captions. "Intellech . . . Intellechal . . ."

"Intellectual," said Danya. "Public Intellectual, they all are."

"What's that?"

"People without a real job," said Danya. "Kiri, can you zoom on the guy at the end there? That's Justice Rosa."

"What's a PhD?" Kiril asked as he did that.

"Something they give people without real jobs." Justice had a long brown face, made longer by his tall, curly hair.

"He looks like a pencil," said Svetlana through a mouthful of ice cream. *"He's writing Sandy's book?"*

"It's not Sandy's book, it's his, but it's about her." If anyone could get a message to Director Ibrahim, Justice could. Or that had been his reasoning in taking the risk to come here. There were probably others, but he had no idea who they were, and without knowledge, couldn't risk it. But Justice, he knew from Sandy talking about it, had contacts everywhere, and had now declared himself firmly against Operation Shield. "Just be careful, Svet, see if he has any advisors or someone you could slip a message to."

Svetlana walked down the slope and into the crowd. If it were a concert she'd have hated it, she only came up to most people's middles and couldn't see a thing on the stage. But today she liked it. Here she could move with complete freedom and slip through gaps no one else could. And do other things unnoticed.

"Hey, Kiril, see if you can get a feed on this." She put her new acquisition in her pocket with the AR regulator, saw the connection made on her vision, blinked on it, linked it to the main feed.

"What's that, Svet?" As the feed reached Danya.

"That's really shielded," said Kiril.

"I bet we could find someone to break it," said Svetlana, licking her ice cream into a more manageable size and shape. "One of Ari's friends."

"Svetlana, what is it?" Warily.

"Just the spare belt unit I lifted from that surveillance lady back there." Squeezing between gaps in the crowd. "I didn't look directly at it, you didn't see."

"Oh, for fuck's sake, Svet."

Kiril laughed. *"Cool,"* he said. And suddenly Svetlana could see new markers appearing on AR. Broadcasters, making a new signal pattern between them, like a grid of interlocking secure pathways.

"What the hell is that?" Danya asked. *"What's making that network?"*

"Don't look at me," said Svetlana. She looked about, pausing for a moment. Each of the new nodes seemed to be located exactly where good surveillance would place a person, to watch the square. "It looks like . . . oh, wow, Kiril, did you just hack the shielding?"

"Um . . . I'm not sure." A pause. *"Yeah, I think I did. It's, um . . . it's really weird, I can't see that network or anything, I mean I can't see a picture? A schematic?"* Which was one of those technical words he'd picked up that he loved to use, in or out of context. *"But I'm getting this different feed now? And I think . . . I think it's coming from them, from the Feds."*

"And that's why we're all seeing it!" Svetlana barely remembered to keep her voice down in her excitement—there were people all about, but mostly the speakers from the stage and occasional cheering were too loud for them to overhear some kid beneath them. "You're processing the feed and sending it back to us! Kiri, your uplinks are really working!"

"And working crazy well," Danya muttered. *"I don't like it, we should pull out, this is much more advanced than any uplinks should be at this level. It could be doing him damage."*

"I feel fine," Kiril protested.

"Danya, this is too awesome," Svetlana said in a harsh murmur. "I can see everything, this is much safer for all of us, I know where they all are!"

A pause. Wild cheers following some announcement on stage.

"*Okay*," said Danya finally. Reluctantly. "*Just stay low and do your own surveillance, Svet. No more stupid risks, okay?*"

"It wasn't a stupid risk," Svetlana muttered, moving forward again. "I made us safer."

She finally reached the front of the crowd and peered through a small gap between arms. From her low angle, the stage was too high, and she could barely see Justice's face as he sat near the present speaker. There were no barriers holding people back from the stage, though, and the volunteer security looked nervous. Shouldn't the cops be protecting the stage? Shouldn't there be barriers? Everywhere else in Tanusha the government seemed to stick its hand in, making everything safer . . . but not here.

She did a slow circle, edging into gaps. It was possible there was even a security person or two down here—they'd have a poor view, but sometimes you needed someone right up close. Funny the things you saw as a kid, down low, that no one else did. Litter on the once-perfect grass. Shoes people wore, from crazy boots to silly heels, to smart leather. She thought it would be funny to tie someone's laces together when they were watching the stage. A tough-shelled beetle, several times stepped on but still undamaged against the soft grass, struggling to find a safer place.

Around the back of the stage were a lot more officials . . . or maybe "unofficials," as they wore no uniform and were scampering back and forth, talking, arguing, trying to organise things. Sometimes Svetlana wondered if adults knew what the hell they were doing, surely it couldn't be this complicated just to have a few people stand on a stage and talk? A few uniformed cops were talking to them, and as she got closer, she overheard something about permits, noise volumes. The "unofficials" wanted some cops around the front of the stage, between the speakers and the crowd.

"Hey, little girl." She looked up and found the man beside her looking down—African, dreadlocks, grey-streaked. "Where are your parents?"

"I'm not little," she replied, with just the right amount of petulant independence. "They're back there." She pointed. "They can see me through these; I said I'd get them a different angle." Pointing to her AR glasses.

"You know, when I was your age," the man said, leaning down to her with a conspiratorial smile, "I'd go and crawl under that stage when there was someone singing. I'd get right underneath them and hear all the musicians talking to each other between songs." Svetlana smiled politely. "But I don't think it's safe to do that today. In fact, I don't think it's safe for a child to be here at all, these are not safe times."

The AR showed him clean, so he certainly wasn't a Fed. He seemed very nice. "Why isn't it safe?"

The man smiled. "When you have pacifists taking the side of those trying to preserve Federal military reach," nodding at Justice Rosa on the stage, "and those who say they're campaigning for individual rights standing against GI emancipation and *for* mass murder on Pyeongwha, you know the world is going crazy. And when the world goes crazy, young girl, you know no one is safe."

Pop pop pop. Svetlana hit the ground before anyone, face pressed into the grass amidst the many shoes. Then, a second later, everything erupted in screams, running and falling as others figured what was going on.

"Svet! What's happening?"

"Someone's shooting at the stage!" Not especially worried, despite her galloping heart—shootings were always dramatic, but she was far enough from the stage, and amidst this crowd would have to be very unlucky. "Ow!" As people ran over her. Then, "Ow!" again as someone landed on her—the dreadlocked man, and he was heavy! Had he been hit?

"Svetlana!"

"Stay down, stay down!" the dreadlocked man was telling her. Svetlana rolled her eyes—she'd *been* down, like a whole four seconds before him, and didn't need him falling on her . . . though it did stop the galloping crowd from kicking her in the face.

"I'm fine!" she said, for his benefit and her brothers'. "I'm fine . . . look, the shooting's stopped!"

"Stay down!" From his desperate voice and trembling, Svetlana didn't think it was *entirely* her safety that worried him. "He could still be out there!"

Looking sideways, face pressed to the grass, Svetlana saw cops against the side of the stage, weapons out, pointing into the main crowd. None were looking skyward, so it didn't seem to be a sniper—logically a sniper would be up high somewhere, and the cops would all have tacnet, and tacnet could find snipers just by cross-referencing the sound of bullets passing different tacnet feeds.

"I have to find my parents!" she shouted. "Look, it's safe, the cops have got him!" And struggled out from under the man, determinedly slipping his grasp, then running, sidestepping, and leaping over all the people lying flat, the others running at a crouch . . . and found a new cover position behind several people in turn behind a tree, more concerned about being seen by Feds than shot.

She could see the stage from here; at least one person down and apparently hit. Justice Rosa was crouched over him, ripping a shirt and applying first aid. A cop was helping, firmly directed by Justice, who seemed to know more what to do than the cop—Svetlana recalled Sandy had said he'd been a war correspondent.

Other cops were converging on a place in the crowd, guns levelled at someone now lying on the ground on the cleared grass. Presumably the shooter. Crap, she thought—she must have gone straight past him, concealed in the crowd.

She looked back to the stage, at officials, volunteers, cops, and others, hiding and low, apparently with no real idea what was going on—keeping your head when there was shooting was hard without practise. She'd had practise, they hadn't. Maybe she could get to one of them, one of Justice's friends, slip him the note Danya had written in pen on a scrap of paper . . .

"*Svet. Look up.*"

She did, at the surrounding buildings. And saw a whole series of red dots that hadn't been there before, linked by encrypted network. Like the sky above the square had suddenly come alive, like a spider's web.

"Holy fuck," she said.

"*Some of those signals are, like . . . computers or something?*" said Kiril, sounding puzzled. "*It's tacnet, but it's like computer signals inside tacnet?*"

He was decrypting tacnet? Again, as Sandy would say, holy fuck.

"*Snipers,*" said Danya. "*They had this square covered so much more than we thought. Svet, get the fuck out of there, that's an order. Head two blocks east and find the kind of store kids might go into, we'll join you there.*"

Svetlana didn't argue with Danya when he took that tone. She took off running toward the nearest road, where cops were yelling and gesturing at everyone else running their way to keep running, and cross the traffic-empty road. She did, then slowed, and walked briskly down the adjoining street.

"If they had snipers," she muttered, "why didn't they shoot the shooter? Why just let him shoot?"

"We don't know they didn't."

"Danya, that many snipers would see a gun as soon as it was drawn. And he'd be dead before the cops even saw him, but all the cops knew where he was on their tacnet. No way is the cops' tacnet linked to the snipers' tacnet, but the cops all knew where he was when he was shooting. I reckon the snipers saw him, and let him shoot until the cops got him."

She was better at this stuff than Danya, and he knew it. She could feel him thinking.

"Hey look, Justice is okay!" That was Kiril, hooking into a new feed. That feed made a square on Svetlana's vision, and she could see Justice not merely okay, but resuming his seat on the stage as the wounded speaker was carried off by medics. And now getting to his feet, taking a mini-mike, and starting to speak himself. Upright and chest out, as though daring someone else to take a shot.

"Balls," said Svetlana. It was what they'd said in Droze when someone had done something brave but almost certain to get him killed.

"Balls," Danya echoed.

"Balls!" Kiril added cheerfully.

"Preeti!" Rami Rahim exclaimed, sitting before his operator's bank with a wide view of Tanusha's night skyline. "Where are you calling from?"

"Hi, Rami! I'm calling from DV8, the new decor is just rocking and there are lines to get in going round the corner! Plus Deepak Gaur was just seen here, rumours are that Augment League football star Jennifer Straughn might be here too . . ."

"Thank God for the Augment League!" Rami announced. "Where tiny women can give huge men an enormous butt whooping and men in the stands even more enormous erections doing it! Thank you, Preeti, also on red we've got Mohammed in Kuta, where you calling from, Mo?"

"Rami, I'm calling from the Wunderbar here on Khan Street. They're having a bikini wax competition tonight, special guest starring the entire chorus line of the hit RK Road musical 'Mardi Gras!'"

"Oh, hell, yes!"

"The best bikini line, as voted by drunken fools in the audience, will win an entire Michelle Mauvin swimwear collection and the undying gratitude of about three hundred men in the audience."

"And a wad of goo in the left eye, no doubt." Behind her sound barrier, Liz the producer rolled her eyes.

"*And I'm going to get you some vision on the Rami Matrix!*"

"Awesome, make sure it's a real low angle, you know? Thanks, Mo!"

His feed meter showed close to a million direct links across the city tonight—a Friday, and every Friday was a party night in Tanusha—and Thursdays, Saturdays, and Sundays—political crisis or not. The ad market feed was showing twenty-three thousand dollars a minute and up to forty-five for premium, not a bad rate of return given the competition from other sources. But when the shit hit the fan in Tanusha, people got drunk and danced. Usually Rami found that admirable. Tonight, less so.

"Here's the news!" he announced, not missing a beat. His night beat style was tempo tempo tempo, never a break save for feed crosses. "Malini Chopra's tits grew a little smaller today . . . can you believe that? Breast *reduction*, Malini?"

"No!" called Angus from the other mike.

"Yes, that wailing sound you hear is a thousand teenage boys throwing themselves out their apartment windows. And if the *old* Malini had been lying on her back on the road beneath them, they'd all survive, dammit!" Angus and Caitee's laughter gave him a beat. "In other news, Finance Minister Richards' penis, just as small as ever."

More laughter. The minister's wife had been photographed in bed with a male stripper three days ago, giving comics three nights of running gags.

"I mean, poor Mrs Richards," said Rami, scrolling through multiple feeds on his board, already scanning ahead for the next three segments. "Four centimeters just doesn't cut it, right? It used to be six, but then there were those budget cuts . . ." Laughter. "Liz, what say you?"

"Five," said Liz with confidence. "Absolute minimum."

The secret to Rami's success, as with most comics, was that he never felt apologetic for what he found funny. Dick jokes, fart jokes, breast jokes . . . hell, he had six hours to fill, and he loved it, and mild literary puns wouldn't fill the time or pay the bills. It was old reflex, and he could yammer on like this all night, the quickest wit in Tanusha and everyone knew it. But tonight, somehow, it didn't make him happy.

"In other news," he announced, "writer and Very Serious Man Justice

Rosa denounced Operation Shield! He said it was all a scam and a con job, and he'd go down to the local park with some friends to protest about it! Two hours later, someone tried to shoot him. So I guess we can just put that down to coincidence, right?"

Liz gave him a wary look.

"Well, the shooter was a well-known anti-GI nutter," said Angus. "Can't really blame the GC for some loon who thinks Rosa's for emancipation."

"In further news," Rami added edgily, "the ghosts of two hundred and fifty recently killed GIs on a remote island in the Maldaris want to know why this guy gets called an anti-GI nutter, while the Federation chairman who had them all killed for no immediately provable reason gets called a hero."

"Oh, great, he's going after the Chairman now. How big's his penis, Rami?"

"Surely much, much bigger after he killed 200 people for no obvious reason."

"No obvious reason aside from the coup plot that they have *recordings* of, Rami, your buddy Kresnov planning in private conversations." Angus's job was to give Rami something to bounce off, and to fill the silences. But this was politics, not dick jokes, and his heart wasn't in it.

"Wonderful," said Rami, "a media professional who listens to a couple of recordings he could cook up in five minutes in this studio, and automatically believes they're genuine. Angus, you're a great loss to the legal profession." Angus made a face. "In other news, there was a lot of shooting in the Supreme Court building today. The authorities refuse to tell us who was shooting, or why, or at whom, because, you know, we're just the public, the people who pay for all this shit, why would we care?

"And in local politics, Callayan President Vikram Singh crawled a little further up the Grand Council's collective butthole today! Who knew there was still room up there? What with all the local media and the Callayan Parliament all crammed in there together . . . way to stick up for Callayan rights guys! That'll show 'em."

On his board, the ad market feed began falling to twenty-two thousand. Thirty thousand links disappeared just like that. He was supposed to be in a perpetual good mood, but sometimes Tanusha made him angry. Behind her window, Liz was gesticulating frantically at the boards.

He took a deep breath. "We've got Juanita on the line! Where are you, Juanita . . . whoa! Vision on line five, what the hell is that behind you?"

"This is Callay's Largest Pizza competition, Rami, and behind me is the biggest pizza on the planet!"

A call light was blinking. And on Rami's uplinks. The blinking was accompanied by beeping, quite distracting; it shouldn't do that. He looked at Liz, as Juanita rambled on about sauces and toppings, and Liz looked puzzled.

"I'm trying to block it," she said on their private line, *"but it won't go away."*

Rami just had a feeling. He wasn't sure. But he felt it was worth the risk.

"I'm sorry, Juanita, we have an unscheduled caller, who is this?" And connected the call.

"Hi, Rami. It's Sandy Kresnov." And the whole studio just stared, as though stunned by some jolt of electricity. Followed by frantic activity, as new links were made to ad markets, to publicity houses, to feeder nets.

"Sandy. Wow." Rami put his boots down off the opposing chair and felt a deep chill. His heart suddenly thumping in his chest. Every now and then, he did serious. Usually he did it on his own terms, rarely if ever on his famous weekend night beats. One of those serious sessions, long ago, had been with Cassandra Kresnov. Since then, they'd done a few more, the only sessions at any length, and away from pure journalism, she'd done with anyone. Some jokingly called Rami "Kresnov's favourite journalist," which was meant as an insult, because he wasn't one. To which Rami had told them all, on air, that he didn't think Cassandra had favourite journalists—she'd talk with anyone whose morals and ethics were superior to a blood-sucking insect, and she hadn't found any actual journalists whose weren't, so she chose him instead.

Beyond the window now, Liz was gesturing furiously for him to continue. So fickle, Liz.

"How are you Sandy?"

"To paraphrase a great writer long ago, reports of my death were greatly exaggerated."

"I can hear that. Or at least, well, we don't have any visual feed of you, but . . . can I just tell listeners that I just received a shock when your call lit up my board, I've no idea how you do that, you got past all the network barriers and I don't know who else could do that but you.

"Sandy, Operation Shield. Is it real?"

"Oh, it's very real, Rami. Justice Rosa said it best, there has been a coup plot executed against the Grand Council, and Operation Shield is it. Rami, I only have a little time before I have to get off . . ."

"Okay okay," Rami rushed. From the corner of his eye, he could see his link meter shrieking upward, passing three million now and on its rapid way to five and beyond. The ad rate climbed to . . . one hundred thousand a minute! New bids rolling in for the next available slots directly after this interview . . . five million for thirty seconds! Eight million! "Sandy, what should we do? Ordinary Tanushans, why should we believe you, and what should we do about it?"

"Firstly, you should believe me because every piece of evidence they've presented is easily fabricated. You work in media, you know this, that stuff of me and others talking in rooms under surveillance, that's scripted work, it's pure fantasy. In itself it proves nothing because it can't be proven real.

"Secondly, who benefits? Everyone who opposes 2389, everyone who could speak out against Operation Shield, has been either arrested, assassinated, muzzled, or subject to attempted assassination, like myself. The GC will now pass amendments that will change the shape of the Federation to suit 2389 perfectly. This should be unconstitutional, but I'm predicting they'll go after the Supreme Court Justices next, they should be put under 24-hour surveillance, but guess who's in charge of that? FSA and CSA, both suspended, so it falls to the OID, who are certainly behind this coup. Clever, isn't it?"

"That shooting in the Supreme Court Building today, what was that?"

"That was trouble, Rami. Trouble that tells me it might be too late even for the court."

"So what do we do, Sandy? What do you do?"

"There's hardly anything I can do, Rami. The network runs on basic codes that the GC now controls, it's very hard even for me to do anything without the net. So I'm calling on all you underground types, all you frauds and hypocrites who say you love your freedom but are now sitting passively while Operation Shield walks all over your faces. Defy them. Get angry, get busy, get arrested if necessary. Bring the whole thing down if you have to. Don't let them steal your freedom from under your noses, because if you lose it now, you might never get it back."

"You're calling for civil disobedience?"

"Yes, especially online. Look, don't do it for me; I know a lot of people are very suspicious of me right now, and that's fine. Take me out of the picture. Look at them. Look at what they're doing, how they're behaving. I'd be angry. Why isn't everyone else?"

"I think maybe because this is dressed up as an anti-Federal cause. 2389 are the anti-Feds, they're trying to limit Federal power, and President Singh of Callay, the biggest anti-Fed there is, is backing it to the hilt so far."

"That's because he's in on it."

Rami could barely breathe. He was a comedian, dammit. That *he* should be dealing with this accusation, from her, was crazy. "That's . . . well, I think he'd say that statement was treasonous."

"Well, then I have a message for President Singh. I'm going to get you, you mealy-mouthed son of a bitch. You should be scared. You know what you've done, and who you've tried to screw, and I'm going to get the lot of you."

Click, and she was gone.

"Holy crap," said Rami. Quite conversationally. "Well, Sandy Kresnov just promised to bring down the entire Federation and Callayan governments on my show. Anyone mind if we stay with politics for a moment more, or should we go back to talking about fucking pizza toppings?"

It was getting late when Danya arrived in Denpasar District. The taxi cruised down a main strip, office crowds now dissipated, replaced by the late-night crowds, out for a meal, a concert, or a party. Lights everywhere, massive ten-storey displays, projected holograms that appeared to block sidewalks and even roads, only to part like some magic waterfall when you passed through it. Cruisers coming in low to a roadside rooftop park, running lights strobing. Crazy fucking city, it still blew him away. Ari had lived here all his life and said the same.

He hit the stop button on the passenger display, and the automated vehicle found the next convenient autopark and pulled over. On Danya's AR glasses, he saw his credit score deducted a small amount. Nothing much, this credit account was seriously maxed out from yesterday, a mysterious pile of electronic money just appearing. Sandy, he had no doubt, having arranged for that to happen automatically if she didn't renew some code in twenty-four hours. These three kids were now loaded, by kids' standards anyway.

He pulled the glasses off as he got out, onto the sidewalk, and immediately he could feel it. This wasn't a typical Tanushan party night, the street music, the enticements, the happy prowling of people just looking to be entertained. Many of the holographics were displaying odd things. Crazy patterns, news images, slogans. A lot of people were just standing about and staring at them, commenting amongst themselves.

On the next corner, a huge wraparound display was showing scenes from the war, battle images, brief flashes of armoured GIs in action, brutal vision, guns blazing, people dying in that horrid way they did on real vision but didn't in the movies—without close-ups, without drama, without clever direction and editing, just dying, with an utter lack of romance. Danya knew real vision from fake, he'd seen plenty of the real stuff himself. And now his earbuds picked up the display audio, *"I'm going to get you, you mealy-mouthed son of a bitch. You should be scared."*

Sandy's voice, from that comedian guy's show she liked. These displays were hacked, at least half of them. Whether they were pro- or anti-Sandy, he couldn't tell. Here on the corner, a police car sat, lights flashing, two cops with pistols prominent standing by their vehicle and just watching the crowds. Danya had never seen that before in Tanusha.

He walked on, a little surprised the air traffic was still flying. There were reports of the traffic net crashing in parts, which never happened. Kiril told him the net was crazy, everything was tangled, a lot of things not working. Not all of it was hackers taking Sandy's advice, a lot of them were taking the other side, but all were causing trouble, and there were attack programs everywhere, smashing official constructs to debris, rerouting automated functions, doing all kinds of stuff Kiril couldn't explain. And the busy Tanushan streets were still crowded but buzzing with a different, darker kind of energy.

Abruptly the cops got back into their vehicle and sped off, central traffic yanking other vehicles out of their path. Chasing someone, Danya thought, walking briskly onward. Ahead there was an argument, one group of strangely dressed people pushing and yelling with another group of strangely dressed people. He did not hang about to find out the nature of it, and just walked faster. Crack, boom! He flinched, but it was fireworks somewhere about, echoing off the towers. Illegal in regulated Tanusha, but tonight that wasn't stopping anyone. The crackle in the air was anarchy, and when he'd first arrived, it had been the last thing he'd expected to find.

"Guys, where are you?" He spoke into the little headset, detached from his glasses, just earbuds and mike.

"We just got off at the station," came Svetlana's voice. *"It's a little bit crazy around here. Some shop windows have been smashed, there's cops chasing people."* The distant sound of a siren. *"That's an ambulance, it's a block away."*

"Just keep your head down and meet me at the rendezvous." They could not travel together lest any person or surveillance program reckon who they might be, and it was Svetlana's turn to mind Kiril. Because Kiril was now insisting that they had to come here, Denpasar District, Patel-Clarkeson intersection. He saw something, he said, and couldn't really explain it . . . except that he saw it so much more clearly than anything else on his uplinks, and it was coming from here. Logically the only thing that might stand out like that was similar technology to what Kiril used. There was only one person in Tanusha with similar technology uplinks, and that was the guy they were looking for—the mysterious Ragi. Danya thought it worth a shot.

"Doesn't do much good smashing windows," said Svetlana. *"Or throwing things at the cops, it's not the cops' fault. Why don't they go and smash some Feds instead?"*

"Because Feds will shoot them," said Kiril quite sensibly.

"It might be useful to Sandy if the cops are spread thin," he reasoned. "I mean there's really not enough of them. Sixty million people could go nuts in this city with this few cops, they're not used to people going crazy."

It could make the people in power nervous. Tanushan defences were designed to stop high-tech special operations attacks, terrorist bombs, and the like. But what would Parliament defences do if screaming mobs broke into the President's house and dragged him away? Or dragged anyone away? Would they order troops to open fire on unarmed crowds? And Ari said weapons were easy to get with all the material printers—what if the crowds didn't stay unarmed for long?

Kiril's destination was a market. It occupied the open two floors of a city block along Clarkeson Street, where architects had left an open space beneath the building. It was nearly 10pm, but still it bustled and thronged, lights ablaze, shoppers spilling onto the pavement. Crisis or no crisis, Tanusha had to eat, and liked to eat fresh.

Danya took a seat at a noodle bar opposite and ordered a bowl, still hungry after a light dinner hours ago. The noodle guy did not blink at a thirteen-year-old out at 10pm, it wasn't uncommon, and with all the residential buildings around, he might have been minutes from home. He sat at the bench and looked through the window at the market, as a couple of cars cruised past, tough-looking underground types hanging out the windows blasting heavy metal music from speakers. Ominous and pounding, it suited the street mood entirely.

He put his glasses back on—wearing them all the time was trouble, Feds looked for that sort of thing, plus they could blind you, make you dependent on technology he'd survived five years in Droze without. But now, sitting with his excellent noodles, he wanted to see what Kiril was seeing.

The feed was crowds, then shoes and bags, then fresh fish. Kiril's hand, tightly in Svetlana's, as she led him through the market throng, people buying, people talking, people laughing. Danya had thought a high-tech city would buy everything at the flick of an icon, but Tanusha loved everything personal and face to face. Things were still bought at the flick of device on device, but here, food was handled, smelled, prodded, questions asked of talkative sellers. You could do that on VR, he supposed, but that was a *simulation*. Maybe it was one of those inverse relationships, where the more synthesized everything became, the more people came to value the real experience. While tech heads saw technology as all heading in one direction, they forgot the people who made it all happen and resisted what they didn't like.

Kiril's uplinks weren't registering any Feds here. Danya didn't trust that, because all those snipers above Russell Square hadn't been visible at first either, only after the shooting started. Meaning that the Feds had modes where whatever Kiril had in his head couldn't see them. But Kiril had seen *something* here. And no one was looking twice at a ten-year-old girl leading her little brother through the market.

It took him twenty minutes to finish his bowl, eating slowly. Svetlana and Kiril couldn't stay much longer, wandering endlessly around the market and not buying anything would eventually get them noticed, assuming someone was watching. He always assumed someone was watching. The trick was to assume it without becoming so paranoid you couldn't move, because you assumed they were watching *you*. When in reality, you were just one of these masses, and they had no way to tell you from them, unless you gave them one. And whatever the IDs put out on Kresnov's kids, those wouldn't be on any Fed's priority list when there were armed and dangerous adults on the loose.

Unless they knew of Ari's sent message and figured it had gone to Kiril. He didn't see how, but then he was new to all this uplink-network stuff. If they had, then they might just figure it was better to make those kids disappear for good.

The guy at the corner display screen hadn't moved for several minutes, he realised. It was raining now, and beyond the hissing traffic, a man tapped icons on a display telling him where everything in the market was. Uplinks did that too, but not everyone had super-high-tech uplinks, or liked using them. The screen glowed blue in sidewalk puddles, and the man wore a smart coat against the rain, while less-organised people ran across the road for cover. Moving icons, moving icons.

"Guys, I see a man on the corner of Clarkeson and Patel who looks like a watcher." His own reflection in the store window showed him no one behind close enough to hear or not involved in other conversation. His position on the corner gave the man a good view down two entire sides of the market. But he couldn't stay there forever in that standing position . . . so whatever he was watching for would logically happen soon.

Running lights flashed above, and Danya leaned forward to peer up. A cruiser was coming down atop the building. It wasn't tall, barely ten floors. And here on the road in front parked another vehicle, three people getting purposely out, all in suits, good coats, sensible shoes.

"Here we go," Danya murmured. "One group coming down on the roof, another parked out the front. There must be someone they want in the building above."

"*Yeah, I see someone moving in here too,*" said Svetlana, above a nearby shouting fishmonger. "*Here, Kiril, look at these crabs, aren't they cool?*"

Danya saw her feed focus on crabs, then slide across to crowds . . . a man and a woman, moving down the next aisle with purpose. They passed, and . . . Svetlana turned to follow down this aisle, losing vision to adults blocking her way. Danya didn't mind that; everyone was looking over her head, and people with guns on high alert just didn't think to notice kids.

The way up to the building above was in the central core, service elevators that brought goods down from the rooftop pads, and smaller personnel elevators for people with access to the middle floors. The people Svetlana was following seemed to be headed there, behind some terrific cheese stalls, various writing in European languages, a couple of empty automated trolleys awaiting the next ride up.

Danya noticed Kiril was eating a chocolate. And recalled a chocolate stall a few minutes back, selling just those kind. Svetlana hadn't stopped to pay for anything.

He must have made some involuntary noise of disapproval, because Svetlana said, around a mouthful, *"I was hungry, and it's in the service of the entire Federation, right? If they can give us a medal, they can give us a chocolate."*

"This is really yummy," said Kiril. *"Let's go back there again later, and pay for something."* Followed by the muffled sound of Svetlana trying not to laugh. Against all better judgement, Danya found himself fighting a smile.

The man and woman Svetlana was following joined several others Danya recognised from the car out front, moved past the cheese stalls and pressed for a personnel elevator. The elevator opened, and a black man stepped out quickly, and sideways, to avoid being hit by the suits walking in. And stood to one side, watching them quite overtly, as none of them even glanced at him.

Danya wasn't the only one to notice. *"What the hell is that?"* Svetlana asked. *"Danya, why is he doing that?"*

"It's like they can't see him," Danya said slowly. Then it clicked. Ari had mentioned something about this. "I know. He's hacked their eyes."

"That's not possible."

"Danya!" Kiril said plaintively. *"That's Ragi! It has to be!"*

The elevator departed, and so did Ragi, walking through the market crowds. Svetlana followed, not having to be told. Danya thought furiously, where had Ari spoken about this? He'd said it was the holy grail of uplink hackery, and that it was completely impossible with existing technology. But that he was certain it *was* possible, nonetheless, in the future. What did it mean, that Ragi could do it? And if Ragi's signal on the net was what Kiril had been following, what did that mean about Kiril's uplinks?

Ragi approached the wet road. Several people at a stall seemed to notice him. Danya saw it about to happen before it happened, and abandoned his stool for the door in a flash.

"Whoa!" on Svetlana's feed, as two men by the road grabbed Ragi, thrust him into a car that screeched to a halt out from nowhere, then sped off again with doors slamming. *"Wow, they're good!"* The timing, she meant, as Danya rushed the street to get a cab. There was one waiting at the autostop just a little up, and he pressed his credit ring to the door. It opened, and he jumped in.

"Please state your journey's destination," said the pleasant voice.

"Follow that vehicle!" Danya tried. "That blue groundcar that was just parked on the verge opposite, fifteen seconds ago!"

"I'm sorry, this request is not allowed. Please state your journey's destination."

"U-turn please, pick up my brother and sister."

Bleep, and the nav screen indicated the manoeuver to be performed. And waited for passing traffic. Danya looked desperately over his shoulder, but the other car had stopped at lights a hundred meters down the road.

Finally the U-turn, other traffic slowing to allow it, then a relatively rapid dart across the road, alarming if not for the knowledge that central controlled everything on the road and couldn't possibly crash. And pulled up at the curb, Svetlana and Kiril running into the rain, then into the car.

"Can we follow it?" Svetlana gasped, in the other front seat as Kiril leaned between them in the back.

"We're not allowed to," said Danya. "Maybe just give a destination and change it to keep following them?"

The light ahead was going green, traffic accelerating. And now the taxi was moving in pursuit.

"What?" Svetlana stared at the nav screen. "Why are we moving, did you tell it to move?"

"No." Danya was similarly baffled. And they both turned to stare at Kiril. "Kiril, is that you?"

"I don't know," he admitted. "It might be. I'm seeing this weird stuff, and I just thought I'd like to follow the car, and we started moving."

"Okay!" said Svetlana, hands up. "Kiril, don't think about it, just . . . just keep doing what you're doing." No reply, just a fixed, straight-ahead concentration. Svetlana and Danya looked at each other. "Don't even talk about it."

"Svet, I don't like it . . ."

"Danya! Don't talk about it, we tried to find Ragi and we found him, right?" Danya made a face. They were at full speed now, which wasn't much in the urban zone, lots of cars, signals and stops. "So what are we going to do? Danya, I saw them put some kind of collar on him, they were that fast. I think it's the kind that blocks uplinks."

"So we know he's got mad hacking skills. Svet, Ari said it's not possible to hack eyes . . ."

"But we saw it!"

"Then he's got to be a GI. I mean, Sandy's so much better at uplinks even than Ari, even she can't hack eyes, but if anyone could, it has to be a GI . . ."

"He's not a GI, they just grabbed him and put him in that car!"

"Not all GIs are combat GIs, Svet. Maybe he's a super-advanced non-combat GI." Sharing similar uplink tech to what Chancelry had put into Kiril. They both looked at him, between the front seats, staring ahead through his AR glasses. Danya had a chill.

"What are we going to do then?" Svetlana asked. Ahead, the car came to another stop. Clearly the Feds weren't about to bring attention to themselves by hacking traffic central and moving faster, probably they felt they didn't need to. The taxi slowed also, stopping at lights one block behind. "We could ram them."

"And then do what?" said Danya, a little exasperated. "Svet, there's armed agents in that car, if we knock them off the road they'll just get out and shoot us. Unless you stole someone's gun as well?"

Svetlana shook her head. Opened her jacket to reveal a fishmonger's knife. Danya rolled his eyes. "What?" She was indignant. "I needed a weapon; I feel better with a weapon!"

"Well, we're not going to stab these guys to death. I don't think we can stop them, Svet. I say we follow to see where they're taking him, then plan from there."

"Danya, they'll be taking him to some Federal agents' headquarters! Getting in there will be like breaking into FSA headquarters; it's not going to happen!"

"Well, getting killed on the road there won't help either. Svet, we don't know this guy, he might be useful, but we don't owe him anything . . ."

"It's not about owing *him*." Svetlana was adamant. "It's about owing Sandy! The people who took over the Grand Council are trying to kill her, and if we can get this message to Ibrahim, Ibrahim can stop them! Ragi might be the only one who can help us, you saw how he hacked those Feds' eyes!"

It was a strong point, Danya knew. Ari wouldn't have sent the message to Kiril if it weren't just that important. But even if they could do something, the risk! It wasn't just him in the car, nor him and Svet, but all three of them. He'd spent the last five years of his life trying to keep them out of such a situation. And for what? For Sandy, sure, but Sandy was alive, and could take care of herself. For the Federation? What was the Federation to three street kids from Droze? What, except for a nice city and a massive life improvement, but that wonderful new life was suddenly trying to kill them all over again, just like Sandy had warned him it one day might . . .

The car ahead, moving out from the red light, was hit at the intersection by a speeding car. In spun wildly, its rear shorn off, shedding wheels and panels.

"Go!" yelled Svetlana, as the taxi came to a concerned halt half the block away. She hit the door emergency, and it let her out, having no choice.

"Svetlana, no!" But she was already gone. "Stay here!" Danya yelled at Kiril, and leaped from his seat onto a road full of suddenly unmoving cars, sprinting after his crazy sister. She was fast for her size, but Danya reached the ruined car just ahead of her, with no choice now but to help, they were committed. Inside the car, everyone seemed unconscious, including Ragi, with one Fed in the backseat, windows all shattered from the impact.

Danya tried the right rear door, but it was twisted and jammed. Svetlana tried the left and found the same. Danya tried to climb on the mangled wreck of the car's rear to drag Ragi out, but there was no safe footing.

"Svet, help!" He wasn't going to get an unconscious man out on his own . . . in fact, the two of them probably weren't either, especially in the slippery rain, but maybe they could wake him up. "Svet!"

She'd gone around to the front of the car, where the second agent, the driver, was waking up. Deprived him of his pistol, reversed it, and pistol-whipped him in the head. Twice, three times. Even a ten-year-old did damage with adrenaline and a pistol butt.

"Holy fuck, Svet! Come here and help!" She scared the shit out of him; she was so ruthless when frightened. And now he was scared she'd just shoot both agents, execution-style. She scrambled up on the other side of the rear dash and tried to get her hands under Ragi's armpit. "Ragi! Ragi, wake up!"

To Danya's surprise, he did. And blinked up at them groggily.

"You're in an accident!" Danya explained. "But the Feds will be coming soon and you have to get out . . ."

A shriek of tires said they were probably too late, another groundcar arriving on manual control, Feds opening the doors and . . . Svetlana, propped on the back of the car, unloaded her clip on them like an action movie. They scattered, bullets shattering windows, puncturing tires, cracking and whining off the road. Danya leaped onto the car roof and over Svetlana's side as return fire came back, Svetlana dropping to keep the car's rear, wheel-less on the road, between her and the bullets, then leaned around the end of the car and sprayed one-handed.

"They're shooting high," she explained to her far more frightened older brother, as she changed that clip for a new one, having somehow had the forethought to get several. "They don't want to hit their guys."

And suddenly Ragi was slithering out of the rear window, and Danya helped him to drop onto the road. "Help me get this off," he gasped, pulling at the collar. Danya tried, but it wouldn't budge.

"Is there some kind of key?" he asked. Ragi had a cut on his forehead and looked beat-up far worse than any combat GI would from a simple crash. Surely even non-combats were tougher than regular people? Maybe he wasn't a GI at all. He did look very normal.

"I think . . . in the agent's pocket."

Danya got up and dove into the rear window, hoping Svetlana was right and the agents wouldn't risk hitting their comrades. He clambered on the rear seat amid shattered safety glass and fumbled at the unconscious agent's jacket until, amid wallets, chewing gum, and sunglasses, he found a very boring metal object the size of his thumb. This agent had a gun too. Oh, crap. He took it and several clips, and slid back out the window onto the wet road.

Ragi caught him, then accepted the metal object . . . and Danya saw another car arrive, on this exposed side, an agent attempting to lean out the window for a shot. He knelt, took the pistol's safety off, and fired. The recoil snapped his wrists, but he lined up another shot, and another. Fire came back, a shot clanged into the door right alongside, and he realised he was drawing fire near Svetlana. He slithered right, still crouching, toward the front of the car, firing again and again.

The car driver had had enough, and slammed on the power, holes now pockmarking his windscreen. Crouched by the ruined car's bonnet, Danya knew he had to go left, but that would draw fire to Svetlana's exposed back. He stood, grasped the pistol in both hands, and fired at the suddenly onrushing car. The best way to distract driver and gunner was to put holes in or near them. He was so focused on that, he barely noticed how crazy fast it was closing, so much faster than anything on wheels moved in Droze . . .

He dove and crack! it hit him, bounced him off the other car's bonnet, then smack face-down on the cold, wet road. Conscious enough to hear Svetlana scream. And then, conscious enough to feel the slow, spreading agony in his leg and his shoulder. He'd been hurt before, but not like this. This pain was horrible.

"Danya!" Svetlana was screaming. "Danya!" And now she was beside him, the pistol clattering on the road, her hands grasping at him helplessly. "Danya, get up! You have to get up, Danya!"

It was over, he thought. The Feds would be on them now. If they were the kind he thought they were, they'd probably not kill kids in public but would take them away to secure keeping, where they'd meet with a quiet accident. After which Sandy would find out and slaughter the lot of them, like she had those League marines at the Droze spaceport, only far worse. That was at least some comfort, as he lay in unmoving agony in the rain.

Footsteps on the road by his head. Were they here already? "Young girl," said a voice. "Stay very close to me. Do you understand?" Ragi. Was that Ragi? "Stay very close to me, and I will get us all out of here safely."

"Don't move!" came a more distant yelling. "Everyone down on the ground, arms out wide!" It continued, from several locations, a chorus.

Danya felt arms beneath him, and then he was being lifted. That hurt indescribably. Unfortunately, he did not pass out. "Leg," he muttered between gritted teeth. "Broken. Maybe shoulder too."

"I can see," said Ragi. Ragi was not a big man, and Danya was no light-weight any longer. So non-combat GIs *did* have some strength, though on nothing like the scale of their combat comrades. "Svetlana, stand very close to me. Hold onto my jacket."

Suddenly the chorus of yells to get on the ground changed. "What the . . . ? Where the hell did he go?"

"Now," said Ragi, "let's walk, calmly, over here." Ragi walked, that faint jolting making more agony.

"He's hacking again! Fuck!" A shot went off.

"No shooting! No shooting, you'll hit one of us!"

"Countermeasures, get control, cordon the area! Get us every reinforcement you can, seal us in!"

"If they get hundreds of people down here," Danya muttered, "you can't hack all of them. We saw you get caught; you're not perfect. They'll get us."

Ragi stopped. Took a deep breath. And turned around once more. Danya tilted his head to one side, so he could watch through slitted eyes, as Fed agents converged on the ruined car, weapons out and wary as though expecting the empty air to spring alive and get them.

"There he is!" yelled one agent, pointing his gun at another agent. The other agent looked astonished. "Get on the ground, get on the ground or I'll drop you!" Frightened, the other agent raised her weapon in defence. Crack! and fell to the road. Other agents turned their guns on the shooter.

"What the hell? You shot Carla!"

"There there! Put it down!" Another outbreak on the wreck's far side, agents screaming at each other. Another shot, and someone else went down, then everyone was hitting the ground, lots of yelling and confusion.

"Kill some more of them!" Svetlana snarled with eager anticipation. "Make them shoot themselves, can you do that?"

"I have no control over motor function," Ragi said quietly. "I only control what they see. I think we have enough confusion for now. Let's go."

He walked back down the road, past cowering pedestrians who might have come to help had not the shooting started. A couple of teenagers sheltered in a building doorway and stared at them passing—too young for uplinks, Danya realised, they saw everything. And here, sheltering beside a roadside tree . . .

"Hello," said Ragi to someone Danya couldn't see, "you must be Kiril."

"Danya!" Kiril exclaimed in fear.

"It's okay, Kiri," Svetlana told him, "it's okay. Danya's a bit hurt, but he's okay. Ragi can make us invisible to the bad guys, so you come with us and we'll get Danya to a doctor."

"Danya, the taxi tried to drive away with me in it!" Kiril said indignantly. "I made it let me out, but it didn't want to! And then I told it . . ."

"That's great, Kiri," Danya muttered. He could really use a pain-induced blackout right about now. In the movies the hero always blacked out and woke up safe in a bed somewhere. That would be perfect. "Just hold Svetlana's hand and we'll go, huh?"

CHAPTER TWENTY-FOUR

"**Y**ou knew about the Supreme Court," Sandy said to Ibrahim. "Didn't you." They stood in an old library between tall rows of hardcover paper books. On Ibrahim's other side, Vanessa leaned against the shelves, hands in pockets.

Ibrahim pursed his lips. "I suspected. I have sources unknown even to Mr Shin."

"In some ways Yadav's right," said Vanessa. "The court can't do its job unless it's protected. When the guys whose job it is to protect them, and everyone else, start fighting amongst themselves, everything stops functioning. Supreme Court included. They took sides to protect themselves."

Ibrahim sighed. Took a random title off the shelf and flicked to the contents page. Gujarat State Tax Law, Filed Casework, 2388 to 2389. Good chance they would not be interrupted in this stretch of the public library VR space. There was no real reason to lay it out like this in old book format, but some people liked the atmosphere.

"I'm like you in some ways, Vanessa," Ibrahim said. "I did not start my career in security. I did odd jobs after school, then a doctorate in public administration."

"I saw the 'Dr' against your name once," Vanessa admitted. "You don't publicise it much."

He gave her a solemn glance beneath arched brows. His natural expression among friends, somewhere between thoughtful intensity and mild bemusement. "My thesis was on the importance of theoretical structural foundation underlying all public administration. It was quite good too. And almost completely irrelevant to what I do today. When the prospect of war against the League began to look real, I realised that without victory there, nothing I'd focused on to that point mattered even a bit. We don't need a theoretical foundation, we need a secure foundation. Which, given the natural state of insecurity in all things, is quite a task. Thus my new calling."

"So you sent me and Rhian in there without a warning," Sandy surmised from his lack of direct answer.

"Would my warning have made your success or failure more or less likely?" Ibrahim asked. Sandy thought about it. And shook her head. "I know your capabilities, Cassandra, and I did not want to make you prejudge the situation. I may have been wrong. And our professional relationship, like it or not, is one in which I will sometimes place you in great danger."

"I know," said Sandy. She looked up at the high ceiling above the shelves. Wondering if this library space was based on somewhere real. It looked impossibly ornate, probably European. Someone's fantasy imagining of what a grand old library ought to look like. Getting here was relatively simple, now that the net was in chaos, thanks to Sandy's appeal on Rami Rahim's show. Whole chunks of the Tanushan network were now essentially unmonitorable, even by the GC. "It doesn't leave us with many options, does it?"

"Well, no," Ibrahim agreed. "Our enemies control the Grand Council and the Callayan Government. We have friends in CSA SWAT, but they're immobilised, thanks to the Callayan Government's control of the CSA. Our own intelligence arm, FedInt, is up to its ears in Operation Shield, and their loyalties are uncertain."

"I wouldn't say that," said Vanessa. "More likely hostile."

"Add to that the forces currently carrying out Operation Shield under GC orders were brought here by Fleet," Ibrahim continued, "indicating large portions of Fleet are involved, probably in response to negotiations with League out at New Torah. If the orbital strike against the Maldaris is any indication."

"You're saying we're screwed," said Sandy.

"No," said Ibrahim with certainty. "I'm saying our options are few. Far fewer than I'd hoped even yesterday."

"I can think of one," Sandy said solemnly. "But it involves popular uprising and blood on the streets. Led by myself, possibly a few others, volunteers . . ." she paused, to let that sink in, ". . . who hit the GC, possibly the Callayan government, and kill some people. Starting with Ballan and Singh."

Even Vanessa paled at that. There was a silence at the sheer magnitude of it. "Sandy, that's political assassination. It's . . ."

"It's a violent coup," said Sandy. "It's exactly what they've already accused me of. They put an awful lot of work into making it seem real. I'll finally give them what they want."

"And then what? Fleet arrives in orbit, with more firepower than you can possibly handle, and kicks you out what, a month later?"

"A month in which we put the record straight," Sandy replied. "Then let people decide what they think the truth is."

"The essential question here is not whether Operation Shield is justified or not," said Ibrahim, putting the virtual tax volume back on the shelves. "It's on the question of the amendments proposed by 2389 and its supporters. I can tell you all the psychological analyses will tell you the same—people will decide the former question based upon where they stand on the latter. Like watching a football game, if your team is accused of a foul, they're innocent. If the other team is accused of a foul, they're guilty. The nature of the foul itself is irrelevant."

"Thank you, Mr Theoretical Foundation," Sandy said drily.

"The problem with your proposal," Ibrahim continued, "is that without a full revealing of the fraud that Operation Shield is, the political space that you will create is one with two opposing sides, separated in violent confrontation. That is how civil wars begin."

"Moral question for you," said Sandy with a deadly intent stare. "Is it worth a civil war to prevent a state, or a federation of worlds, from building a foundation of constitutional law based on dangerous lies? A foundation that may last hundreds more years, and lead to much larger wars, civil or otherwise, in the future? Or do we retreat in fear of conflicts and let our enemies use that fear of conflict against us and just hope that it never gets that bad?"

Ibrahim looked at her for a long moment. And took a long, thoughtful breath.

"Wait a moment," said Vanessa in dawning horror. "We're not actually going to do this, are we?" Ibrahim and Sandy looked at her. "No! I'm not going to launch a fucking coup! That's the whole point, don't you get it? The point is that they're wrong! We'd never do something like that, any of us—if we do this, we just prove them right!"

"They were always right, Vanessa," Sandy said quietly. Vanessa stared at her. "I wasn't planning a coup. But I was always capable. If pushed far enough."

"Well, I'm not!"

"You are. You've not thought it through far enough."

"Sandy! This is Tanusha! I was born here! I swore an oath to defend its government and I extended that oath to the Federation . . ."

"You did not!"

"And I'm not going to make a bloodbath in my own fucking city!"

"You swore an oath to defend the constitution!" Sandy shouted, eyes blazing. "These people just wiped their ass on the Federation and Callayan constitutions both, then set them on fire! You think you swore an oath to defend the *government*? Good God, Vanessa, you're not that stupid!"

"Stupid?"

"Governments are the first and primary threat to constitutions, and institutions like ours were designed from inception to be a knife at every government's throat! That's why they tried to take us out, don't you get *that*?"

"Sir!" Vanessa stared at Ibrahim. "This is your plan? Violent insurrection?"

"Last resort does not mean unthinkable, Vanessa," Ibrahim said solemnly. "It means the last resort. I sent Cassandra and Rhian to the Supreme Court despite suspecting it was a trap because I wanted to be sure. But I think we're there. The last resort."

"Sir . . . it's just not possible that the Federation can come to this!" Vanessa said desperately. "This is the Federation! We don't do that here!"

"And yet they've done it. To us, to everyone. We did not start the violence, Vanessa, that was them."

"And that makes a difference?"

"It makes every difference. We are the speed break. The buffer that absorbs the impact of rapid change and colliding political forces. Our purpose is essentially conservative, an irony lost on 2389, who style themselves the true conservatives, restoring the original constitution and all. We preserve, we do not initiate. So it is here."

"Sir, you were the one lecturing that we had to hold back until we had proof!" Vanessa reminded.

"Proof would be lovely," Ibrahim admitted. "It's quite possible our lack of action is the reason it cannot reveal itself, as the enemies of proof hold all the levers."

Vanessa blinked, staring at him. "Or was that just an act? To throw everyone off, in case there were leaks?"

Ibrahim's heavy-lidded eyes gave nothing away. Vanessa swore to herself and looked about in exasperation.

"Letting them get away with it," Ibrahim said carefully, "is not a viable defence of the constitution. Security is not results, Vanessa. Security is process. Results are for historians. Soldiers do not decide results. Soldiers fight. Allah decides."

"Well, then you and Allah have a problem," Vanessa retorted. "Because you're talking a military coup, and we're not the military! We're the FSA, we've precious few resources left, and the actual military, the Fleet, is still in orbit over us! What are we going to use, harsh language?"

"If so," said Sandy, "you're on point." Vanessa glared at her.

"My harshest assessments of the Federation's governing structure," Ibrahim said quietly, "I've never published, nor even mentioned. If they'd been known, I'd never have been given this position."

"You saw it coming," said Sandy.

"I have sources," said Ibrahim. "Sources even Chief Shin does not. Sources I share with no one, not even you. This system has always been dysfunctional, we've just never noticed the dysfunction until now because circumstances have never pushed its limits far enough to force a system failure. But I've taken precautions, ever since I took the office."

"Assets?" Sandy asked. Hopefully.

Ibrahim nodded. "Let me show you."

President Vikram Singh entered Ambassador Ballan's large Grand Council office, assistants and bodyguards remaining outside.

"Mr President," said Ballan, coming to shake his hand. "Good of you to come. Refreshments?"

"No thank you, I can't stay long." Singh settled his broad self into the waiting chair. "Trouble in Parliament. Opponents to Operation Shield are moving to table censure motions; we're expecting a concerted assault over the next week."

Ballan took his own seat with a frown of concern. "Can they succeed?"

Singh made a face and shook his head. A big, serious man with a thin beard and imposing charisma, despite his infrequent smiles. His turban was dark blue to match exactly his expensive suit, no flashy colours for the President of Callay. "They've had a sudden shot of courage with all this protest and mess in Tanusha. But the popular support isn't there, and soon they'll realise it. The Callayan public has never gone for this sort of thing, protest politics, agitation. We are a population of professionals, everyone is expected to do their job efficiently, not break windows and make trouble. They're at least fifty votes short, and they know it."

"Good to hear," said Ballan. "Thank you for all your help on this. It couldn't have been done without you."

Singh waved the thanks away. "Putting Ibrahim in charge of the FSA was stupid. The man considers himself a law unto himself, it was always going to make trouble. I've been speaking with some of the ambassadors involved in this—Callayan ambassadors, you understand, on behalf of their world governments, not the Grand Council—and we'd like some sort of guarantee that the selection criteria for FSA Chief is strengthened."

"What sort of person would you prefer?"

"Someone who respects the primacy of elected bodies," said Singh with certainty. "No one elected him. I daresay if he was put to a vote, after all he's done to promote Kresnov and her little gang of subversives, he'd lose by a wide margin."

Ballan kept a straight face. Singh was an intelligent man, but like so many intelligent men, once elected to high office, he put on a fair impersonation of a blustering fool. Talk of popularly electing intelligence chiefs was ludicrous.

"And Director Chandrasekar?" he asked instead. "How is he holding up to the pressure?"

"There's no sign his little mutiny is going anywhere." Singh folded his hands on his middle, tugged his suit jacket. "Could use a little more useful Intel there though, we're not getting much from the CSA. Our only other source of Intel is the SIB, and they're bloody useless. Ibrahim was right about that much.

"Where are we on the amendments? I need those amendments passed, Allessandro. Once they pass, I'll be able to point to an achievement in the whole mess, a means of preserving Callayan independence from Federal overreach. Which is damn hard to do right now with Federal overreach shooting up my city," he nodded sourly to the windows, another tuck at the jacket, "and shutting down my security agencies. But I can turn it to my favour once the amendments pass. I can point to this as a real example of what I'm trying to protect us from, and say never again."

Again, Ballan let pass the measure of the man's smallness. All he needed Singh for was to keep the domestic agencies, particularly the CSA, in line.

And to assist in keeping all network codes open to Operation Shield and the Grand Council. Which reminded him . . .

"Mr President, we're having a lot of difficulty at present stabilising the Tanushan network . . ."

"Look," said Singh with volume that promised temper if pushed further. "You had so much control of the network to start because everyone was surprised. Every software structure that runs on the net has to interact with the matrix codings to some degree or they won't work, that's one of the basic security systems we engineered into it from the start. That's what lets you see so much at the beginning. But now the programs here are evolving."

"Well, can't you stop the people who are doing it?" Ballan pressed. "We can't start losing control of the system now when we're so close . . ."

"*People* aren't doing it," Singh snapped. "The system's doing it itself. Or so my own techies tell me. The software's evolving its own defences, they're blinding themselves off the matrix, and now the hackers are making that evolution move faster, thanks to Kresnov's little appeal."

Rami Rahim was not put on the first list of targets, Ballan pondered. That may have been a mistake. But how did arresting a comic who'd interviewed Kresnov a few times strengthen the credibility of Operation Shield?

"If I were you," Singh continued, "I'd be a little more worried about how Ibrahim has responded to all this. I'd have thought he'd be cleverer than this. But as I've been waiting for his other shoe to drop, nothing. Has he truly given up?"

"Oh, I doubt that," said Ballan. "But I don't know what else he can do. The Supreme Courts were his last chance of suspending the amendment voting, but just as our simulations predicted, the courts will value their security first if threatened, and in a conflict between security agencies, that grants the power in charge the upper hand. Courts cannot exercise neutrality without security, Ibrahim should have seen that immediately."

"Who's to say he didn't?" Singh said warily. "What if you're playing into his hands?"

Ballan raised his eyebrows, heart beating a little faster at the prospect. Mouth dry, palms sweaty. Every thump in his chest reminded him of the repair work done there, the technology that now kept him alive. So many forces pushing on this result. He'd never counted on being in the collision zone of so many forces at once.

"Well, I've no idea what that could be," he said. "The voting will be in less than a week now, now that we can be reasonably certain that the Supreme Court will not overturn the schedule."

"Ibrahim won't bother to appeal?"

"I'm reliably assured by Chief Shin that there is no way that Kresnov went to the Court without Ibrahim's blessing and was most probably ordered by him. Ibrahim believes in institutional purity and will now distrust that in the courts. He may use an appeal as a distraction, but there is no chance he'll place any weight on his prospects there. And his window of opportunity for other action grows very small."

Singh nodded, thinking hard. "It could work out," he murmured, mostly to himself. "It could all work out. And it's good work, because we were headed for another war. It's the problem with the bureaucratic administration that surrounds democracies, Ambassador. Too many unelected people like Ibrahim and Kresnov holding far too much power. And with another war coming, it would favour all the unelected people with the guns, just like them, they could ratchet up their powers as much as they liked. Combine them in the FSA special forces arm with this new influx of combat GIs from the League . . . it could have just been devastating. It's far too much power for any one institution to have, so close to the center of Federal government."

Ballan nodded slowly. And repressed a roll of the eyes that Singh completely failed to acknowledge that it was exactly such an unrepresentative bureaucratic structure that was currently implementing Operation Shield. On Nova Esperenza it was known as the GC lobby, politicians and interest groups, big businesses, professional lobbyists, all pushing not only at Ballan but at his senior staff. Sometimes it seemed their opinions mattered more than those of his own President, and he knew for a fact that at least half of his GC staff here in the building were selected almost person for person by the GC lobby, not by the Nova Esperenza President, nor the Parliament.

Those people were in turn representing a lot of people who were now very scared of a new war. Scared enough to start pushing very hard for amendments that made it impossible. And threatening all kinds of things to people who got in their way. The phenomenon was, as far as Ballan could make out, Federation wide.

"One more thing," Singh added. "I'd like to request some of your best Operation Shield people to add to my personal security detail."

Kresnov's threats would do that to a man, Ballan supposed. His own thudding heart beat a little louder. "I'm not certain that we have any to spare," he said.

"You've got some. I see them outside."

"The Grand Council has to rely on outside security personnel. Are there not sufficient people on Callay?"

"The best are all in the CSA," Singh growled. "And no longer reliable."

The door to the office opened, and the secretary put his head in. "Mr Ballan, Director Ibrahim is on his way in person."

Ballan nodded, and the secretary left. "Ibrahim's coming here?" Singh asked, frowning.

"Says he has a compromise plan. A way out of the current mess."

Singh's frown grew deeper. "That doesn't sound like Ibrahim. Be very careful of that man, Ambassador. He's full of tricks."

Ballan smiled tiredly. "I'm aware of that. But I am an ambassador by training. Talking is what I do. If Ibrahim has something to talk about, that is how I move the ball forward."

CHAPTER TWENTY-FIVE

Agent Teo flicked Ibrahim a sideways glance from the driver's seat of their groundcar. "Sir, why exactly are we talking to Ambassador Ballan?"

Ibrahim's lips twitched, the faintest smile. "Chief Shin wishes to know, does he?"

"Not really, sir." Agent Teo's voice, his normally calm demeanor, showed little. That in itself told Ibrahim that the young man was hiding something. Normally Teo was more expressive. "I'm just required to update my movements for FedInt's equivalent of tacnet."

"Mr Teo," said Ibrahim with faint amusement. "I understand you are a spy. I would not like to think that you are spying on me."

Teo was wise enough to smile and say nothing.

They passed the security point between FSA and Grand Council grounds and descended the long ramp to underground parking. Ibrahim glanced at Amirah in the backseat. She seemed calm, observing the passing of parked cars, security staff, automated baggage servers, flashing lights.

Teo pulled up at the securest central elevators. More security eyed them leaving the car, heavily armed. *"K13,"* came Amirah's formulation on his uplink. *"They've changed."*

"They must have considerable resources here if they can afford to place personnel on GC guard duty," Ibrahim observed.

"Or maybe they're expecting something."

They entered the elevator, three together, and watched the wall displays show them their moving location. They would emerge at the central ring corridor, main thoroughfare between major ambassadorial offices, high above the actual government chambers, which were on the ground floor, closer to the carpark. As usual in political offices, the real action took place well away from the most famous chambers.

Ten seconds. Ibrahim closed his eyes briefly and thought a small prayer. No doubt the many who served under him, and respected what wisdom he'd managed to accumulate, would expect something profound. For matters of judgement and wisdom, he may have managed such. But today was not a day for judgement and wisdom. Today would exercise more fundamental instincts. And so he offered his personal version of a prayer he understood to have originated amongst American aviation test pilots in the twentieth century.

"Please Allah, don't let me fuck this up."

The elevator opened. His uplink activated once more—Chief Shin. *"Director, I apologise for the intrusion, but I need to know the purposes of your visit with Ambassador Ballan as a matter of urgency."*

"And why do you need to know that, Chief Shin?"

There were many people in the gently curving hallway. Staffers mostly, a few senior. Here an Ambassador, flanked by several staff and security. All were looking at the passing FSA Director and his small entourage.

"Director," Shin tried again, *"we have reports of anomalous activity in the Western Delta. I think you should see this immediately."*

Ibrahim kept striding. *"It can wait until after I have seen the Ambassador."* Another hundred meters around the bend. Amirah was linked to his communications, most irregular for personal security. She heard every word. Her stride was easy, her weapon comfortable on its shoulder strap.

"Director, please do not go any further. Something is going on."

"Reaction," Amirah said quietly. *"GC primary defence grid just alarmed. It's still in query mode."*

Was Shin causing that? Ibrahim wondered, quickening his pace just fractionally. Or was he reacting to it?

Ballan came online. *"Director, GC defences just went to phase one. There are reports of movement beyond the city perimeter, and orbital surveillance blackouts."*

"I'm watching that too, Mr Ambassador," he said aloud. "Very curious." Fifty meters.

"Phase two." Amirah. *"They're on us. Tell me when."*

A line of security appeared across the corridor, weapons out, a moving wall. Five of them. Thirty meters. *"Go,"* said Ibrahim.

Amirah opened fire. The line of five went down, crumpling, sprawled, a row of heads snapping back in quick succession, blood spraying. Ibrahim ran. He'd been fast once, in his youth. Now, he hoped merely not to be slow.

Amirah was firing behind now, staffers screaming, falling for cover. Approaching Ballan's door, Ibrahim saw more security farther around the bend, fired to keep heads down, and ducked right, into the Ambassador's waiting room. Most here were staff, frozen in horror, ducking, sitting, scrambling out of the way. But several were security staff, armed if not especially competent. Two were drawing. Ibrahim shot one, two-handed, center of mass only, and he fell back against a wall and slid bloodily.

The other scrambled about sideways, buying time as he pulled clear a pistol and aimed. Ibrahim pivoted, firing steadily, putting holes in the wall that finally reached the target, who took a bullet to the arm and side, and fell.

Ibrahim kept moving, past cowering unarmed staff and into Ballan's office. Ballan was risen from behind his desk, fumbling in a draw.

"Hands!" Ibrahim demanded, as more gunfire erupted in the room behind. Amirah had arrived and was now covering the entrance from counter attack. Ballan showed his hands, face white, arms trembling.

"My God, Shan!" he exclaimed, hoarse and shaky. "Why?"

"Because there has to be one who takes his vows seriously," said Ibrahim. "Command codes to the Operation Shield matrix. Now."

"I can't! They're embedded!"

"I thought as much." Ibrahim shot him in the head. "Matrix codes embedded," he announced with uplinks open, moving behind the desk, now blood-spattered. Stood over the ambassador's body, accessing the desk console, not expecting much. "Target is neutralised."

"*It should be enough*," came Verma's reply, leading FSA net tech. Behind him were a whole team, many of whom had planned the Pyeongwha operation. "*Ballan was the key, without him the matrix is unstable. Get me a link in and we can get the GC mainframe.*"

Ibrahim set about doing that. "Amirah," he said, again relying on uplinks, though speaking aloud to avoid the difficulties of formulation under pressure. "This may take a few minutes. Situation?"

"*Oh, just peachy sir.*" Thunder of automatic gunfire from the room behind, the crackle and vibration of incoming rounds. Fortunately none of the GC guards had thought to notice her extra mags on the way in, accustomed as they'd become to her presence at Ibrahim's side. "*They'll move the heavy stuff up soon. Then you'd better get away from those windows.*"

The windows behind Ibrahim, now spattered with blood and indented with a single non-penetrating bullet hole, opened onto the central space in the

GC Building's donut design. Soon enough there would be incoming fire from across that space, and while bullets would not penetrate the glass, explosives would.

"What happened to Teo?"

"*I've no idea. I'm not Cassandra; I can't watch ten things at once.*" And that was that, neither of them had any idea where Teo was, or what had happened to him, and they had no time to look. Most likely he'd been hit in the initial exchange of fire. Though with FedInt, anything was possible.

SWAT grunts dropped whatever else they were doing and crammed around the ready room screens, recent tactical surveys overlaid with the big transmission from FSA overriding all channels. They could have watched on personal uplinks, but somehow the situation compelled them to cluster, fighting for space in unarmoured tac gear.

"*. . . act of high treason,*" Ibrahim was saying. It was a recording, of course, Ibrahim would be busy right now. But recorded live to lense. "*The Federal Security Agency, charged with the duty to protect the Federation constitution at all costs, commands that all personnel currently engaged with Operation Shield shall stand down and offer up their weapons for immediate confiscation. Failure to do so will result in elimination by force.*

"*All sitting members of the political faction known as 2389 are henceforth declared under arrest until cleared of charges. All Grand Council sittings and procedures are suspended until further notice. Callayan President Vikram Singh is henceforth under arrest upon the charge of complicity in high treason against the Federation. He will present himself to Federal Security Agency forces or risk all possible consequences.*"

"Holy fuck!" someone shouted, unable to restrain it longer. "They're going to fucking kill him!"

"Quiet!" demanded Captain Singh.

"*. . . Callayan citizens of Tanusha, please remain indoors for your safety. Shortly you will observe why. I know some of you may wish to participate—please do not. Leave this matter to the professionals. We in turn shall be answerable to your lawful and democratic demands soon enough. This message will now repeat.*

"*I, Director Shan Ibrahim of the Federal Security Agency, officially charge those commanding and facilitating the fraudulent assumption of command known as Operation Shield with an act of high treason.*"

Singh swung on them all. "Condition red!" he shouted. "Everybody move!"

Half left at a sprint. The other half stared about in confusion. "Why?" one asked. "Are we joining in?"

"No," said Singh. "But Operation Shield might think we are and hit us first to be sure."

"But if they see us mobilising, they *will* think we're joining in!"

Singh's grin was evil. "Then we'll tell 'em we're joining in to help."

Sandy and Vanessa stood atop a nondescript residential tower in Powgai District on the western edge of Tanusha. There amidst rooftop parking and a small garden space with a children's slide and swings, they watched the attack coming in. It was low, fast, widely spread, and entirely tactical. No strategic targeting, no hardpoint infrastructure. Tanusha itself was not being assaulted, just cleansed.

"Whoa," said Vanessa, watching through AR glasses, locked into a growing-strength FSA tacnet that was now beyond the GC's ability to interfere with. "That's Vita Formation. Quad sixteen's on a diamond spacing. Fucking clearance pattern."

"Here we go," said Sandy, watching the same thing but without glasses, seeing the first missiles fire. Out in the dark above the jungle perimeter, flares lit in multiples, accelerating fast, dividing and dodging as they came. Then hissed by, rapid staccato thuds of sonic booms, WHAM as one rushed directly overhead, both women turning to watch it go. Sandy nearly laughed. She couldn't help it—she was many things, but she was this too, always this, this rush and buzz like an adrenaline junkie on a roller coaster, or a rock metal fan at a huge concert. Combat reflex reddened her vision, and she felt like she could just explode with energy.

Boom, b-b-b-boom, b-boom! A spread of detonations amidst Tanushan towers. Like nothing this city had ever seen before. "Airburst, they're just flushing."

"Gonna be a fuck of a glass bill," Vanessa murmured. Sandy glanced at her. She looked taut with anxiety, pale and drawn. Tight. Sandy wondered what all those augments felt like at times like these; Vanessa said they ached sometimes.

"Yeah, well," she said offhandedly, "glad you're not coming." Vanessa looked at her. Sandy looked her up and down.

"Who said I'm not coming?" asked Vanessa.

"Your doctor, for one." More missiles tracking, ten Ks south, picking up speed before zooming into the city proper. Multiple detonations.

"I'm fine in a suit, the augments don't strain at all."

Crackle and contact on audio, someone on tacnet established a link. *"Hello, Cassandra, I've a fix on your position, please confirm?"* Sandy recognised the voice immediately.

"Rishi!" she laughed. Even Vanessa grinned. "How the fuck are you? We thought you were dead!"

"A few of the Director's people came to us in the middle of the night and told us to move," Rishi explained. *"All of us. I didn't know who to trust, but I recalled you said the Director would never betray us."*

"Yeah, he can be a devious little bastard though."

"Okay, I'm fixed on your location, full tacnet access coming through now." It unfolded across Sandy's overlay vision, IDs and status of units, like she was in command. All the names, all the GIs from Droze and Chancelry, all the ones resettled in the Maldaris, Ibrahim must have seen Ballan's move coming, God knew how. And moved a good chunk of FSA spec ops arsenal out of FSA HQ well before it was locked down. He must have had some secret hiding places, rendezvous spots out there in the jungle somewhere . . . wow, she thought, as the scale of it hit her. Ibrahim must have been implementing this just after he was appointed Director, no way was this a rushed, last-second job. Had Ballan been entirely wrong to suspect someone, somewhere was moving forces covertly for possible action against the GC? Surely Ibrahim was too smart to have inadvertently triggered the very thing he'd been protecting against? *"I see Commander Rice is with you too, I'll get two suits to you in a minute."*

Sandy glanced at Vanessa. More sonic booms thumped and crashed. Vanessa made a face. "Not like I fucking get to choose," Vanessa muttered. "I knew that when I signed."

"If you can't do it," Sandy told her, "sit it out. Don't worry about me or Rhi, we love you for life no matter what."

Distant airbursts half-lit Vanessa's profile. "I know," she said. And turned as the first return fire came back. "SX2s. Now we're in the shit."

They were met halfway by counter-fire, more airbourne detonations across a wide front, several close enough that suddenly cover seemed like a good idea. From down the sides of the resi building, Sandy heard people shouting and yelling—civilians, staring out at the fireworks with what sounded like a healthy mix of fascination, terror, and excitement. On the net somewhere, Ibrahim's message was repeating. Stay the fuck inside, you fools. Preferably well away from the windows.

With a howl a combat flyer was upon them, coming up from beneath and rotating, rear hold opening and all black, not a single light showing. With it, utterly silent beneath the roar of engines, the first hopper suit, a flare of jump-jets, a low trajectory between buildings, seeking a new grounding point. Then another, well below . . . and suddenly one flared and landed on the rooftop beside them, a massively automated, almost insectoid armour, huge cannon mount on one arm, triple-barrelled launcher diagonally across its back, pivoting even now as tacnet made new targeting assignments, just in case something came its way. The visor popped to show a familiar face.

"Coming?" Kiet asked her.

"Two minutes," said Sandy, even pleased to see him. "You in command?"

"No, you," said Kiet. "If you want it."

Sandy grinned dangerously. "Oh, sure. Chancelry HQ, Tanusha, Federation Grand Council, why not?" Kiet did not smile back, but his eyes did, with fire.

Sandy leaped to the flyer's rear ramp and could not resist turning to catch Vanessa as she landed too, utterly unnecessary as it was. The flyer held four hoppers, they were nearly twice the size of regular armour, and ten times the weight, any more than four, and a smaller flyer wouldn't get off the ground.

Her hopper's core was already humming when she got in, someone had aligned the fittings to her size and shape, folding in on her legs as she wriggled them in, then settled her seat on the crotch and wrestled her arms in like hauling on a giant metal overcoat, all while the flyer fell for the ground away from the vulnerable rooftop. The restraints grabbed her at the necessary points and fastened tight, an embrace she'd always found vaguely erotic, a few FSA girls laughed that if the machine just vibrated a little more in the right spots they'd marry it. And all this power was more than a little orgasmic.

Legs sealed, then arms, a wriggle of fingers to get the gloves humming, then the torso sections sealed with a final, tight yank of harness that pulled pelvis hard onto saddle, any slippage there and you'd bounce inside like a nut in its shell. Men did not look forward to that manoeuver, but women hardly minded.

"Well, that always cheers me up," Vanessa remarked as her armour reached the same point. She sounded better, adrenaline had that effect on both of them . . . or in Sandy's case, pseudo-synthetic adrenaline.

Helmet and visor last, a flash of electronic vision with multi-layered depth, a universe of interactive function and sensory awareness. Cannon mount, ammo feed, coolant . . . the six mini-missiles in the back rack counted off and ready, then sim-gyros as the drive train engaged, environmentals breathed warm air at her neck, coolers flushing hot air from the core into the surrounding cabin. The flyer would get damn hot inside if they stayed too long.

The flyer was just hovering now, cabin open, above a park surrounded by residential towers, not daring to advance into what was unfolding ahead. Sandy pulled clear of the hold restraints, clomped for the rear with Vanessa following, performed a quick thruster check, and jumped. A five-meter fall ended neatly balanced on the downthrust, then a gentle touch on the grass, Vanessa joining her as the flyer powered away once more, presumably to find two more FSA grunts to pilot the two other suits, certainly there would be others out tonight, dispersed from hiding toward the city's western edge.

Surreally, with no immediate missile fire or explosions, it suddenly seemed that just the two of them were standing alone in a deserted park in Tanusha one evening. Unusually deserted, certainly, normally at this hour there would be people here, walking the dog, jogging, some old folks strolling after dinner, a couple making out on a bench. But unusual or not, everything suddenly looked so mundane. People lived like this, Sandy thought, never seeing the forces that ruled them. An apartment here, in one of these buildings, a park to play in, restaurants to eat in or grab takeaway from. Sports on weekends, VR club on weeknights, holiday plans around the corner. And here was she, with all of these lives in her hands.

"We good?" she asked Vanessa.

Vanessa bounced and swung her arms as though limbering up. The suits' dexterity was ridiculous, you could tango in them. If you could tango. "Seem to be."

"Not what I meant," said Sandy.

Vanessa shrugged, for the suit shrugged too. "I know. Let's go." As tacnet inserted them properly into the formations. They jumped.

Sandy kept low, a power cruise at ten meters, kicking the thrust again and again for course change and velocity boost. It made a trajectory like a drunken blowfly, rising and falling, just avoiding towers at the last moment, and largely unpredictable to any watching armscomp. Ahead, the forward wave was just starting to get seriously engaged, where the defending tacnet established an outer kill zone and defensive fire became kinetic as much as self-propelled. That was five Ks in from the perimeter. Tanusha was seventy Ks across, and roughly circular by design, not as big a footprint as a lot of old Earth megacities, but many times the population of most—an even spread of density, not the traditional thick in the middle and thin around the edges.

The Grand Council and Federal District were in Montoya, which was on the far eastern edge, right up against the jungle. A ground assault had to go right across the city because coming in over the jungle put you in the kill zone of a truly brutal aerial defence grid that could erase everything above bird size, irrespective of number or velocity. But they couldn't employ that system west, because of all the civilians who lived here. Even coming in from north or south was fraught, because although it made the distance shorter, it also severely limited the ability to manoeuver, one flank vulnerable to counter-hooks under the cover of that aerial grid, the distance of which was then also shorter. All the sims, or for Sandy just a casual glance, told her that doing it the long way from due west, across the entire city, was far smarter—it took the aerial grid out of play, opened up the full expanse of Tanusha's urban terrain to manoeuver in, and forced the enemy to defend in depth and width, spreading them out and making gaps, just what a mobile attacking force wanted.

Unfortunately, they weren't the only ones with hoppers. In fact, looking at what was rising up ahead of them, it looked like they might be outnumbered. It was hardly surprising, no one really knew what Fleet had been bringing insystem the last few days and weeks through Balaji, no doubt a lot of heavy stuff in case things went belly-up. Behind those, the ubiquitous A-12s. Around Montoya and the GC, it was well known, a lot of mobile defence grid units. Plus all the installed aerial and ground defences Callay itself had built at great cost to the Callayan taxpayer, now employed against Tanusha's own liberation. And now, just to mess things up more, here came the UAVs, lots of them, some for potshots, others for recon and tacnet expansion, others for jamming and disruption . . . expect tacnet to get wobbly when they started taking parts of the network down. But two could play at that, and defenders were somewhat more entrenched and immobile in what facilities they could employ . . .

"Good evening, boys and girls," Sandy said calmly as the scale of this particular assault began to wash over her, three-dimensional and crazy mobile. "Welcome to Tanusha, my name is Sandy and I'll be your guide this evening, as we are about to pass through some of the most wonderful tourist spots in all the galaxy, have your recorders at the ready and your weapons loaded at all times."

She grounded on a footpath beside a road, there was still too much traffic out, crazy fucking Tanushans still driving, across from this urban square were people pointing as she landed. "Our plan tonight," she continued, "is small-unit action, four by four, I want pairs and squads to advance by Vita Formation, we move fast and penetrate, get in amongst them and back our reflexes over theirs. That simple."

Satisfied she'd retained good position, she leaped again, a slam of Gs and she was off, screeching past neighbouring towers. Ahead was Baidu District, towers, a nice bend of river . . . and shit, she remembered an evening here with Ari, music and dancing, Ari rarely danced, but he'd danced with her, sat up ages talking and kissing, then home for some great sex . . . and now Ari was in intensive care, and these people had put him there, and were now occupying *her* city, because it was her city, and she loved it like she loved Ari, and Vanessa and Rhi and everyone else who'd become so vital to her life in this place.

And these fuckers who'd done it, they were going to die.

"No no!" Rami was shouting from his penthouse living room, a huge thing under three storeys of heavy floors and well away from the windows. "Use the secondary network, not the primary, that'll take the local security grid out of play! And boost this fucking signal, I can barely get a feedback reading!"

"If we boost it," his producer Liz came back in his ear, "we could get traced."

"Well, I'll fucking risk it!" He sat on his sofa, banks of screens randomly arrayed about him. Trying to get the wireless net to sync them all wasn't as simple as it should have been. In the studio all this shit worked seamlessly, but despite Tanusha's crazy mobile tech aptitude, it never quite came together so smoothly on its own. "Anyone who doesn't want to be here can leave!"

"Holy shit!" said one of the techs, watching a feed screen while trying to get the local construct gens synced. "Look at this, it's a fucking war!" As the feed showed missiles ripping and dodging between Tanushan towers, exploding from counter-fire, now tracer and mag rounds glowing white hot with velocity. Still little sign of who was shooting; in modern war you saw a lot more shooting than shooters.

"Yeah, well Sandy fucking warned us, didn't she?" Rami muttered, making frantic adjustments. The local feeds wouldn't match with the net security construct; if he went live like this he'd be asking for an Operation Shield high-explosive round through the ceiling for sure.

On cue, his uplink blinked—his personal link, the ones only close friends and family knew. *"Rami,"* came Sandy's voice. *"Challenge to the netsters, break the Operation Shield tacnet."* She must have been speaking aloud, her voice strained abruptly, as though she were pulling Gs. Then the unmistakable sound of mag fire, thud-thud-thud! Given how Sandy aimed, that probably meant someone just died.

"Sandy, they don't all work for you!" he exclaimed.

"Rami, we can kill their hoppers, but they're buying enough time to deploy a mobile defence grid, which is going to get real nasty the closer we get to the GC. The GC's no longer controlling the main network protocols, but I'm still looking at eighty percent casualties before I reach the GC defences, and that won't leave enough to breach it. Some tacnet confusion would be great right now, and we grunts just don't have the time." And, *"Hang on—Ceta Squad, evade and redirect, target 255 left, watch your line of advance!"*

Pause as counter-chatter came back, Rami couldn't hear what. Then, *"Rami, gotta go, about to get seriously busy. Get it done, I'll promise them anything, up to and including wild sex with all of them, just do it!"*

Hoppers were useless against entrenched forces in urban combat, you overflew sophisticated weapons systems you hadn't seen, and they killed you. But Operation Shield forces were not entrenched, and Tanusha was not entrenchable, and for rapid ground assault hoppers were unmatched.

Tacnet showed her a line of confirmed and semi-confirmed dots, a line of possibles behind that, and a whole bunch of question marks farther back, dots flickering and shifting as the system updated itself. Even now tacnet was trying to sift the local nets for data feeds from Tanushan civilians, filming hoppers, artillery, A-12s, and feeding that input into the grid, but the Feds had a bunch of programs finding that data and destroying it before they could access.

City-level topography suggested blind spots, and she took one with a wingman, tearing past low- and mid-rise buildings, then grounding with a skid and run on the road where they ended, aiming past building sides as two other pairs similarly advanced. An eruption of missiles, six Ks behind the lines, probably an A-12, never quite close enough to hit. Accelerating fast, as the targeted suits took rapid cover, and the missiles airburst close rather than take out civvie buildings, showering them with shrapnel . . . but two made it far enough to draw fire from another building rooftop, revealing a location properly. Someone lobbed a missile from a shoulder rack, the shooter jumped, and Sandy's cannon boomed—a two-K shot, but the mag round got there in less than a second, the enemy hopper spun like a crazed top and fell from sight.

"Gamma Five, Gamma Four, move move!" She left cover and ran up the road, then leaped—this crescent of higher buildings terminated ahead at Porcetti District center, big towers and gleaming lights—going through it would run them into close range defence, going around it would leave them exposed.

Gamma Five dodged in mid-air as missile fire nearly had him. Gamma Four took out the offending UAV with a mid-air spin, hiding behind a building and awaiting opportunities. Sandy saw more long-range fire coming in, kicked harder and turned the hopper into a rocket, speeds over 600 kph toward the big buildings at barely treetop height past lower buildings, glimpses of flashing suburban houses and swimming pools . . . then blew a UAV on reflex as it appeared at five hundred meters, ten o'clock low behind a rooftop.

Then she hit the brakes, feet first and thrusters howling, fired an airburst blinder grenade above an intersection, a white flash to temporarily blind sensitive night vision, and nearly nailed an enemy hopper that leaped from a taller rooftop in time, skimming his armour with a shot; missing was acceptable if you achieved results by fear. She hit a big city road at eighty Ks, bounded like a kangaroo, just missing some hastily abandoned vehicles, then leapt abruptly skyward as sensors showed indirect fire . . . a missile blew a hole in the street as she rocketed up fifty floors and blew a hopper off the rooftop on the way past, a split-second snap. Cut thrusters and coasted up the glass front of a 140-storey mega-rise, gravity for brakes as her teammates arrived below, flashing rapidly moving fire as they chased other hoppers down the canyons, a twisting of missiles, a shower of glass from a detonation.

Approaching zero velocity at apex, Sandy slammed another round down at a fleeing hopper . . . it was dodging, and she made a hole in the road instead, at these ranges and speeds, accuracy even with 50mil armour-piercing mag rifles wasn't certain—she never missed, but targets often weren't where they should be when the round arrived.

Another short kick took her to the top of the mega-rise, grounded with heavy boots on the roof amid com and transmission gear, and took a look out at her city. Flashes, shooting and missile trails across the tower-studded horizon. Not every munition was detonating early; in a few places, things were burning, and emergency crews were braving the night in flyers and cruisers, IDs on full blaze and hoping no one blew them from the sky by mistake.

The net she could sense was a mess, conflicting security protocols destroying each other, out-of-control code eating other constructs, data channeling to relatively secure pathways and feeders. Lots of vid feeds, lots of interrupted regular broadcasts, lots of emergency announcements, shouting, politicians, personalities, regular folks screaming for the shooting to stop, can't we all just talk about this?

Been talking, Sandy thought with contempt. Now shooting. People who didn't care then but suddenly cared now, rated on the moral minus scale. Fuck off and shut up, the grownups are working.

Suddenly she had at least ten incoming missiles from a variety of ranges. All angling for the top of this tower. She jumped off, turned head down and kicked, ripping down the towerside at building speed enough to make a fatal crater if her thrusters died . . . but she righted, kicked again, and they slowed her at a bone-crushing 18Gs amidst the smaller towers. The Gs made her synthetic muscles clench, just to stop her internal organs from rupturing, and then the missiles were streaking in, and these were not airbursting but ripping into walls, blasting huge waves of debris across the roads as Sandy cut thrust, fell again, bounced off the road then kicked again into rapid flight at no altitude . . . a missile streaked an intersection ahead and blew out a wall ahead, as she dodged wildly over the top of it, wreckage showering off her armour.

"*I reckon they know this is you,*" Gamma Two suggested.

"Fair bet," said Sandy, bounding again, then kicking up to a well-sheltering cover of gardens and parking atop a fifteen storey, and crouched while taking another look. And violated all tacnet protocols by opening to an external net link, which quickly propagated into broadcast across multiple channels. "Yeah, here I am, cocksuckers. Come and get me."

No immediate reply of missile fire. In fact, a noticeable pause across the immediate five-K front. Fear had its uses. Soldiers facing her would demand more support, weakening other sectors. Some might panic, with reason. They might throw more soldiers this way, thus losing more. In war as in chess, you made your opponent do something they'd rather not. Something different, out of their comfort zone. If she was bait for that, so be it.

A broadcast channel opened. "*Hello, Tanusha, this is Rami Rahim, going live in the middle of a FUCKING WAR, isn't this fun?*" Everyone who liked Rami, and there were millions, were now receiving uplink alert of an unscheduled show running off black code. "*Now we've got some great shit lined up for you folks who wanna know what the fuck is actually going on, suffice to say that this violent removal of parasitic scum is brought to you by Director Ibrahim and Sandy Kresnov, that same duo who previously brought us such hits as 'Die Feddie Fifth Fleet Die,' and 'Die League Assassins Die,' and are now bringing you their brand-new single, 'Die Operation Shield Fuckholes Die.' But before we bring you the good stuff, here's a little track to warm you up—this is for you, Ambassador Ballan!*"

And the audio erupted to the thudding percussion and power chords of Death's Door, Tanusha's best metal band, the best power riffs this side of the Federation; Sandy had nearly damaged walls dancing to it when no one else was home. It had always had the alarming but fascinating effect on her of dropping the red mist of combat vision, like she suddenly wanted to kill someone—so she hadn't heard it since the kids arrived.

Now she used her own uplinks to bounce the signal off about three thousand major relays, just to make sure everyone had it. "DIE MOTHER FUCKER DIE!" roared the pounding opening, before the ball-tearing rhythms cut in. They'd know that signal came from her too. Psych warfare was not usually her style, but this time it seemed appropriate. Even more so, given that by now, Ambassador Ballan really would be dead.

Ibrahim sat in the green room and stayed low, as the walls shook and rattled with incoming fire. Ballan's office had been hit several times from across the vast open space across the GC building donut and was now a flaming ruin, but the intervening walls to the waiting room were thick enough to keep the blasts out for now. He kept AR glasses on, uplinked through several systems into the GC mainframe, newly liberated with Ballan's demise and FSA attack codes, and tried to manage things from the little portal he'd set up there, surrounded by hostile defences. At the front doorway, barely four meters away, Amirah was holding off assaults from two directions at once, currently crouched in the doorway and reloading, hair a-mess from dust and debris kicked up by incoming fire. But the bend in the main hall made it hard for assaulting forces to get an angle, plus putting them at severe risk of hitting their friends farther up if both sides fired at once.

A grenade hit the far wall and showered her with debris. Amirah barely flinched. "Sure could use a grenade," she suggested.

"They barely let you in here with guns," Ibrahim replied, hands flying over visual icons in the air before him; it was too dangerous for a full emersion dive when he might need to move so suddenly. "With grenades, no chance."

Amirah stuck her arm out and fired a burst, just to keep heads down.

Hando tried to reach him for the third time. *"Sir . . . work unstable . . . pound under fi . . . spond if poss . . ."*

"Certainly seems the FSA compound is under attack," said Ibrahim, trying to get a clearer picture with the various command functions available to him. It was difficult; he wasn't a net tech, he could only rely on the superior coding given to him for use in this sensitive location, behind the primary barriers. "Hando can't get a clear connection here, we're on our own."

"Was always the plan, sir," said Amirah. Watching GIs under fire was a learning experience, even if he wasn't truly watching her. Incoming fire provoked not fear or flinching but thought process, he could see her looking at the rounds blasting holes within hands' reach of her head and immediately calculating return trajectories. "Sir, if they decide to simply wipe out this entire section of building, I can't stop them."

"These things work by procedure, Ms Togales," said Ibrahim, as heavy rounds hit the wall separating Ballan's office. "Taking out a section of the building will require high-up clearance, even in these circumstances. That will take time, and with any luck, Cassandra and company will be here by then."

And if not, they wouldn't. He didn't need to say it, Amirah understood.

"Yes, sir. Excuse me a moment."

She rolled, then leaped into the hall, firing both ways simultaneously. Then disappeared. More firing, crashing, and then screaming, that stomach-turning moment when a soldier's mind went from tactical professionalism to the realisation that he had a split-second of life remaining. Relative silence in the hall, then grenade fire whistling past the doorway, detonations farther away . . . a thunder of fire as Amirah returned, crashing in so fast she impacted and spun off the doorway. And sat, back to a wall, head cocked as though listening for indications of the damage she'd done.

"You're hit," Ibrahim observed.

Amirah made a face, as though wondering how anything else was possible. There was a clear hole in her clothes to the front of her hip, though no visible blood. The other blood on her fist, Ibrahim reckoned, was not hers. "That'll keep that side clear for a few minutes," she said. "They had too little defensive gunnery; they won't make that mistake again."

CHAPTER TWENTY-SIX

Danya sat watching the wide windows of the presidential suite and wishing he could stand with Svetlana and Kiril for a better view. They were not especially high up, perhaps twenty storeys, but their view north of central Tianyang District showed them zigzagging missile trails, darting magfire rounds and rapid tracer sprays. Explosions lit the dark towers in silhouette like some approaching lightning storm.

"Ragi," Danya tried again, "you have to help them!"

"I'm not intervening in a civil war," Ragi said quietly. He stood farther from the windows, a drink in hand, surveying the deadly view with somber resignation. "I have sympathy for what Cassandra and her friends have had done to them. But her side wishes to pursue the option of war against the League. For the moment, I'm unable to choose between them."

"You stayed out of it because you didn't want to risk starting a war between the FSA and Operation Shield!" Danya retorted. "But look! War came anyway! And it'll come again against the League no matter what you do, if that's what's going to come."

"Odd sentiment for a street kid who's spent his life staying out of the way to stay alive," Ragi suggested.

"Yeah, well, this is the first time I actually *could* make a difference."

"Seductive, isn't it?" said Ragi. "To be so powerful? I do not trust it."

The underworld doctor who had put the cast on Danya's leg and his arm in the sling had departed. Danya did not question how Ragi had contacted her, any more than he questioned how Ragi could get this massive hotel suite. He suspected that with Ragi's network skills so advanced, the more sophisticated an entity's network, the more vulnerable they were to takeover. Big hotels like this didn't even require you to turn up in person—if you had sufficient network ID and security, they just presumed you were real. And most of the time, unless the guest was Ragi, they were right.

The doctor had done the cast well though, and the sling—it only hurt now when he moved. Or breathed. She'd been a Jain and served the underground types who'd rather suffer than go to hospital.

"Danya!" Kiril exclaimed, peering through his AR glasses. "I can see missiles!"

"Can you see what's going on, Ragi?" Svetlana asked.

"The FSA are advancing quickly," said Ragi. "But they're going to struggle to get past the final defences. Every minute they take, those defences get stronger."

"That's Sandy leading that attack, isn't it?" Svetlana demanded. "Ragi, if the attack fails, she's going to be killed! Operation Shield would rather kill her than anyone else!"

"I'm sorry," said Ragi, spreading his hands helplessly. "I'm not going to take sides in this war. Cassandra understands what it means to have principles; I'm sure she'll understand this one."

Svetlana stared at Danya. Demanding of him. Pleading. *Do something!* She had the pistol with her still; Ragi had not attempted to take it from her. Perhaps Ragi was naive in his own way, not understanding how far even a child might go. Danya took a deep breath. Every instinct he possessed told him Ragi was right, in tactics if not in strategy—look out for yourself first, minimise your risks, don't bring trouble down on those you love. But one of those he loved was already in trouble, and here it was, the great dilemma he'd faced upon first meeting Sandy—that by increasing the number of people in your close little family, you increased the amount of risk you'd have to take to keep all of them safe.

But it was too late now, because if he didn't try everything to try to help Sandy, when he had the means at his disposal, and Sandy died . . . well, that was just unacceptable. The same way it would be unacceptable with Svetlana or Kiril.

He pulled his AR glasses over his eyes, saw the local network connect to his portable, and Svetlana's and Kiril's, which boosted the local network to something sizeable. "Well," he said, "even with Operation Shield's control of the city net reduced, it's still going to be impossible to make contact with the FSA or Director Ibrahim. But I reckon if his network works the way I think it works, we can reach Rami Rahim."

"Danya?" said Ragi, frowning with alarm. "Danya, you shouldn't do that; you boost the local signal size any bigger, Operation Shield will see it."

"Well, then why don't you help and make sure they don't?" Danya suggested. He was in the network now, he could see the constructs displayed before his eyes, appearing to float in mid-air. Ari had shown him basic techniques, the kind of thing any Tanushan kid knew real young but were still a novelty to a kid from Droze—how to match a net construct with a physical location. A simple search showed him where Rami Rahim's studio office was . . . of course he wouldn't be there, Operation Shield would put a warhead in it anytime. Private houses? Well, he was rich, he'd have a lot. So where was this signal coming from?

"Kiril," he said, "can you see where Rami Rahim's network is operating from?"

"You won't be able to trace his immediate location," Ragi said with mild frustration, "he's got a lot of very smart people working with him; all of Operation Shield won't know his location."

"But he gets outside calls all the time," Danya retorted. "It's a talkback show; he talks to people all over Tanusha. I'm betting he'll still have talkback function enabled. We don't need to find where he is, we just need to be able to talk to him."

"Danya, you can't do that." Ragi was properly alarmed now. "You can't upload Kiril's information to him anyway. Kiril's wireless uplinks aren't advanced enough to upload to a civilian network . . ."

"No, but we can just tell him what we've got," Danya retorted. The glasses put rows of icons in the air before him, but it was hard to manipulate them fast enough with only one hand. The viewpoint flashed and rotated, then darted to a different part of the network, then ran multiple search functions on different strands of data . . . it was frustrating to see just how much data there was. He felt he was moving very fast, but in reality he was barely scratching the surface.

"Danya, if you tell him what you've got," Ragi replied, "everyone will hear. Including Operation Shield. They'll trace back to here, and they'll probably put a missile into this room, do you understand that, Danya? Or anywhere else you move to, they can trace the transmission."

"Not if you stop them," said Danya, still working.

"I told you I won't. Now stop this immediately."

"Or you'll do what?" Danya asked. "Stop me yourself?" Ragi was staring at him. Standing against the wall, looking increasingly cornered, eyes wide with alarm. Danya didn't know exactly what he was doing, except that it was instinct, and it seemed to be right. Ragi didn't know how to handle confrontation. Sitting on the sidelines was one thing. Having a gun put to your head and being forced to make instant decisions, that was something else. Danya had experience of it. Ragi didn't. Speaking of guns . . .

"Svetlana," he added, "make sure he doesn't try to stop us."

Svetlana pulled her pistol and aimed it at Ragi, quite calmly. "You're not a combat model," said Svetlana. "And we don't have uplinks you can hack. I wouldn't try it."

A promising lead turned into a dead end. Danya swore beneath his breath. "I'm not going to help you," Ragi repeated.

"You don't have to," said Danya. "There's the door."

"No way!" Svetlana protested. "Danya, he can really help, we can make him!"

"I'm not going to make him do anything," Danya said firmly, and distant explosions shook the windows. "He insists on being allowed to do what he wants. That's fine. He can't stop us doing what we want either. But he can leave."

"It is my hotel room," Ragi pointed out.

"We're street kids," said Danya. "We steal. Sorry."

Rami was aware that Liz was having an increasingly agitated, wide-eyed conversation with someone while seated before her production bank arrayed before the sofa. Her hands flew through multiple icons at once, as on the display screens, their crude imitations of tacnet software tried to translate multiple incoming data sources into some kind of tactical picture. That feed was running on multiple self-randomizing net feeds throughout Tanusha, which in turn was getting them millions of ongoing links throughout the city from frightened citizens desperate to know what was going on. Those citizens were now in turn adding their own data into the feed, vid images out windows, audio recordings of nearby shootings that software was triangulating into location points . . . Tania and Anjul, his two main net geeks, were running furious interventions over by the indoor garden, trying to keep the whole system synched as feed-ins kept multiplying.

"Remember," Rami was saying now, watching the feeds unfold, "don't contact us directly even if you know how. Operation Shield has murdered before to keep their shit intact; we figure there's a good chance they'll just lob a missile onto your location. We are *not* the CSA or FSA, we can't guarantee anonymity, and if any of you netsters listening out there can help run interference for us, that'd be bilkool awesome, capish?"

Liz was gesturing to him frantically now. "Kirpal, tell us what's happening?" Kirpal Singh took over, former CSA SWAT and friend of Rami's, he'd come knocking on the door of this Rami's "other" house ten minutes ago, figuring Rami might be here, and was now offering strategic insight, but only into what Operation Shield were doing. FSA analysis he left alone in case he gave the bad guys ideas.

"Got a kid on the line says he's Danya Kresnov!" Liz hissed at him. "It's encrypted, but it's, like, only grade 3 at best . . ."

Danya Kresnov? "Oh fuck!" said Rami, and linked fast. "Danya, what's up, buddy? Are you safe?"

"Rami, you know how Special Agent Ariel Ruben was nearly killed a few days ago?" A boy's voice, but not a young boy. A teenager, cool and serious.

Rami blinked. "I . . . hang on, who?"

"Special Agent Ariel Ruben, good friend of Sandy's, Police Inspector Sinta was nearly killed with him, Operation Shield blew up their car on the freeway . . ."

"Oh wait, shit, I remember that on the news . . ."

"Yeah," the boy interrupted, *"well, Sinta was investigating Idi Aba, the lawyer who was killed by the League. Only he wasn't killed by the League, he was killed by Operation Shield because he'd been in contact with an activist in the League who'd given him a vision of a secret new League facility for mass-producing GIs."* Rami tried to process that for a moment. *"It's against all the treaties that ended the war, probably it would restart the war, and Operation Shield is trying to force these anti-war amendments through the Grand Council, you get it? This would kill the amendments dead."*

"Well . . . well, shit, Danya, that's . . . that's a great story, but I don't know if . . ."

"Rami, we have the damn vision. Ari Ruben sent it to us just before his car crashed. The League GI production facility, we've got it. You show it, Operation Shield's finished."

Rami's jaw dropped. "Danya . . . Danya, hang on, I'm going to put you onto our technical people . . . wait, what's your format?"

"Well, that's where it gets tricky."

Sandy flanked hard left across the defensive grid assembling on Santiello District, herself and five others streaking low over suburban neighbourhoods, coming down on apartment towers, moving rather than shooting, and making it quite obvious to the defenders. UAV presence directly opposing her had tripled since she'd made her identity known, and tacnet showed defensive depth boosting dramatically—it was taking tips now from Rami Rahim's independent network, which was now getting open-source feeds from all kinds of places, including some crazy fools out in their cars filming out the window and daring Operation Shield to shoot them. If they kept piling up resources here they'd leave a flank exposed.

Only now her net sensors were warning her of new tacnet alerts, but these weren't strategic, they were audible, meaning tacnet had overheard something and was feeding it to her . . . and her eyes widened with a shock that nearly caused her to miss her next landing on a roadway and crash through a street-light. Danya's voice. Tacnet said he was talking to Rami Rahim, something about Ari and Sinta, and . . . and if she could overhear this, Operation Shield could too.

She gridsearched frantically, that confusion of emotion trying to override the deadening weight of combat reflex . . . who was closest? It was Tianyang District, almost squarely in central Tanusha, ahead of their line of advance for now but about to get pulled onto the friendly side, and if Operation Shield wanted to do something about a target there, they'd have to do it soon or risk losing the capability. Vanessa! Vanessa was closest, taking 9th Company in a typically aggressive hard push through the guts of the defences . . . but she couldn't tell Vanessa to abandon her command priorities just to save her kids.

"Sandy, I got it!" Vanessa yelled, and kicked off the pavement behind apartment buildings, blasting low over the adjoining park and watching hard for the source of autocannon fire hovering behind buildings in Tianyang just over a K ahead. "Sandy, get back in fucking command, I got it, your kids are a strategic fucking asset, now get your head together and go!"

Because she already knew how Sandy would react, the ruthlessly logical tactical side hitting the powerfully emotional side and freezing. But her own tacnet sensors were showing her the same thing, the link coming from somewhere within a hundred-meter radius, maybe five possible buildings over two kilometers ahead . . . and crap, if Operation Shield decided to put a round in there, she was in no current position to stop it.

"Blue 3, push hard on grid-31, draw some counter-fire and light 'em up!" Because the usual catch of infantry combat still applied here—in order to see the enemy, you usually had to get them to shoot at you first. The smart ones would hold their fire until they wanted to shoot, not when you wanted them to.

She grounded hard behind another building and didn't like doing that because these were residential and occupied, but if people were clustering in central stairwells and basements as advised . . . tacnet showed her Blue 3 drawing fire ahead, grounding now and returning fire, several of the enemy displacing under cover from farther back . . . and suddenly there was magfire hitting the ground directly in front of her, huge eruptions of dirt and grass from gardens showering her armour as she pressed herself to the wall and tried to ignore it—it was a warning that enemy tacnet knew where she was, knew it couldn't hit her but wanted to delay her. She couldn't delay, not here.

"Go go!" she shouted. "Two by two, next cover!" And half of her squad displaced, running and leaping, Vanessa jumping straight over the line of fire from incoming mag rounds, they were taking two seconds to reach this location, if she didn't fly in a straight line for longer than two seconds they couldn't hit her. Theoretically.

Here a rooftop raced up, she made as though to land on it, then as it raced up she kicked again, a mid-air burst of thrusters as a mag round tore pieces from the rooftop where she would have landed. And here it was, two Ks off, airbourne and moving as it fired, and Vanessa put her own magfire onto it, then kicked sideways in mid-flight behind a taller resi tower, saw fire skipping and racing at other targets ahead . . . a flash as Blue 5 went down, no telling what did it, Gs crushing her as she kicked again and thrusters red-lit across her vision as temps reached critical, land or burnout.

An out-positioned enemy hopper tried to run, was blown spinning into a towerside by one of Vanessa's squad, as Vanessa hit, stumbled, and slid on knees to slow, then up and running for building cover, realising only as she reached it that she was in a school yard, and her cover was a classroom building. One K to target, and tacnet showed her fire passing Blue 7 that could only have come from behind a particular tower . . . she fast-programmed a missile, fired, saw it loop high, and said to her man with the best angle, "Blue 4, watch for fast target behind tower grid H-98." As tacnet highlighted that point. The missile searched, found, and dove, the enemy hopper dodged, firing frantic countermeasures, and was blasted into a backward spin by Blue 4.

"Good call, Skip," said Blue 4, and Vanessa jumped as incoming magfire began to shred the school building. Damn, there was going to be a damage bill. And now she could see an A-12 at long range, seven Ks ahead, firing a whole spread of missiles that did not appear to be directed at specific mobile targets, but the bigger warheads for taking out building floors . . . and her heart nearly stopped. Oh, no.

"Danya!" Kiril shouted. "Danya, they're firing at us!" They were at the back of the huge room, by the big bed farthest from the windows, but that wouldn't save them here. Ragi stood in the middle of the room, no doubt seeing everything that they saw.

"Ragi!" Danya shouted. "You can suicide if you want, but you don't have the right to take us with you!"

And then on his own glasses, he could see the onrushing missiles suddenly turn upward, five of them, fanning out like the petals of some flower. And continuing onward, streaking into the night. Ragi turned to look at them resentfully.

"You're a very manipulative boy," he told Danya.

Danya stared, heart thumping. Ragi could turn missiles around. He hadn't known that, but he'd been hoping. Surely Ragi would have run somewhere else if he couldn't, seeing what Danya was doing, drawing attention to this spot.

"You haven't seen anything yet," he told Ragi breathlessly. "Because Operation Shield just saw that, and they'll guess what did it." Ragi sighed and muttered something under his breath. "Svet, put the gun down. Ragi's on our side now whether he likes it or not."

Her back to the wall by the bed, Svetlana lowered the pistol but kept both hands on it by her side. And Danya found time to marvel that hyperstrung

Svetlana seemed the calmest one in the room. It was the gun that did it, he knew. Some kids liked a safety blanket, Svet liked an automatic . . . or even better, Sandy.

"I'm not sure you quite realise what you've done," Ragi said somberly to Danya. "This choice is far from optimal."

"Ragi," Danya retorted. "There's no good and bad choices. Just bad and worse. Deal with it."

"Oh, I'm dealing with it," said Ragi, exasperated. As one after another, five distant A-12 combat flyers were hit by incoming missiles and exploded.

"Woah!" Kiril shouted. "Danya, that was Ragi! He turned their own missiles around on them and . . ."

Crash! as something big and fast-moving plowed through the big glass windows. Danya grabbed Kiril with his good arm alongside him on the bed, as Svetlana dropped to a simple crouch and aimed . . . it was an FSA hopper, brutally armoured and protruding with cannon, launcher, and antenae, thrusters and power train howling and now a metal chank! chank! chank! as it ran across the floor, half as tall again as a regular person.

The visor popped, and here was Vanessa, alarmed and out of breath. Ragi, Danya saw, hadn't even flinched, had probably seen her coming. "You guys okay?" Vanessa asked.

"We're fine," said Danya, as Vanessa noted the sling and foot cast.

"Guys, you gotta get out of here, you're targeted! Get in the central stairwell and . . ."

"They're in no danger," said Ragi, as Vanessa stared at him.

"He turned their missiles around!" Kiril explained. Vanessa blinked.

"Vanessa," said Danya, "can that suit generate a com net? Kiril's uplinks are working just enough to pick that up; you can transmit it on the net and . . ."

"Don't bother," Ragi said quietly. "I'll do it. The best way to save lives now is for one side to win quickly, negotiations and deals will only prolong the conflict and increase suffering. Kiril, close your eyes."

In ready room one by the landing pads, Captain Arvid Singh, acting Commander of CSA SWAT, watched the feed pouring in. Rami Rahim's voice narrated, a surreal counterpoint if there ever was one for those more accustomed to dirty jokes on a Saturday night.

"... okay, we understand Detective Sinta and Special Agent Ruben were nearly killed in that big explosion Operation Shield blew in the L35 freeway four days ago—and here we can see what they were trying to get back to HQ past the net blockers, and what Operation Shield doesn't want you to see. Folks, this is a brand-new GI production facility in the League, we don't know where, but we're talking to some experts here who can tell you it's genuine ... Harley, jump in here ..."

And Rami's newly linked expert proceeded to tell them what they were looking at. There were a lot of vats, a lot of sealed units, machines lining walls, white and sterile. Bio-synth growth and fabrication, even the average Tanushan citizen knew them to look at them, they'd featured in enough news vids and bad movies over the years, and a few good ones. The handheld camera moved down corridors, past sealed doors marked "secure" and "sanitised," and the narrator continued to explain why a biosynth full production facility would be laid out like this and not like something else.

"Sinta thought they had Idi Aba killed for this." Arvid turned on Chandrasekar, leaning against the wall by a display. SWATs One, Five, and Six were here, the rest in the other ready rooms or sitting against the walls in hallways, waiting. The place was crowded with clattering, whining armour, even as they tried to keep still. "She's awake and talking, says she has a clear evidence trail that goes back to Operation Shield. Idi Aba was meant to get this footage."

"I know," said Chandrasekar somberly, arms folded.

"And he would have used it for the emancipation cause, and that's the end of the amendments, because obviously once the public learns the League is back mass-producing GIs again, possibly higher-designation ones, there's no way they'll allow amendments that will handcuff the Federation's response."

"They've been trying to keep this quiet until the amendments pass," the Director agreed. On their separate tacnet feed, they were now receiving an overview of FSA tacnet, showing the general location of the front, and defensive forces. It showed them arriving at CSA HQ in several minutes. "We can't do anything about the Grand Council, it's not our jurisdiction. But President Singh's administration is plugged into the current GC network; all Callayan civil service and government apparatus, including us, are at least nominally supporting Operation Shield."

"He has to stand down," said Arvid with a direct stare. "Tell him to stand down."

"He's not responding," said Chandrasekar. "The entire administration's gone autistic. I think they're panicked."

"He's complicit in a coup. He's helping them now, and he was involved from the beginning. At the least it warrants arrest."

"A coup against the Grand Council," Chandrasekar countered. "A federal crime. We enforce Callayan law, not Federal."

"He allowed a foreign force to occupy Callay and take over its security," Arvid retorted. "That's treason. That foreign force has since assassinated, or attempted to assassinate, members of Callay's security forces and civil service whose interests the President is supposed to protect. At the very least it presents Callay with an immediate security emergency, which the Callayan government can't respond to because it's partially the cause. This administration must be removed as a matter of immediate security emergency. If they won't go quietly, we'll kick them out loudly."

Chandrasekar thought about it. On the incoming tacnet, FSA forces were advancing fast now. "Caretaker administration," he murmured. "Opposition leader heads, CSA Director as deputy, new election immediately following full and public investigation." And he nodded, once and firmly. "Wait a few minutes and FSA will have forced Shield back enough you'll have a clear space. Then you can fly to the Parliament."

Arvid gave one hand gesture, and everyone moved to their flyers, in determined, orderly lines.

"Go go go!" Sandy yelled, and kicked herself onto a high trajectory through uncovered airspace that would have got her killed a few minutes ago. But not only had Operation Shield's own missiles been turning back on themselves to destroy their point of origin, her own side's missiles were now getting through the defences, destroying airborne and ground units and leaving Shield units without support. Those were now running, falling back in disorganised flight, and if ever there was a moment to drop everything and charge, this was it. If she'd had bayonets, she would have fixed them. "Max speed advance, kill everything!"

She drew fire on this trajectory, or attempted fire, but with her reflexes most of those were dead before they could pull the trigger. Still she had to land, thrusters were reactor-powered, so fuel was no problem, but temperature was. She landed atop a residential with a running thud, coolant gens running at a howl that nearly rivaled the engines, took a knee and pumped mag rounds after an escaping hopper at fifteen hundred meters' range—it dodged once, twice, and she guessed with the third, a flash as the ammo ignited, then a flare of falling debris. Missile fire ripped past her, but from behind heading forward, all one way at the moment; Shield were scared to fire. And now, their networks were disintegrating, though whether that was the same thing that was turning their missiles, or local hackers, or something else again, she had no idea.

". . . *ssandra?*" The link told her it was Hando, from FSA HQ. "*Cassandra, can you . . .*"

"I hear you, Hando! Situation?" Temp readings touched blue, and she jumped. A UAV targeted her from behind a building, and she put a round through it at six Gs acceleration.

"*The compound's a smoking mess, Cassandra, but we're all in the bunkers, so we're okay! The Director and Amirah are still pinned down in the GC!*"

"I copy that, I'm . . . nearly twenty minutes away."

"*He's not going to last five by the sound of it!*" Hoppers weren't equipped for sustained long-range flight. Ahead, tacnet showed an A-12 hit, spin, fall into buildings and explode.

"I'll get there. I've got an idea." And flashed over onto main net again, as an announcement came through. It was Li Shifu, Grand Council chairman himself. The closest thing the Federation had to a President.

". . . *Federation Grand Council is currently under attack!*" The picture setup was not professional, a bit lopsided, the lighting poor. Li looked scared. That would freak people out, they weren't used to seeing the GC Chairman genuinely frightened and hearing that authentic wobble in his voice. "*I urge all Federation patriots, including all available elements of the Federation Fleet, to defend your capital with your lives. We are under attack by League GIs, synthetic soldiers who have declared war on their organic creators. All who value their freedom must defend the Grand Council from this new wave of tyranny that descends upon us.*"

Sandy slowed her cannonball descent, braked hard across some trees and rooftops. "Hando, put me on main net!" Flicker of static connection, and she was on. "This is FSA Commander Kresnov to the Grand Council." Roar and thud, as she landed on a suburban street with a jolt, no longer worried about incoming missile fire, and now uplinked in search of automated taxi services. "Any individual directly assisting Operation Shield will be killed, by me personally if necessary. Federal employees are advised to sever all network connections at this time and assume an unthreatening posture. We apologise to Federation citizens for this temporary break in Federation democracy. Normal service will resume as soon as possible."

Fleet didn't bother her: they couldn't do anything from orbit. Getting through that final defence grid without losing nearly everyone bothered her. And the prospect of doing so while Ibrahim and Amirah were still alive did too. There were pedestrians here in the 'burbs, she noted, hiding in their yards, filming her with devices. A few, seeing the FSA insignia on her armour, were waving, yelling encouragement. Good lord, one incoming artillery round, and they'd all die.

She kicked thrusters again as a new rendezvous point established, and now she had a Fleet frequency incoming, as the burb blasted away beneath her . . . Captain Tsien of the carrier *Danube*. "*Commander Kresnov, this is an act of war against the Federation. This action will be met with counter-attack by Fleet, you cannot hope to hold your objective even should you achieve it.*"

"Hello, Captain," she said, zipping past the top floors of low-rise residentials. "The first thing I'll do when GC is captured is gain full control of planetary defences. The second thing I'll do is remove you and your warship from Callayan space by ground-to-orbit strike. If you start running now, you might get clear in time, reaction missiles move much faster than carriers."

Well, at least Operation Shield's friends in Fleet were revealing themselves. Then she saw the rendezvous site ahead and landed hard to cool before one last kick.

CHAPTER TWENTY-SEVEN

The explosion blew in the wall to Ballan's office waiting room and took all merely human visibility with it. Ibrahim had been expecting it, thanks to Amirah's warnings that it was imminent, and was hiding under the heavy secretary's table, two legs collapsed to make a shield. Even so, the force of it deprived him of air and sense, ears ringing and only barely aware of shooting now in the neighbouring room, from where the explosion had come. Amirah had warned him of this too.

The shooting stopped. Amirah could be dead in there, but this was the plan, so he scrambled from under the table, slipping on shattered wall and dust, hand over his mouth, AR glasses shielding his eyes from the worst of the dust, they and uplinks giving him some kind of fragmented vision overlaid onto swirling dust . . . here was the hole, roughly a meter and perfectly circular, the wall not wide enough for multiple entry points without risking bringing down the roof.

He scrambled through, into a nearly identical office waiting room, the visibility much better here, and found Amirah already arming herself with better weapons. The armoured corpses of the assault team who'd blown the wall were splayed about the room, their injuries horrific, armour crushed. Explosive entry into a room containing a high-designation GI was ill advised at such close ranges, because she could be through the hole before your follow-up grenades and flash bangs. And then, at point-blank range, you got this, a slaughter.

Amirah tossed an automatic at him, then a pair of attached mags, which he somehow caught, then went to the hallway door and tossed out a couple of newly acquired grenades on an impact fuse. They blew the corridor beyond to hell, and then she was gone again, with another flurry of shooting, into the hall from one doorway farther around the bend than she was supposed to be.

Then a yell, as they were still without uplink coms, "Sir, on me!" Ordering him like a private, and he ran, expecting to be shot in the back at any moment from someone Amirah had missed in that direction, but nothing came. And here against the inner curving wall, as he kept running, were more dead personnel, nearly all headshots, five of them . . . but their weapons and armour were nowhere near as advanced as their previous opponents. This was all?

And here at a junction hall was Amirah, standing left shoulder to the outer wall for the best angle both ways, rifle ahead left-handed, big auto pistol on the right hip in case someone came at them behind—she'd see that on her headset's rear cam, literally eyes in the back of her head, and her right hand could draw that weapon and put rounds precisely on target within milliseconds. And to think that Amirah was dismissive of her abilities next to Sandy.

"Where to, sir?" she asked, seeing from his run that he was relatively unhurt. His suit was a mess, he had cuts and bruises everywhere, but on this much adrenaline with all augments hypercharged, he barely felt a thing. "I'd like to put some armour on you, we're so exposed to shrapnel out here, but we're short of time."

"Only five in the hall?" he asked, crouched low by her leg so he wouldn't block her line of fire in either of direction.

"Plus five more in the assault team," said Amirah. "I think five more up the other end of the hall, but they'll be having a crisis of confidence by now." Given that every time one of them showed himself or got a bit too close, he died. "They'll be moving most of their numbers to the outer defences now, they thought fifteen was enough to bottle us up."

And then made the mistake of trying an assault with numbers only sufficient for containment. "We'll only have a clear run until they realise we're loose," said Ibrahim, checking his rifle, AR glasses trying to display GC schematics, but the GC network terminating the graphics before they could fully form. "Our best bet is strategic command, you know where that is?"

"The war room, yes, sir. Sir, try to stay forty-five degrees on my forehand flank . . ." she indicated his present position.

"I know, and keep low." He was baggage to her, though thankfully self-propelled baggage. He wasn't sure his dignity could survive being thrown over her shoulder. "Let's go."

With one hopper clinging to each side of its bodywork, the taxi cruiser could barely get airbourne. But once airbourne, it could maintain 300 kph at low altitude without having to stop every few hundred meters. Sandy hung off its right side, Gamma 4 off its left, like two giant insects hitching a ride on some unwilling host. Steering was by uplink, largely reflex, and now as a number of other units copied her manoeuver, they were rushing onto the enemy hoppers faster than they could retreat. Deprived of network cover, FSA troops were lobbing mini-missiles at them that countermeasures were no longer defending, and enemy hoppers were either hiding or dying.

"This is Red 1. I've got some surrenders here!" came a call, six Ks north.

"Make them crack their armour and climb out," Sandy replied. "If they don't comply immediately, it's a trick, so kill 'em." And switched to Ragi's link. "Ragi, get me some progress on the GC, we can't control planetary systems without it."

"It's a heavily secured command system, Cassandra," came Ragi's voice. *"It's mostly output and very little input, I must admit it's very hard to penetrate, even for me."*

"Well, get it done, because that grid has magfire defences; you can't just turn them around like missiles once they've been fired." Though God knew how he'd been doing that, because those missiles were supposedly autistic too . . . though she knew of some technologies that used main net frequencies in urban areas to penetrate even missile guidance . . . but take *control* of them?

They were six Ks out from Montoya District now, and she knew there were units on the streets that extended the air grid, probably tanks or AMAPS of some sort, the towers would block line of sight of those extended units, but there were precious few fire shadows showing on tacnet, and most of those shadows became traps once you were stuck in them . . .

Another feed showed her CSA SWAT now descending on Callayan Parliament. Parliament hadn't shut down aerial defences either, so SWAT had simply bombarded them from range, and for whatever internally chaotic reason, anti-missile defences weren't working. It was creepy, seeing those red brick arches and domes obscured by smoke from massive explosions. In the midst of the confusion there was more shooting, flashes of staccato fire as SWAT stormed various entrances, but she didn't have time for a direct feed and had to trust Arvid could handle it . . . which she had no doubt.

Suddenly a new feed, tacnet couldn't ping the location, so that meant somewhere heavily shielded, ID coding lost somewhere in the replication. *"This is Agent Teo, FedInt, I have an outside line for the moment. Mr Ragi, can you backtrack this connection into the GC main grid?"* So Teo was with Ibrahim, Sandy supposed. And FedInt were suddenly being useful . . . only now that it was clear who was going to win.

"Mr Teo, I can't gain direct access from here, but I can overload their processing, hold on . . ."

Sandy's visual managed some fast gymnastics, showed her the massive graphical shield of Grand Council's construct, and around it . . . something ridiculous, golden and clinging like some hyper-dimensional parasitic vine, flickering and replicating around the barrier, destroying interactive functions before they could even propagate, with careless flicks of golden tendrils. But Ragi couldn't fully penetrate. Capabilities still somewhere short of Cai then.

"Cassandra." Ragi again. *"Their internal feeds are now self-replicating; they'll have to devote massive processing to shutting it down. It should slow down everything by a second or two. Including fire control."*

On the other side of the cruiser, Gamma 4 looked at her. Marco, his name was. "Should?"

"Okay, guys, time the approach. Full speed down the middle." She illustrated what she meant, a fast manoeuvering of icons, tactical formations, and how it ought to play out. If Ragi was right.

"That looks interesting," Rishi remarked drily. Sandy did a fast double check—she hadn't even noticed Rishi was one of those who'd grabbed a taxi cruiser; everyone was using unfamiliar IDs, and she hadn't had time to check everyone's identities. Or perhaps was subconsciously preferring the luxury of not knowing who was dying when.

"You guys are all volunteers," Sandy replied, broad-net. "You can opt out if you want."

"If I ever meet the people who made me," Rishi replied, *"I'll be sure to thank them for volunteering me for everything dangerous and scary."*

Sandy was astonished. Not that Rishi showed no signs of bailing, but at the obvious and intentional sarcasm. A high designation, Rishi. Like Amirah. A few months ago she wouldn't have understood something that sarcastic if spoken to.

"Hey, Rish," said Sandy, still on broad-net. "Love you guys. Thanks for coming."

"Those Krishna priests who lived where we were building our houses said none of us are in control of our destinies anyway," said Rishi. *"So what the hell, right?"*

"Hey, did they get out?"

"No." A silence from Rishi. *"They refused to leave. Another reason why I'm not bailing."*

"We may yet prove them right," Sandy murmured.

Ahead lay Montoya. Even now, several defensive missile emplacements were firing, and almost immediately the missiles looped back upon themselves, or took abrupt turns, and blew each other to pieces.

"Damn, that's a nice trick," said Lorenz, one of Rishi's friends. *"Can you do that, Sandy?"*

"Sure," said Sandy. "Give me a week to plan and half an hour to execute." And one-handed, pumped three magfire rounds into another battery that was holding fire. Her rounds streaked two kilometers, a brief high-velocity arc toward the base of an apartment building, then two small explosions followed by a massive one as the ammunition detonated. She hoped the civvies in the building were well gone from there. The recently free-and-lively net was full of warnings for locals to get away from anything that might be targeted, and showing easy-to-read locations. There were commercial buildings nearby that would have served as cover just as well, all empty, but Operation Shield wanted propaganda corpses for the cause.

The Grand Council was three Ks out, invisible at this low altitude, weaving now between lower buildings, over a stretch of suburban houses, a lake, some sports fields by a school. . . . "We need to overload them, everyone max v, mix up the altitudes, crisscross vector so we overlap their fire zones." With real-time illustration, assigning roles. There were only five cruisers, ten hoppers total. And now tacnet was finding more information on defensive emplacements, cross-referencing from her own schematic files, plus all the additional wheeled units Shield had been placing around it. Magfire, not missiles . . . and even without tacnet drawing all the kill zones onto the map, Sandy could see that without Ragi's armscomp delay, they'd be one hundred percent KIA within ten seconds of entering range. With the delay . . . well, local armscomp could realise its circumstance and recalculate. They had to take out most of those units on the way in. And if they did . . . she figured sixty percent casualties.

Meaning the odds suggested that, most deadly combat GI ever built or not, she was more likely than not about to die. She took a deep breath.

"Hit 'em with everything," she said. "We need as much distraction as . . ." And suddenly tacnet was showing vehicles airborne about Montoya, abruptly changing direction and heading toward the GC. Some civvie cruisers, taxis, all on automation—empty, she presumed.

"Got you some help," said Ragi. *"Good luck."*

GC defences opened up on them as soon as the complex became visible, the big O-shaped building emerging behind towers amidst a drifting cloud of glowing, incoming fire. Sandy stayed with the cruiser as long as possible, as the first magfire flashed past at armour-shredding speeds, explosions on proximity charge . . . then leaped, as Marco jumped from the opposite side, hit the thrusters and smashed at ten Gs as the cruiser was hit repeatedly, smashed instantly to pieces that got progressively smaller as fire shredded the wreckage of the wreckage, leaving nothing more than an expanding cloud of metallic debris.

Tacnet returned missile fire on automatic, their remaining missiles leaping from back racks, hoppers streaking along a deliberate scatter of trajectories as suddenly defensive fire was readjusting to the unburdened cruisers that came rushing at them from the surrounding towers. And then it was all crazy, cruisers exploding, anti-missile defences erupting about the grounds like some crazed, explosive sprinkler system, and Sandy herself pumping magfire as fast as she could into the mess, calculating how many shots it might take to penetrate the heavy armour of defensive emplacements, and reckoning most of the use might be in distraction. She twisted repeatedly as magfire ripped close to her path, Gs levelling out as thrusters reached maximum and rapidly overheating, took shrapnel from proximity blasts, saw one of her friendly icons on tacnet abruptly vanish, then another.

And found herself clearing the top of the building, fire chasing her toward the apex, and she dove, spinning even now to pump fire from her white-hot rifle into emplacements, hitting all but silencing only one . . . and now the bottom of the big circular building, right in the bull's-eye, a central floor of glass surrounded by walkways and gardens. Sandy hurtled at it like a missile, upending at the last moment as she passed roof level, battery fire ceasing so it wouldn't hit the building, and crashed feet first through the glass at 300 kph.

Luckily the Grand Council's main chamber had a high ceiling. But she was still travelling at 200 kph when she hit the central floor right on top of the Chairman's table. And smashed, blacked out, and came to her senses even as she hit the floor face-first. Struggled, aware that others had hit the ground around her, chairs in the grand circular chamber, the most famous in all the Federation, now burning and smashed from thruster-blasting crash landings.

And now they were under fire, as armoured troops rushed the chamber's perimeter doors. Sandy levered her broken suit into a roll, fire pinging and cracking off her armour, then a concussion of grenades, levered herself up on an awkward knee, and discovered her big magfire rifle was still working when it had no right to be, and thank god for Tanushan arms tech. And began unloading her remaining ammo at infantry troops with armour to withstand medium-caliber small arms, but nothing like this two-meter-long tank killer. Two exposed soldiers disappeared in pieces, others diving for cover or sheltering behind door frames, which Sandy summarily blew apart, pivoting in a continuing circle, shell feed clanking and humming, leaning into the recoil like a sailor in a gale. Her comrades joined in, five besides her, several with street-clearing grenade launchers put fragmentation rounds into walls, ripping a thousand holes in representatives' seats across swathes of chamber.

Incoming fire ceased, and Sandy cracked her broken armour, rolling onto her back to free her legs from the suit's unresponsive limbs. Wriggled out amidst smoking-hot steel and the stench of scorched thrusters, found her personal weapons mangled on her armour rack, and so scrambled up an aisle between chairs, willing her hypertense leg muscles to work properly, found a dead Shield soldier with serviceable weapons. And found the GC network relatively open to transmission.

"This is Kresnov," she snarled to all defenders. "I'm in the building with friends. Good luck, assholes."

Ibrahim gazed up from his chair in the war room at the end of a long table with all kinds of high-tech displays and implants. Mostly dysfunctional for now, but he'd been following as much as he could and issuing commands where possible. He *had* been. Now he gazed dazedly at the blurred figure before him and recalled that he'd left the short rifle on the table before him . . . but he could not see it clearly, not quite recall how it operated on short notice. He'd known such things as a younger man. But it had been so long ago. And if the figure before him now was hostile, there was little he could do about it.

The figure crouched and put a hand on his shoulder. Blonde hair, messed askew. Blue eyes, calm intensity. Not especially beat up this time. "Director," said Cassandra. "Are you okay?"

"I think so." He blinked, eyes resolving blurs into clear shapes. "I don't know what happened. I was here, on the displays, and then . . ."

"Augment stress," said Amirah on his left. Ibrahim stared, not having seen her there. She was seated, far more bedraggled than Cassandra. Unaccustomedly, for a GI, she looked exhausted. "It happens when you push an organic body harder than it could normally take. You're not a young man any longer, sir."

"No." He rubbed his face. "Evidently not. Cassandra, what . . . ?"

"They surrendered," she said. "Once we got inside. I did write a paper on that a while ago, on the flaws in the GC architecture, let us get directly into the main chamber. They were finished once that happened, they can't match us in the corridors. Had a hard enough time with Amirah by the looks of it."

"Indeed," said Ibrahim. And looked at the other GI with admiration. "Extraordinary, Amirah." Given her first real taste of combat had been only a month ago, had nearly killed her, and caused her considerable trauma. "Quite extraordinary."

Amirah nodded, face strained. Took a deep breath, elbows on knees, attempting composure. Sandy said nothing.

"Amirah?" Ibrahim pressed.

"I don't like fighting," she managed, voice strangled. "I don't care how I'm built, or how good I am at it. I don't like it."

Ibrahim leaned and extended a hand. Amirah took it. "I'm so sorry," he said quietly. "But I had no choice. You were an asset I desperately needed."

Amirah nodded. Tried to reply but couldn't. Gasped again for air, and composure, tears streaming.

"Sir," said Cassandra. "Someone needs to talk to the media. Now. Not some broadcast message, I mean face to face. The people need to know what's happening, the population's roused now, and if they think it's just another coup, they could be storming the walls."

Ibrahim nodded. "It should be me. Let's give them enough time to assemble . . . are the grounds secure enough? It should be here."

"Yes, sir. Sir, I've already taken the liberty of summoning them. You've been unconscious for fifteen minutes at least?" She looked askance at Amirah. Amirah nodded. "I'm not sure you're in any condition."

"Sir," Amirah added, "your pulse rate is very elevated." They could see that, Ibrahim realised. Infra-red vision, watching pulses of heat, blood, and tissue. "With respect, I'm not sure the first thing people see of the new authority is a man who can barely stand."

"Well, then I can get a shot to keep me on my feet."

"Absolutely not," Amirah retorted sternly. "That's against all medical regulations for a man your age with augment stress. Need I remind you what happened to Commander Rice? And she's young and fit."

Ibrahim repressed a tired smile. Amused at this new condition in his life—female GIs who could kill with the flick of a wrist, now scolding him like his wife and daughter.

"And Commander Rice is well?" he asked. And looking at Cassandra, knew the answer immediately. "Of course she is, good." Because Cassandra would be considerably more distraught than Amirah if it were otherwise. "Well then. If it must be immediately, and it cannot be me, it must be you." With as firm a stare as he could muster. "Cassandra."

A year ago, she might have protested. Six months ago, even. Now, she just gazed at him with that familiar, calm blue stare. "I know," she said. "There's a few things I want to say."

She strode the back hall to the media room off the lower main entrance, adjusting the armour suit she'd borrowed for the occasion. A GI was guarding the doorway ahead, watching the newly arrived and arriving media outside, weapon at cautious cross-arms. Kiet now pressed past him, coming to see her. From his face, she sensed bad news.

"They found Rishi," he said quietly. She'd disappeared off tacnet, one of four from Sandy's final assault to do so. Marco had been found alive, his suit winged, he was hurt but would live. They'd been hoping a similar story for Rishi. Kiet's expression said otherwise.

Sandy hugged him. They clung to each other for a long moment, repressing the occasional tension tremor from the armour.

"There wasn't much left," Kiet said quietly. "So at least it was fast."

"She was the first to rebel," said Sandy. "Others fought back, and some like me escaped, but she led the first true rebellion. I'll see that that's remembered. That they're all remembered."

Kiet pulled back to look her in the face. "How?"

Sandy managed a faint smile. "Watch," she said.

She moved past and strode into the media room. And here they were, rows of some of her least favourite people in the world, journalists. Net casters, source collectors, independent traffic aggregators. With modern tech anyone could be a journalist, could gather news themselves, but still most people went through the aggregators for convenience. And the aggregators packaged and spun, this way or that, because a firmly stated opinion gathered more viewers than bland objectivity. They pretended to be independent, but most of them were sheep, the groupthink elite, who interacted mostly with each other and thus viewed the universe from within that cage, peering through their narrow bars.

Sandy walked to the podium behind which one or another Grand Council importance would normally stand, the GC logo behind, and Federation flags. And placed her assault rifle deliberately upon the podium where all could see it. Rows of nervous faces confronted her. Rows of cameras, large 3D spectra-lenses, small portables, active-pulse laser scanners that her combat vision disliked, a distracting flicker on hypersensitive synthetic retinas. They hadn't liked being called in like this, Dahisu had done it, had said there'd been exclamations and disbelief. She was putting their lives in danger, they'd said. She was going to make threats. Surely they should wait another hour or two to confirm all was safe?

Fine, she'd relayed through Dahisu. There will be an announcement in thirty minutes. If you don't want to cover it, don't come. Your competitors will get the live feed, it's not my problem. She could see the fear and excitement battling on faces, the instinct for self-preservation against the desire for the story. About two hundred of them, all told, crushed to standing room only at the back.

"You've seen our evidence against Operation Shield," she told them without preamble. "I'm not going to rehash it. I'm not a spokesperson, I'm a soldier. If you still need one of us to convince you of what Operation Shield really was, with everything we've shown you, then you're probably beyond our ability to convince anyway."

"Why was this necessary then?" called out some vaguely familiar face, who was probably famous or something, Sandy wasn't sure and didn't care. "It's one thing to accuse Operation Shield of wrongdoing, and maybe you're right. But a full-scale war in Tanusha? There are at least a hundred civilians dead so far, hundreds more injured . . ."

"You," said Sandy, pointing a finger at the maybe-famous journalist. "Shut up and wait your turn."

"You can't just threaten a journalist!" shouted another.

"I can," said Sandy. "And I'll tell you why. None of you raised your very opinionated voices against Operation Shield. Not one. It took independent media operators like Rami Rahim, and traffic shunters like Splinter Group and Kalita Constructs, to get subversive and ask questions. There will be investigations. Not done by us, we're just soldiers, but by independent judges, probably not even Callayans, since a Callayan could be considered compromised given the emotion of what's just happened. But investigations will happen, into Operation Shield, and into the role of everyone who backed it, or supported it, or was otherwise suspiciously silent with the questions, when it's supposed to be your job to ask them. Now a lot of you are probably just spineless and compliant rather than guilty, but we've evidence against some who were definitely Shield mouthpieces, bought and paid for, possibly even some in this room. So am I threatening you? You better believe it. With justice, independently administered. We're dealing with treason here. That's about the only thing people are still put to death for. Think about it."

They thought about it. There was fear on a lot of faces. Good. Sometimes these jokers forgot that theirs was not merely a power but a responsibility to at least attempt objectivity and not take sides. And responsibilities forgotten, or abandoned in the name of personal preference, Sandy was learning, were only truly recalled beneath the blade of an axe, metaphorical or otherwise.

"Second thing. The same people who will determine your fates will now certainly determine ours. Ours, of course, meaning we who have just forcefully removed the current leaderships of Federation Grand Council and Callayan Parliament from office. Again, there will be investigations. Should we be convinced that those investigations are fair, we will submit to them, as humble servants of the Federation should. Should the same people who implemented Operation Shield be running those investigations, however, they'll find us resisting them with every weapon at hand. And once they hear the weight of our evidence, I'll hope that the majority of the people of Callay, and indeed the people of the Federation, will join us in doing so.

"Next thing. People will accuse us of launching a coup. A real one this time, not the utter fabrication of the one we were previously accused of. And they're right. This *is* a coup."

She ran her gaze over them. The assembled faces stared back. Sandy supposed she was going out live, certainly she couldn't take anything back. But she hadn't thought to check.

"There's no denying it. A group of unelected soldiers took it upon themselves to overthrow the acting Federation and Callayan governments by force of arms. If you consult a dictionary, it'll tell you that defines a coup. But this was a *counter*-coup." She raised a combat-gloved finger. "Important distinction. The first coup destroyed the democratic legitimacy of both governments, attempting to ram through massively important amendments without due democratic process. *That* was why we acted. Not, and I'll repeat this so that everyone understands, *not* because we didn't like the amendments. That's none of our business; we're not elected, we don't get to choose what either government chooses to do through due democratic process.

"It was the *lack* of such process that made us act. The forceful suppression of alternative views, the assassination and attempted assassination of several such figures. A coup by stealth, disguised as a security action. Innocent people have died in Tanusha today, and we all regret that. But this was not our choice. We were doing what we all swore an oath to do—defend the Federation constitution at all costs. If people want to change the constitution by legal means, wonderful. But if you have to threaten, suppress, and murder to do it, we, and others like us, will kill you. I apologise if that seems blunt to some people. This seems the time for blunt talk. We'll kill you. We're good at it. If you try it again with ten times the forces, we'll kill them too. And then we'll trace it back to the people who ordered it. You know who you are, and you should be frightened.

"It's clear to the Federal Security Agency, and others with us, that something has gone wrong with the way the Federation works. Perhaps we never truly paid Federal governance the attention it deserved. True power always rested in the hands of independent worlds, and given the distances and delays, the Grand Council, and the way it elected its representatives, was usually second priority. Add to that the distortions created by the war, and it's clear we have a mess.

"The Federal Security Agency has some suggestions how to improve matters. It is not the FSA's intention to tell Federation member worlds how they should govern and elect representatives to the Grand Council. But it is the FSA's purview to further the security interests of the Federation, given that we're the ones who have to sweep up the mess when it goes wrong. When our replacements arrive, as they shortly will, those replacements will assume governance of the Federation. Until that time, the FSA will form its own emergency government for the Grand Council, while it is my understanding that the Callayan Security Agency, under Director Chandrasekar, will do the same for Callay. You'll have to question him personally if you want those details, I understand there will be a conference similar to this one at the Callayan Parliament shortly.

"While holding this transitional power, the FSA will lay down the security fundamentals for the future Grand Council electoral system as it sees fit. Firstly, there will be a full security audit of all Federation member worlds. There will be a full investigation into the role of the Federation Fleet in recent events. Military complicity in political and factional schemes is unacceptable. I invite all Fleet Captains to recall again, what is being discussed here is treason. The military should not play politics. If the barrier dividing military institutions from political ones needs to be electrified to make any crossing of that barrier fatal, so be it. Current measures are clearly not strong enough. I repeat, military officers using forces in any form to subvert democratic outcomes is treason, whatever the nature of the subversion and outcomes. And I warn Fleet, the FSA's patience is ended. Captains who will not play by established democratic norms will be removed or eliminated, by one means or another. I can't be more plain than that."

She imagined Captain Reichardt cheering when he heard those words. Or at least nodding with fierce satisfaction, since he was not a man to cheer. She and he had had this discussion before, in Ibrahim's presence, had even listed names of reliables and unreliables, and said loudly how completely sick and tired he and like-minded Captains were of the latter giving the rest of them a bad name. He'd all but volunteered to provide the bullets. She would thank him later for sending the message that may have saved her life and, more importantly, those of her kids.

"Also very important," she continued, "we're going to set up a working group to look at the Callayan information net. This is normally the responsibility of Callayan Parliament alone, but events have demonstrated that some Callayan infrastructure affects the security of the Grand Council as well. We all thought the net was far too large and free to control, it turns out it wasn't. The working group will invite leading experts from all across Callay with an eye toward making the net completely and totally uncontrollable." Pause again to let that sink in. "That might seem an odd policy from a security agency, but as we see it, freedom on the net is the best guarantee of freedom on Callay. Such a policy will certainly make our lives more difficult on the level of lower operations. But on the larger scale, any network whose central protocols can be taken control of by a central government is more a danger than a benefit, its all-encompassing nature not only allowing all citizens to reach their government, but more worryingly, the government to reach all citizens."

She thought about mentioning FedInt. That was a huge one, the FSA was going to finally have to work out its relationship with Federal Intelligence—either hive them off into a separate entity or merge them fully into the FSA. Because right now, she was prepared to bet the house she didn't own that Chief Shin had been in this up to his eyeballs, only to back out at the last moment when it was clear his team was losing, and deftly switch sides. And slippery as Chief Shin was, it was likely they wouldn't find a damn thing to pin on him in the wrap-up.

So she wouldn't mention FedInt. Some battles were yet to be fought, and revealing one's hand too early, against the likes of Shin, was a bad idea.

"So this is a genuine coup," one of the assembled journalists interjected, with self-impressed boldness. "You're in charge, and now you're going to make all the rules."

"On security matters, yes," said Sandy. "That's our job. What we implement can be tweaked at a later date, as we learn more."

"And what if an elected government wants to change what you implement at a later date?" asked a woman. "Why shouldn't we be just as worried about a Federation where the FSA has too much power? Isn't this really just a coup to give the FSA the final say on Grand Council security? And if you have the power to threaten whoever you want, doesn't that give *you* the ability to influence policy?"

Actually a very good series of questions, Sandy conceded. A fast uplink visual matched the questioner's face with an ID—she was an independent, one of those activist academics with small but loyal followings who evidently *had* been questioning everyone, because the link showed she'd been on Operation Shield's watchlist.

Sandy nodded at the questioner. "That's why we're going to start a new Federal security agency. You won't see them much, they won't be very glamorous, because they'll be the internal investigators, the ones who keep an eye on internal functions of big institutions, including the FSA. They'll watch us, and the GC, and all institutions, for illegal and unethical behaviour."

And weren't they all going to regret that at a later stage, Sandy had no doubt. But it seemed there was little choice. Institutional bureaucratic process could undo them all, and the FSA was ill-equipped to specialise in it. If the damn thing had to exist, better the FSA had the prime role in writing its constitution, so it didn't turn into the kind of pain-in-the-ass, semantical, hair-splitting idiocy seen in the SIB.

"And who watches them?" the journalist pressed.

"We do," said Sandy. "And others like us. Call it the institutionalised version of mutually assured destruction. It's messy, but it works."

"Cassandra," came a familiar voice. Sandy looked and found Justice Rosa against one wall. He must have been deliberately keeping out of sight for him not to have registered until now. Sandy couldn't help but be pleased to see him well, whatever their differences.

"Mr Rosa," she replied with a faint smile. Some of the journalists, recognising him and recalling their relationship, turned their cameras toward him.

"Cassandra, it appears that most of those implementing this secondary coup today are GIs like yourself. And it appears that you have removed this very powerful force that Operation Shield had assembled with relative ease."

"I've been in actions before that dismissed many dead friends as 'relative ease,'" Sandy said somberly. Thinking of Rishi.

"In military terms," Justice persisted. Sandy nodded reluctantly. "This follows recent events on the New Torah world of Pantala, and the synthetic uprising against the Torahn branch of Chancelry Corporation. The same uprising, in fact, that these same GIs with you here today were involved in. It is the same people, yes?"

Sandy gave an inward sigh. Justice just had to build it up into some kind of dramatic point. "The ones we were attempting to peacefully resettle as a part of negotiations with League in New Torah, yes. And that Operation Shield tried to kill and make look like a coup attempt."

"Thus sowing the seeds of the counter-coup that would remove them, yes," Justice replied. "Director Ibrahim has a sense of irony." Rustlings from the other reporters. Get to your fucking point, Justice. "Two hundred GIs? Against many thousands of regular troops, and one of the most advanced aerial defence networks ever established anywhere. Yet you make it look easy. GIs are apparently forming the nucleus of the FSA's special operations capability here on Callay. You yourself have noted to me that GIs are fundamentally unequal, compared to normal humans, and acknowledged the difficulties that this presents, socially and politically. Can it not be said that the FSA runs the risk of becoming the Federation's unequal, dominant institution simply based upon the unmatched military capabilities of its primary combatants? So much of strategic manoeuvering, whether between states or institutions, depends upon underlying capabilities. Who would now dare to bluff the FSA? Given that the FSA now has the power to eliminate anyone it wants, in the event of a fight?"

"The idea is to avoid fights in future," Sandy began.

"By the imposition of an FSA-led puppeteer dictatorship?"

"Our advantage only comes into play when people start shooting at us," said Sandy. "Best that they don't. I can promise that the FSA will never shoot first."

"Perhaps we need more GIs?" Justice suggested. "To spread evenly between institutions?"

Sandy nearly smiled. "I suggest to Federation citizens that the defection of GIs from League to Federation is a vote of confidence in our system. And that we should all try our best to justify their faith in us."

"Spoken like a politician," said Justice. "All these GIs look up to you. Do you lead them?"

"My two hundred–strong democratic constituency?" Sandy replied with a faintly dangerous smile. Don't play these silly games with me, Justice. I know you want your book to sell more, but if that involves "controversialising" me in the public eye even more than I already am, you'll be sorry. "Wouldn't get me very far, would it? I think I can speak for all Federation GIs when I say that we left the League because we thought the Federation way of doing things looked better. In the Federation, we could make up our own minds and not just do what any single person told us. Don't typecast us as brainless followers. We're individuals. Some of us lost our lives today, defending Federation democracy and freedoms. That was a choice, not a command. I hope that one day, it will be respected as such."

CHAPTER TWENTY-EIGHT

The surf was really a little too big for beginners, but the thing with Danya and Svetlana, once they'd overcome the initial fear of the unknown, they became hair-raisingly brave. Even Danya, whom Sandy had suspected would retain his usual caution in the surf, now threw himself deliberately at rides he knew would dump him, as though he had something to prove. To himself, Sandy supposed. Or perhaps it was just the usual sibling rivalry, safe to indulge in now that the activity was proven non-lethal. Or maybe he was just finally acting like a typical thirteen-year-old boy.

He took off on one now, paddling hard when Sandy urged, got to his feet as the board began to run, corrected his balance with a frantic windmill of arms, and was then set as the wave built behind him, only a little over a meter tall, but plenty large and fast enough for someone who'd only first stood up two weeks ago.

"Go Danya!" Sandy yelled, echoed by Svetlana alongside on her flower-patterned longboard. He stayed on it until the wave broke, which upset the board and dumped him in the wash. And when he came up, he gave a whoop of delight, regathered his board with the ankle rope, then clambered back on. Sandy had never before seen him just having fun for such a prolonged period. He didn't like movies much, TV even less, and found most use for his AR glasses looking up League-Federation war footage, security reports, weapon specs, or other uncheerful business. He was reading more now, but that was mostly spy thrillers. He liked to exercise, but went at it like a SWAT grunt in training, running and swimming every morning, one of his only activities Svetlana would not immediately join in with, reluctant to drag herself out of bed at that hour. Surfing was the only thing he did that was not "necessary."

"He's better than me," Svetlana complained. She'd been standing first, not surprising given her dexterity and light weight on a big board. But the advantage hadn't lasted long.

"Well, he is three years older," Sandy reminded her. "He's also bigger and stronger, so he can power that board around a lot more. You're so light on a big board you're just a passenger."

"I want to move up to a short board like you," Svetlana decided.

"You still won't be better, once he's on a short board too. Strength makes a difference. And he's a boy and you're not."

"I want augments too!" Svetlana added. Sandy laughed. And worried, thinking of all the things that would entail. Fortunately, Svetlana was many years from being legal. She'd have to tolerate Danya being better than her at surfing through her childhood at least.

In the shallows beyond, Kiril was paddling on his boogie board, catching the wash of broken waves up to the sand. And somewhere up the beach, Ari and Raylee Sinta had gone for a walk. Svetlana still didn't like that.

"I know they've just been hurt and everything," she'd said when Sandy told her she was bringing them, "and it's nice that you'll take them to the beach for some space. But, I mean, they're boyfriend and girlfriend now! Doesn't that bother you?"

"No," Sandy had said. And when Svetlana had looked puzzled and a little frustrated at that, she'd added, "Look, Svet, I'm a GI. I'm wired differently. Don't waste time bothering whether that makes me right or wrong, or you right or wrong—I'm me, you're you, we're different, and whatever we feel, that's fine. You don't like it, that's fine for you, don't doubt yourself. But Ari's one of my best friends, I'll always love him whether we're together or not, and Raylee's pretty cool too. They've been through hell the last month, Raylee's got a new arm and half a new face. If I can help out just a tiny bit by giving them a lift to somewhere nice that's not a hospital, I'm going to do it."

Ari had supported Raylee all through her recovery, had sat by her bedside despite his own mending bones and talked to her, even urged her to take the opportunity to get higher-level upgrades, now that the CSA was willing to allow it for her, given her new centrality in sensitive security matters. She'd taken him up on that, though more because it would make the transition to a more powerful synthetic arm easier on the rest of her body. By all accounts she'd been tough as hell, and Sandy found she couldn't begrudge either of them a thing. She'd left the League for a life unconstrained, and she was grudgingly beginning to see how Ari may have felt that about her. Being what she was, his loyalty to her locked him into a lot of positions that were, for him, a matter of personal choice and conviction. On Pyeongwha, he'd risked his life for those convictions. Having to tiptoe around his points of difference with Sandy, given that he then needed to work with her on matters like Pyeongwha, pulled him back and forth in ways he couldn't have enjoyed.

Raylee was nice, smart, worked in a field probably more similar to Ari's own than Sandy did, and was so pretty that Vanessa, upon meeting her recently with the reconstructive surgery more or less complete, had admitted to momentarily tearing up her heterosexuality membership card. Given Sandy herself had gained her own looks by unfair means, she could hardly begrudge her that, nor its effects on men. Plus, Ari *impressed* her, in ways that men could rarely impress Sandy. Not that Raylee Sinta was the kind of girl who wanted a man to sweep her off her feet. But most regular human women seemed to like it at least being an option, some of the time. Ari had been her protector and mentor in hospital, and now out of it . . . and in time, Raylee would no doubt return the favour. And no doubt that would feel good to Ari, to be able to look after her in that way. He'd tried with Sandy, and expressed frustration with it sometimes, that she didn't listen or barely noticed. And now, here was someone who needed him. Sandy had been with Ari by choice. She'd never truly *needed* him, not like that. And to Ari, that lack could have felt like . . . distance.

The realisation now didn't even upset her. It was what she was. What was it that Justice had remarked to her, upon learning of her and Ari's relationship, and its recent breakup, through another of his secret sources? *It's the solitude of Kings*, he'd said. *There's only room for one person atop the pinnacle.*

No, Sandy had disagreed. *You just find other pinnacles to place your own alongside.*

"Sandy, look!" Kiril yelled now from the sand, holding up something squishy. "A jellyfish!"

"That's a big one, Kiri!" Sandy yelled back, vision zooming on it to be sure it was safe. Now that her kids were gromits, she was suddenly taking an interest in dangerous marine life and had catalogued them all in a memory file. "Just be sure you don't pick up any jellyfish with blue spots on it!"

"This one doesn't have any spots!" Kiril replied.

"When's his appointment?" Svetlana asked.

"Three-thirty," said Sandy. "We've hours yet; we can go straight to HQ from here." The Shield bombardment hadn't destroyed HQ's med labs, which were functioning even as the rest of the compound howled and hammered with construction activity.

"What if they find he's getting smarter?" Svetlana wondered. "What if he ends up like some kind of boy genius?"

Sandy made a face. "I'd rather no change at all, thanks." A passing swell lifted them, nothing worth catching.

"But they can't really tell, can they? I mean, it's all so new."

"With Ragi's input they can tell a lot more than they could." His brief interaction with Kiril had somehow allowed him to compile a graphical map of how Kiril's uplinks were working. The FSA's biotech doctors were a little more excited about it than Sandy liked, but at least it was helping.

Svetlana saw another swell coming and turned to set herself up for a run. "Not this one," said Sandy. "It's too flat." Sure enough, it passed under without ever really building.

"You know," Svetlana volunteered, "with Kiril going to the doctors regularly, if you get really busy, we could take him ourselves. Danya and me."

"Danya and I," Sandy corrected.

"Crap, you say 'someone and me' all the time!"

Sandy grinned. "Do as I say, not as I do." Svetlana snorted. "Well, that'd be great, Svet, if I get really busy and I absolutely can't do it. But for now I'd like to do it myself."

"Do what yourself?" Danya asked, finally reaching them after his paddle back out. The increased exercise was beginning to show in his arms and shoulders, especially all the surfboard paddling. And his birthday was in two weeks, he was nearly fourteen, and increasingly strong for his age. Svetlana had had to remind him of the date; he'd genuinely forgotten. Sandy was wondering if there should be a big party with new schoolfriends, but Svetlana had cautioned her against it—Danya didn't exactly not get along with kids his own age, he just didn't have much to say to them and wouldn't consider a party full of them to be a very fun time. One older boy had tried to make a thing of it, show he was a tough guy, pushing around the quiet Kresnov kid before his friends. Danya had beaten him up, quite quickly, no fuss, just a methodical punch in the head and several kicks on the ground to make sure the message stuck.

And Sandy had told the principal unapologetically, *I told you it would happen to the first kid who went after him. You promised me no kid would go after him. But here we are.* And Danya had calmly shaken the other boy's hand the next day, no hard feelings, though he'd flatly refused to apologise and gave the quiet impression the same thing would happen to anyone else who tried him. Thus far, no one had. Svetlana said with glowing worship that she didn't think it ever would. And Danya, ever methodical, had admitted to Sandy that he'd deliberately not hurt the other boy too much, calculating how much force was sufficient for deterrence alone.

Svetlana now reported that many older girls, and some younger ones, were now approaching her wanting to talk about Danya, and how a girl might gather the courage to strike up a conversation with him. Sandy wondered what a teenage Tanushan girl would make of him. He wasn't a "bad boy," he was actually a very good boy, never broke the rules if he could help it, studied hard, was absolutely devoted to his brother and sister, was more disciplined than most adults, more than some SWAT grunts even. It was just that his rules were his own, and those personal rules preceeded the other rules every time. One of those personal rules was zero tolerance of threats that were within his capability to personally deal with. If he was threatened, then conceivably his siblings were at risk as well. He just wouldn't put up with it. Couldn't. And those who thought that made him violent were missing the point—he wasn't; in fact he hated violence. And so engaged in minor violence to protect those he loved from the worse violence that could follow if he didn't.

That some Tanushan teenage girls found that hot only increased Sandy's opinion of the taste of teenage girls. But good luck prying him away from Svetlana. Maybe girlfriends would have to wait until Svetlana discovered boyfriends. And where the hell *that* would end up . . . it made her head spin just to think on it. Thank God it was all so far away for Kiril at least. Kiril was all hers for years yet.

Danya was now on official probation with the school, however. Sandy didn't mind that. As she'd told him, *So long as you don't start it, don't throw the first punch, and don't use other kids' fear of you to push them around or make them feel bad. You're the school tough guy now. It's not just a power, it's a responsibility. Don't abuse it.*

"Take Kiril to the doctors," Sandy answered him now. "Svetlana was saying you guys could do it alone if I was busy."

"Yeah, good idea, Svet," said Danya. "And don't forget to get some spending money for the shopping tour along the way." Svetlana splashed him.

"What would you rather buy when I'm not there?" Sandy asked quizzically.

"Nothing!" Svetlana insisted. "Just . . . stuff."

"Girly stuff," Danya said knowingly. Svetlana looked a little embarrassed.

"Hey," said Sandy. "Svet, just because I'm a butch broad doesn't mean you have to be."

"You're not a butch broad!" Svetlana protested. "You're just not very . . . well, you know. I like decoration." Looking at the purple flowers on her surfboard.

"Well, I know what I am, Svet," Sandy reasoned. "And it's hard to paint flowers on an assault rifle. But you're still discovering who you are, you're supposed to try things out at your age. Tell you what, let's go shopping together next weekend, you can buy *me* some girly stuff too."

"Deal!" said Svetlana. "But you gotta wear it."

"Well, you think of an appropriate occasion, because I'm not wearing it to tac simulation."

Danya grinned, watching Kiril in the shallows all the while. "Ari said Fleet will be here soon," he said. "A few days." The other reason Sandy wanted to keep close ties with Ari, aside from the personal, was that she'd seen how good he was with Danya. Not just the male role model thing, more the normal-human role model.

"They're overdue," Sandy confirmed. "I think it's a good sign. They're not rushing in with all guns blazing."

"Or a bad one," said Danya, "because it means they're preparing a big force."

"Thanks, Danya, very cheerful," said Svetlana.

"Yeah, but where?" Sandy replied. "Earth's out, no one trusts them after the relocation. Callay became the default center of colonial space. Fleet has no real concentrations other than Pantala, and that's out . . . and how do they round up that much political consensus? Normally they'd all come here to do that."

"So . . ." Danya thought about it. "Anyone who came here without consulting anyone would be accused of another coup. Because it's unrepresentative. So they have to take their time, but with the space lanes so big and messages going only one way . . ."

"Exactly. It's a nightmare. I expect they'll start trickling in, hold up in the outer system and talk about it there. It's the only way."

"You mean that by taking the GC, you really do control the center of the Federation," Danya reasoned.

"Yep. And now control the agenda, because we can demand they agree with or answer any security points we've identified. And since most of the Callayan population have grudgingly accepted we did the right thing, they're behind us, so any military resolution of our occupation of the GC would be a Fleet hostile invasion of the capital world, which isn't going to happen. We'll talk, it'll work out. You'll see."

"Can we not talk about work while we're surfing?" Svetlana complained.

"Absolutely," Sandy agreed. "Danya, stop it."

"Me stop it?" He grinned. He was doing that so much more these days. "You were talking more than me."

"Yes, but you started it. Look, here comes a good wave. Let's catch it together."

"And no cutting each other off!" Danya demanded, paddling to position, watching the wave approach. "Svetochka!"

"It's not my fault!" Svetlana protested, also paddling. "I'm too light to control the board, Sandy said so!"

"Okay, ready?" Sandy watched the green wave building nicely as it approached. "Okay, go go!" As Danya and Svetlana both paddled like crazy. Sandy let it come to her, thrust twice and stood, looking fast left and right to see Svetlana, then Danya manage shakily to get to their feet, then rushing down the face, all up together. On the beach, Kiril saw and cheered loudly. Sandy laughed and made a couple of little weaves on her short board between them, up close to one, then the other, all grinning.

Until Svetlana tried to balance on one leg, lost control of her board, which plowed into Sandy, then across into Danya, as all three fell or jumped clear. And resurfaced laughing.

"You're an idiot," Danya told his sister, swimming to her and grabbing.

"I nearly did it!" Svetlana laughed, struggling.

"You know, that was all a lot more 'happy families' in my head," said Sandy, with an amused glare at Svetlana.

"Isn't it always?" said Danya. Svetlana stuck out her tongue.

ABOUT THE AUTHOR

J oel Shepherd is the author of four previous Cassandra Kresnov novels—*Crossover*, *Breakaway*, *Killswitch*, and *23 Years on Fire*—and four previous novels in the Trial of Blood and Steel series—*Sasha*, *Petrodor*, *Tracato*, and *Haven*. He is currently midway through a doctoral program in International Relations and has also studied film and television, interned on Capitol Hill in Washington, and traveled widely in Asia. Visit Joel at www.joelshepherd.com.

Author photo
© Impact Image, South Australia